'THAT WILD LIE . . .'

NAOMI JACOB

'That Wild Lie . . .'

The Gollantz Saga 2

Futura

A Futura Book

First published by Hutchinson & Co (Publishers) Ltd 1930
New hardback edition published in Great Britain in 1983 by
Judy Piatkus (Publishers) Limited

This edition published in 1985
by Futura Publications, a Division of
Macdonald & Co (Publishers) Ltd
London & Sydney

ISBN 0 7088 2656 3

Printed and bound in Great Britain by
Hazell Watson & Viney Limited,
Member of the BPCC Group,
Aylesbury, Bucks

Futura Publications
A Division of
Macdonald & Co (Publishers) Ltd
Maxwell House
74 Worship Street
London EC2A 2EN
A BPCC plc Company

For
OLIVIA ETHERINGTON SMITH
With my love and gratitude
to remind her of Salo, Malcesine,
Gardone and Lake Garda

Contents

Book One

Emmanuel

1

Hermann Gollantz came to Vienna—from Heaven only knows where—in 1838. He brought with him a considerable amount of money, some excellent pictures, and a small, but admirable collection of old furniture. He also brought several introductions to persons of quality from old Fernando Meldola of Paris, whose reputation, both for integrity and knowledge in the world of connoisseurs of art, was unassailable. Hermann Gollantz always asserted that his father, Abraham, was an even greater expert than Meldola, and that he was well known in Paris; but when Emmanuel visited that city in 1864 he was unable to trace his grandfather, or to find anyone who had known him.

Hermann Gollantz, a moderately handsome Jew with a good manner, was a man of considerable education, and exquisite taste. Not only did he buy to sell, but, when any piece of furniture, any picture, any piece of china made a special appeal to him, he bought it for his own collection. He was both popular and successful, he invested his money, sold his wares and married in 1840 Rachel Hirsch, the daughter of a well-to-do wool merchant. They had two sons, Marcus, born in 1842, who was drowned in a skating accident, and Emmanuel, born in 1844.

Emmanuel was barely twenty when his father died; a week later his mother followed her husband. Her death was regarded as the final proof of wifely affection and devotion by her friends and relations. When young Emmanuel came to wind up his father's affairs he found that, contrary to expectation, they were in the worst possible state. He investigated further and discovered that for the past twenty years his father had been steadily bled by his mother's family. Ishmael Hirsch, his uncle, had speculated and lost; Hermann Gollantz had made good his losses. Money had been lent and given to the whole Hirsch family, and Emmanuel found that his father had left him little but debts, and the furniture and pictures which the huge Viennese house contained. True, there was still sufficient money in the bank, from various investments which could be realised, and from outstanding debts to pay what was actually owing, but Emmanuel knew that after such debts were paid he would be left practically penniless.

Two things were outstanding in young Emmanuel Gollantz, his pride and his good looks. He was, at twenty, undeniably the most handsome Jew in Vienna. It was said that when he entered a ballroom, women had been known to swoon for love of him; and it was further stated that these ladies were not only the daughters of Israel, but women of the ruling Gentile.

His manners were perfect, perhaps just a shade too perfect, his gestures a shade too flamboyant; but his figure, his clear-cut features, his dark, wide eyes, his small feet and beautiful hands were things of which the young womanhood of Vienna might, and assuredly did, dream.

His pride equalled his looks. His first thought when he realised his deplorable financial position was one of dismay. His second emotion was fear; fear that anyone might pity him.

He spent days with the lawyers in order to ascertain his position. He refused, quite firmly, but with perfect courtesy, the offers of extended credit from people who had liked Hermann Gollantz and trusted his son.

He paid all his father's debts, all his own—which included an immense tailor's bill, for he was the complete dandy—and arranged for the sale of his father's house. The furniture, the pictures, the china, the tapestry, the brocades, and the beautiful carpets he decided should be the foundation of his own fortunes.

He never saw any of his mother's family again. Years afterwards they wrote to him that his grandfather was dead, and Emmanuel sent money for prayers for his soul. A month later, when he felt that decency permitted, he wrote, coldly and unemotionally, that he refused to answer any further communications from his mother's family.

When his business was conducted, Emmanuel took farewell of his closest friends—four women and one elderly man. It was said that one of the women, a Countess, went into a decline after his departure; that another contemplated entering a convent, only to discover that she lacked a vocation before it was too late. The absolute truth of these statements cannot be vouched for, but it is certain that Emmanuel entered one great house to make his farewell by the balcony, which he reached by the aid of the festoons of ancient ivy which covered the house. That he left hurriedly is probable, for in descending he slipped and fell, and left Vienna two days later with his arm in a sling and with a dislocated collar bone.

The one man whom he visited was his father's old friend, Marcus Breal, the banker.

'I have to say "good-bye",' Emmanuel said. 'Tomorrow I leave for England.'

The old man blinked at him from behind his horn-rimmed glasses. 'Why England?' he said. 'And why have you your arm in a sling?'

'To answer the last question first,' Emmanuel said, 'because I was forced to—run away. A meeting with pistols for two and coffee for one might have delayed my departure and my plans were already made. The second question—why am I going to England? Because I have seen pictures of English houses. They are quite unbearably ugly. I cannot believe that the English can bear to live in the middle of such horrors for very long, there must—sooner or later, and I trust sooner—be a revulsion of feeling. Presently they will begin to invest their money in objects of beauty, which I shall sell them. I shall call myself a dealer in furniture, pictures, and antiques. I shall offer them my taste in house decoration in exchange for money.'

Breal blinked his eyes again. 'What do you know of these things?'

'I have lived with them all my life. I have listened to

my father speaking of them, I have learnt to recognise good from bad. I speak English quite well—thanks again to my father—may his soul rest in peace. I speak French very badly, and, as you can hear, German exceedingly well. My father's furniture, pictures, and so forth are sufficient to start me in business. Oh, I shall do very well.'

The old man took snuff from an old gold snuff-box and dusted the grains from his white waistcoat. 'It is the trade, Emmanuel bar Hermann, which has bred more rogues and tricksters than any other. You are neither a rogue nor a trickster . . .'

'I shall be unique, and my success will be unique also.'

Marcus Breal nodded. 'It may be. I am going to make you an offer, and tell you what will be the outcome if you accept it. Listen. I have no sons—I have always hated women, they bore me. I am very rich. If you will stay here, in Vienna, I will make you my heir. You shall be free to come and go as you please. You will mix in society—oh yes, even in exclusive Vienna it can be arranged if a Jew is sufficiently rich. You will hear this and that which affect the money market. Wars and hints of wars, disagreements here, friendships there. You will report them to me. I shall act upon them. Women like you . . .' he nodded, his eyes dancing, 'I hear many things, Emmanuel bar Hermann, many things. Women tell the secrets of their husbands to their—friends. Now, what do you say?'

Emmanuel stood upright. He struck an attitude, throwing back his head, conscious that he looked both noble and indignant, and indeed he felt the latter and—in a lesser degree—the former.

'I thought,' he said slowly, 'that you told me that selling pictures and furniture bred more rogues than any other business in the world?'

'I did. It does.'

'And banking . . . ?'

Marcus Breal chuckled. 'Banking has bred one, to my knowledge—myself. I, too, like to think that I am unique, but,' he shook his head, 'I am dreadfully afraid that there may be others. Well, you won't accept my offer? Don't make a speech about it, I only want "Yes" or "No".' Emmanuel swallowed the speech which he wished to make, hid his disappointment and said 'No' with decision and firmness.

'All right, that is closed,' Breal said. 'Now I shall give you a small piece of advice. The Englishman is a strange creature. In his heart he always keeps a dislike and fear of the Jew. Jews remember, English forget. They forget that their God was a Jew, and when the unpleasant thought comes into their minds, they pray that next time he will have the good taste to come as an Englishman. But,' he held up a pale hand, 'even though they dislike Jews, they dislike still more the Jew who is ashamed of being a Jew. An English lord came to do business with me the other day. He said, "Be Gad"—they all say "Be Gad!" He said, "You're a Jew, Breal, but, damn me, if I wouldn't rather do business with you than with half a dozen Englishmen I could name." He went on, "I always say that when a Jew deals straight, when he's honest, be Gad, damn me, if he isn't the straightest and honestest man alive!" Now that, Gollantz, is rubbish. An honest man is an honest man, no more and no less whatever his race. But once get an Englishman to believe in a Jew— and they aren't fools, oh, dear me, no—and he'll trust you with every penny in the Bank of England. They may fear you, they may dislike you—but once they trust you, you're a made man. Good-bye, come and see me when you are in Vienna, and should I hear of any good pictures —I do hear of these things—I will buy them and sell them to you at a commission of five per cent, which as you know is only nominal. I, too, profited by your father's —may my last end be like his—dissertations on art.'

Emmanuel never failed to call and see the old man when he went to Vienna. He frequently found that he had bought goods on his behalf which were of great value, and when he died in 1870, he left the greater part of his fortune to Emmanuel Gollantz. The remainder was left to various Catholic churches to purchase candles, stating that as no one now went about with candles— looking for honest men—they might well be localised and serve as a reminder from the altar, that honest men need finding. The will was much disputed, as was Marcus Breal's sanity, but the Church was victorious and the altars were brightly lit in consequence.

Emmanuel arrived in London on March 9th, 1865. He thought London the most gloomy, miserable, and depressing place he had ever seen. As he drove to his hotel in the Strand he could have wept, and only when he was alone in his room did his courage begin to return. He unpacked, ordered a bath to be made ready, and dressed with great care. As he stood before the foggy, insufficient looking-glass, his courage rose completely. He had come to conquer London, and looked every inch a conqueror. His fine black cloth suit was exquisitely cut, his high collar with it's projecting points, his white tie, his linen, his jewellery could not have been improved. His hair, his small moustache, his carefully trimmed side whiskers looked unbelievably dark against his pale skin. His cloak swung elegantly from his shoulders and gave a touch of romance to his appearance. Even the black silk sling for his arm seemed to add to, rather than detract from, his appearance. He took his gold-headed cane and descended the gloomy hotel staircase conscious that every man and woman turned their heads to look at him twice.

Within a month, he had established himself. What money he had was safe in the Bank of England; his beautiful pictures, his furniture, his carpets, brocades, and tapestries, his china were shown to the best possible advantage in the dignified house which he had taken, on a long lease, upon Campden Hill. He had rejected the idea of a shop as being unsuitable for the class of business which he desired, and as—to the English mind—ticketing him too definitely as a tradesman. He visited all the antique dealers of standing, introduced himself, mentioned his father's name, and behaved with such modesty, offered such deference, yet withal spoke with such authority upon matters of his business, that he gained respect and good-feeling.

Old Gelbe in St. James's was so taken with the good-looking young fellow that he wrote, tentatively, offering to take him into partnership along with his stock. James Marchant, whose sale rooms were world famous, came to Campden Hill and offered to buy three pictures for a client at a figure which was very little less than the one which Gollantz asked. Later, he offered to buy the whole stock, sell it on commission, and send the young man travelling in search of new treasures. Gollantz smiled, bowed from the waist, thanked them—and declined.

He did not sell a single article for six weeks after his arrival in England. He was not disheartened, he knew that his goods—like his knowledge—were excellent. He could wait—patiently and with serenity, for deep in his heart was the belief, which he never lost, that ultimately

Fate, Destiny, God—call it what you might—was on the side of the Children of Israel.

At the end of April, a sunny morning, Emmanuel stood in Hammet's Sale Rooms, carefully noting prices and at the same time the credulity of the buyers who were not actually in the trade. He presented a noticeable figure in his tight brown frock-coat, his brown and white check trousers tightly strapped under his patent leather boots, his cravat of brown satin decorated with two scarf pins joined by a slender gold chain. He realised that two very small, very bright blue eyes were watching him, and half turning discovered that they belonged to a man rather older than himself, a man whose face was burnt to a brick red, and whose hands—one of which held a catalogue—were the colour of mahogany. Cautiously, Emmanuel, suddenly curious as to what this obvious country dweller was doing in Hammet's Rooms, edged nearer. Presently he could read the catalogue in the man's hand, and noticed that 'Lot 137' was marked with a cross. 'Four occasional chairs. Queen Anne. Original needlework seats.' Emmanuel grimaced. He had seen the chairs. The auctioneer was ready to sell them, he was eulogising them at length. The man with the blue eyes stood to attention suddenly. Once again his eyes met those of Emmanuel. They smiled as if to say, 'Watch me, I'm a knowing one.' The auctioneer's voice boomed out. 'Four Queen Anne occasional chairs, original needlework seats. Unique—quite unique. What shall I say, gentlemen, for these very fine, very remarkable chairs?'

Emmanuel listened for the dealers to open the bidding. From somewhere near the rostrum came a Cockney voice, 'A fiver the lot!' and a smothered giggle from a group of Jews. The auctioneer raised his eyebrows, looked round the sale room, his face pained and surprised. Emmanuel glanced at the man with the blue eyes, saw him stand more erect than ever, he was preparing to bid. Carefully Emmanuel edged nearer, he resented that this obviously country lamb should be shorn for the benefit of Messrs. Hammet.

He caught the man's eyes, lifted his finger and whispered, 'No.'

The blue eyes ceased to twinkle, the man came nearer. 'What?' he said.

'No,' Emmanuel whispered again, 'they are no good at all. Leave them alone, please.'

'Good Gad!' the words came like a small explosion. 'Can you show me better ones?'

'Infinitely. Please follow me.'

He turned and walked from the sale room, never doubting that the man would follow him. And follow he did, reaching Emmanuel on the steps of Hammet's and embarking on a long stream of questions, never waiting for replies. 'Amazing! . . . Gad, stopping me just as the bidding started! . . . What d'you do it for? . . . Think I shall have lost 'em? . . . Damned annoying if I have, eh?'

Emmanuel felt that the man, for all his engaging blue eyes and his pleasant twinkle, was a fool. His mind was of the type which walked but never jumped, that was evident. He ought to have realised that only a man who was an expert would have checked his bidding. Emmanuel smiled tolerantly, half amused.

'You did not need to have followed me,' he said.

'Damme, and I don't quite know why I did,' the Englishman said, 'except that somehow I liked the look of you.'

Emmanuel bowed. 'I, also,' he said, in his slow, careful English, 'if it might be said, liked your appearance. T'ose chairs, they are bad ones. Queen Anne—maybe—but only smallest pieces of them. They are,' he sought for a word, 'they are restorated chairs.'

The blue-eyed man stiffened. 'Gad,' he said, 'you're a dealer! You've got chairs of your own to sell, I'll be bound, eh?'

Emmanuel drew himself up and stared blankly at the man. His stare was so cold, so disgusted, that the other was visibly shaken. When Emmanuel spoke all the friendliness had left his voice.

'I r-regret,' he said, 'I spoke as von gentleman to another. I find my mistake a little late. I haf no Qveen Anne chairs, and I vish you a very pleasant "Good morning".'

With that he lifted his broad-brimmed hat, turned on his heel and walked rapidly away towards the Strand. The other man stared, his red face turned a deeper scarlet, his blue eyes bulged; then, cramming his catalogue into his pocket, he made after Emmanuel as quickly as his rather bow legs would carry him.

'Hey!' he cried, and again, 'Here, please, just a moment. Wait.' Emmanuel stopped, waited until his pursuer drew level, then stared at him as if he had never seen him before.

'Here,' he said again, 'don't go off like that. How the devil was I to know you weren't just a dealer's tout? Damn it! Made a fool of myself. Take my card—and my apologies. Shan't make the mistake again. Sorry.'

Emmanuel smiled, took the card, read 'Sir Walter Heriot', and in the corner the mystic word, 'White's'. Heriot was talking again, asking him to take something with him, assuring him that Romano's was quite close. Adding, 'And let's forget that damned silly mistake of mine, shall we?'

'I have forgotten what occurred,' Emmanuel said, 'it nevere happened. May I tell you my name? It is Emmanuel Gollantz, once of Vienna, now of this city.'

'And—now, don't lose your head, keep cool—you're a dealer in antiques?'

'Indeed, yes. Also an expert in house decoration, in pictures, in old silver and gold.'

In Romano's, which Heriot affectionately called 'The Roman's', he reverted again to the subject of the chairs. Emmanuel explained.

'The chairs which I had in my mind,' he said, 'were in Carter's of Bond Street. Perfect chairs. He asks a hundred and fifty for four.'

Heriot scratched his chin with a stumpy forefinger. 'See here,' he said, 'Carter don't—employ you?'

'Indeed no. I saw the chairs by chance yesterday.'

'But you'll want commission or whatever you call it?'

Emmanuel shook his head. 'That had not occurred to me,' he said. 'You see I did not meet you in business. I ventured to speak with you. I looked at you, I said to myself, "T'ere is a man who likes real t'ings. Odder kinds . . ." he paused, "he can't—digest them." That is my excuse, my explanation and my apology.'

'Very handsomely said, be Gad!' said the other. 'If you've finished your wine, let's go and see these chairs, and then p'raps you'll honour me with your company at luncheon, eh?'

A few days later Heriot came to Campden Hill. He confided to Emmanuel that he was about to marry the most beautiful girl in the world, and that he wanted the furnishings of his town house to be worthy of her. He admitted that he had certain taste, but that he lacked knowledge. Emmanuel had both. Later, the baronet told his friends that he had found an honest Jew. 'And when a Jew *is* honest,' he said, 'damme, if he isn't the most honest fellow on the face of the earth. This man—Gollantz —handsome as a picture, straight as a bit of string— and as proud as Lucifer. And, Gad,' he added, 'the man's got a manner that would carry him anywhere. It's going to carry him as far as my dining table and my wife's drawing-room at all events!'

Outside Heriot's house, in Grosvenor Square, among the ladders and scaffolding a small, very neat board was displayed. 'Gollantz. Decorations and Furnishings. 92 Campden Hill.'

2

During the years which followed, that small board was to become familiar to Londoners. It became the hall-mark of exquisite decoration and beautiful furniture. Ninety-two Campden Hill, together with the house next to it— which Emmanuel had acquired—became the fashionable centre for people who had a taste for lovely things and money to gratify it. Emmanuel Gollantz became the vogue. Men liked and respected him, women admired and trusted him, even, in some cases, loved him.

His personal attractions, his knowledge and his culture opened to him doors which would have admitted no ordinary art dealer. He neither pushed nor stood humbly in a corner; he was at his ease, confident, charming, and amusing. He walked warily, far more warily than the men and women who invited him to their houses ever knew. That he had conquests was believed, hinted at, but Emmanuel never spoke of his private affairs.

Only once did he come near to making a grave mistake, and that one occasion might have caused disaster. The Earl of Crawley was old, he was dissipated, he was a drunkard, he was immensely wealthy. His young wife was beautiful and very silly. It is difficult to say whether Emmanuel loved her. It is certain that beautiful women attracted him, and Alice Crawley was like an illustration from a Book of Beauty. It is certain that she loved, or believed that she loved, him.

She collected old embroideries—copes, altar cloths, pattern covers, chair seats, and samplers. She came to Campden Hill in search of them—and found Gollantz. She was twenty-six, Emmanuel was a year younger and very handsome, Crawley was nearing sixty and repulsive. The copes, altar cloths, pattern covers, and so forth were taken away in Lady Crawley's carriage for closer inspection at Portman Square. The rejected pieces were returned and Emmanuel unpacked them himself. Hidden in the linings were notes in Alice Crawley's sloping, elegant, Italian hand. Other selections were sent to Portman Square. When Emmanuel wrote letters he wrote them delightfully, and as Alice read German, he was unhampered by his somewhat stilted English.

Then—someone suspected, someone whispered to Crawley, and not Alice but her lord came to Campden Hill, Crawley hinted, Emmanuel was obtuse. Crawley spoke frankly, Emmanuel smiled and expressed careful surprise that his lordship should listen to servants' gossip.

'Then—if it's moonshine—why does she cry at night?'

'My lord, surely you can answer that question better than I.'

'She refuses food.'

'If I may suggest, these delicate creatures . . .'

Crawley lost his head, and forgot that he was speaking to a damned tradesman. 'Her door is closed to me! Damme, she refuses me entrance to her room. Her husband—I have rights . . .'

Emmanuel looked at the dissipated old-young man in disgust.

'She's in love with some other man,' Crawley spluttered, 'it's obvious.'

'Not of necessity,' Emmanuel said gently. 'Her ladyship is fastidious.' Crawley blinked his red-rimmed eyes and spat noisily into a fine cambric handkerchief. 'Damned offensive,' he said. 'Blasted Jew furniture dealer!'

'The offence,' Emmanuel said, 'lies with you, my lord. You offend me. You offend my sight, my hearing, my sense of smell—I detest brandy, and stale at that, at eleven in the morning. Your wife is my esteemed patron. I am her sincere admirer. I always admire people who have a knowledge greater than my own. Her knowledge of sixteenth-century needlework is—profound. For your pr-rivate ear,' he spoke as one gentleman to another, 'I-am to be married in a month's time. I wish you, Lord Crawley, a very good morning.'

Late that evening, a lady in a hired carriage drove to Campden Hill. Emmanuel received her, she wept and he comforted her.

'He said,' she sobbed, 'that you were going to be married.'

'I am.'

'To whom?'

'That I cannot tell you. I do not know. I shall be married in a month's time. That is all.'

She stared at him with wide blue eyes. 'Heartless! Do you want to break my heart?'

Emmanuel lifted her hand to his lips. 'No,' he said softly, 'only to safeguard you from evil tongues. I can do it best by this—all too small—sacrifice.'

As he closed the door of the coach, and turned back to the house, he smiled. 'The first time—and the last—that I have written letters,' he said softly. 'Never again.'

For the next forty-eight hours Emmanuel gave the matter of his marriage careful consideration. He was twenty-five, and already on the road to becoming a rich man. He had no particular wish to marry, he had made the assertion from a misguided sense of chivalry to Alice Crawley, and—he admitted—to safeguard himself. Having made it, however, he decided that no retreat was possible.

Seated in his great carved arm-chair, which bore the date 1640, with breakfast—which consisted of excellent coffee and two small rolls which his German housekeeper baked every morning—before him, he considered the various women he knew. Rachel Leon, the sister of Hermann Leon, the engraver. She was clever, witty, but—he smiled at his reflection in the mirror which stood on the table before him—she was too clever. She would never take him seriously, she would make fun of his small dignities. Miriam Bernstein was too pious. Her life was spent in keeping fasts and feasts, in prayer and observation of small ceremonials. Emmanuel was intensely proud of his race, but he accepted its religion with an easy tolerance. He went to shule twice a year and kept Black Fast—that was the extent of his religious activities.

Adah Lewis was too sallow. He fancied that her legs were slightly bowed. He detested plain women. Esther

Salamon was too rich, he did not want a wife whose bank balance made his own insignificant. Elizabeth Davis —he paused, his cup half-way to his lips—Elizabeth Davis, daughter of Reuben Davis, the notary—he corrected himself—lawyer. She was small and quite attractive. She was always glad to see him. She was well educated, musical, and admired his pictures—or said that she did. Fate was on his side! That very evening he was dining with the Davises at their house in Westbourne Terrace. Elizabeth Davis should be the woman he would marry before the month was out.

That evening Emmanuel dressed with more than usual care. As he dressed he sighed. He liked Elizabeth Davis, indeed he could think of no one he had rather marry, but—again he sighed—he had dreamed of romance, of great love, wild admiration, tenderness, passion. He eyed his severe breastplate of linen with disfavour and thought regretfully of his frilled shirts already out of fashion. The waistcoat of his dress suit was cut too high. The coat itself was not waisted sufficiently. He disliked the new fashion of stuffing a handkerchief in his waistcoat, with a fold displayed. He looked at his reflection and sighed. Took a white gardenia and placed it in the lapel of his coat, took up his broad-brimmed hat, laid it down again while he delicately sprayed his hair and small side whiskers with eau-de-Cologne, took up a pair of virgin white kid gloves with one button—and he was ready.

His housekeeper met him in the hall and stared with undisguised admiration.

'Master,' she said, 'you look like a bridegroom.'

'S-sh,' Emmanuel whispered, his finger raised, 'the truth is hidden sometimes in a jest. Wish me Mazzoltov.'

'So! That is why you look as you do! Mazzoltov, Emmanuel Gollantz, and may the God of thy Fathers bless thee.'

Emmanuel picked up a hansom, and sat with his arms folded on the apron, dreaming and still a little sad. Firmly he meditated on Elizabeth and her admirable qualities— her musical ability—her good housekeeping—her kindness of heart—and still he sighed. He would marry her and settle down. He would be serious, successful, and sensible. He would have preferred to be gay, romantic, and just a little foolish.

The old man who was footman, valet, and butler combined admitted him.

'I'll announce you, sir,' he whispered. 'It's a formal party on account of the lady.'

'Lady? What lady?'

'The Countess, sir, the Countess Lara.'

He was announced and made his way carefully over the parquet flooring to where Miriam Davis stood under the great cut-glass chandelier with Elizabeth beside her. Emmanuel lifted her hand to his lips, then turned to Elizabeth and repeated the gesture. She was almost pretty, he thought, with smooth dark hair, great deep eyes and a neat figure. Emmanuel wondered if his heart fluttered for a second as he watched her, then knew that it was perfectly steady and regretted the fact.

Reuben Davis came forward. 'We're waiting for the Countess,' he said.

Rachel Leon smiled at Emmanuel. 'Ah, Emmanuel,' she said, 'you look like some young man in a Disraeli novel, all perfection and carefully trained personality.'

He smiled and her fine dark eyes smiled back at him. 'No one,' she said, 'has ever called you "Manny", have they?'

Emmanuel raised his eyebrows. 'My dear Rachel—never!'

Hermann Leon glanced at the clock, his mouth a little peevish. Mrs. Davis said, 'I know, Hermann, we're shockingly late. It's the Countess.'

'Who is the Countess?' Emmanuel asked.

Elizabeth answered, speaking very fast and with the colour deepening in her cheeks as she talked. 'She's a client of Uncle Walter's in Paris. She has property in England, and Uncle Walter sent her to papa.' The Davises were carefully English and never said 'Fadder' and 'Mudder'. 'She's going to stay here until it's disposed of—the property—so I suppose we shall be late for dinner every evening. She's brought a maid, who talks nothing but French, and her boxes are simply too enormous . . .'

Reuben Davis checked her. 'Elizabeth, what a yen you make of everyt'ing. It's all not'ing, this Countess. She is the vidow of Count Leone Lara of Perus, Walter's important client. Nothing at all, a foreign title!' he stuck his hands in his trouser pockets. 'Not the same as an English Countess. I should say not!'

'But,' Hermann Leon said, 'How infinitely more romantic.'

'Pooh, foreign titles—two a penny.'

'Good value for the money.'

Emmanuel nodded. He despised Reuben, he knew that in his heart he was triumphant that he should entertain a Countess, glad that the two clever Leons, Gollantz, the rich Salamons and their daughter, the young Bernstein —who boasted that he should change his name to Burns and discard Judaism as it impeded his career in society— should witness his triumph.

The door opened suddenly, old Isaac mumbled something half inaudible, and the Countess Lara entered. She took Mrs. Davis's hands in hers, and in a warm husky voice protested that she was terribly ashamed, but that her maid, 'a half-wit, poor creature, mislaid all my chemises. It has taken her—and me—literally hours to find them. I contemplated coming down without one, but the problem presented itself what was I to wear instead! Not that its absence would have been apparent, but the moral effect upon me might have been—would have been—disastrous.'

Miriam Davis was shocked, so was Elizabeth. Reuben went scarlet, young Bernstein stretched his thick neck in his high collar and sniggered, the Salamons were busily examining an Empire clock. Emmanuel caught Rachel Leon's eyes and laughed aloud. The Countess swung round and faced him; and Emmanuel knew that this time his heart not only fluttered but actually missed a beat. Her long narrow eyes seemed to dance as they watched him, the thin pencilled eyebrows above them were arched, the eyes themselves were faintly mocking. Her mouth was wide, generous, and full-lipped, the parted scarlet lips showing big, strong, and very white teeth. Her nose was short and rather wide at the nostrils. Her hair, unlike the smooth tresses of the other women, was short and arranged in small, fair curls all over her head.

She stared at Emmanuel, then said in the voice which had already charmed him, 'A catastrophe, was it not?'

He bowed. 'On such apparent trifles—as the loss of a —garment, the fate of Empires rests.'

'But it was found eventually . . .'

'Empires have ceased to shake.'

Reuben came forward and make belated introductions, he offered his arm to the Countess and they went in to dinner. Emmanuel sat on her left, with Elizabeth on his right. He tried to talk to her, tried to remember that he intended to ask her to marry him. He almost laughed. It was ridiculous. He was going to marry the woman with the narrow eyes and impertinent nose who talked in public of her lost chemise. Half listening to Elizabeth's account of some play which she had seen, he listened to the husky voice on his left. Presently Elizabeth turned to speak to Horace Bernstein, and Emmanuel, his eyes on his plate, listened to the voice in peace.

'Are you very hungry or very stupid?' it asked suddenly.

He turned. 'Certainly not very hungry,' he said, 'and, I hope, not unbearably stupid; but only incurably romantic.'

'Romantic! And you keep your eyes on your plate? Oh!'

'To listen the more intently.'

'To what, if you please?'

'I might dare to tell you—if I was not certain that you knew already.'

She laughed. 'Perhaps I do.' Then, 'Oh, this is such good food. I am so happy to be a greedy woman. Only Jews understand the art—not of cooking, that belongs to the French—but of eating.'

'You are a Jewess?'

'Oh, yes.'

She turned back to Reuben Davis. Emmanuel talked to Elizabeth, and was, to outward appearances, himself. Inwardly, he felt that he had suddenly come to life; that he stood on the edge of the world; that he was about to plunge into the romance which he had always sought. It would be cool, soothing, exciting, its calms broken by tempests—but it would be living romance—he could have laughed aloud.

Later, when he sat in the Davises' drawing-room, Rachel said softly, 'What has happened to our young Disraeli hero? I have never known you so—human.'

He said, 'Rachel, my dear, you are a very clever woman. I have always thought of you as heving the br-rains of a man.'

'Pooh! Thank you for nothing! Hermann would never have made that mistake!'

'Nevertheless,' he persisted, 'that is how I t'ink of you. And, therefore, it is qvite possible that already you hev guessed, eh?'

'I thought,' she whispered behind her fan, 'that it was Elizabeth.'

'So did I, until I saw—her.'

The Countess, being led from group to group by Reuben Davis, rather like some strange but rare animal which is on exhibition, came to where they sat. She took Emmanuel's place on the brocaded sofa, sighed, and said to Reuben that she refused to go any further.

'I like your nice friends all so much,' she said, 'but I am tired. I shall bore them if I talk any more. Let me sit here and rest. Miss—Leon and Mr. Gollantz will forgive me if I am dull.'

Emmanuel stood before her, making his stiff little bows when he spoke.

Rachel, watching him, thought that she had never seen him look so attractive, had never found his careful, rather difficult English so charming. Even his slightly artificial dignity seemed to have slipped away from him. He listened with great gravity while the Countess confided to him that she wanted—'above all things' to see the sights of London.

The Tower, the Houses of Parliament, the Abbey, even Madame Tussaud's Waxwork Exhibition in Baker Street. She wanted to understand English history and 'these things are part of it. Mr. Davis says that he knows nothing of them. I must find an escort.'

Rachel Leon pointed to Emmanuel. 'Here is the man,' she said, 'no Englishman knows more about them than he does. He even knows his way to the British Museum and the National Gallery'

'Perhaps it might bore him. He looks as if he might be easily bored.' Emmanuel, who had never seen the Tower, to whom the Houses of Parliament were nothing but a Gothic outline, the British Museum only a place of reference, and Madame Tussaud's merely a name, protested that nothing could give him so much pleasure as to escort the Countess.

She arranged that he should call for her the following morning, and Emmanuel suggested that if she would consent to lunch with him they might continue their sight-seeing during the afternoon. He was conscious that Davis looked at him coldly, that young Bernstein was annoyed, that the Salamons were speculating what he was going to sell the Frenchwoman in addition to showing her the sights of London—he remained unmoved, smiling and impassive.

He drove Hermann and Rachel to their home that

evening. As he left them at the tall house in Bloomsbury, he said softly to Rachel:

'That old paste ring which you admired the other day will be sent to you in the morning—with my love. Tell me, before you go, have either you or Hermann a book on the Tower of London, and how do I get there?'

Hermann answered for her. 'The authorities provide excellent and most picturesque guides,' he said, 'and any hackney driver knows the way. Leave it all in the hands of people who are paid to know these things, Emmanuel. You can find a better use for your time.'

Rachel lingered to speak to Emmanuel while Hermann was opening the door.

'My dear,' she whispered, 'be careful. Walk—don't slide.'

Three days later, Juliana Lara visited Emmanuel's house in Campden Hill. She was escorted by Mrs. Davis, who disliked old furniture, and almost immediately sought out the housekeeper to obtain a receipt for pickling herrings, leaving them alone together.

Emmanuel showed his treasures. He spoke well, though his English was slow and over careful. He was amusing and never tedious, the Countess was interested and intelligent. Twice she opposed his opinion, and once he was forced to admit that she was right. His admiration grew at every second. She held a miniature of Ninon l'Enclos in her hand. 'The most beautiful woman in the world,' she said, musing.

Emmanuel shook his head. 'Scarcely that,' he said. 'Great charm, that we cannot doubt, but not the greatest possessor of that commodity.'

'Authorities disagree with you.'

'I am an authority. Their knowledge was limited.'

'So is yours.'

'So—was—mine,' he corrected, 'until three days ago. Now,' he snapped his fingers, 'that for Mademoiselle Ninon.'

She frowned. 'I hate flattery.'

'But so do I!' he said, 'so do I. If I say what sounds like flattery, it is because I lack experience. I use words badly. I am clumsy. I want to say such beautiful t'ings, romantic t'ings, and instead, I am talking like a shopman or an ector. I should wish to speak like a poet.'

She sat down in the big, carved oak chair, her hands looking unnaturally white against the dark wood. Emmanuel stood humbly before her, his affectation left him, his pose disappeared, he stood as he might have stood before a great queen who was granting him an audience.

'Emmanuel Gollantz,' Juliana Lara said, 'I know what you try to say. I should be a fool if I did not. You want to tell me that you love me, and ask me to marry you. Do you think—listen carefully—that I should make you happy?'

'I know that I could not be happy without you. The chief thing is, surely, that I should make you happy?'

She shrugged her shoulders. 'I doubt if anyone can make anyone else happy. It's a stupid idea—we make ourselves happy. You think that you would be happy if we were married. Ah! You believe that you love me. I think, perhaps, that you do. I do not love you—frankly, I love no one but Juliana Lara. I like you, you are handsome—and I abhor ugly men. You are romantic—and I adore romance. But—you are an Austrian Jew, and I am a French one. Your French—thank God, you do not speak it often, is deplorable. I am a Countess, you are a —merchant. What have you to say?'

Emmanuel said, 'I am glad that you find me—handsome, and romantic. There are at least two t'ings which you like about me. The language—I will learn French, but most important is this—love is international, and has an international language. I am a merchant—I am more, I am a collector of beautiful t'ings, and I cannot bear that I should lose the most beautiful t'ing in the whole world. Please marry me—I am a very impatient man.'

She smiled, showed her white, strong teeth. 'I am not easy, Gollantz,' she said, 'I want a lover—not only a husband. Can you be both? Can you go on being a lover for ten, twenty, thirty years? I am older than you are. I am three years older than you are. Reuben Davis told me your age. I must have attention, admiration, adulation—and it must be clever. Not that heavy, treacly love and affection of English husbands. Not the proprietory attitude of the Frenchman, or the solid, kind superiority of the German. I do not know even if I could always be faithful to you—I do not know anything, except that I will not—now or at anytime—endure boredom. Will you promise never, never to bore me?'

'I will promise anyt'ing,' he said, 'but what is more, I will try to keep my promises. Give me my answer—please . . .'

She smiled again, shook her head, and turned back to

his curios, asking questions about them, making comments, even laying two or three aside saying, 'I will have that, please.'

Only when he escorted the ladies to their carriage, did she speak of the subject which was torturing Emmanuel. She laid her hand on Miriam Davis's arm and said, 'One moment, dear Mrs. Davis. Emmanuel and I have something to tell you. We are engaged to be married.'

Miriam Davis stood, gasped and asked in a breathless whisper, 'When?'

Emmanuel answered. 'Next week,' he said. 'I am going now to look for a suitable house. When I have made a selection, perhaps you will come and choose the one which you like best?'

3

On May 16th, 1869, Emmanuel Gollantz and Juliana Lara were married. They spent their honeymoon on the South of France, and to Emmanuel those three weeks were always the most perfect time of his whole life. His wife was charming, amusing, and affectionate. He found that she was widely read, and had many and varied interests, loved music and pictures and possessed an energy for seeing and exploring new places which equalled his own.

He wrote to Rachel Leon from Nice, 'For twenty-five years I have been in the world and never lived. Now I live every second. I have only one wish, and that is to reorganise the measure of time, so that each day might have forty-eight hours, each minute a hundred and twenty seconds.'

They visited Paris on their way home, and for the first time Emmanuel was admitted into the society of men and women who looked upon art, music, and the drama as necessities, not luxuries. Whatever his wife's friends might have felt at the news that she had married a merchant, they accepted him as their equal in every way. Indeed, it would have been difficult for them to have found any obvious faults with him. He was handsome, charming, his manners were perfect, and his devotion to his wife almost pathetic.

They returned to the house which Emmanuel had taken on a long lease in Regent's Park. He had furnished it to please both himself and his wife. It held treasures which he had collected with the greatest possible care, and Juliana declared that it was the only house which she had seen in London that did not offend her taste. He had spent money freely, but his business was doing well, and Juliana had a considerable income of her own, with which she insisted upon being remarkably generous. In 1870, old Breal died and left Emmanuel his entire—or almost entire—fortune, together with a small collection of books, pictures, and manuscripts which were almost without price.

Throughout the winter of 1869-70 they went everywhere. Juliana loved gaiety and Emmanuel loved her. He had learnt to dance, as a boy, in Vienna and made a conspicuous figure in a ballroom. Englishmen who did not like him said that he danced too well; those who were his friends envied him for doing it so perfectly.

Walter Heriot put him up for White's, where he was blackballed on account of his race. Heriot made no secret of his annoyance and stated openly that Gollantz was the finest gentleman he knew. Emmanuel was deeply hurt and his pride suffered terribly. He refused to allow his name to be brought forward as a candidate in any club for the remainder of his life. Juliana laughed, called the committee of White's 'fogies' and 'parochial'. Emmanuel defended them.

'What they know of Jews,' he said, 'they know from Jews. I am paying for the mistakes of men like Bernstein. He has changed his name to Burns, and the men who know him call him "The Sheenie".'

She agreed, hating the men who had refused him admittance far more bitterly than Emmanuel did.

'Sheenie,' she echoed. 'How like the English. They have a silly nickname for every nation they cannot understand, and that means every nation under the sun but their own. I like them—and I despise them.'

'I like them without despising them,' Emmanuel said. 'That very evident stupidity is their greatest asset. They are a great nation because they have been too stupid to realise when they were beaten. Men like Walter Heriot are worth their weight in gold.'

In the early summer of 1870 Emmanuel was at the height of his popularity. He was only twenty-six, and his name was a household word among artistic Londoners. He was besieged with orders, not only for decoration, but for antiques and furnishings. He had an immense correspondence with various Continental towns, whence his agents sent him news of any valuable work of art which was for sale. In the autumn of 1870, he told Juliana that he felt that he ought to make an extensive tour of the Continent to buy new stock, get new ideas, and generally get into personal touch with his agents. She dismissed the idea. It was ridiculous, his place was in London, his ideas were never less in want of renewing. He was satisfying London, why should he want novelties.

'To satisfy myself,' he said. 'I am standing still.'

'You are making money, you are successful socially and financially.'

'I want to be successful in my art.'

She shrugged her shoulders. 'If you go, I shall come with you.'

Emmanuel was horrified. He protested that he should be moving all the time, he would be going to towns, villages even, where there was no accommodation for a lady. He would be busy, unable to devote his time to her. He could not allow her to face discomfort, hardship, and even danger.

She narrowed her eyes, showed a line of white teeth, and smiled—a smile which did not reach her eyes.

'I want you with me. I never wanted you so much. I hate being alone.'

'But,' he said patiently, 'I am going, r-really, for you, my dearest.'

She caught his hand, drew him to her and put her arms round his neck.

'I love you,' she said, 'I can't bear you to leave me. Take me with you.'

'Three months, perhaps,' he smiled, 'and the rest of our lives together.'

'Poof! The rest of our lives! How do I know how long that will be? I may die of congestion of the lungs, you may be killed in an accident. I will not, cannot, be robbed of three months. Take me with you.'

Finally, he decided not to go. Instead he sent Julius Salamon whom he had taken to learn the business when he left school. Julius was clever, he worked hard, but he had not Emmanuel's flair for precious things. He had not Emmanuel's courage, and let an El Greco slip through his fingers because he doubted if that painter was 'popular' at the moment.

Emmanuel listened. 'Great paintings are never popular,' he said, 'there are not sufficient of them. But they are always valuable.'

So the summer slipped away, and that winter Emmanuel and his wife danced, and entertained, heard music, saw plays, and sat at other people's tables. Juliana was very happy, and Emmanuel was satisfied that she loved him. His one wish was that they should have a son. It seemed to him that the birth of a child would put the final seal on his happiness. He found himself making a small collection of things which would be suitable for a child. In the deep drawer in his desk, which was always kept locked, he hid an old silver rattle and bells which some child had swung before James I fled to France; a string of beautiful deep red corals, a tiny silver porringer which bore the date 1558, and old flattened silver spoons which carried the marks of small sharp teeth. These things he treasured and loved, handled and wove his dreams round them.

In April, 1871, he was visited by an American millionaire. Emmanuel had met Americans before, he had even seen them travestied upon the stage both in Paris and London, but he had never had extensive business dealings with any of them. George Parker Hewett was a little man with a parchment-coloured face, small dark eyes, and a thin-lipped mouth. He had made money, more money, he told Emmanuel, than any man had any right to have. He wanted to gather things which would be of interest —'artistically and his-torically to pas-terity.'

'I want pictures—I-talian, Spanish, Dutch—they tell me that the Dutch painted interiors excellently. Now what kind of interiors will that re-fer to, Mr. Gollantz? Nothing indelicate, I trust.'

'Rest assured,' Emmanuel said, 'nothing in the least indelicate.'

'French, and if there are any—German. I want furniture of those nations, manuscripts—whatever your ex-pert knowledge tells you is of note and characteristic. Do I make myself plain?'

'Perfectly,' Emmanuel said. 'It would sound to me that you were willing to spend a great deal of money.'

'You apprehend my meaning perfectly. So much that I will only en-trust this to a workman whom I can trust. I was assured by Frank Moresby that I could trust you. He said—I have no wish to be offensive, Mr. Gollantz—"The man's a Jew, George, but he's an honest one, and you don't have to have me tell you how honest that is." '

Hewett was prepared to spend at least twelve thousand pounds. Emmanuel was interested not only for the sake of his commission. He could combine his own interests with those of the American, and gain in experience, in ideas as well as in goods. Again he broached the idea of a Continental tour to Juliana, again she begged to come with him, or refused to let him go.

Emmanuel spoke to Julius Salamon of the trip, adding, 'My wife wants to come with me. I say that it is too dangerous, too uncomfortable.'

Julius twisted his little moustache, and pursed his red lips. 'I should take her, Emmanuel. She's a damned sight too attractive to be left at home.'

Emmanuel sprang to his feet and faced the younger man. For a moment Julius thought that Emmanuel was going to kill him. He had never seen a man so changed —his eyes blazed, his face was livid, his whole frame shook with anger. When he spoke it was scarcely above a whisper.

'God of my Fathers', he said, 'I could so very easily kill you, Julius. Never again, so long as you know me, dare—dare to say such a thing as that. The implication is damnable—disgusting—an insult to me—to my wife.'

Julius, a decent enough fellow, stammered an apology. Emmanuel regained his composure, nodded an acceptance, and the matter ended.

Finally he consulted Rachel and Hermann Leon. Hermann was already making a name as an engraver. The brother and sister lived in their tall house in Bloomsbury; they were both constant visitors to Emmanuel's house. Juliana liked Rachel for her intelligence, and Leon for his sympathetic understanding and his evident admiration.

They listened to Emmanuel's difficulties, Rachel sitting perfectly still on the big sofa covered with a printed linen which Hermann had designed and had executed for her; Hermann standing by the empty fire-place, a pencil balanced in his hand, with which he fidgeted as he listened.

Rachel said, 'Emmanuel—take her with you. She has said she wants to go. Juliana knows what she wants. She will never reproach you for any discomforts, but she may reproach you for not allowing her to share them. Women are much less delicate than you believe—when you love them. She is afraid of nothing except being bored. With you she may be uncomfortable, but she will be interested—amused. Take her.'

Hermann, still balancing his pencil on his finger, said, 'No, Rachel, you are wrong. I'm thinking less of Juliana then of Emmanuel. Men are—I admit—greater cowards then women. Juliana might not mind the discomfort, but can you imagine how Emmanuel would hate it for her? Holland, France, parts of Italy—are all very well; but think of some of the Spanish inns, think of the roads—where there are roads—in North Italy; think of Russia, Servia—it's impossible for any woman to travel there. Not only dangers from people—brigands, cut-throats, and so on, but from sickness. Suppose that Juliana was ill—very ill—fever in Rome, bad water in Spain, infection in Russia—No, Emmanuel, leave her here, safe in London.'

'I don't agree,' Rachel persisted. 'Take her out with the fixed belief that she is going to be ill—stricken with fever, poisoned by water, infected from dirty peasants, bitten by bed bugs and lice—and she will assuredly suffer from them all. Disregard them, disbelieve in them, discredit them and she will escape them. Hermann, I'm ashamed of you for being an alarmist.'

But Hermann's advice carried the day. Emmanuel went back to Regent's Park and had his first real quarrel with his wife.

'T'ree months is not'ing,' he said.

'Three months may be everything,' she returned.

'Hermann agrees with me. You value his opinion, Juliana.'

'Hermann! How dared Hermann Leon offer his opinion, please?'

'I asked for it.'

'You fool!' Suddenly she became herself, smiled, treated the whole matter as an affair for teasing. 'Go,' she said, 'go and leave your wife behind. But—if I'm not here when you come back—you will have yourself to blame. I may find old Salamon, or his precious baby Julius, young Bernstein—I beg his English pardon, Burns—will supplant you in my affections. "Where is the Countess?"' she mocked his voice and gesture. ' "Gone, sir, left yesterday with all her luggage, in a hired carriage with the blinds drawn." How much good will your old pictures do you then?'

Emmanuel kissed her. 'I will scour Europe for jewels worthy of you,' he said.

'Jew!' she laughed, 'how could there be jewels worthy of—me! You know it.'

'You're right,' he said, 'I shan't find them—but I shall try.'

He thought that she had forgiven him, that her smiles meant that the sun shone again after the storm, but that evening when they sat at dinner, she went back to the subject of his travels.

'Emmanuel,' she said suddenly, 'tell me again, for the last time, why you refuse to take me with you?'

'Because I love you too much to expose you to discomfort and danger.'

She made a gesture of impatience, then folded her white arms on the dark, polished table. Emmanuel stared at her, thought that he had never seen her look so lovely, never noticed how white her skin was, how wonderfully the light from the candles became tangled in her hair, how her long, narrow blue eyes lit up so that they looked like pieces of sapphire. She watched him, staring back at him, her mouth hard and tightened at the corners.

'Discomfort! Danger! Discomfort cannot frighten me, and danger—I laugh at it! Emmanuel—there are dangers here—in London—plenty of dangers. Shall I tell you that greatest of all—for you? The danger that I may be bored!'

He rose and came over to her chair, stood beside her, holding her hand in his. He said nothing, for one moment wondered if he dared take her, wondered if he could bear to leave her behind. Three months was a long time.

'Emmanuel—take me with you . . .'

He was his own master again, he lifted her hand and kissed it.

'I do take you with me—in my heart,' he said, 'that is as much as I dare to do.'

Juliana tore her hand from his grasp, pushed back her chair and faced him.

'Meshuggah! Go, then—you're kotzon already—make more gelt. See that your gelt can buy you everything! Take your advice from Hermann Leon—the schmuck! I have said everything. Now, ask me to go with you and hear me say "No." I know myself better than you know me. I once tried to tell you. When you asked me to marry you. I told you then that I didn't love you as you loved me. That was—then. Now, it was almost beginning to grow different. I asked to come—I get arguments, second-hand arguments from Leon. I beg to come and I get a droshe from you, like some rabbi talking. No, don't say anything —go!'

That night he took her in his arms and begged her to understand and forgive him, but she lay cold and un-responsive. He whispered that he loved her beyond the bounds of reason, she shrugged her shoulders and said, 'Nu—prove it.' He said that he should miss her, should think of her every moment he was away, she laughed softly and said, 'I may not remember to miss you for so long.'

When he left, she bade him good-bye, wished him God-speed, and smiled. He put his arms round her, said, 'Tell me that you love me, Juliana,' and she laid her head on his shoulders and said, 'I do—but I still think that you are quite mad. Good-bye.'

For two months he scoured Europe. He found the furniture, the pictures, the materials, the silver and gold which he sought. He slept in hard beds, dirty beds which stank, damp beds when he was forced to wrap himself in his great travelling coat; he ate coarse food, badly cooked food, food which was so saturated in rank oil that his stomach almost turned against it—and with each dis-comfort he found reason for congratulation that Juliana was not with him. He experienced intense cold, great and stifling heat, he was bitten by mosquitoes, he was soaked to the skin, his hands and feet were numbed with cold. He wrote all these things to her, wrote of them with humour, making a yen which should amuse her; he begged her to enjoy herself, to entertain, told of the jewels he had found for her and literally counted the days until he should see her, speak to her again.

On the seventh of October, 1871, he wrote that his work was almost ended. He would return by way of

Brussels, would she meet him there and they would have
a second honeymoon. He was still moving from place to
place, and knew that it was uncertain that any letter from
her could reach him. She would wait for him in Brussels.
He went to the hotel, they told him that Madame had
not yet arrived. He was disappointed, but found a thousand reasons which might have delayed her. He went out,
called upon Louis Moise, the picture dealer; and his smart
young son, Isadore Moise, had a manner which equalled
Emmanuel's own. Isadore knew everything and everybody.
He bowed and smiled, and asked why they were denied
the pleasure of seeing the Countess.

'She is not yet in Brussels,' Emmanuel said. 'I am going
back to the hotel now, hoping that I may find her there.'

'Not yet . . .' Moise said, then added quickly, 'No, I
forget that she had not accompanied you on your tour.'

Emmanuel returned to the hotel. Juliana had arrived. She was waiting for him in their sitting-room. Emmanuel forgot to be dignified, he raced up the stairs
three steps at a time, he burst into the room, and held his
wife to him half-way between laughter and tears. He
had never realised what the separation had meant to him,
had not understood how hungry he was for the sight and
sound of her—never known how much and how intensely
he loved her. For a week he was like a schoolboy. Together they went everywhere. They watched plays, they
heard operas, they saw pictures; they drove together, then
dined at the fashionable restaurants. Emmanuel visited
dressmakers and spent money like water. Nothing could
be sufficiently good, sufficiently expensive, sufficiently fashionable for his wife.

They went back to London, and in December, Juliana
told him that she was going to have a child. She came
into his library, stood by the fire-place with one foot resting on the high steel fender, smiled, and said, "Emmanuel,
listen—I have something to tell you. I am going to have
a baby in—I expect—six months' time.'

He stood up, turned, his hands resting on the big desk,
his face quite colourless, his eyes immensely dark, and
said, 'My wonderful adored . . .'

She lifted her hand. 'Wait,' she said, 'let me tell you.
Perhaps you had better sit down, it may be difficult.'

'You're not ill . . .'

'No,' she laughed, 'you see I am a very strong woman.
That is why I could so easily have gone with you on

your tour. However—I was in Brussels for three days before I met you. Isadore Moise saw me—at the opera. I wasn't alone, of course. No, don't interrupt me. I was with my cousin, Jules Alessandri. I was—as I told you I should be—bored in England. He came to see me, talked of Brussels. I said, "Jules—take me to Brussels." That is what happened . . .'

Emmanuel stood with his hand pressed over his mouth, he felt that he must keep back the words he wanted to say. He might scream, might lose control, he bit the back of his hand until he could taste the sharp, acid blood. He let his hand fall to his side, the fear was past, he felt numb, stupefied. He licked his lips, swallowed convulsively.

'Then—this child—it is—his—not mine?'

Juliana shrugged her shoulders. 'That is where I am being honest,' she said. 'I do not know. Perhaps—it is his, but very probably it is yours. How can I tell?'

'Have you told him?'

'Told Jules? No, why should I tell him? Whatever you do—and you must do what you think best, Emmanuel—I shall not tell Jules. He is nothing but an attractive, amusing halfwit.'

'You don't love him"

Juliana laughed. 'Love him! No . . .'

'But—but . . .' Emmanuel muttered stupidly.

She clenched her hands, he saw the knuckles show white. 'Oh, how stupid you clever Jews can be,' she said. 'I was bored—bored—bored. Now, is that enough? Tell me what you are going to do. I have nothing more to say, except that I shall not reproach you whatever you decide to do.'

'Do . . .' he echoed stupidly, 'what can I do?'

'Divorce me.'

'I t'ink that I could kill you.'

'Then do that . . .'

Emmanuel stared at her, then gazed wildly round the room. He felt that he was standing in an unknown place, that all the objects within sight were strange to him. He was dreaming, this was a nightmare, presently he would wake, rub his eyes and know that this horror had existed only in his imagination. His dignity, his sureness, his elegant pose had been stripped from him. He remained, a young man stricken by a terrible blow—puzzled, wounded, dazed, and mortally hurt.

Again his eyes went back to Juliana. She stood, still with

her foot resting on the polished steel fender, her face calm, her eyes watching him steadily. He saw her as the woman of his dreams, the woman who had come into his life and changed it, given it colour, light, and music. Juliana—he frowned—trying to concentrate upon the matter before him. Juliana had ceased to love him, she had given herself to Jules Alessandri—a man she ticketed a half-wit. It was impossible—unbelievable, something too horrible to be understood by a human being. Fantastic —unreal—ridiculous. He heard himself speaking. His voice was thick, muffled, as if he were drunk.

'You don't love me any more?'

Juliana's voice came back to him across the distance which separated them, it came over a desert, over leagues of hot sand, over rivers, mountains, so that it reached him thin and pale, like the voice of a ghost.

'I love you—I told you that I loved you before you went away. I haven't changed.'

'But you must have changed . . .'

He saw her move, leave the fire-place and sit down in one of the big chairs.

'No, I never change. Half of me becomes sick—ill when I am bored. I am like that. I can't give reasons—I can only tell you that it is true. This happens to have serious consequences, but it was never serious in itself. There was no love affair. It was only an adventure.'

'You have never done—this before?'

'You never left me before, you never allowed me to be lonely.'

For the first time he moved, left the support of the desk, and stood swaying on his feet. His hand was smeared with blood. It gathered and fell on the carpet. He felt that the earth shook under his feet. He realised that he dared not look at his wife, that he must keep his eyes averted. Even when he spoke he did not look towards her.

'Do you wish me to divorce you?' he asked.

'Honestly—no. That is for myself, that is thinking only of me. I have no wish to leave you. But you must do what you feel is right. It is for you to decide. After all, I have told you quite honestly, the child may be yours. Probably is yours.'

Emmanuel flung back his head. 'God of my Fathers!' he cried, 'the child! That adds to the horror of it all—the child. I must think. I must get away. When I am with you, when I look at you, I lose my sense of what is wise and right. I love you so much—still, always. I want to kill you so that you can never, never belong to another man. I'm in torment . . .'

She rose and walked to the door, opened it and without looking back, left him. Emmanuel sank on his knees before the chair where she had sat, buried his face and cried as if his heart was broken.

4

Emmanuel raised his head, his eyes, swollen and inflamed, stared round the beautiful room. He stood up, swaying on his heels, and looked at first this thing of beauty and then that: the carved chairs, the wonderful bronzes, the four small pictures—Dutch interiors—which hung on the walls, the heavy velvet curtains which he had brought from Genoa. Each thing perfect, almost all of them unique; chosen with immense care because everything in the house which held Juliana must be the best and most costly of its kind. Still swaying unsteadily, he stretched out his hand towards the deep drawer of his desk, as if he would have opened it. Then, with a shudder which shook him from head to foot, turned away and began to pace the room.

He tried to order his brain to work calmly, to reason, to weigh up arguments, to come to a decision. It was impossible. Whenever he forced himself to remember what Juliana had said, extraneous things came rushing into his mind. He found that he was remembering ridiculous things—things which had happened when he was a boy. The Danube—some tune ringing in his head—himself dancing with Mina Strafeldt—he couldn't remember anything except her name. He cleared his mind violently of dances, the Danube and Mina Strafeldt. Juliana was going to have a child—she was unable to say who was the father. Jules Alessandri—once in Paris Emmanuel had seen him. He remembered that he wore a soft silk tie, checked silk; he carried an ivory-headed cane. He didn't care much for ivory, it so easily discoloured, looked dirty. Somewhere he had an ivory box carved with reliefs of Saint Anna. Who was Saint Anna?

He moved his head impatiently, it ached terribly, his eyes smarted. Not only his head but his whole body ached. He moved his shoulders, straining them back to ease the pain. Not his shoulders alone, his heart ached as if something gnawed it. He could not breathe, the room was closing in upon him, the walls coming closer and closer, the floor rising up to him, the ceiling descending slowly. He threw back his head, dashed to the door and flung it open. He stood in the paved hall, where the light shone down upon him from the old Moorish lantern which hung from the roof.

Before him stretched the white marble staircase, with its broad, gleaming banister. Somewhere up there, behind one of the heavy mahogany doors, Juliana sat. He made a movement as if he would have ascended them, then turned and went out into the darkness, closing the front door behind him.

It was too much to carry alone, too great a secret to lock in his own breast unshared. He wanted advice, counsel, wanted someone to reason with him, to keep his mind from wandering off into unknown places full of old half-forgotten memories. He thought of his many friends, discarding each name as it came to him. Davis, Heriot, da Costa, Rabbi Israels—again he shuddered, he couldn't confide in a man, couldn't allow any man to know of his degradation, his loss, his disgrace. If they knew—if any of his friends knew, he could never face them again.

'Poor Gollantz, fooled by his wife,' or 'Emmanuel cheated by his wife's cousin,' or, again, 'he couldn't hold her, she preferred a Frenchman.' Even to Hermann Leon, kindly, sympathetic, cultured as he was, he couldn't confide the shame which had come to him.

His feet rang on the hard pavement, the sound of his steps beat out words which hammered on his brain. 'I must tell someone or I shall go mad.' He walked on and on, down into the Marylebone Road, towards Islington, past a church where great caryatids stood looking down on him, into a dim square.

A voice said suddenly, 'Emmanuel—what are you doing here?'

Emmanuel lifted his heavy, inflamed eyes and gazed stupidly at the speaker.

'Rachel—my dear Rachel . . .' his hand went to his head, then he remembered that he had no hat, he had come out without one.

'Emmanuel, are you ill? Juliana—she isn't ill?'

'No,' he said, 'Juliana is quite well. I am well.'

'But what are you doing here—without a hat—without an overcoat?' He looked at her stupidly, for a moment she thought he had been drinking.

'I want to talk to you,' he said. 'Not Hermann, please, not Hermann, only to you, Rachel.'

She slipped her arm through his and led him back to her house. Without asking any further questions she took him into her own sitting-room, and gently pushed him into an arm-chair.

'I shall be back presently—wait,' she ordered.

She sent a servant back to Juliana, saying that Emmanuel had called. She came back to him with hot coffee and stood over him until he had drunk a cup, before she would allow him to speak.

'Now,' she said, 'tell me.'

Slowly, like a man who has almost forgotten how to speak, Emmanuel told her. He told the story without comment, without emotion.

' . . . and she tells me that she does not want—him. She will stay with me. If I wish. If I wish to divorce her, she will be willing for that, too.'

He spread his hands, palms upwards. 'How can I tell— I don't know.'

'You love her?'

He hesitated. 'I did love her—intolerably.'

'Why? Because she was—yours?'

'Not because she was mine, because she was—Juliana.'

'She still is—Juliana, Emmanuel.'

For the first time he laughed. 'The mistress of Jules Alessandri!'

'But she, herself, is the same. She is amusing, attractive, clever, cultured, sympathetic to you. Since you came home, you have noticed no change in her. She has not grown hard, or stupid, or dull? You do not love men or women for what they do, but for what they are, Emmanuel.'

'Surely what she did proves what she is,' he argued.

'She was sufficiently honest to tell you.'

He moved impatiently. 'Fear that I might discover it for

myself. Fear that this child might be like Jules Alessandri. That is not honesty, Rachel.'

'She begged you not to leave her in England.'

'Because she said she would be bored! Can boredom be an excuse for adultery, please tell me?'

Rachel shrugged her ample shoulders, 'Pah! Emmanuel,' she said, 'do not talk like the Law and the Prophets! Boredom is an excuse for most things from bad temper to murder, and you know it.'

Emmanuel flushed. 'The Law! The Law! Moses made a law how to deal with women who are unfaithful. The Law! If I followed the Law, I should put her away, and you know it.'

Rachel Leon turned and poured herself out a cup of black coffee in silence. When she turned back to him, her eyes were half-amused, half-contemptuous. 'Emmanuel Gollantz has become froom suddenly,' she said. 'Stoning was the penalty, wasn't it? Or was that only "taken in adultery"?'

He stared at her, hurt and angry, then rose, recovering some of his old suavity of manner. 'I came,' he said, 'in g-great distress, for help and advice. You find it amusing to make fun of me. I had thought better of you.'

'Emmanuel Gollantz,' she said, 'sit down and listen. Let me tell you. You will do what you wish and nothing more nor less. Already, your mind is clearer, already you know—in your heart—what you wish to do. You are very successful, very rich and very, very proud, Emmanuel, and—however much this has hurt your heart, it has hurt your pride even more. Perhaps you don't realise that yet. One day you will look back and see that I was right. I do sympathise—with both of you. Life isn't going to be easy for Juliana. Nu, in this case, do what you think wise —not right. I hate people who are constantly doing— right. Obey your own heart. Not the sentimental heart, but your soul. Whatever you do, do with a good heart. No reproaches, no recriminations, and, above all, magnanimity if you decide to remain as you are. You are not quite free from blame, Emmanuel.'

'I!' He was incredulous. 'I have never t'ought of another woman.'

'You were too much of a coward to take her with you. You came to a decision. Juliana warned you. Now, do what you think will be best—divorce Juliana, or put this behind you, and go on together.'

Very simply, with no trace of his ordinary dignity, Emmanuel said, 'My dear, I dare not t'ink of my life without her.'

'Even now?'

He nodded. 'Even now, Rachel.'

'Then she isn't really changed after all?'

'I don't know. It's—not going to be easy, Rachel.'

'If it were, then it would not be worth doing. But remember, Emmanuel, real forgiveness means forgetting, wiping out. You'll not—go on, only for Juliana's sake. You will remember that, won't you? You are saving yourself the pain of living without her.'

'Yes.'

'And sometimes it may be pain to live with her.'

'Indeed—yes.'

'Now, go home. Juliana will wonder why you have stayed so long. She knows that you are here. I said that you had come to see Hermann. Mazzoltov.'

Emmanuel stood before her, his face was still pale, but the traces of his tears had gone, his features had lost their ravaged look. He took one of Rachel's hands and kissed it, then stood upright.

'This . . .' he paused, 'this confidence, Rachel, will always remain a confidence? Whatever happens—this child—may be mine; probably is mine.'

'Ah,' Rachel said softly, 'the old Emmanuel begins to live again! Then you have decided?'

'This child will be mine,' he said, 'I shall make him mine.'

'Him?' she said. 'You've even decided the sex shall be what you wish. Good night, Emmanuel. I have forgotten all you told me.'

'Yosher-Kowach, you are a good friend, my dear.'

As Emmanuel walked home, his hands clasped behind him, his head held high, his steps firm and steady, he reviewed the reasons which had brought him to his conclusions. His mind was made up, there would be no separation, no divorce. He smiled. No separation from Juliana; that would have been unbearable. Rachel was right, if this misfortune were due to lack of morality, he had not married Juliana because he felt that her moral code appealed to him. He had married her for her charm, her personality, because he had fallen head over heels in love with her.

Then again, he knew that his friends envied him his

position, his wealth—and his wife. She was no overblown Jewish woman, no hide-bound devotee debating whether as a married woman she ought not to assume a hideous shietel; she did not spend all her time in her kitchen driving the servants wild, or in her linen cupboard counting sheets. She was different. She could listen intelligently to Heriot when he talked of his stables, she could amuse old Professor Heinemann who boasted that he detested women, she talked of art to Hermann Leon—she was a woman of the world, a perfect hostess, a much-sought-after guest. To have lost her, to have admitted to the world that she had not found Emmanuel Gollantz sufficiently strong to hold her. He shivered. He would have been pitied, commiserated with, and—behind his back —sniggered at!

He had boasted that everything in his house was as nearly perfect as was humanly possible. To have admitted, publicly, that his wife had betrayed him would have been insupportable.

The child—the son—who was coming should never know that there was an element of doubt as to his parentage. Emmanuel prided himself upon his justice, he would see that it was done to the last farthing.

'After all,' he mused, 'if this child is Jules Alessandri's then I am robbing him of his father. Though from what I remember of the fellow it is the most petty of larcenies. If, on the other hand, he is indeed my son, then, God forbid, that I should rob my own child. My conclusion is the right one, I shall abide by it.'

He walked up the marble staircase, and knocked on the door of his wife's room. He wondered how he would find her, almost hoped that he might be forced to comfort her, to wipe away tears, and tell her that he was determined to forget and forgive. The sentimentality of the Jew rose in him. He heard her voice call to him to enter, and waited for a moment to wipe away the tears which sprang to his eyes.

She lay in bed, reading. As he entered she raised her eyes from her book and smiled; then closed the book and held it out to him.

'Emmanuel,' she said, 'you must read these poems— Swinburne. His names are amazing—Algernon Charles; but his poems . . . ! They have made me drunk.' Emmanuel took the book, still warm from her hands, and held it carefully.

He loved books, adored poetry. For the moment his resolutions, his conclusions were forgotten.

He said, 'I bought, the odder day, a first edition of *Atalanta in Calydon*. Have you read it? I must give it to you—wait, I'll run down and get it from my room.'

'Not now, Emmanuel . . .'

'But now and no odder time!' he turned and ran downstairs to get the book. He found it, mechanically opened it, then walked over to his writing desk, took up a pen and wrote on the flyleaf, in his meticulous German script: 'To my adored wife, from her husband, Emmanuel.'

He blotted it carefully, and carried it back to her.

'There!' he said, 'with all my love. Please read what I wrote.'

She read it, shut the book and held out her hands to him.

'You mean that? Really—you know what you want? This is not chivalry, or nobility?'

'It is love that is stronger than I am.'

She smiled. 'You will try to forgive me?'

'I have forgotten that there was anything to forgive.'

But very often during the winter months, and when the winter changed to spring, Emmanuel Gollantz found it very hard to forget, found it difficult to drive thoughts from his brain which tortured and wounded his spirit. Poseur he might be, ridiculously dignified and self-conscious he certainly was, overwhelming pride and immense self-satisfaction he possessed to an amazing extent; but during those months he was a great gentleman, who having given his word, having come to a decision, never allowed anyone, even Juliana, to see that he suffered. He accepted congratulations from his friends with a smile and some well-turned phrase. He engaged the finest accoucheur in London, and worked harder than ever to make money that the future of the child—which was to be his child—should be assured.

A son was born on June 9th, 1872. Emmanuel, when he was shown the child, could scarcely bear to look at him. His relief when he saw two tiny slits of blue as the infant opened its eyes, was immense. He was certain that he was like Juliana.

When the question of his name arose, Emmanuel suggested Julius, but Juliana shook her head. Her father's name had been Louis, she hated the name; Emmanuel's father had been Hermann. She disliked the name Hermann.

She laughed. 'I have it! Call him Algernon, after Mr. Swinburne.'

'Elchernon,' Emmanuel repeated, for he still found certain words presented difficulties.

'Not Elchernon,' she corrected, 'Algernon. Can you learn to say it?'

'Certainly I can. I can say it now—Elchernon.'

The child was baptised 'Algernon Walter' and Emmanuel to the end of his life called him 'Elchernon.'

Juliana recovered quickly, the child grew and waxed strong. He was a beautiful baby, with fair curling hair, and blue eyes. The likeness to his mother was remarkable. Emmanuel never found it possible to love him, but he was always kind and generous. The boy was denied nothing, and it was always Emmanuel who insisted that he must have the best and only the best. Sometimes he would go into the nursery, and stand looking down at the child, trying to find in his baby features some faint likeness to himself. With his arms folded, his eyes half closed, frowning, he would stare down at the child, and after some moments' scrutiny turn and, sighing, leave the room on top-toe.

Juliana seemed to have forgotten. She was as she had always been, gay and loving life. She was able to dance again, she went everywhere, and upon every side Emmanuel heard praise of her. He was intensely happy with her, even the child's advent seemed unable to mar his happiness. She was never an adoring mother. She loved the child, visited him in his nursery, played with him and brought him toys; but she never became maternal, and Mrs. Davis—the traditional Jewish mother—never failed to insinuate that Algernon was neglected.

'Neglected!' Rachel Leon said. 'I never heard such nonsense. Can you imagine Emmanuel Gollantz allowing any child to be neglected!'

'Emmanuel has eyes only for his wife,' Miriam Davis said, 'he is foolish about her. She takes him to Paris to buy her clothes, and never yet have I seen her in skule— never!'

Rachel shrugged her shoulders. 'I should doubt if either of those things will damn Juliana—or Emmanuel.'

Emmanuel had never been deeply religious His feeling for his race was one of intense pride, he loved to see Jews successful and never refused help—and that of the most generous kind—to any Jewish charity. His attitude towards religion was detached. It was very excellent for those to whom it made an appeal; to Emmanuel Gollantz it made none. The small forms, ceremonies, obligations, the lesser points of dietary laws irked and irritated him. To him the fight between Orthodoxy and Liberalism meant nothing, he could never understand Hermann Leon's passionate interest in the struggle.

Once he was approached by a clergyman of the English Church, with the suggestion that he might change his faith. The expression was unhappy.

'Change my faith,' Emmanuel repeated. 'The difficulty is that I have no faith to change.'

'But you are a Jew . . .'

'I have never denied it, why should I? I am thankful to be a Jew. It was the greatest piece of good fortune that ever came my way.'

'I am told that you attend no synagogue?'

Emmanuel bowed. 'I don't. They are all so new—so hideous; I cannot feel that the Almighty can enjoy visiting them any more than I should.'

The clergyman smiled, and Emmanuel disliked his tone of slight patronage.

'The God whom I worship,' he said, 'thinks nothing of places. His Son was born in a stable . . .'

Emmanuel nodded. 'Ah,' he said, 'but stables are interesting places. Only last month, when I was in the country, I found some old carving—oak of the early sixteenth century. Thrown there, you understand, forgotten, left dusty and for worms to eat. I saved it. It is beautiful. You never know what you may find in stables. Bits of good old iron, old chests, a dozen things.'

'You know what we—the Christians—found in a stable, Mr. Gollantz.'

Emmanuel froze suddenly, the man refused to take a hint, he talked as if his hearer was a half-wit. Emmanuel became automatically a Jew.

'You found?' he said. 'I t'ought that the discovery was made by t'ree Kings from the East and some Jewish agriculturists. I am unorthodox, I know your Testament as well as my own. My wife declares it to be the most beautiful literature in the world.' He paused and smiled. 'She loves it as much as the poems of Mr. Swinburne and Mr. William Morris.'

Once the Rabbi himself came to persuade him to attend to his religious duties.

'Duties mean nothing,' Emmanuel said, 'religion should be a joy, not a duty.'

'It can be both, Emmanuel Gollantz.'

'The Germans say that religion without piety has done more mischief than anything else in the world.'

'Piety may be cultivated.'

Emmanuel made a gesture which included all the beautiful things in his room. 'I care only,' he said, 'for originals. I lack original piety.'

The Rabbi shook his head. He found Emmanuel flippant, he disliked flippancy.

'Listen,' Emmanuel said. ' "Wisdom is the principal thing . . ." and you remember how the precept ends? "With all thy getting, get understanding." I have no understanding of religion. All I can say is that, as a Jew, my cheque book is always at your service—for Jews. Now, let me show you a picture which I bought yesterday, it will interest you, I think.'

So they left him alone, and troubled him no more, except when they wanted money or help for any project. Then, Emmanuel would listen, ask questions, and give generously. If the money asked for was for other than Jewish charities, he referred them to his wife.

'My wife,' he said, 'is the most cheerful of cheerful givers. Only tell her that someone is uncomfortable, and she sympathises. She loves comfort terribly.'

Juliana would come to him afterwards and tell him of the people who had come to ask for charity. She disliked the clergy of any religion.

'That old Rabbi, Emmanuel—tell me, does he really wash? His beard is like a dusty hearth-rug.' Or, 'What was his name, that fat man—Father Leary? I could read the menus of the past week on his waistcoat.' Or again, 'I gave what he wanted very quickly to the Reverend Mr. Peacock. He exuded oiliness. His hands felt as if he held a poached egg in each palm. Ugh!' But to small, tired, shabby people she was infinitely kind, and never imitated them to Emmanuel afterwards.

Hermann Leon said to Emmanuel one evening, while they waited for dinner: 'Juliana is a good woman, as well as an attractive one. I hear constantly on all sides of kind things done—so quietly—so sympathetically.'

'She is wonderful,' Emmanuel said, 'and yet never

"given over to good works," which means a dowdy bonnet, and a badly cut skirt. She loves giving, and loves taking.'

Leon nodded. 'It's a great success, your marriage,' he said.

'I am very grateful to Juliana for making it one.'

'And how is the wonderful Algernon?'

Emmanuel stood very erect. 'My son,' he said, 'grows more like his mother every day. That says everything.'

5

Almost the last public function which Juliana had attended with Emmanuel before the birth of her son, had been the Thanksgiving Service for the recovery of the Prince of Wales. Emmanuel had been much moved by the national thanksgiving, he had taken expensive seats, and had even wiped his eyes after the Royal carriage had passed.

Juliana watched him, smiling. 'Crying—and he isn't your prince.'

Emmanuel, still dabbing his eyes, said, 'I feel as if he were, and I am thankful for his recovery.'

Juliana slipped her hand into his. 'I only feel that he's a handsome fellow, he loves life—he wanted to live and I'm glad he has!'

Walter Heriot, who stood near, laughed. 'Gad, what a way to speak of His Highness!'

In 1880, she insisted that Emmanuel should take out naturalisation papers. Emmanuel objected, brought up reasons of patriotism for his own country, but she argued him down.

'It is in England that you make your money, it is in England that you have made your home. You are not a soldier; then it might have been different. Now, you read the papers, your eyes shine when you read of that man— what is his name?—Wolseley. You speak quite excellent English—except when you are excited. Be made an Englishman, and then you will be able to sing, "God bless the Prince of Vales" with real fervour.'

They saw a great deal of Heriot and his wife during the years which followed. Together they saw Salvini as 'Hamlet', and the next year Henry Irving and Ellen Tree in the same play. Juliana disliked Irving, and said that Salvini 'left him in the shade'; Heriot liked neither of them and found the play much too long. Emmanuel said that Salvini was 'all voice and no heart.' 'Irving,' he said, 'thinks and feels. He is "Hamlet." ' Heriot much preferred *Little Doctor Faustus* or some other play which offered him amusement.

Once Heriot proposed that they should visit a music hall. His wife was scandalised, and regarded the suggestion as another proof of his eccentricity. All the Heriots were eccentric. Emmanuel frowned and looked dubious, but Juliana was delighted with the idea.

'Don't dress,' Heriot ordered, 'and wear thick veils.'

They drove to the Oxford music hall, in a hired brougham, for Emmanuel refused to allow his own coachman to know that they had visited the place. He sat well back in the box, nervous lest Juliana should be seen and recognised, annoyed at Heriot's guffaws at the broad comedy and still broader jokes and hating Lady Heriot's sibilant whisper which he felt could be heard all over the the house. The performance bored him, though Juliana said it was the most entertaining thing she had ever seen. Once she turned and took his programme from him. 'Who is the man who has just sung? He hasn't any voice, but he and the girl who is on now are the cleverest people on the programme.'

Emmanuel leant over her shoulder and found the names, he read them in a cautious whisper. 'The man is called—Art'ur Roberts,' he said, 'and that girl is—perhaps French, is she?—her name is Marie Loftus.'

Juliana shook her head. 'She is not French; he might be—if he wasn't obviously English, he has not only comedy but audacity.'

When Algernon was seven years old, they took him to the pantomime at Drury Lane, where the wonderful Vokes family carried the whole performance on their own shoulders. He was a beautiful child, vivacious and intelligent. His love for his mother was evident, he was never really happy unless he was with her and near her. There were times when Emmanuel was almost jealous of him, for though Juliana never spoilt him, it was apparent to everyone that she adored the child. As the years passed, Emmanuel found it increasingly easy to forget that there was a doubt as to the boy's parentage. Neither he nor Juliana ever referred to it, and Emmanuel, true to that promise which he had made to himself, never allowed his attitude to the boy to be anything except that of a devoted father. He, although he never loved the boy as he had hoped to love his own son, found reasons for pride and congratulation in his mentality, his good looks, and his intelligence.

A governess was engaged for him when he was six years old, and when he was eight, Emmanuel installed in her stead a tutor who had been in charge of the education of the children of an archduke.

In January, 1881, Juliana told him that she was going to have another child. He had never known her so affectionate, so appealing, so wonderful. He sat in his chair, at his desk—afterwards he wondered if she had chosen that setting to atone for another scene which had been played in that same room—when she came and leant over the back of it, laid her arms around his shoulders, and told him her news. His first impulse was to be delighted, thankful that his unspoken prayers had been granted, and that he was to have a son of his own. His second sensation was that of fear. Algernon was nearly nine years old, Juliana was almost forty. True, she looked, to him at least, as young as ever; she was gay, and still loved gaiety as she had always done. But—forty . . . He rose and took her in his arms, his face suddenly very pale.

'You're glad, Emmanuel?'

'Dear God!' he said. 'Glad is such a small word.'

'Then,' she touched his pale cheek with her finger, 'what does this mean?'

'It means that I love you—terribly. There! I have the right word—terribly—and that love makes me frightened.'

She laughed. 'Poof!' Then, 'Algernon will be jealous.'

Under her smile, under the tone which seemed to half excuse, half pardon Algernon, Emmanuel caught something else. He heard the jealousy of her own heart which feared that her son might be overlooked, slighted, pushed aside. He felt the old pain as he remembered, then mastered it, smiled and reassured her.

'Elchernon shall never, never have cause to be jealous. Am I so small that I cannot love my two sons?'

All through that spring and summer, Emmanuel Gollantz felt that he had never known before what love was, had never realised how precious his wife was to him. He scarcely left her side, he neglected his business and put more and more authority into the hands of Julius Davis, so that his own time might be free. For the first time for many years, he opened the deep drawer in his desk and brought out, carefully sealed and wrapped in paper, the little things which he had collected before Algernon was born.

He took them to Juliana and gave them into her hands.

'There,' he said, 'those are for him.'

'How do you know it will be—him?'

He shrugged his shoulders. 'A girl could only—at best —be a poor copy of her mother.'

Juliana unwrapped the parcels, examined the little gifts smiling, then said, 'When did you get all these treasures?'

'I have been collecting them,' he lied, 'since that evening you told me.'

In May, when London, to Emmanuel's fancy, began to be airless, he closed the house in Regent's Park and took Juliana and Algernon down to Brighton. Juliana protested that Brighton was hotter and far more noisy than Regent's Park, but Sir Isaac Montague, the specialist, agreed that the air was better, and, he added, ideally bracing.

On June the seventh, Emmanuel had been to a sale of pictures in town; as he travelled down, he let his thoughts wander to the coming child—his son. He sat, in a corner of the carriage, while the fields and hedges passed unseen, building castles in the air, making plans for the child's future, seeing himself and Juliana growing older and taking a pride which should grow each year in the boy's achievements. Juliana—the thought of her pushed even that of his son into the background. Emmanuel smiled tenderly and contentedly. Juliana was perfect; she was, as he had known when he saw her first, the one perfect woman in the world.

He decided to walk from the station, but he was scarcely a hundred yards from it when he decided to call a cab and drive home. Seated in the jolting, rattling carriage, fear came over him, quite suddenly. He found that his heart was beating heavily, that the palms of his hands were wet, and that a great sense of oppression overwhelmed him. He longed to shout to the driver to go more quickly, then his will subdued his unknown fears, and he leant back—shaken but calm again.

He let himself into the house with his latch-key, and stood in the hall breathing relief that he was home. As he laid down his hat, he smiled to think how amused Juliana would be at his fears. Only last night, when he had begged her to take the greatest care, always, she had laughed and said that he was foolish, adding, 'Me! I am the strongest woman in the world. When Algernon was born—it was nothing worse than toothache!'

Someone was coming down the stairs towards him. He looked up and felt a sudden disappointment that it was not Juliana. It was a man whom he did not know, a stout, elderly man with clipped side-whiskers, and a dark coat. He came down the stairs and stood in the hall, staring at Emmanuel.

'You are Mr. Gollantz?'

'That is my name. Yes?'

'I am Dr. Whittaker, of Hove.' He paused and Emmanuel knew that his heart was hammering against his side. 'They sent for me an hour ago, when your wife had the accident.'

'Accident,' Emmanuel said. 'Please—what accident? Is my wife—ill? Where is she? Take me to her—at once.'

The doctor raised his hand. 'Gently, gently, Mr. Gollantz. Your wife slipped and fell. It appears that a horse bolted, dashed on to the pavement, she slipped in avoiding it. I came immediately. I should like—if you have no objection—another opinion.'

Emmanuel stood, stunned and stupefied, then recovered himself, and turned and beckoned to the doctor to follow him. He sat down at the desk and took up a wad of telegraph forms.

'Get whatever opinion—or opinions—you wish,' he said. 'Send one of the servants. I should like to send for my wife's own doctor. Sir Isaac Montague. He can get a special train.'

Steadily he wrote out two telegrams, both very full and explicit. One to Julius Davis, ordering him to place himself at Sir Isaac's disposal, to arrange for a special train, the other to the great doctor. When he laid down his pencil he turned to Whittaker.

'May I see my wife, please?'

'For a moment.'

He stood by Juliana's bedside and looked down at her. She was terribly ill, in dreadful pain, but she smiled at him, and Emmanuel with a great effort smiled back at her.

'You said to me,' she whispered, 'be careful. But I never have been careful of anything. Forgive me.'

He knew that she was not thinking of her fall, of her pain, only of the one thing she had ever done for which she might ask forgiveness. Still smiling. Emmanuel said, 'Forgive? I have forgotten. Get well—quickly.'

She said, very softly, 'Emmanuel—dear Emmanuel—don't let Algernon be unhappy, will you?'

'Let my son be unhappy—no! Now, rest. I will come again presently.'

'Kiss me—good night.' He bent and kissed her cold forehead. She put her arm round his neck and he heard her catch her breath with pain as she did so. 'Good night, dearest, I do love you.' She laughed softly. 'I married the handsomest man in England. You're far better-looking than the Prince of Wales.'

An hour later, before the special train which brought Sir Isaac Montague arrived, the doctor with the side-whiskers came and told Emmanuel that she was dead. He expressed his sorrow and his sympathy. Emmanuel, his black eyes sunk deep in their sockets, checked him.

'Was it—difficult?'

'Death?' Emmanuel shivered suddenly. 'No—she slipped away. We could scarcely believe that she had gone.'

'I see. Thank you.'

The doctor remembered that he had heard that Jews loved their sons better than their wives. He cleared his throat. 'The child—it's a boy—is doing well. Small but perfectly healthy. Perhaps you would like to see him?'

'Not yet, please.' He turned and rang the bell, and when the servant answered it, said, 'Is Master Elchernon all right?'

The girl sniffed. Emmanuel saw that her eyes were red. 'He's crying, sir. Wanted to go to his . . .' she sniffed again, 'mother. Says he wants to say "Good night".'

'Bring him down here to me,' Emmanuel said, then turned to the doctor, 'Elchernon in my—eldest son, doctor. Good night, and t'ank you.'

They brought the fair-haired little boy down to him; Emmanuel looked at his tear-stained eyes and teased him gently for being a baby. He took him on his knee, gave him biscuits, and made him drink some milk. The boy was nearly nine—was he eight or nine? Emmanuel could not remember. His brain ached, his whole head felt sore.

He said, 'I want to tell you a secret. It's terr-ribly important. Mother has been called away to London on business. I sent for a special train.'

'What is a special train, Father?'

'A train especially for her. She said to me, just now, before she started. "Don't let Elchernon be unhappy." '

'Did she say that . . . ?' he was obviously pleased, 'only she never says "Elchernon". She says "*AL*-gernon".'

'I know . . . Now go to bed quickly and don't make a noise, and you shall go to London in the morning—quite early.'

The child nodded. 'Back to Regent's Park? I'd like that. Good night, Father.'

The next morning, Emmanuel travelled back to London, taking Juliana with him. Julius Davis met him at the station, found him calm but looking terribly ill. Once, as they walked to the carriage which awaited them, Emmanuel swayed, and would have fallen had not Julius caught his arm. During the drive home, he neither spoke nor moved, never turned one backward glance to see that the hearse had left the station, only ordered the coachman to drive home quickly, taking the shortest possible route. As the carriage turned into Regent's Park, he turned to Julius and spoke. 'You laid down the carpet as I ordered?'

'Yes, Emmanuel, and an awning.'

'Flowers—you got flowers?'

'Masses of them.'

Emmanuel nodded. 'That was right,' he smiled. 'She always liked a fuss made of her.'

So when the coffin arrived, Emmanuel met it, dressed ceremoniously, and walked beside it over the red carpet through the hall where flowers were banked, into his study, where it was laid upon the huge oak desk. His friends came, bringing their condolences, offering sympathy; he would see no one. Even Rachel Leon went away without a word from him, only a message of thanks from his secretary.

After the funeral, Julius expected that Emmanuel would Sit Shiva, and abstain from work, but when he hinted this Emmanuel shook his head.

'Sit Shiva,' he said, 'Julius, I shall do that all my life. I must work or I shall go mad. Tell Elchernon's tutor that neither will I have the boy taught to say Kaddish for his mother. Let him remember her—and be happy, not weigh down his mind with prayers for the dead, who can probably take care of themselves better than those of us who are left.'

For the first time, he consented to see his son. He walked up to the nursery, and had the child placed in his arms. It was small, pitifully small, but—so the nurse assured him—perfectly healthy. Emmanuel looked down at the tiny face, saw the dark eyes open and stare back at him, saw the black down which covered the child's head and touched its cheek with his finger tip.

'He is like you, sir.'

'Yes, I suppose he is.'

'What name shall you give him?'

'Name?' Emmanuel said, 'I haven't t'ought what name.' He looked down again at the scrap of humanity in his arms. 'Call him Max,' he said, 'short for Maximus, because he is so little. A paradox of a name, eh?'

For six months Emmanuel went nowhere except to his business, and about his business. He refused to see his friends, refused to rest; when his work was finished he would sit for hours alone, his head resting on his hands, staring blankly before him.

It was Rachel Leon who forced him to take up his life again. She came, one frosty December evening, and walked into Emmanuel's study unannounced. She was a beautiful woman, a trifle over stout, but with magnificent hair, fine eyes, and—what so few Jewesses retain after their first youth—a wonderful skin. Emmanuel frowned, then stood up, offered her a chair and said, 'My dear Rachel, this is a pleasure.'

She sat down. 'It might be, for me,' she said, 'if you meant it.'

'It is always a pleasure to see you.'

'A pleasure of which you so seldom avail yourself. We never see you, you shut yourself up here and live like a hermit. Poor Juliana, how you would have bored her!'

'Rachel—please!' He held up his hand, hurt beyond words.

Rachel shrugged her shoulders. 'Nu, think of it. You are thirty-seven—a young man. Are you going to live like this for the rest of your days? How abominable for your poor children. Do you ever see them?'

'I see them once every day,' his tone was dignified and cold.

'I should think they dread it. Even Max must feel this gloom descend upon him. Poor Algernon, small wonder he looks peaky.'

'I had not noticed that he did.'

'Do you notice anything? Listen to me, Emmanuel Gollantz. For ten years you lived with Juliana, for ten years you enjoyed life, for ten years she loved you and you loved her. Now she is gone, and you live in a way which would be in direct opposition to her wishes. To live —to laugh—to be happy—is not to forget. This gloom— it pushes itself outside your study walls, up the stairs to the children's rooms. Is that kind? Is it just? You feel that your life is over—well, that is as you feel. But Algernon, Max—their lives are beginning. Don't you owe them anything?'

Emmanuel clasped his hands, the thought of trying to be gay without Juliana was torment to him. Rachel saw his white face, his strained eyes, his drawn mouth, and the new lines which had gathered round it. She came over to where he stood, and took his hands in hers. The warm contact comforted him, he relaxed, and the frown on his face disappeared.

'What do you want me to do, Rachel?'

'First,' she said, 'sit down, then listen. You told Julius that Algernon was not to say Kaddish, you wanted him to remember his mother and be happy. Are you helping him? Can't you hear him say that you are changed since his mother died? Have you no faith, Emmanuel?'

'No, Rachel, none.'

'You think that you have lost Juliana for ever?'

'I am afraid so.'

'You can't say, "The Lord giveth, the Lord taketh away, Blessed be the Name of the Lord"?'

'I can say the first part,' he said, 'but I refuse to bless the name of a God who gives only to snatch away, Rachel.'

'I see. In justice, Emmanuel, admit that if He left the decisions with you or with me, He would scarcely be a God. But—we'll leave that. Let me go back. Either you believe that you will meet Juliana again, or that she is lost to you for ever. If the first—then you must live—sanely and humanly, so that when you meet she shall not find you changed; if the second, then you must remember that Juliana belongs to the past, Algernon and Max to the future, and that you are responsible for them. Don't shirk your responsibilities, your liabilities.'

'What do you suggest that I should do?'

'First,' she said, 'it is December. You are a Jew . . .' she smiled, 'after all, you *are* a Jew, Emmanuel; but this is what Mr. Dickens in his *Christmas Carol* calls the "Festive season". Make it festive for Algernon. Get a Christmas tree. You lived sufficiently long abroad to know how children love them. Send for Walter Heriot's two little girls, for little Miriam Davis—oh, I will find you a dozen nice children. Old Mudder Davis will screw up her face and accuse you of being "link"—that won't trouble you?'

He nodded. 'Perhaps you are right. And after this—Christmas tree?'

'Come and see Hermann. He longs to see you and show you his newest pictures and books. Go and see the Heriots, poor Sir Walter is so terribly anxious to, what he calls, "bring you round". Live, Emmanuel, and do, do remember how it must bore Juliana, if she can see you, to know you live in this gloom.'

'I t'ink,' Emmanuel said slowly, 'that you are right. I have been selfish. Have you seen Max? He really begins to grow.'

'Send for him,' she said, 'I should like to see him.'

Emmanuel went to the bell and rang, then turned and said, 'And you'd like to see Elchernon too, wouldn't you? He is so intelligent, that boy.'

Book Two

Emmanuel and Algernon

6

Emmanuel Gollantz took up the threads of his life again. With grave distaste, he began again to accept invitations. He forced himself to amuse his sons, and gradually found that Algernon was very dear to him. The child was so like Juliana, he loved gaiety, adored music, and one of the first presents that Emmanuel gave him after his mother's death, was a curious music-making machine. A huge square box, upon the top of which were laid discs, made of strong cardboard and perforated with oblong punctures. These were placed upon the top of the machine, a handle was wound, a spring released and music was produced. The affair was declared quite wonderful, and visitors were frequently taken to the nursery to hear it play. Walter Heriot, his legs straddled before the fire, declared it to be 'a damned wonderful invention', while his wife gave it as her opinion that 'nothing could be more natural'. Only Algernon, listening to the sounds with grave attention, said, 'It's not quite right, is it, Father? Not real music like pianos and violins.'

The baby, Max, grew slowly. He was strong enough, but never had the intense vitality of his elder brother. At seven, he was a slim child, with beautiful eyes, serious, and a little shy; his hands and feet were small and slender, his manners charming. Emmanuel, in his heart, idolised him; but sternly repressed any impulse to make more of Max then he did of the elder boy.

When Algernon was twelve, he was sent to school. Emmanuel felt that a prejudice still existed in public schools against Jews, and to safeguard the boy against any additional hardship, sent him to an expensive private school which was run by the younger son of an Earl.

Here Algernon—automatically becoming Algy—mixed with boys who had no pride of race in particular, but heartily despised Jews, whom they regarded as following the trade of money-lenders and pawnbrokers to the exclusion of all others. The very thing which Emmanuel had hoped to avoid grew and flourished in the exclusive school to which he sent his elder son.

Algernon, on being questioned as to the nationality of his name, and having enough intelligence to realise that to admit his Jewish birth would be fatal, declared that his father came from a noble family in Vienna, and that his mother was a Frenchwoman. When he returned home at the Christmas holidays, and Emmanuel pressed him to invite his friends to a party which should be given in his honour, the boy turned sulky and swore that none of his friends lived in London.

'Not live in London!' Emmanuel said. 'But the Wrottleseys live in Berkeley Square, and Frank Benson has a house in Mayfair. Ask them, Elchernon; let me give you a great party!'

Algernon stuck his hands in his pockets, scowled, and said that he hated parties. Emmanuel shrugged his shoulders, and left the boy alone. Later he sent for him to his study. Emmanuel sat at his desk, the same desk upon which Juliana's coffin had rested, and smiled at his son. Emmanuel had grown heavier, but was still remarkably handsome, his figure was still elegant, and his clothes immaculate. He always looked back with regret to the frilled shirts, the embroidered waistcoats, and the strapped trousers of his youth; still dressed with a touch of extravagance and—still—swaggered.

To Algernon, full of the belief that no gentleman should ever look in the most minute detail unlike other gentlemen, his appearance was shattering. He eyed with distaste his father's grey frock-coat, his huge tie with its diamond pin, and the black and white check trousers. Emmanuel laid down the cigar which he was smoking and drew the boy to him.

'Listen,' he said, 'I have somet'ing to say to you.' After Juliana's death, when there was no one to correct his accent, he had slipped back and spoke more like a foreigner and less like an Englishman every day. A fact which added to Algernon's fear that his father might ever meet any of his school-fellows. 'You got holidays—fife weeks, eh? Now, I want you to enjoy yourself, to go back and tell all the odder boys what a grend time you've had. Tell me how you'd like to plan your time, please.'

Algernon struggled away from Emmanuel's encircling arm. 'I want,' he said, 'to go to concerts, and hear music, Father. I don't really like pantomimes at Drury Lane. I don't think Herbert Campbell's very funny, really.'

'Music!' Emmanuel said. 'Music—you like music? Well, you shall have it. Uncle Hermann loves music too, he will take you whenever you wish.'

Hermann Leon was the one Jew who did not rouse shame and dislike in young Gollantz, and it was Hermann Leon who went with him to hear every concert which could be crammed into the holidays. It was Hermann Leon who told Emmanuel that the boy must have lessons in violin playing.

From that day, Algernon Gollantz neglected everything except his music. His masters declared that he learnt nothing, his writing was abominable, his mathematics deplorable, his knowledge of history nil. Only his violin playing improved. Emmanuel heard him play during the Easter holidays, and admitted to Hermann Leon that the quality of his playing was a surprise.

Leon nodded. 'That is nothing,' he said, 'to what he will do. That boy is clever, Emmanuel. More—he's brilliant.'

Emmanuel agreed. 'It's a splendid accomplishment for a young man. It will be a gr-reat asset to him in society.'

'He won't want to use it only as a leg-up in society, Emmanuel.'

'Not? Then where would he use it?'

'As a profession, perhaps.'

Gollantz laughed. 'A professional violinist! My good Hermann, what nonsense. Fiddling for a living when he can take over a business like mine.'

'But could he take over a business like yours?'

'If he's trained. The boy is intelligent.'

He talked to Rachel about Algernon. Rachel, who had

grown very stout, but was still very beautiful. A modern woman, reading pamphlets issued by the Society for the Extension of the Franchise to Women, smoking expensive cigarettes and, strangely enough, appearing to enjoy them. Physically she was the laziest woman Emmanuel knew, mentally the most active. It was on Rachel's advice that he invested in two paintings by Manet, and one by Degas which has since become famous and been bought by an American millionaire.

'Renoir, Emmanuel,' she said, 'buy Renoir.'

Emmanuel shuddered. 'Oh, those fat pink women! I hate them. The earlier ones—how charming. Children, women, men—even Paris, but later they are terr-rible.'

'They will sell,' Rachel said, 'people can remember his name, and say it more or less correctly. The rich ignorant will prefer him to Ingres. They can never make up their minds whether to say "Angre" or "Ingrez"—that annoys them. For that reason—apart from any other—the multitude will always like Hals.' She settled herself more comfortably against her cushions, knocked the ash from her cigarette on to the Persian carpet, and leant back contentedly.

'Algernon is seventeen this year,' she said, with apparent irrelevance, 'what are you going to do with him?'

'I t'ought, perhaps, Oxford or Cambridge.'

Rachel shook her head. 'He could never pass the most simple examination. Why waste time and money? He wants to go to Germany to study, he told Hermann so.'

'This music playing again, eh?'

'Again—always—forever apparently,' she said, 'you will let him go?'

'I don't like it,' Emmanuel said, rising and pacing the room, his hands clasped behind him. 'Rachel, I don't like it. There are reasons—big reasons. Not money—for he shall have share and share alike with little Max.' She heard his voice soften suddenly when he spoke of Max. 'Don't t'ink that I don't want him to have what he wants. It is not that. I hev been chenerous—I t'ink, I have been just, I hev been affectionate. I love Elchernon. But music—to study out there alone—it makes me afraid for him. T'ere would be no one to watch him, no one to say, "Do this", or "Do that".' He came and stood before Rachel, and stared at her with his dark eyes full of trouble. 'Elchernon likes odder t'ings besides music, Rachel.'

'Don't we all like more than one thing?'

'Yes,' eagerly. 'I do. I love—what?—t'ousands of t'ings. Books, fun, comfort—but I'm willing to work for them, and pay for them.'

'Ah—that's how it is, eh? It's difficult, Emmanuel, isn't it?'

Algernon was difficult, Emmanuel had found that his difficulty increased as he grew older. First there was his hatred—the thing amounted to an obsession—of his father's race. Emmanuel wondered, puzzled, and worried over it, reflecting that even Jules Alessandri had been a Jew. He was scarcely civil to Emmanuel's friends, with the exception of Hermann Leon.

Emmanuel had overheard a conversation in the hall, not long ago. Algernon had come home late, during his holidays. Old Moses, the butler, had warned him that he must hurry.

'Dere's a dinner party tonight, Mr. Elchernon. I laid out your t'ings.'

'Dinner party! Oh, Lord. Who's coming? A mob of damned Jews, I suppose.'

Moses had chuckled, 'Damned or not, they're arriving at eight, Mr. Elchernon.'

That hurt him, but after all, if the boy hated Jews, that was his affair. There were other matters which disturbed Emmanuel more. Bills from school, accounts from tradesmen, curious accounts for women's things. He had demanded details before he paid them, the tradesmen had given the details. Now, the last straw, a letter from the Headmaster. Emmanuel had no great opinion of that gentleman, but the letter made him anxious. He drew Emmanuel's attention to the fact that Algernon was seventeen, that he was old for his age, that he refused to apply himself to any work except his music. He suggested that, perhaps, the time had come for his father to remove him. He hinted that he would be glad of the vacancy, there were numerous applicants for places in his school houses.

Emmanuel thinking over these things, rang the bell and asked that Julius Davis might be sent to him. Julius was installed in the house as his secretary and manager. He divided his time between Regent's Park and Campden Hill. Julius came, stout, well groomed, and effective. Emmanuel greeting him, reflected that Julius would never set the Thames on fire, and congratulated himself on the fact. Julius was honest, Emmanuel seldom found that brilliance and honesty went hand-in-hand—in business.

'Julius, take a cigar. Sit down, I want to talk to you. It's about Elchernon.' For a second he fancied that a shadow of uneasiness passed over Julius' face. 'His school bills are all paid? Yes. His bills—t'ose damned tradesmen's bills? Yes. Let me have them and the receipts, please. Now, Julius, what opinion have you of Elchernon?'

Julius moved uneasily in his chair. 'With regard to coming into the business? I don't know that he has any great flair . . .'

'Business, no!' Emmanuel said. 'Kerecter—that's what I want to hear about.'

'He's affectionate . . .'

'So are dogs. Affection won't get him far.'

'He is intelligent . . .'

'So are monkeys. Julius, Julius, don't be a fool. If you had ten t'ousand pounds, would you trust it to Elchernon?'

'No, Emmanuel, not as he is now.'

'Ah!' a long drawn sigh of enlightenment. 'How much does he owe you?'

'I didn't say he owed me anything.'

'I know you didn't. I said it. I want an answer, please.'

'I couldn't say—off-hand. I couldn't, really.'

Emmanuel nodded. 'All right. Please go and reckon it up, and bring it back to me here. As quickly as you can.'

Julius rose. When he got to the door, Emmanuel called, 'Send Moses to me, please.'

Moses came and stood just inside the door, shifting from one foot to the other. Emmanuel went on writing for a few moments, then looked up.

'Ah, Moses—why did you lend money to Mr. Elchernon?'

'Me lend money to Mr. Elchernon! Vy would I hev to, sir. Mr. Elchernon alvays hev plenty of money.'

Emmanuel raised his hand. 'That will do, Moses, we're not in the Ghetto lying to each other to sell a pair of boots. How much is it?'

'Tisn't a lot, sir. Not a great deal. I didn't hev a lot to lend him, already. P'reps—p'reps—five or six pounds. Don't say notting to him, sir. Boys is always being boys, it's an old head what doan't rejoice.'

'That will do. Send Elchernon to me, at once.'

'Mr. Elchernon's just gone to hev his bath, sir.'

Emmanuel glanced at the great black marble clock on the mantelpiece.

'What—at a quarter to eleven! Tell him I want him in ten minutes.'

Until Algernon came, Emmanuel sat and stared at the picture of Juliana which always stood on his desk. He knitted his brows, and set his mouth firmly. At last he lifted the picture and examined it more closely. He scrutinised every line of the laughing face, looked into the eyes which even after nine years smiled back at him.

'Help me to be wise,' he said softly. 'I never wish to make Elchernon unhappy.'

He put down the picture and turned to face his son. Algernon stood in the doorway, his handsome face was sulky, his whole attitude was nervous as he faced the man who had always been his father. Emmanuel smiled, and beckoned him to the desk.

'Sit down, Elchernon,' he said, and the boy resented that his father could not even say his name correctly. 'I want to hev a little talk with you.' Algernon felt depression descend upon him. 'A little talk'—how horrible. He prepared to listen, mentally criticising Emmanuel's clothes as he did so. How awful to have a father who dressed like an actor or a glorified ring master! A grey frock-coat with satin facings, that huge black pearl pin, yards of white cuff showing, a tie which looked like the breast of a pouter pigeon. All too rich, too opulent; even his father's voice sounded too rich, too full—like an organ, you didn't want men's voices to sound like organs. He talked like an actor . . .

'Elchernon,' Emmanuel said, trying desperately to conquer his nervousness and speak naturally and as like an Englishman as possible, 'I've got a lot to say to you. You're seventeen, you're almost a man. Nu (the Jewish word slipped out before he could check it), you got to play fair. It isn't playing fair to run up bills, and borrow money from Julius Davis and old Moses. That isn't—playing the game.' Algernon shuddered, he had waited for that expression ever since his father began.

'They've sneaked, have they?' he said. 'That's like them. Would you call that playing the game?'

Emmanuel fought hard to keep his temper, he looked at the handsome, angry face and smiled. 'I asked them, I made them tell me. Is it five or six pounds to Moses? Six. And Julius? Fifteen-ten.' He took out his note case and counted out four five-pound notes, then drew his sovereign case which was attached to his braces buttons by a gold chain and extracted two sovereigns. He pushed the money over to Algernon. 'Please settle with them.'

Algernon took the money, and weighed it in his hand. 'Do you want the ten bob change?'

'No, you can keep that. Now, about the bills from Herringway. From hosiers, stationers, and tailors.'

'I have to look decent, and I must have books.'

'I agree. Since when did you wear silk garters, and two pairs of'—he read from the bill before him—'fine cambric chemises and drawers?'

Algernon flushed. 'That was a joke—that's all.'

'Your jokes are expensive, Elchernon. More expensive than listening to Dan Leno's—who doesn't amuse you. Well, they are paid for now. Settled.' For the first time the boy softened. 'That's very decent of you, thanks awfully, Father.'

'It has cost me,' Emmanuel began, and Algernon sank back into his sulky, half-ashamed annoyance. Why must his father spoil it all? The first gesture had been so good, now he was going to talk like a money-lender. 'It has cost me—twenty-seven pounds, eighteen shillings, plus the twenty-two pounds which I hev given you. Forty-nine pounds, eighteen—nearly fifty pounds. Now that is over —forgotten—wiped off. Let us talk of other t'ings. Only remember, Elchernon, this must not heppen again. I mean that, please.'

'All right, Father, and thanks awfully.'

Emmanuel settled himself in his chair, lit a cigar, and made his suggestions to his son. He had settled the bills, he had said that it must never happen again, but he was dissatisfied. He felt that he had said either too much or too little, he had been weak because he was afraid of making Juliana's son unhappy. Only yesterday, Max had flown into a passion, had screamed with temper at his governess, thrown his books to the floor, and dashed the inkpot after them. Emmanuel had been sent for. He had spoken sternly to Max, Max had sobbed with deep contrition, and today it was reported that Max was behaving like an angel. He had never been able to deal with Algernon in that way; always, when the boy had been naughty and Emmanuel had rebuked him, his words had been checked by the memory of Juliana saying, 'Don't let Algernon be unhappy.'

Now, making his suggestions, offering advice, voicing promises, he was conscious that he was trying to win Algernon's affection, trying to make him love him, trying—most of all—to make him happy. Munich, a famous teacher of the violin—'very expensive, but very good indeed'. Algernon should live with a family known to Hermann Leon, nice people, cultured people. 'Not an ordinary lodging house for young students. It will cost more, but you will be more comfortable and it will be well-spent money.' A new violin, Hermann had said that the old one was not good enough. There was one which Hermann wished Algernon to try—'very old, apparently violins are like wine, they improve with years. Like good wine, too, their price goes up. This is—to my mind—a terr-rible price, but you must hev the best.'

Everything, the boy thought, ticketed 'very expensive'—'terr-ribly costly', and so on. His father's friends—excepting old Heriot, who was a half-wit, talked of money, of what they bought, and for what they might sell it. Heriot was forever talking of horses, dogs, his racing stable, and his wonderful daughters. Davis, Goldsmidt, Simmons, and the others with their comic names, Belisario, Omyshund, Samuda, and Pireira, always boasting that they were Jews, or else using Jewish words as if they constituted a joke.

The other day when they had dined with old Davis and his wife, Emmanuel had been offered some new dish. Old Davis had chuckled and said it was all right. 'Kosher, Emmanuel, kosher.' His wife, fat and hideous, had giggled and said that they all knew that his father was 'link'. Little Miriam, the daughter of Julius, had been brought in. Ten years old, with long curls and bright dark eyes. His father had petted her, taken her on his knee and said, 'What eyes! No need for the shadchan here, Davis.'

The unsuccessful were shlemihl, the men who asked for favours were 'good schnorrers', goy and goyim were applied as terms of slighting reproach. Algernon hated them all, hated their self-satisfaction, their success, their evident admiration of each other.

Upstairs, alone in his own room, he stuck his hands in his pockets, and scowled at the memory of the offending race. One day he would be free of them, one day he would discard the name of Gollantz, he would deny, as he had denied at school, that he had any Jewish blood in his veins. He looked with satisfaction at his reflection in the mirror. Touched his fair hair approvingly, noted his blue eyes, his bright colouring, and his wide mouth which lacked the fullness of the Jew.

'I might be an Englishman or a German,' he said complacently.

So Algernon, at seventeen, went to Germany, and Emmanuel was left alone with Max—Max who at nine was already begging that he might go to school as his brother had done. Emmanuel debated over the choice of schools, he disliked the idea of allowing Max to follow Algernon at the exclusive school where he had apparently learnt nothing. He decided to send his own son to a school in London, which had been the training ground for so many Jews whom Emmanuel revered and admired.

Max returned after his first day there and was allowed to sit up to dinner to give his impressions to his father. He was a nice-looking boy, like Emmanuel but lacking his extraordinary good looks. Max was well-built, his features were clear cut, and unmarred by racial exaggerations. He would never excite comment as Emmanuel had done, he would be an average, well-built, good-featured fellow, with an amazingly pleasant smile. 'Lots of Jews at my school, Father.'

Emmanuel nodded, smiling. 'Do you like Jews, Max?'

'I don't know . . .' the boy hesitated, 'I like—people, you know.'

'Jews are the Chosen People.' Emmanuel blew a delicate stream of blue smoke from his cigar, eyeing the boy as he did so.

'I think that's rather mean—to choose a few people and give them extra chances, don't you? If God made them all, He should have treated them all alike. That's fair, isn't it? You wouldn't treat me differently from Algy.'

'In strict confidence,' Emmanuel said, 'speaking as one man to anudder—I don't believe He does. I doubt if He ever did. That is between ourselves.'

Max nodded gravely. 'Oh, of course. After all the Jews wrote the Bible themselves, didn't they? I mean, all that about the Sun standing still and those other things. Oh, that reminds me, may I go to the Egyptian Hall on Saturday? There's a wonderful conjuror there called Maskelyne.'

7

Algernon was coming home, coming home for good. Twice he had returned on a visit, each time appearing less and less satisfactory in Emmanuel's eyes. He had left the family were Hermann Leon's introduction had placed him. There had been trouble—one of the daughters, and Emmanuel had paid a considerable amount to settle the matter. He had sent for Algernon, had spoken to him seriously and coldly. Algernon, very frightened, had looked white and pinched, had pleaded and given a dozen unsatisfactory explanations. His eyes, his fair hair, his beautiful skin had sent Emmanuel's eyes flying to Juliana's picture. He had seen her in the young man who faced him. His coldness had turned to warm affection, he had spoken with kindness and tenderness; Algernon had wiped away his tears, his colour had returned, and he had despised his father because he still called him 'El-chernon'.

'This music isn't any good,' Emmanuel said to Rachel and Hermann Leon, 'it's doing the boy harm, making him easy-going, sleck, and impractical.'

Rachel yawned, showing her white teeth. 'Scarcely impractical, Emmanuel. It's not impractical to manage to live—and live very well—at someone else's expense.'

Emmanuel shook his head and made a little gesture of protest with his beautiful white hands. 'That's hard, Rachel. I don't like you to be hard on him.'

'It's not the music,' Hermann said, in his rather high weak voice, 'it's—it's something in him that doesn't respond to the influence of the music.'

'Somet'ing, somet'ing!' Emmanuel echoed, 'but what—can't we find it?'

'I can tell you,' Rachel said, 'I can tell you, and you may not like it. It's that bogey of Juliana's—boredom turned sour. She liked gaiety, he likes orgies; she liked excitement, he likes vicious danger; she liked exquisite luxury, he likes sensual comfort. That's what is wrong. He is Juliana shown in a distorting mirror.'

Emmanuel stared at her in horror, his eyes wide, his face pale.

'Rachel! Do you know what you are saying—you're accusing Elchernon of being a—a—libertine.'

'So he is,' very calmly, 'a libertine in the making; and you are helping to manufacture one.'

Hermann Leon laid his hand on Emmanuel's arm. 'Take no notice, Emmanuel. Rachel talks violently. Ever since she wanted women to have a vote, ever since she interested herself in slums and factories she is—violent.'

'Agreed,' Rachel said, 'it is only fanatics who get things accomplished.'

The two men sat in silence, while Rachel continued to smoke calmly. Hermann rose, walked to the huge sideboard, unlocked the tantalus and poured out a drink for himself and Emmanuel. He brought them back, handed one to his friend without speaking, and sat down again. Emmanuel took the glass, nodded his thanks, and the silence endured.

Rachel rubbed the end of her cigarette on a metal tray and extinguished it, she looked at the two men and smiled, a wide, very affectionate smile.

'I said, just now, what you have both felt and known for months. Deny it, either of you. What shocks you is not the truth, which you know, but that I should speak it. Listen to me, Emmanuel. Ever since Algernon was born—I can speak frankly—you have spoiled him. Since Juliana died, you have ruined him. You told me what she said, "Don't let Algernon be unhappy." Are you so stupid as to believe you are making him happy?'

'I hev tried, Rachel.'

'No, my dear, that is just what you have *not* tried. You have played for safety. You always do—since you became rich and successful. You have tried to make Algernon love you; the result is that he neither loves nor respects you. Playing for safety—always. When we played whist two evenings ago with Ike Samuda and Adah Mercado, you played for safety and lost fifty pounds.'

Hermann stayed his glass half-way to his mouth. 'Fifty pounds! What were you playing?'

Rachel moved impatiently. 'Forty on the rubber and a pound a trick.'

'Far too much. You gamble abominably, Rachel.'

'I know—I know. I like gambling. I can afford it.'

Hermann mumbled, 'Forty on the rubber—a pound a trick.' Then said suddenly, 'Then you lost more than fifty, Emmanuel?'

'I know, it don't metter. Let's get back to Elchernon. What shall I do?'

Rachel sat upright, sending the ash tray and her box of cigarettes flying on to the floor. 'Make him work,' she said. 'Disraeli once said that the man who does not work, has no right to live. He's a hero of yours, follow his advice. Make Algernon either work or make his living less easy.'

Algernon came home, he brought boxes which weighed down the carriage because they were full of music, he brought strange clothes, stranger pipes, and his violin. Max thought him wonderful, watched him with pride, and boasted of him to his friends at school as the greatest violinist in the world.

'Sarasate is the greatest violinist in the world,' a boy declared.

'Sara—*what?*' Max said. 'I never heard of him!' He made an examination of the whole class and discovered that only two boys had ever heard of Sarasate. 'There,' he said in triumph, 'what did I tell you!'

Emmanuel interviewed Algernon alone. The interview was stormy, and in the end, Emmanuel felt that he had been hard and unjust.

'You can't judge artists by ordinary standards,' Algernon said. 'It may sound ridiculous to you, Father, but it's true none the less.'

'I want you to work,' Emmanuel said. 'From what Hermann hears, you don't work. You play what you like to play, when you want to play, and how it amuses you to play. Thet isn't how violinists are made.'

Algernon twisted his little fair moustache and said 'Oh . . .' in a tone of superiority which made Emmanuel's blood boil.

'No,' he said violently.

'You know, of course.'

'I know a gr-reat deal more than you t'ink.'

'How do you know what I—t'ink?'

Emmanuel heard the imitation, as he was meant to do, his hands clenched, and he felt suddenly a little sick. He turned and faced the young man, speaking very softly. For the first time in his life, Algernon was frightened of his father. This tall, pale-faced man who towered over him, who spoke in a whisper, was a stranger.

'Now,' he said, 'I will tell you somet'ing else that I t'ink. You are a schnorrer, that's what you are. The horse-leech had not only daughters but sons, and you are one of them. You hate Jews, you despise them—then go to your friends the goyim and see what they will do for you. I have never made you a Jew—never imposed fasts and observances upon you; go and see if the Christians can do better than I have done. You're free, you can do as you like—you hev always done as you liked. I am done with you—finished—ended.'

Algernon turned and went out, slamming the door. For three days the sound of his violin was heard through the house. Emmanuel, still smarting under the belief that he had been hard and unkind, listened with delight. At last he had made an impression on the boy! Then the playing ceased, and Algernon was out early and late, coming home silent with no information as to how he had spent his time. Max followed him about the house whenever he was at home, with adoration in his eyes. Algernon always smelt of tobacco and beer. To Max the combination was wonderful, exciting, and delightfully manly. He tried to smoke one of his brother's pipes, was caught, and—incidentally—was terribly sick.

Two days later, while Max was still a little pale from his attempt to emulate his brother, the storm burst. It was just before dinner. Max was in the study with Emmanuel explaining carefully that his misdeeds of two days previously ought not to be weighed against the long-standing promise of a Star bicycle. Emmanuel listened, gravely amused, stroking his chin, and smiling.

'Well,' he said, 'I'll meet you half-way. How much have you in that gelt box of yours, Max?'

Max shuffled his feet, played with a pencil and sniffed.

'You said that you would give me a bicycle, Father.'

'You hedn't been a bad boy then. How much hev you got, and I'll make up the rest. Thet's fair.'

'I haven't got anything.'

'You spent it?'

'I haven't got anything. I did something with it.'

'What did you do with it?'

'I can't tell you. It's not fair to ask me. I can't break promises.'

'Ah, you promised not to tell me. How much was there? That's not breaking a promise, Max.'

'Four pounds, sixteen, and fivepence, and two French pennies and a German mark. You can have the pennies and the mark, Father.'

'No,' Emmanuel said, 'I'll change them into English money for you. You can hev the bicycle, Max. Tell Moses to go with you to the shop on Saturday. Good boy, never br-reak promises.'

'You're not cross? Not really?'

'Not a bit, Max. Gentlemen don't break promises.'

Max traced a pattern on the carpet with the toe of a dirty shoe, then looked up and said, 'Jews can be gentlemen if they try, can't they?'

'Anyone can be a gentleman—if they try hard enough.'

Max smiled, and turned to go. Emmanuel caught his arm and pulled him to him. He felt very tender towards the little boy, wanted to take him in his arms and talk to him about his mother. He didn't dare to do that. He said, rather thickly, 'How old are you—twelve? Time you hed a watch, a good watch. You'd like to have a watch, eh?'

'Yes, I would, but,' hastily, 'I'd like a bicycle, and, oh, I would like a little dog, if I might.'

'One t'ing at a time, please. You shall hev a watch tonight, a bicycle on Saturday, and the dog—well, your birthday's over.'

Max said, hopefully, 'Yes, but there is Christmas. Lots of Jews give presents then, and it's a very good time to give people dogs. You see, they get used to you all winter, when they're in the house a lot, and then in the spring when you take them walking they don't run away. Not if you've treated them prop'ly.'

'You'll make a lawyer, Max, or a politician. We'll see, we'll talk of this dog later. Let's get the watch.'

Juliana's watch, a small hunter which he had given her before women wore diminutive things pinned on their breasts as they did now. Max should have it, he should know it had been his mother's. For years Emmanuel had kept it, with a dozen other small bits of jewellery in a trinket box in his dressing-room drawer. Together he and Max mounted the stairs and entered the room. Max wandered about, picking up things, asking questions while Emmanuel opened the drawer and found the box.

'Now, Max, this is your mother's watch, and I . . .' he

stopped short. The watch was not there, neither were the dozen almost valueless trinkets which had lain with it. Emmanuel laid down the box and stared at his son. 'Max,' he said in a queer shaking voice, 'it's—gone. They've all gone. A brooch I gave her with silly little pearls, because she liked the shape; a locket . . .' he choked suddenly, coughed, and laid down the box, said again, 'They're gone, Max, so you can't have the watch. I'm sorry.'

Max drew a deep breath. 'I don't mind,' he said, 'I shouldn't mind too much if I was you. I don't often look at the time, you know.'

Something in his voice made Emmanuel look at him sharply. 'We don't know who took them,' he said quickly.

''Course we don't,' Max agreed. 'Prob'ly a burglar did one night.'

That night Emmanuel could not sleep, he paced his room hour after hour, assuring himself that he must not be unjust, he must not suspect everyone before—his son, Juliana's son. He tried hard to imagine that old Moses might have been horse racing, that Rebecca the cook, Miriam the parlour maid, Rose the housemaid, Grant, who carried coals and cleaned boots and knives, the coachman, even Julius Davis might have robbed him—and failed miserably. He came down in the morning, heavy-eyed and short-tempered.

Max was late for breakfast. Emmanuel snapped at him. 'You'll be late for school. Why don't you get up when you're called?'

Max smiled. 'I meant to, but I went to sleep again. I dreamt I was riding a bicycle and it turned into a dog.'

'Where is Elchernon?'

'Why, he never comes to breakfast, Father! I egspect he's still asleep.'

When he finished his breakfast, Emmanuel was still hidden behind *The Times* pretending to read. Max came and touched his father's arm. 'Good-bye, Father.' Then added, 'I don't think that I would worry too hard about —things.'

Emmanuel sat and sipped his cold coffee. Max guessed. That was where his money-box contents had gone—the same way as his mother's trinkets. Somehow the thought of Max's money hurt Emmanuel more than anything else.

'Sir,' it was old Moses, 'Mr. Morrison would like to speak to you.'

'Mr. Morrison? What Mr. Morrison? The bank manager?'

'A gentleman with great dignitment,' Moses said, 'wearing a frock-coat and side-viskers.'

'Say that I am at breakfast, ask him to join me. Bring fresh coffee.'

Morrison would take coffee, he complimented Emmanuel upon it, he praised the air in Regent's Park, he said that Emmanuel looked well, and that 'The Star Bicycle' shares were a good investment.

Emmanuel said, 'Good. My boy's going to hev one on Saturday. They'll go a bit higher. Now, what did you want to see me about, please?'

'These,' Morrison said, and laid a pile of cashed cheques before Emmanuel. Emmanuel felt that he was being strangled, that the room was closing in on him; he forced himself to look at the cheques slowly, one by one, with great care and attention. He had examined four, when he stopped and said,

'These are all quite in order.'

'I know. Please continue, Mr. Gollantz.'

Emmanuel went back to his examination. Suddenly he stopped. 'But not this,' he said, 'and not this—never in the vorld.'

Morrison picked up the two cheques. 'This one,' he said, 'is fairly clever, the other is an impertinence. Both cashed outside the bank, you notice, both made out to Albert Goodman. Now who is Mr. Albert Goodman?'

'I'm not clever enough to tell you,' Emmanuel said. 'I don't know.'

'Then shall I deal with it?'

Emmanuel nodded mechanically, then said, 'No, no —I'll see to it. Leave them with me. I hev means of my own, machinery which I can set vorking. It will be very easy for me. I will communicate with you.'

'Very good. It's considerable, Mr. Gollantz. What are they? Seventy the first, and two sixty-nine the second. Nasty business.'

'Very nasty. Thank you for coming so promptly.'

He saw Morrison out, smiled and bowed to him as he went down the steps, then went back to his own room, and sat with his head in his hands. His face was wet, he took out his handkerchief and wiped it, rubbed his hands, leant back in his chair and closed his eyes. The sound of someone whistling brought him to himself. Outside the door, someone was walking whistling a tune. He sprang to his feet, flung open the door, and saw Algernon.

'Come here, please,' Emmanuel said.

'Won't it do after breakfast?'

'No, I want you now. Come on, shut the door. Now, tell me, if you can, what you have done with t'ree hundred and t'irty-nine pounds, sixteen and fifepence. That is what I want to know.'

Algernon stood with his hands in the pockets of his velvet smoking jacket, and under the velvet Emmanuel could see that his hands were clenched; saw, too, that his knees under their elegant striped trousers were shaking. 'Three hundred and thirty-nine pounds, sixteen and fivepence,' he repeated, 'what *are* you talking about?'

'It's not any use,' Emmanuel said, 'that's bluffing, and I can't be bluffed. What did you want it for?'

Algernon thrust out his chin, and squared his shoulders. 'Because I wanted it! Why—is my business.'

'But it was my money,' Emmanuel said softly.

'That's what hits you,' the other returned, 'losing money. God, you live for money! What are you going to do?'

'Not'ing, not'ing that will metter to you. I mean I am not going to the police or anything like thet. I should like the address of the place where you sold your mother's jewellery. I want to buy it back. The rest,' he shrugged his shoulders, 'is well spent, to be rid of you.'

'You think you're going to turn me out? You're too late. I was going, anyway. I'm sick of living in the Ghetto. I'm going to live with decent people, to marry a decent girl, a Christian.'

'Do you mean a Christian—or a member of some other religion than Judaism?'

'I mean what I say—no more, no less. You won't hear from me again, I'm changing my name—have changed it, if that interests you.'

'Very well—Mr. Elbert Goodman.' Emmanuel sat down, he felt that his strength had left him. He was as if he had recently recovered from a long illness. Shaken. He was losing Algernon, Juliana's son whom he had promised to love as his own. He had loved him, did still love him. It was terrible.

'It's as good a name as *ELCHER*non Gollantz.'

'I agree. My name, your name, has got badly stained during the last years. When are you going, and what are you going to do? Three hundred pounds won't keep you for ever.'

'I am going now. What I do is my business, and how I live is my business. You can get back the jewellery—it's worth nothing, I might tell you—I sold it at Manning's in the Strand. Precious little it brought, too.' His voice suddenly grew shrill, he took his hands from his pockets and moved them convulsively. 'I'm going, and I thank God that I am. I'll be rid of the Jews once and for all, finished with Hebrew superiority, with Yiddish conceit and self-satisfaction. I hate this house, hate the pictures and the glass and the furniture. I hate your friends, with their lisping voices and fat wives. I hate everything, even, he laughed hysterically, 'your beastly clothes. How my mother stood it for nine years passes my comprehension. I wonder she never found someone else—someone who didn't look like a third-rate actor and talk like a money-lender.'

'Perhaps, if you don't mind,' Emmanuel whispered, 'we might keep your mother out of it. Now, go. Don't wait to pack your things, Moses can do that. I shall keep nothing of yours. Your boxes can be sent on.'

'You want my address—no you shan't have it.'

'I want not'ing. They can be sent to any railway station you prefer.'

'And that's all?'

'That is all. Look!' he picked up the two cheques, and tore them in small pieces. 'That evidence is gone. Wait, one t'ing more.' He took out his cheque book, hesitated a moment, then wrote quickly. Tore out the cheque and held it out to Algernon. 'Four t'ousand, six hundred and sixty-one pounds,' he said. 'It should have been fife t'ousand, but I deducted the money you—appropriated.'

Algernon hesitated, scowled, and looked sulky. Emmanuel longed desperately that he might show some sign of weakness, that he might offer him some excuse to take him back, forgive him, and begin afresh. He waited, the other eyed the cheque, then said:

'No—it's a trick to buy me back. I don't want your damned money.'

'But you will take it,' Emmanual said. 'I will not allow it that you go to the goyim saying that your father sent

you out penniless. Even now, if I wanted to buy you back
I could do it. I don't want to. I wish you good morning.'

'That's all, eh?'

'Good morning.'

Emmanuel turned and began to fill in the counterfoil
of his cheque; he did not raise his eyes, and presently
Algernon turned and went out, closing the door behind
him. Emmanuel could hear his voice giving instructions
to Moses, and later heard the front door shut, and knew
that he was gone.

That evening, he gave orders that Max was to dine with
him. When the boy entered, wearing his evening suit with
its broad white collar, his father pointed to the foot of the
table.

'Sit there, Max. Every night I wish you to dine with
me—unless I have a dinner party.'

'That's Algy's seat, Father.'

'That is where you sit. Come here. There, that is the
watch I promised you. Take care of it—your mother's
watch, Max.'

Max examined the watch with satisfaction. 'It's a glorious watch,' he said, then remembered. 'Then you found
it?'

'I found it, or rather Julius found it.'

'Where? Where was it, and the other things?'

'They had been left, by mistake, at a shop in the
Strand.'

'Whew . . .' he whistled, 'bit of luck to find them. I'm
jolly glad.'

Not until the dinner was over, and Max struggled to
peel an apple without breaking the skin, did his father
refer to Algernon. He sat very erect, carefully cutting a
cigar. The light fell on his bent head, touching the temples with silver. Max, staring up the long shining table at
him, thought his father the handsomest man he had ever
seen—better even than Algy. He was rather like the man
he had seen playing at the Avenue Theatre, or last year in
a play called *The Idler*. Rather dignified and sad-looking
like the last act. His clothes were lovely, too, smooth-
looking and dark. He sighed, he was beginning to get a
little sleepy.

Emmanuel looked up from his cigar. 'Tired, Max?'

'Not really. I do like your clothes, Father.'

'Do you? I'm very much pleased.' He smiled. 'Elchernon dislikes them.'

'Where is Algy tonight?'

His father braced himself, and said slowly, 'Elchernon and I have agreed that we don't get on, Max. He's gone to live somewhere else. If you don't mind, I would rather that you didn't talk about him to me'.

'Won't he come back here?'

'I don't think so.'

Max swallowed hard, he admired Algy, loved him dearly. Something was wrong somewhere. If it was over his moneybox, he gave it when Algy wanted it. Perhaps his father blamed Algy. Again he swallowed with difficulty.

'I can do what I like with my own money, can't I? It's not—anything to do with me and Algy, is it?'

'Nothing at all.'

'Can I go and see him when I like?'

'When you are eighteen, not before.'

'Whew! Six years.' He sat silent, cutting his apple into small pieces. Suddenly he looked up and met his father's eyes steadily. 'Well,' he said, 'I *like* Algy. I always will. I can't help it.'

'So do I, Max. That's the trouble. Come and say "Good night." '

'Good night, Father.' Then he added, 'I'll always like you too—awf'lly. Even more than Algy. I think you're like Lewis Waller—or, no, Wilson Barrett, only your hair's shorter than his.'

'Thank you very much. Good night, Max.'

8

Emmanuel's fifty-fifth birthday. A new butler, for old Moses had been superannuated, was giving the last touches to the dinner table. He stood back, his hands resting on his hips, admiring his handiwork, and finding it good. He prided himself upon being something of an artist in his work, and certainly the huge sheet of looking-glass, surrounded by a hedge of trailing smilax, and decorated with small bunches of scarlet and white sweet peas, had succeeded beyond his hopes. Beside each small cluster of wine glasses, stood a narrow vase containing the scarlet and white flowers, and in addition a tiny silk Union Jack.

The door opened and Emmanuel entered, he stood looking at the table, his eyes shining, his mouth smiling.

'Admirable, Judson, admirable.'

'If I might say so, sir—patriotic. That was the note which I wished to strike on this most auspicious occasion. Pity, I was just saying to Masters, that Nature don't seem to produce blue flowers—with the exception of "Forget-me-nots". Otherwise I should have dispensed with the flags and relied upon natural colours.'

Emmanuel nodded. 'Still, it would hev been a pity to dispense with the flegs. People hev to hev flags, you know. There would be no fighting in Sout' Africa, if t'ere were no flegs. T'ere very pretty, Judson.'

'Thank you, sir.'

Emmanuel walked back to his study, took a cigar and stood before the fire-place, smoking. Watching the thin streamers of blue smoke dip and wave and disappear before him. He had heard that people saw pictures in smoke. He never could, though he tried very often. Pictures—he looked towards the desk where Juliana's picture stood. Eighteen years ago since he had lost her, and he had never seen another woman to equal her for charm or character. If he had, he mused, he would have married again. He was lonely, there was no doubting that. Max was at Cambridge—dear Max—and for half the year the house was empty but for himself and the servants. Algernon, Heaven only knew where Algernon was. Once, Emmanuel thought that he had seen him, second fiddle in an orchestra in the West End—at the Adelphi. He had stared, satisfied himself that the player was Juliana's son, then had left the theatre. He regretted losing the boy— Emmanuel checked his thoughts—well, he was no boy now. Algernon was twenty-nine. Max was eighteen—dear Max. His frown disappeared, and he smiled again. Max was very dear to him. Max never criticised his accent, or his clothes. Max liked him, and loved him. Not that he and Max had never had differences of opinion—Emmanuel chuckled—from the very first. Over the dog, that was the first one. He had promised to give Max a dog at Christmas time. Then Max had found a dog—well, scarce-

ly worthy of the name, a disgraceful mongrel, dirty,
travel-stained and distinctly smelly.

Emmanuel remembered how he had looked down at
the shivering creature with disgust, how Max had
chuckled and opined that it was 'a bit of luck to find such
a dog'.

'I can keep him, can't I?'

'Max, that's not a dog, it's a mongrel.'

'I read that they're the most intelligent, Father. He
will wash.'

'He needs it. Now—he smells.'

Max sniffed the muddy coat. 'Yes,' he agreed, 'it's a fascinating smell, isn't it. I can keep him, can't I?'

'I don't think so. I promised to give you a dog, a real
dog with a pedigree, and—good looks.'

'I don't care. I found this one, myself. This is the dog I
want.'

Max, he remembered, standing over the offending dog,
with his eyes suspiciously shining, his mouth trembling at
the corners. 'This dog came and chose me, he might
have chosen a hundred other people to take care of him.
He didn't. He liked me. It's—it's a kind of trust.'

'People will laugh at a dog like thet one, Max.'

'Not twice they won't laugh,' Max said, 'not twice they
won't.'

'Suppose that I laughed at him?'

Max drew a deep breath before he spoke. 'Knowing
how I feel about him, I should rely on you—as a gentleman—not to let me see you laugh.'

Emmanuel looked at the boy, met his eyes squarely,
and said, 'I beg your pardon, Max. Please give the dog
all that my house can offer him. Only—wash him in the
kitchen, not in the bath, if you please.'

They had never quarrelled, they had differed, and
settled their differences and remained friends. Max had
wanted to go to France when he was fifteen to study
the language. Emmanuel disliked France and the French.
They had argued, Emmanuel had lost his temper, Max
had kept his. Finally, they had compromised—Max had
gone to Germany for a year and then had a French
tutor at home. Now—and again Emmanuel's face clouded
—Max wanted to go to South Africa and fight.

He had announced it yesterday at dinner, without any
preamble.

'Father, I'm eighteen. I want to go and fight.'

His father had stared, open-mouthed. 'You're med,' he said, 'quite med.'

'Walter Heriot's gone, he's nearly sixty. He's taken fifty men with him.'

'That's Walter's business.'

'Then my going is my business, Father. Lots of men I know have gone.'

'More fools they then.'

'That's not part of the argument. It's not their mentality but my wishes.'

Remembering it all, Emmanuel walked restlessly up and down the room, his cigar cold between his teeth, his hands clasped behind him. He would not let Max go, Max was all he had, he couldn't risk losing Max. He had heard dreadful things, not only death, but bullets which were tampered with, enteric, dysentery . . .

'I'm demned if he shall go!' he said. 'I'll not allow it.'

At dinner, the thought of the coming fight with Max spoilt his food. It ruined his wine, it made his cigar tasteless. Max himself seemed oblivious of the storm which was brewing. He sat at the end of the table and sent a smile down the length of it to his father. He proposed his father's health, standing straight and slim, with his glass raised, bowing to him. Emmanuel flushed with pride, caught the glances of approval from his friends, remembered that neither old Davis, nor Julius could ever hope to have such a son; saw that Hermann Leon, his white hair catching the light and shining like silver, nodded with pleasure; that Lady Heriot, thin and fretful, threw a glance across the table to where her own son, Walter, sat. She must be wishing that Walter was like Max, instead of the heavy, stupid weakling that he was. Rachel, her inevitable cigarette spilling ash on the white cloth, smiled, and glanced at Emmanuel.

'Very well done,' she said softly.

Julius leant forward. 'Is it true that he wants to go to the front?'

Emmanuel growled. 'He may want, he's not going.'

Rachel said, 'That's right, Emmanuel, let him stay at home and kill Kruger with his mouth, like the rest of us!'

Hermann caught the quotation. 'I heard Mrs. Tree recite that the other day. She did it beautifully. I designed the cover for the programmes, a big charity affair. It's not good poetry, that "Absent-Minded Beggar", but it's astonishingly good journalism.'

Rachel dislodged the stump of a cigarette from her holder, and inserted a new one. 'It's going to be very popular,' she said. 'Lots of people this winter will give away coals and blankets. The most expensive are cheap.'

Max called down the table, 'I thought you were a pacifist, Rachel dear. Why the bitterness?'

'I am a pacifist,' she returned, 'I think the whole business is nonsense, vile nonsense. But I can still admire the men who know it's going to be vile, who believe it's necessary and who don't think half-a-dozen pairs of blankets clear their bill.'

'Young Harris went last week,' Elizabeth Berman said, 'he told me that it was nothing but a glorious rag. Hilda's going to make bandages, aren't you, darling?'

Old Davis puffed out his chest and took another sip of port. Max watched him, comfortable, secure, enjoying the good wine, and almost hated him.

'De Boers,' he said, 'hev esked for a lesson. Now they'll get it. They'll get it from the Heart of England, und the C.I.V.'s will give it 'em. De Empire's got to be made safe, already.'

'And,' Rachel said, with mock piety, 'please God, the South African Market.'

'I honour every man who goes,' Davis said, 'und I'm not ashamed to say it.'

'Why should you be?' she asked. 'Julius going? Too old? Hard luck—very hard luck. Well, let's be happy that we're all too old to go.'

Max's voice struck in, 'I'm not, Rachel.'

'Oh,' she said, 'you, Max. I'd forgotten you. Emmanuel, the younger generation is knocking at the door.'

'I won't allow him to go,' Emmanuel said.

'Brother pacifist, Emmanuel?'

'Pacifist,' he echoed, 'no, certainly not. Max is still being educated. He's going back to Cambridge at the end of the week.'

'Do you want to go, Max? I mean—you think it's the right thing to do?'

Max wriggled in his big chair. 'I think—well, Rachel, lots of men *are* going. Uncle Walter for one. It seems a bit low down to stay out of it.'

She stared at him without speaking, then turned to Julius Davis, and asked if he had seen *The Message from Mars*.

That evening, when Emmanuel was helping her on with her cloak, she said:

'Be wise, my dear. He'll never forgive you if you stop him.'

'I should never forgive myself if—anything happened to him.'

'Don't play for safety,' she said softly, 'I've told you that before.'

That night, Emmanuel called Max to him. He laid his hands on the boy's shoulders, looked at him with intense concentration, then said, 'Max—if you want to, really want to—not just thinking it's a reg, and fun—you can go.'

Max stared back, his mouth a little open. His face flushed suddenly, then he gasped, and took his father's hands in his.

'Father, I am grateful. I'd have hated . . .'

'Me?'

'Not you,' smiling, 'I couldn't do that. I'd have hated to meet Uncle Walter, or Bill Harris, or—any of them, afterwards.'

So Max went out, and Emmanuel was left in the big house alone. He threw himself into his work with renewed vigour, he bought and sold, he conceived new schemes of decoration, and even took Max's old and rheumatic dog for slow and tedious walks in the park. He read and re-read Max's letters until they almost fell to pieces, he sent out parcels, which, if they never reached Max, provided undreamed-of comforts for other men who needed them.

He was very, very proud, and under his anxiety his pride was evident; and he swaggered as he had always done. 'Damned near sixty,' his friends said of him, 'and as straight as a ramrod.'

As a matter of fact he was fifty-seven when the new century came in. His hair was white, but thick, his figure still slim and straight. Men who disliked him said that he wore stays, which was never true. He despised men who neglected their figures and got paunchy. He lived well but carefully, and kept a record of the readings from the weighing machine which stood in his bathroom.

His mind, his imagination, were as active and receptive as ever. He boasted that he did not follow public taste, he forestalled it. He had watched it change, watched heavy Victorian furniture begin to fall from public favour; he noticed the installation of art hangings, the eruption of crockery on the walls, and still collected his Chippendale, his Sheraton, and his Hepplewhite.

Julius shook his head, and wailed that it was dead stock, no one wanted it except a few collectors. Emmanuel smiled.

'It will keep, Julius,' he said, 'they'll get so tired of the hengings, and the fens, and the blue plates. They'll get sick to death of white enamel and blue enamel. Buy me old chairs, Julius, old tables, old—anyt'ing. Even if they're broken, buy them. We'll mend them, we'll sell good restored stuff to the people who can't afford the real stuff. There won't be enough Chippendale in the world to satisfy them—one day.'

'But the pictures, Emmanuel. We're overloaded. The warehouse is full.'

'T'en get another warehouse and fill that. Leave pictures to me, Julius. I understand pictures. I buy before Victoria, and efter Victoria, never Victoria.'

Julius thought that he was mad, and said so. People clamoured for pictures and Emmanuel would stock none of them. He bought old paintings and new pictures, never what Julius called 'contemporary art'.

Julius took him to the Academy and pointed out six good investments. Emmanuel chuckled and shook his head.

'No, no,' he said, 'Mr. Pears wants them for his annual. Let him hev them.'

He was making money, even his investments paid, and with each entry in his bank book, with each security added to his stock, Emmanuel congratulated himself that Max would be a rich man. Only at long intervals he thought of Algernon, and then as something which he wished to forget, something to be banished quickly from his mind. Even the memory of Juliana's words could not make him reproach himself now. He had done his best, he had given the boy his name, his protection, his love. Algernon had hated his name, despised his protection, and flung his love back in his face. Algernon belonged to the past, Max to the future; Max was, in himself, the future.

In March, 1900, Max came home. He was ill, had almost died of enteric, and was invalided out. Emmanuel, once he was home, made no secret of the fact that he was glad. While Max had been in Africa, he had hidden his anxiety and misery, had concealed his fear of every

telegram and his dread concerning each letter. It was
over, Max was home, and Emmanuel's swagger became,
once again, real and not assumed. Max found him
changed, older and softer. His manner was more gentle,
he listened to arguments, and gave more considered
judgments. His hair was whiter, the whites of his eyes
were a little yellow, the veins of his hands stood out more
noticeably. When Max, growing stronger every day, said
that he did not wish to go back to Cambridge, Emmanuel, instead of saying, 'You will go back to Cambridge'
and then asking why he didn't want to go, said,

'Why don't you want to go back? What are your
reasons?'

'I want to work.' Max had a dozen reasons, but this
seemed the best of them.

'Don't you work at Cambridge?'

'I want to learn business, Father. Your business, if
you'll have me.'

Emmanuel was deeply flattered. This was what he had
hoped for, what he had planned, and here was Max wishing it too. He hid, or believed that he hid, his delight,
and said, cautiously,

'You wouldn't be a gr-reat deal of use to me—not at
first, Max.'

'No, I don't suppose I should. I shouldn't ask you to pay
me very much—at first. I expect that there's a lot to learn.'

'Indeed, I should t'ink so. I hev been learning all my
life. I am still learning every day.'

Max watched his father draw down the corners of
his mouth, look dubious, and realised that this was a
game, which his father was enjoying very much. That
strange bargaining game which Jews seemed to like.

'If it's so hard, perhaps I'd better try something else,
Father. What about this new motor-car—carriages without
horses. There might be a future there?'

'No, no. I don't t'ink that's much of a joy, making
carriages without horses.'

'I could go to Hermann Leon, learn lithography.'

'Thet's no use at all. There'll be no future there. Making imitation pictures. Cheap business—and t'ere isn't so
much engraving now.'

Max sighed. 'I expect you're right. I'm not much use,
you'd better set me up in a shop, a tailor's or a hosier's.'

His father stood up and came over to where he lay, he
put his hand on Max's shoulder. 'Not much use!' he said.

'Don't, please, ever say that again. Every use, all the use in the world. Come with me, Max. I'll teach you everyt'ing.'

So Max went into the business with Emmanuel and absorbed knowledge as a sponge absorbs water. He was clever, his artistic taste if not original was at least sound and his memory was excellent. Emmanuel paid him exactly what he had paid Julius Davis twenty years before: fifteen shillings a week for the first year, a pound for the second, and in the third raised it to three pounds ten, and commission. Max found nothing at which to grumble, he had his allowance, from which his father deducted fifteen shillings each week, stating that it was for his board and lodging. That kind of thing amused Max, it was so childish, so ingenuous, so laboriously living up to the traditional Jew.

Early in September, 1904, Max heard from his brother Algernon. Max was at breakfast. Emmanuel was away on the Continent. The letter was posted from Camberwell. It asked him to meet his brother by the bookstall at Charing Cross that afternoon at three. Stated that his business was urgent, and was signed 'Your affect. brother Algy.'

Max read the letter again, consulted his engagement book. There was a sale of furniture at three in St. James's Street. It must wait, or he must send Julius. He knew that he was excited and pleased, that some of the admiration of a little boy for his elder brother remained. He began to speculate as to how Algy would look, if he would know him, and what he wanted with him. Five minutes to three found him standing impatiently by the bookstall, scrutinising the faces of the passers-by anxiously. Five minutes past three. Max became anxious, fearful lest he had mistaken the place of meeting, then at seven minutes past someone laid a hand on his shoulder and he turned to face his brother.

'Hello, Max.'

'Hello, Algy.'

The tall florid young man laughed. 'Long time since anyone called me that. Didn't you know that I changed my name? Cost me twenty quid—and well worth it. Well, come and have a drink and I can talk to you.'

He caught Max by the arm and led him away to the restaurant. Max glanced at the man who walked beside him. He was tall and heavily built, his face was handsome, florid, and thick about the jaw. His hair was very

thick and fair, he wore a small fair moustache. His
clothes were smart and not too well cut, in the fashion
that was called 'Bohemian', which meant loose, over-loud,
and running to soft collars and flowing ties.

Seated in the restaurant, Algy talked. He talked quickly,
and laughed a good deal, talked too loudly for Max's
taste, and drank his whiskies and sodas as if he was
thirsty.

'I've seen you, young Max, doing the plutocratic in the
stalls, while your poor brother fiddled in the orchestra
for a living. Saw you sitting there like a lord with that
over-dressed old peacock, our respected parent—beside
you. He doesn't change much, does he?'

Max said, as he had said once before, 'You know, I
like his clothes, they suit him.'

'Do you? No accounting for tastes. Now, listen, Max.
I'm in a hole. I'm leaving, packing up, vamoosing.
Going tonight. Can't stand another day of it. I've had
trouble, old boy, bad trouble, not of my own making.
You know I married? Not? Well, I married soon after
I left the parental roof. What—twelve years ago. It can't
be twelve years—by God, it is though. Time flies, eh?
Got a kiddie—what is he?—well, as a matter of fact he's
a bit older than he ought to be, if you get me. He'll be
twelve in a couple of months. I wasn't good, and I wasn't
careful, Max boy. She made the running. Queer thing,
women never can leave me alone. Bits of skirts always
ready to drop into my arms.' He drank his second whisky
and repeated, 'Queer thing. They think I'm attractive.'

Max said, 'You still play beautifully, I expect, Algy.'

'Play—that's the trouble. I might play if I wasn't
eternally money grubbing. That's the curse of it. That's
why I'm going.'

'Where are you going?' Max asked, 'and how will going
affect your music?'

Algernon pushed away the glasses which stood in front
of him, folded his arms, and tapped Max on the arm
with his finger. 'This way,' he said. 'You've heard of
Elman, this prodigy, and this young German or whatever he is, Kreisler? You have. Well, without conceit,
young Max, and God knows I have something to be
conceited about, I have them both beat, licked to a frazzle. I've played in orchestras, never for long, and why?
I've been too damned good. I've been told so. I throw
the balance out. I got a chance the other day. I went to

see Sandermann—you've heard of him, the impresario from Vienna. He literally gasped. He took my hands and called me "Master"! That's what he said, "Master". England's no damned good to me. That's why I'm going.'

'Did he say he'd give you work out there?'

'Give! That's amusing, Max. Give! He and a dozen others will beg me to take what they've got to offer. Beg me—implore me. God, what's the time? Ten to four. I must go. Oh, that reminds me, have you any money on you? Lend me what you've got, I'll send it back within a month, with interest. Tell the old man that. My things are in the cloakroom.'

Max took out his note case. There were two fivers, and in his pocket a couple of sovereigns. He handed them to his brother, with a half-murmured apology that it wasn't more. Algernon took the money, stuffed it into his pocket, and said,

'All right, young Max, all the less for me to pay back, eh?'

Max followed him to the cloak-room, saw him take two bags and a violin case. Took the bags from him and walked to the barrier. There Algernon turned and took the bags.

'Good-bye, old chap. I'll write in a few days. I shouldn't mention this to my respected parent. Good-bye and good luck.'

'But,' Max cried, 'Algy, why did you want to see me? What about your wife and the boy? Are they going with you?'

Algernon threw back his head and laughed. 'God, how like me! That's why I wanted to see you. I want you to go down and see the wife and the boy. She's fed-up with me, wants a divorce or some fine thing. See to it for me. I must go—good-bye, Max. You'll like the boy. He's a regular Yid.'

He turned and ran down the platform to the train where the guard was already waving a grimy flag and where porters were slamming doors. Max saw him hurl himself into a carriage, saw the train begin to move out of the station, then turned and walked back, reading the address on his brother's letter as he did so.

9

Max walked out of Charing Cross Station, wondering what he should do next. The news that his unknown sister-in-law wished to divorce his brother had shocked him. Divorce was all right, Max supposed it was inevitable, but when it touched one's own people, it seemed queer, unsatisfactory, and rather beastly. He turned out of the station and began to walk along the Strand, turning things over in his mind.

It was queer, all of it. Queer to meet his brother again after twelve years, and to say 'Good-bye' again in ten minutes. Algy was queer too, noisy, and highly coloured. Still handsome, and still, Max felt, a fascinating person. He wished that he might have seen more of Algy. His wife was going to divorce him. That meant that Algy was in the wrong, unless through some sense of chivalry he was permitting himself to be divorced. There was a boy, too. 'A regular little Yid.' Max wondered if he looked like a Yid. Not that he cared—his father's race was good enough for him. The boy was twelve. 'A bit older than he ought to be.' Max frowned, not that the swerve from conventionality bothered him, but the fact that his brother should have admitted it so readily. It didn't seem quite fair on his wife or the boy. Still, he mustn't criticise Algy, Algy was different—a great artist, a musician, probably a bit eccentric. He continued his walk down the Strand, wondering what course he should pursue. Should he tell Emmanuel upon his return, or should he go and see Algy's wife and report to his father later? It was all very difficult. If he saw the girl, what was he to say to her? He stopped and dived into a sweetshop, and asked for a large box of chocolates.

'I want one with an attractive picture on the lid. I mean one that a child would think attractive.'

The girl smiled and laid a selection on the glass-topped counter before him.

Most people smiled at Max when he was twenty-three. He had a voice which aroused smiles, a voice which was so pleasant that girls in shops took more than usual trouble to get him exactly what he wanted. He would never be as handsome as Emmanuel, in fact Max could never be called anything but—good-looking. His eyes were dark, but not particularly large, his nose was well shaped but not distinguished, his mouth was Juliana's mouth, wide and flexible, and filled with very white and rather large teeth. His figure was good, but a trifle too heavy about the shoulders, he was tall, his hands and feet were excellent. His smile—when he did smile—was charming, his voice soft, full and strong without being over-loud.

Rachel Leon said that he was idiotically kind-hearted; Julius Davis said that he was as hard as nails. Emmanuel said that he was artistic, but Hermann Leon said that his knowledge of values was financial, his knowledge of artistic values insignificant. The porters in the warehouse could have told tales of his generosity, the dealers in the sale rooms said that he drove a tighter bargain than most men in the business.

He examined the boxes before him, said, 'I'll have that one, please.'

Back in the Strand, he called a hansom, and gave the address, 'Sixty-four Upper Camberwell Road.' He had decided to go and see his sister-in-law first and report to Emmanuel later. The cab moved off; Max leant back and speculated upon his unseen, unknown relations. Over Waterloo Bridge, on through grim streets to the Elephant and Castle, into the Walworth Road, with its endless series of undignified shops and gorgeous public-houses. Camberwell Green. Max sat upright, and began to feel nervous. More smaller shops, smaller houses, miles and miles of houses all built to pattern, ugly, mean, and pretentious. He felt a sudden spasm of pity for Algy!

The hansom stopped, Max climbed out and wondered if he should tell the man to wait, then remembered that he had given practically all his money to Algy. Had a sudden panic that he had nothing left, except the change from the chocolate box. Found another half-sovereign in his waistcoat pocket. The fare was four shillings. He decided not to ask the man to wait.

The cabman glanced at the house, glanced at Max and grinned. Max looked at the house, noticed the bright pink curtains, rather begrimed, the blinds trimmed with dirty

coarse lace. His eyes met those of the driver, he wanted
to make an explanation, realised that it was impossible,
flushed, and over-tipped the fellow.

'Like me ter wait, Cap'in?'

'No, thanks.'

The driver winked heavily. 'Pre'ps you're right, Colonel.'

Max knocked on the door, where the suns of summer
and the winds of winter had reduced the original
colour of the paint to a nondescript hue. He was conscious
that someone looked out, drawing aside the pink curtain,
and then darting away quickly. The door opened, and he
remembered that Algy had changed his name, but what
name he had chosen Max had not the remotest idea.
He looked at the elderly, hard-faced woman, with her
sandy, grey hair scraped from a protruding forehead.
Her eyes seemed to bore into him like gimlets, and her
hoarse voice demanded who and what he wanted.

He said, 'My name is Gollantz. I have been asked to
call here and see a lady and a little boy.'

'Lidy an' a little boy,' she repeated with evident suspi-
cion. 'D'you mean our Julie? She's got a little boy.'

Max decided that in so small a house there were not
likely to be two ladies and two little boys. He said, 'Yes,
if you please.'

'If it's about the pianner, you can tike it awai. 'Er
'usband's gorne abroad, an' she 'as no use fur it.'

It was Julie!

'I have not called about the pano,' Max said. 'I am her
husband's brother. He changed his name, that's all.'

The woman turned and faced down the narrow, dark,
and stuffy passage.

'Julie,' she shouted, 'I never 'eard nothink abart Bert
chaingin' 'is nime. Did you? There's a feller 'ere, says
that 'es Bert's bruvver. What d'yer know abart that?'

A voice, young and vital, called back. 'Never mind
what you know or don't know, Ma. Show the gentleman
into the front room. I'm coming.'

Max had been in cottages very often. He had been down
in Dorset, where he found a Jacobean day bed, in Wales
where he expected and hoped to find Welsh dressers, and
found only manufactured antiques from Birmingham, he
had been in crofters' cottages in Scotland, in dalesmen's
homes in Yorkshire; he had seen poverty, scarcity, he
had realised in which homes there was a constant fight

to keep going—but never, in all his life, had he been in a room such as he entered then.

It was small, papered in a dull red, the ceiling discoloured and patchy, the paint on the doors and window frames dirty and drab. He had not believed that so much furniture could be crowded into one small room, and wondered why in addition to the red plush and fumed oak suite, someone should have superimposed a bicycle, a sewing machine, and a gramophone with the largest tin horn he had ever seen.

The gimlet-eyed woman said, 'Sidown willyer. Julie'll be 'ere in a minute.'

Max thanked her, wondered if he dared open a window, the atmosphere was suffocating. He wandered to the mantelpiece and looked at the photographs. Revolting faces attached to comic bodies, relics of Margate and Blackpool; couples taken in strained attitudes with pots of ferns in the background, stout children lying in semi-nakedness upon sheep-skin rugs; old men and older women in, so it seemed to Max, the last stages of senile decay. Ornaments—dreadful vases filled with red and blue grass full of dust, distorted animals, dogs who smoked pipes, cats wearing bonnets—all senseless, ugly rubbish, gathering grime and overcrowding a shelf which was already full before their advent.

With a kind of desperate bewilderment he stared round the room again. This was where Algy had lived, the gimlet-eyed woman was Algy's mother-in-law, it was impossssable, fantastic. The door opened and Julie entered. She was a blowsily handsome young woman, with masses of untidy dark hair, fine, bold eyes, and a skin covered with very white powder. Her mouth was big, generous, and loose, with red lips which looked as if she had just licked them. She stared at Max and smiled. The smile made Max wish that he hadn't come. He had disliked the older woman, the younger one frightened him, she was overpowering.

She said, 'So you'll be the rich brother, eh?' Her voice was thick, but alive and warm. 'Bert's rich brother. He tole me that he'd written you.'

'Yes,' Max said, 'he did write. I saw him this afternoon at the station.'

She looked at him, her eyes sharp. 'Anyone with him?'
'I saw no one. He asked me to see you, and your son.'
'Did he? He's a one is Bert. Believe me or believe me

not, after all that Bert's done, you can't 'elp laughing at his nerve, can you?'

Max pointed to one of the dusty chairs. 'May I sit down? Will you tell me—it it's not too painful—the exact position? I hadn't seen my brother for nearly twelve years and I know nothing. Please tell me.'

She laughed. 'Well I never. Bert's deep, isn't he? I'll tell you the sad story. I was on the stige—that is, I was a chorus lady. Bert met me when I was playing in *The Sunbeam Girl*—touring company—at Kennington. He went cracked about me, an' I was balmy about 'im. To make a long story short—we blotted our copy-books. Dad an' Mum made a row. Dad was a local preacher then, disapproved of the stige, an' said it served me right. You know what local preachers are, don't you?'

Max had only a dim idea as to the functions of a local preacher. He said, 'Yes—quite—yes.'

'Mum's strict-ish, not too bad. I always say that 'er bark's a lot worse than her bite. Bert 'ad money then, y'know. Neely five thousand of the best.' She threw back her untidy handsome head and laughed. 'What a time we had the first two yeres, even after Frankie was born! He and me lived in a loverly flat in Brixton. Tip-top it was. I will say that Bert was free with 'is money. I s'ppose I was in love—I soon got over that, believe me or believe me not. Bert hadn't any money left, there was me and Frankie to feed. He got a job in an orchestra in the West End. He's one of those fellers who can't stick at a job, can't Bert. A rolling stone, and precious little moss he ever gathered, I can tell you. We left the flat—that neely killed me, that did. Dad an' Mum said we could come 'ere an' live with them. That was all right, only Bert put on his la-di-da airs and got their monkey up prop'ly. Came that "gentleman" stuff, you know.'

She paused and looked at Max, smiling. 'Smoke if you like,' she said, 'an' you might offer me one. Thenks. Well, to get on with the serial, part two. That's gorne on for the best part of ten yeres. Once I went on tour—but Mum tole me that I'd better come back. Bert was chasing a bit of skirt—not only chasing neither, believe me. He caught her all right. Then I went into a shop in the West End—well, not reely the West End, it was in Holborn. Bert saw me walking out with one of the shopwalkers, an' played hell.

'He got one job an' then another, some of them good

jobs too. One at a swell restaurant. That was 'is larst
effort, that was. He chucked it an' came home 'ere, said
that it was interfering with his art. Can you beat that?
Money came from somewhere—I didn't trouble where.
He went out to give lessons. Went to a room off Bond
Street, over a big pianner shop. Lessons . . .' she laughed,
'I'd like to know in what. Not music, I give you my word
of honour!

'Then—three months ago—I'll be candid, I be'leve in
plain speaking, an' I always say Life's 'ere and we've got
to live it. I met a feller, a chap from Canada.' She
smiled and for a moment Max liked her. She was
coarse, common, and probably stupid, but for a second
he had it in his heart to envy the 'chap from Canada'.
She puffed at her cigarette, then went on, 'He's grand.
He's a worker, an' I like workers. I like fun, but I like
work too. Now Bert, he likes work that much he'd lay
down beside it, Bert would. Ted's different. I'm mad about
Ted, and Ted's mad about me. Bert found out, and
played hell. I said, "What you got to play hell about?"
I said. I said, "You've played the gime often enough,
an' you know it," I said.

'One thing brought up another. Bert came the swell
over me, said that I'd ruined his life. I said, "Well, if
you come to ruining, you played that business first. Only,
thanks to Mum an' Dad," I said, "that young Frankie
ain't a bastard." You see what I mean?'

Max said, 'Yes, I see. It's all rather awful, isn't it?'

'Awful!' she said, 'I can laugh about it now, but that's
because I've got Ted. Believe me or believe me not, I
neely broke my heart at first, Mister . . . I didn't get
your name.'

'Gollantz,' Max said, 'Max Gollantz.'

Julie stared, then burst out laughing. 'Gor',' she said,
'what a name. I don't blame Bert for changing his.
Though, as I said to him, "Why Goodman?" I said—I
knew that he'd changed it, but he never tole me what
from—I said, "You do right to call yourself 'Goodman',
for it's what no one else, barring a born idiot, would call
you, an' not then if the poor begger knew you." Well, to
bring everything up to date. Bert started to drink—Dad
hated that, he never had no money—though he always had
silk socks, mind you, an' money for smokes and drinks
and clothes. Mum hated that. I knew he had a fancy lady
somewhere, who paid up and looked pleasant, and till Ted

came, you couldn't expect me to do a song and dance over that, eh?

'Ted wants me to go with him to Canada—I'm going to be frank with you. Bert says that once he's out of the country I can divorce him or do what I like. Well, Dad's all against divorce. Mum don't like it much either. Ted,' again that wide smile, 'well, Ted don't care one way or the other. He said to me larst night, "Julie," he said, "yore as much my wife now," he said, "as you ever will be," he said, "in the sight of Heaven." He said, "Wedding rings don't make a wedding, nor parsons a marriage," he said. So that's how things are, Mr. What's it. Bert gone off to Germany or France or wherever he has gone, and I'm going to Canada with Ted. That's that.'

Max nodded. 'I see,' he said slowly, 'and what about your son?'

'Young Frankie? He'll stay with Mum and Dad. They love 'im to death. Bit strict, mind you. That's the one thing Ted won't have. He said, "It's all right, Jule, but I can't face watching another feller's kid beside you. It's more," he said, "than flesh and blood can stand," he said. Mind, I'd like to take young Frankie, though I never was what you'd call a fool over him. But, Ted won't have it, and I'm not giving Ted up for Bert's son, so there!'

Max rose, and threw his cigarette into the empty grate. He looked round the room, thought of the hard-eyed woman, and of this unknown little boy, living here with the ex-local preacher and those hard eyes. He turned and faced Julie.

'Could I see—Frankie?'

'If you like.' She rose, opened the door and shouted, 'Frank-ee! Here!' Max heard the sound of feet in the passage, and a small boy entered. He was small for his age, and his shabby suit was too short in the sleeves; his boots were clumsy and kicked through at the toes, his stockings hung in folds round his legs. He stood in the doorway scowling, his dark eyebrows drawn over his darker eyes. His nose was small and well-shaped, his mouth curved and mutinous.

Julie said, 'Go on. Shake hands. That's your uncle.'

The dark eyes were lifted, the boy looked at Max, then said to his mother, 'Garn, you're kiddin'.'

'Go and shake hands,' Julie repeated, 'he *is* your uncle. Don't call me a liar.'

The boy looked again at Max, then said, 'You aren't, are you?'

'Yes, I am. Your Uncle Max.'

'My father once said,' Frankie said, 'that you were a Jew. He hates Jews. I do, too. They're mucky. My teacher says they killed our Lord.'

His mother laughed. 'God, he's cheeky. That's Bert taught him that!'

Max looked at the child gravely. 'And what else did your father teach you?'

Frankie's mouth relaxed into a smile, he came a little nearer.

'He taught me this,' he said, and chanted, 'Gerra bit of pork an' stick it on a fork, an' give it to a dirty Jew, Jew, Jew. That's what.'

'You think that is pretty? Or funny?'

The scowl came down again. 'Not pretty—Father taught me it.'

'You said so.' Something in the man's tone made Frankie wish that he had not chanted his song, made him feel conscious of his dirty hands, and wish that he had stopped to wash them at the sink. He felt small, and hated this clean, well-dressed man who was his uncle.

Max went back to his chair, he sat down and held out his hand. 'Come here,' he said, 'come and let me talk to you. Don't be afraid, I'm not going to hurt you.'

'I'm not afraid. I'm not afraid of anything, I'm not.'

Julie said, 'No more he is, I will say that for him. Go on, Frankie.'

He came nearer; Max made no movement but continued to hold out his hand. Presently Frankie stood by his knee, watching him as children who have been used to an abundance of cuffs, and playing in the streets do watch. Max began to talk softly, almost as if he spoke to himself.

'Your grandfather—your father's father lives in Regent's Park. He is a Jew, your father is a Jew, so am I. So is a small piece of you.'

'I never *am* a Jew!' But the tone was more astonishment than disgust.

Max went on, 'Your grandfather is a very wonderful man. A very honest man, kind, and charitable. I think you would like him.'

Frankie came a little nearer. 'What's that chain for—that one what goes into your trousers pocket?'

'It has a little purse at the end of it, to hold sovereigns.'

'Gurr! Are you rich?'

'Not very,' he smiled, 'but quite clean.'

He looked up and caught Julie's eyes watching him. The laughter had gone, and they stared at him, half-puzzled, half-resentful.

'What are you getting at?' she asked. 'What this trying to make up to the kid? You've never clapped eyes on him before.'

Max did not answer her, instead he turned back to Frankie. 'Run along,' he said, 'I'll come and see you another day.'

Frankie kicked the fender with his dirty boots. 'I'd rather stop here,' he said. 'I didn't mean that you was dirty, only Jews like Abie Rose.'

'I accept your apology,' Max said, 'only don't sing that rubbish again. It's silly, and offensive. Promise?'

'Cross my heart an' wish I might die. D'you want me to go?'

Max nodded. 'Until next time I come. Good-bye.'

He held out his hand, and smiled. Frankie hesitated, then offered his and Max took it. 'Goo'-bye,' he said. 'See you later.'

As the door closed, Max turned to Julie.

'You're going to Canada,' he said, 'you're going to have a chance to be very happy with Ted. Give Frankie a chance, won't you? Let him come to me—to us.'

'What! An' leave Mum and Dad. They'd never let him go. They love him to death. Gor, it 'ud break their hearts.'

'He *is* at the moment,' Max said, 'a remarkably dirty small boy, talking like a gutter child, and you know it.'

'We're not fussy, and a bit of dirt's healthy enough.'

'Frankie should have a constitution of iron,' Max said. 'What is your father? I mean what work does he do?'

'Dad? He's a painter and paper-hanger. Used to be his own boss, but now he works for Adams in the Loughborough Road. Dad makes his couple of pounds a week.'

Max thrust his hands into his pockets. He was desperately nervous, terribly afraid that he was going to hurt Algy's wife—and he had begun to like Algy's wife very much—but he wanted the boy. He liked the boy, liked even his impudence, his scowl, his cautious withdrawal of the statement that he hated Jews.

'Wouldn't you like to leave your father and mother safe

and comfortable,' he said, 'when you go to Canada? Wouldn't you like to know that they did not have to work, that they could live in a nicer house, and have assured incomes for the rest of their lives? Wouldn't you like to go to Canada—to Ted—with enough to help him to buy new machinery or whatever he wants for his work? A man likes a woman no less because she brings him some additional capital. If you leave Frankie at all, why not leave him where he can have everything—education, a good start? You don't want him to turn into another . . .' he paused, then said quickly, 'another Bert?'

'Bert! I'd sooner see him dead.' She sat silent, then rose and walked to the window, and stood looking into the squalid street. 'It's brib'ry, that's what you're offering. Brib'ry. Trying to buy Frankie.'

'Trying to buy Frankie,' Max repeated.

'This,' pointing to the street, 'this isn't much of a playground for him, eh? Dad and Mum's all right, but they're old. Suppose Dad died—died while Frankie was still at school—Gor, it 'ud be a bad job for Mum and Frankie, wouldn't it?'

'A very bad job.' He came over and laid his hand on her arm. 'Julie,' he said, 'think it over. Reckon it out, get Ted to work it out for you. Enough to help Ted and you to start well, enough to make your father and mother safe for always. Give me a photograph of Frankie, if you have one. Talk it over. Let me come in two or three days. Have you a photograph?'

She came a little closer, and turned her face up to him. 'Lord,' she said, 'you're a one, aren't you? I'll give you a photo, taken with me at Brighton last year.' She giggled suddenly. 'I say, I'll tell you what, it's a damned good thing for Ted, that I met him before I met you—Max.'

Max knew that his face flushed. 'Thank you,' he said. 'May I have the picture?'

'Oh, all right!' She found it among the debris on the mantelpiece, and gave it to him. 'Look,' she said, 'there's Frankie and there's me.' Max bent his head to look more closely, she put her arm round his neck, pulled his face to hers, and kissed him. 'There—rub that one off!'

It was the first time that Max had ever been kissed by a woman other than Rachel Leon and old Mrs. Davis. The experience was disturbing. He disliked it, but immediately wondered why he disliked it, and how much, and if he

really disliked it at all. He drew back, rubbed his cheek
with his hand, and said,

'I say—you shouldn't do that, please.'

'Go on, old starchy,' she returned, 'go on home to
Father! Don't worry. I'm on your side. You're right. Come
again in a few days and I'll have them eating out of your
hand.' She laughed. 'You can give me back then, what
I've just given you, if you like.'

Max walked away with Frankie's picture in his breast
pocket, determined that when he did come back, Emmanuel should come with him.

10

Emmanuel had come home. All his life Max could remember those homecomings. The slight stir about the house all
the morning, the increased smell of polish, and the atmosphere of expectancy. Fresh flowers—for his father liked
to have the house full of them—the odour of cooking,
boys with baskets running up and down the area steps,
Julius nervously putting in meticulous order every book,
invoice, and letter. Himself, pleased and happy, not nervous, only rather excited as if his father's return was a
pleasant event.

The carriage, for Emmanuel preferred it to the auto-
mobile, leaving for the station, returning and, as it drew
up, himself opening the door and running down to meet
his father. Emmanuel, tall and dignified in his long travelling coat, taking his hand, and saying,

'Nice to be back, Max. Are you well?'

'Quite well, thank you, Father. And you?'

'Grend, my boy, grend.'

Orders to Judson, and the 'handy man'. 'Take my begs
up, Judson. The small case can stay in the hall, it can go
to Campden Hill in the morning. The leather case—take
it into my study; take that long wooden box with it. Carefully—carefully—it's breakable. That's better. Now,
Max . . .'

Arm in arm they would enter the house, Max would help his father off with his coat, and they would enter the study and talk.

This time, Emmanuel was full of a dinner serivce which he had bought.

'Made for the Duc of Angoulême at his private fectory, Max. Complete—only one piece chipped. A couple of pictures—one by a man I don't know—Matisse. It's very good. A triptych, fourth century—I'll show you presently, it's in that case there. A beautiful t'ing. One or two other larger pieces that are coming direct to Campden Hill. Now,' Emmanuel leant back, and crossed his long, beautifully trousered legs, 'now, what hev you done?'

Max flicked the ash off his cigarette and smiled. 'Me? I've made a discovery, Father. I've found you a grandson.'

Emmanuel sat upright, frowning. 'Is this a joke? What do you mean, Max?'

Slowly and carefully Max told the story, told how he had met Algernon, and gone to see his wife and child. Described the house, the old woman, and—less fully— Julie. Told of Ted and that they decided to leave Frankie behind in England. Added that he wanted to bring the boy home and give him the opportunities which were his right.

'Julie . . .' Emmanuel said, softly. 'Like your mother's name, only not so pretty. But, this child—I don't know. What hev I to do with Elchernon's son? Not'ing. I ended t'ings with Elchernon years ago. This child, a little goy, he hes not'ing to do with us, Max, not'ing.'

In his heart he was saying that Algernon's son was nothing to him. He had always felt that Algernon was the son of Jules Alessandri. He had tried to love him, to be good to him because Juliana had wished it, because Algernon was her son. This child—he was too far removed from Juliana to have any right to claim anything from Emmanuel Gollantz. He never wanted to see Algernon, or Algernon's son. Leave the child where he was. He shook his head and said, 'No, Max, no. I'll give them some money, if you like, but leave the boy where he is. It's only raking up old t'ings—very old t'ings which hurt me. It's—it's over. Let it alone.'

Max came over to him, he held the photograph in his hand. 'I'd like you to see what Frankie's like, Father. This is taken with his mother, last year. At Brighton or Margate, I think.'

'I don't care to see it, thenk you.'

'To please me . . .'

Emmanuel stretched out his hand and took the picture. He put on his eyeglasses and with an air of touching something intensely unpleasant, which amused Max immensely, took the picture over to the window to examine it.

There was a long silence. Max could hear the big marble clock ticking out the seconds, he could hear his father breathing; the room was filled with a sense of tense expectancy. After, what seemed to Max, an hour, Emmanuel turned and came back to the desk. Max caught sight of his white face, and felt that the recollection of past unhappiness had hurt him. He came nearer and put out his hand for the picture. Emmanuel shook his head.

'No,' he said, 'leave it, Max, leave it. Wait and I will show you somet'ing.'

'It's upset you, you're not well.'

'It's upset me. It's shaken me. It has proved to me that I had never enough faith. I can't explain, my dear. Leave it alone. Go and bring me a small brandy, will you? Not much, just a little.'

Left alone, he leant forward and took Juliana's picture in his hands.

Lifting it to his lips he kissed it passionately.

'I should have hed more faith,' he whispered, 'I should hev known that love like ours would protect us. Alessandri was—as you told me—just an incident, a nothing. Forgive me, if I made mistakes with Elchernon—oh, my dear, Delight of my Heart, forgive me.'

He put down the picture, unlocked one of the drawers of his desk, and after a short search found a small, rather faded photograph of a little boy, dressed in the fashion of 1850. A little boy, dark-eyed, dark-haired, who stood beside a low, velvet chair, staring at nothing in particular.

Max came back with the brandy, Emmanuel thanked him, drank it, and then offered him the little picture.

'Who is that, please, Max?'

Max looked at it and laughed. 'Good Lord! I suppose that it's you, but it might be Frankie. It is you, isn't it?'

Emmanuel nodded. 'It's me, Max. Taken in Vienna when I was—what?—seven, I t'ink. Look at both the pictures—it's astonishing. It's wonderful. He must come home, Max.'

'That is what I want, Father.'

'That young woman, that is Elchernon's wife, eh? I don't

think I could face having her here, Max. She's a terrible young woman, isn't she?'

Julie—Max's hand went suddenly to his cheek, while his eyes were fixed on the photograph. Julie by the sea, smiling, and clutching Frankie by the hand. Her whole figure full of vitality, a certain harsh courage, a determination to 'live life'.

'She is not terrible,' he said, 'she's—not educated, but she's quite kind. She wouldn't want to come here, she's mad about Ted. She's going to Canada with him quite soon.'

' "Mad about Ted",' Emmanuel repeated. 'Is that what she said? She's his mistress, I suppose. God of my Fathers, what a house for my grendson to be living in. Max, tell Judson to send for the carriage. I am going to bring him home—now. Each hour makes a difference.'

'Today, Father!' Max said. 'But you're tired. You've had a long journey.'

'Tired! Who said I was tired? And if I were, even then I should go and bring home your mother's grandson—and mine. Order the carriage, Max.'

During the drive, Emmanuel sat silent. He was shaken, he was full of regrets, tortured with the recollection that Algernon was his own son, and that he had—in some way—neglected his duty. He was certain that in his grandson he might find the chance to rectify the mistakes which he had made. By care and love and wisdom extended to Frankie, he might and would atone for whatever faults he had committed. With all his remorse came a sense of joy that Algernon was his son, and that Juliana had been the mother of his son, not the mother of Jules Alessandri's child.

The little house shocked him, he stared at it as if it were some unpleasant curiosity. As he walked from the carriage to the blistered front door, Max thought that he had never seen his father look so tall, so distinguished, so dignified. They were admitted by the gimlet-eyed woman.

'Come in,' she said. 'Dad's 'ome. 'E's just cleanin' isself in the back.'

Emmanuel seemed to fill the dingy little room. He stood on the hearth-rug, and stared round him, his face full of amazed disgust. Max stood by the window and watched him.

'Max, can you open that window? The air is terrible in here.'

'I don't think they'd like it, Father.'

'Ah! Perhaps you're right.'

Julie—Max cursed himself for turning scarlet as she entered. She looked at Emmanuel, smiled, and said,

'Bert's dad, I s'pose. How are you? Hello, Max—back again.'

Emmanuel bowed, his heels together; Max tried to smile and felt the effort was not altogether successful.

'Know what you lef' the other day, Max? Box of chocolates. I wondered if they were for me, or the other lidy you called on afterwards. Anyway, Frankie an' me finished them.'

'I'm very glad. I brought them for Frankie.'

'Next time you can bring some for me. Oh, here's Dad and Mum. Grandpa, this is Dad an' Mum, Mr. and Mrs. Orpes.'

The shock of being addressed as 'Grandpa' shook Emmanuel visibly. He recovered himself, bowed to the gaunt woman and the small sandy man who followed her. Max, looking at them both, wondered where Julie got her hair, her eyes, and that big, soft mouth.

Emmanuel stood very upright, looking from one to the other. Mr. and Mrs. Orpes sat side by side at the table, Julie lounged against the door, and stared at Max, who still stood near the window, and tried to avoid meeting her eyes.

'Now,' said Mr. Orpes briskly, 'it would appear that you and that gentleman in the winder, 'ave a idea of takin' young Frankie awai. Is that correck?'

Emmanuel bowed again. 'Quite, Mr.—Mr. . . .'

'Orpes, to rhyme with corpse. Nah, 'as it struck you that this is a most unnatural thing ter suggest? 'As it struck you that when Bert behaved as 'e did me and Mums 'ere was the first to sai, "Suffer little children ter come, etcetera"? This 'ere is Frankie's 'ome, and be it never so 'umble, etcetera—there it is. Added ter that, there's me an' Mum to consider. Julie's leavin' us ter go to the farest flung outposts of the Empire, and only Frankie is lef' an' you "seek 'im ter tike 'im awai." 'E is a manner of speakin', Mum's one ewe lamb—allus admitting that the sex is altered. She'd be like Rachel weepin' for her children and would not be comforted, without Frankie.'

'Indeed,' Emmanuel said, 'you surprise me. Perhaps I was selfishly only thinking of the boy's future, not his grandmother's affection. Forgive me.'

'Granted,' said Mr. Orpes pleasantly. 'I grant you that you can give Frankie riches, gold, jewels, and the things of this world. But what abart that treasure which moth and rust cannot corrupt, Mister? Tell me that?'

Emmanuel stared at him blankly, 'Moth . . .' he said. 'Moth? Rust . . . I'm not a rag-and-bone dealer, Mr. Orpes.'

'I was refering to Heavenly treasure, Mister.'

'Oh, I beg your pardon. I cannot guarantee that, naturally, but I should do my best to make the lad a decent, law-abiding citizen.'

Mrs. Orpes spoke for the first time. 'The Law,' she said, 'ain't enough in Dad's eyes. 'E was referrin' ter Gawd's laws.'

Emmanuel's manner changed suddenly, it became less suave, more brisk and business-like.

'Quite,' he said. 'I do not propose to discuss theology with Mr. Orpes. Now, what is the figure?'

Julie, lounging against the door, laughed suddenly. Mr. Orpes scowled at her.

'Figger,' he said, 'wot figger?'

'The figure which you decided upon with your wife and daughter after my son's visit two days ago.'

Again Julie laughed, her eyes met those of Max, who immediately became engrossed in the sickly fern in the window. She said, in that warm, hoarse voice which had rung in Max's ears for two days:

'Garn, Dad. The ole gentleman's got you beat. Slap your cards down.'

'Hold your tongue,' Mr. Orpes returned, 'and mind yer own business an' I'll mind mine. Arfter prayer an' supplication, Mister, after pondering an' considering 'ow I might apply salve to Mum's bleeding heart . . .'

Julie said, 'Bleedin' heart's good, Dad.'

'I decided that the sum—for selling Frankie, a birthright as you might say . . .'

Emmanuel smiled. 'Ah,' he said, 'now I can follow the Biblical allusion. What is the cost of the mess of pottage?'

'Six thousand pounds, Mister.'

'Nonsense!'

'Isn't yore grandson worth six thousand pounds?'

'Certainly, Mr. Orpes. But the money goes to you. It's your worth, not my grandson's. Listen'—Emmanuel held up his hand to stop the flow of quotation which obviously rose to Orpes' lips—'if I go to law, even if I write to my son, Elch—Elbert, I can get this boy with a very trifling expense. Corroborate that, please, Max.'

'My father is right, Mr. Orpes.'

Julie said, 'An' I be'leve he's right, Dad. Take it from me.'

Orpes' Adam's apple moved spasmodically in his throat. 'Wot is yore figure, then, Mister?'

'Three thousand pounds for you and your wife, a thousand for your daughter to take to Canada. The three thousand to be invested for you, you receive interest but no capital. That comes back to Frankie at your death. Your daughter's is hers absolutely.'

'Int'rest only,' Orpes said, 'I never 'eard such perishin' cheek in my life! Never. I refuse—absolutely and entir'ly. Now then!'

He rose to his feet, Julie moved for the first time, caught him on the chest with the back of her hand and sent him into his chair.

'Less of it,' she said. 'Now—I've let you all talk, Dad, an 'Mum shoving her oar in and even you, Mister. Now, suppose I talk. 'Oo's is young Frank? Did you carry him for nine bloomin' months, Mum, or you, Dad? Did you 'ave a 'and in the making of 'im, Mister?'

'Yes,' Emmanuel said, 'a little. Not much. You are quite right—go on.'

'Then I'll settle about young Frank, an' no one else. He's mine—get that straight, will you? Max come and *asked* me —*asked* me to give 'im a charnce—but you come 'ere and jore your 'eads off and leave me out of it. I never was much, was I? Frankie goes with 'is grandpa an' 'is uncle Max. I get a thousand Jimmies, an' if you get enough interest to get you two quid a week, you're damned lucky an' don't you forget it! Mister Gollantz, that's settled. There'll be papers and whatnots I s'pose? Make them out in my name—not Dad's. Send Max along with them, an' I'll sign and you can take young Frank. Six thousand quid—like 'is cheek!'

She turned towards Max. 'Come along with the pipers,' she said, 'I'll sign 'em for you. You'll like my writing— very classy it is.'

'Thank you,' Emmanuel said. 'And the boy? I should like to take him with me.'

'Not before the papers is signed,' Orpes said.

Julie turned on him, half snarling. 'Stop yore talking in church,' she said, 'always chipping in out of yore turn, you are. Frankie's ready. He's got on 'is best suit, and his Sunday boots. I 'aven't sent 'is others, Mister, they're not up to much.' She opened the door and called, 'Frankee, come on.'

Max saw Emmanuel stiffen, saw his hands clench as he waited. Frankie entered, wearing a hideous Norfolk suit, with over-long knickerbockers, black stockings, and leather boots with patent toe-caps. Round his neck he wore a blue sailor collar, decorated with anchors and coils of rope. He exuded a smell of yellow soap, his face shone and his dark hair was plastered and sticky. He stood and scowled, until his eyes caught sight of Max.

' 'Ello,' he said. 'Come back, 'ave you?'

Max said, 'Speak to your grandfather, Frankie.'

Frankie looked at Emmanuel, then back to Max. ' 'Im,' he said, 'that my grandfather? Gor, 'e looks a proper toff.'

'Come here, Frankie,' Emmanuel said, and held out his hand. The boy took it, and smiled. 'Don't look much like a Jew,' he said, 'do you?'

As they drove home, Emmanuel watched the boy, a smile of content on his face. Frankie sat, his short legs swinging, his eyes still wet from the parting with his mother. He had clung to her, and screamed that he did not want to leave her. She had kissed him and said, 'Garn, young Frankie, don't be a cry-baby. Look at the carriage and all!'

'What do you weigh?' Emmanuel asked suddenly. 'Do you know?'

Frankie sniffed. 'Yes, I do know. My muvver 'ad me weighted at the station. I weigh five stone an' two ounces.'

Emmanuel turned to Max and smiled. 'Over two pounds an ounce,' he said, 'and well worth it. A good tutor, a good tailor and—that accent attended to, and we shall be proud of him. He's plucky,' he added softly. 'I liked the way he pulled himself together.'

'That's the mother,' Max said, 'she's got grit.'

'Poof!' Emmanuel breathed, 'what a trollop she is! Dreadful! Poor Elchernon.'

Max whistled a little tune. 'I don't know,' he said, after a moment's pause, 'she's—she's like the boy—plucky.'

'I call it effrontery,' Emmanuel said.

Three days later, Max went back to the little house for the last time. His father handed him the papers, saying, 'She signs here, and here. Make her write legibly—if

she can. The money is in the bank for the two Corpses, it
will be paid quarterly. The girl can have hers now. Remember, Max, make it qvite plain, they have no further
claim upon me. That is in the agreement.'

Max hesitated. 'You wouldn't care to come yourself?'

His father shuddered. 'My dear Max, no! It has taken me
three days to get that terrible house, those horrible old
people, and that dreadful young woman out of my mind.
Send Frank to me, will you? Already I see an improve-
ment in that boy.'

Frankie was absorbing new ideas. At first the house had
oppressed him, he had been frightened of the large rooms,
the servants had overawed him, and he had been either
sulky or impudent to them. Max had never seen his father
so patient, so gentle or so understanding. He would stand
and watch his grandson moving slowly round one of the
big rooms. Looking at this, asking questions about that.
Once he had halted before a Greek bronze, a slim delicate figure of a young man, his arms upraised, his whole
body beautifully poised. He had passed brightly coloured
china figures, the product of Chelsea and Dresden, unmoved, he had turned away from a golden triptych inlaid
with precious stones, intricate Chinese carvings had made
no noticeable impression upon him—but the Greek statue
held him silent and entranced.

'Look,' Emmanuel whispered, 'the really perfect t'ing
holds him. You see what happens, Max. The soul of the
man who made that is speaking down all the years to that
child. What hev I always said—leave the mind of a child
alone, and it will find the best, always the best, and like
only the best.' Raising his voice, he said, 'Do you like
that, Frank?'

Frankie turned, looked, for a moment, suspicious and
half-sulky, afraid that someone was going to make fun of
him; then seeing Emmanuel's smile, he was reassured.

'Yes,' he said, 'it's all right, that is. Looks as if 'e was
going ter fly, don't 'e?'

'I fancy that part of him is flying,' Emmanuel said, 'he's
praising, worshipping somet'ing bigger than himself.'

Frankie nodded. 'That's it,' he said. 'I can't see the part
what is flying, but I knew it was, didn't I? It makes you
feel nice ter look at it.'

'Perhaps you would like to have it?'

Max gasped, the statue was worth its weight, if not in

gold, certainly in silver. Emmanuel had refused many offers for it.

'For me own? To keep? Garn, you're kidding me.'

'For your own, to keep and I am, indeed, not kidding you. Take it and put it in your bedroom. It has been waiting for you to come and claim it for more than a thousand years.'

Frankie stared, then went back and took the worshipping boy in his hands very carefully. Emmanuel, still smiling, turned to Max.

'Do you remember your first dog?' he said. 'You said that he might hev chosen anyone else, but that he chose you. You said that he was a trust. History repeats itself, eh? Take care of him, Frank, and never admire anyt'ing less beautiful. Promise me.'

Frankie clutched the bronze to his chest. 'Shouldn't think there was many things as beautiful as 'e is.'

'Exactly, then don't admire very many t'ings.' He laughed. 'T'ere, Max, he's hed his first lesson in antique dealing!'

When he had first seen Max's old dog, who lay asleep most of the day, with the burden of his years heavy upon him, Frankie had hailed him as an object suitable for teasing and tormenting. The dog had snarled and finally snapped and caught the child's wrist in the few teeth which remained to him. Frankie had screamed with fright, and Judson had brought him to Emmanuel.'

'Tip bit Master Frankie, sir.'

'Show me.' Frankie, sniffing, exhibited the scratch on his wrist. 'Get some carbolic, Judson, and bathe it. Why did Tip bite him? He never bites anyone.'

'Master Frankie was teasing him, sir, I'm afraid.'

'Grandfather, I only . . .'

Emmanuel swung round, his eyes cold. 'Go away,' he said, 'I have nothing to say to you. Let me tell you this, please, then go. For many years, Tip hes been a guest in my house. He belongs to Max. I never allow anyone to insult my guests. Please remember thet. Go, and let Judson bathe your hend.'

Half an hour later, Frankie knocked on the door, and Emmanuel bade him come in. He walked to his grandfather's chair, and stood, his head hanging.

'I've come to beg pardon, Grandfather, for teasing Tip.'

'I wonder what Tip thinks of you?'

Frankie came nearer and sniffed loudly, he was still tearful.

'I went an' give 'im 'is dinner. Cook let me. I cuddled him, he liked it. Patted 'is 'ead, I did.'

'Ah, Tip is like his master—a gentleman, Frank.'

'Are you a gentleman, Grandfather?'

'I hope so. I try to be one.'

There was a silence. Frankie drew a pattern with his foot on the carpet.

'Would you say that I was—a gentleman?'

Emmanuel surveyed him carefully. 'No, I don't think so, Frankie. Gentlemen don't hurt animals, and when the animals rightly punish them—howl. But,' his voice softened, 'give us time, we'll make not only a gentleman but a man of you.'

The little boy nodded. He liked to be talked to by his grandfather, it gave him the sensation of being a man amongst men. Something stirred inside him when he looked at this handsome old man. He smelt nice, not only of soap but, Frankie decided, of cleanness. He sniffed with deep appreciation. Emmanuel looked up and asked if he wanted a handkerchief.

'No, I'm not sniffin', Grandfather, I'm smellin'.'

'Smelling what?'

'You—I like the smell of you. I like a good lot of things about you.'

'I am very flattered. Thenk you.'

'I do, strite.' Something was battling in Frankie's soul, he wanted to make a gesture, and with an effort succeeded. 'Did Uncle Max tell you wot I said—about— Jews?'

'Jews, no,' Emmanuel lied. 'What did you say?'

His ears were red, his heart beat terribly fast. His grandfather might be very angry and send him back to Camberwell. He didn't care, he was going to risk it. 'I said as Jews was mucky. I sang a song about putting pork on forks an' giving it to Jews. I shan't ever sing it again, cross me 'eart and wish I may die. I think—I think yore a proper toff, an' so is Uncle Max for not sneaking on me.'

When the door had closed behind him, Emmanuel rose and went to his desk. He bent down and spoke to the photograph which stood there. 'The birth of a gentleman,' he said. 'How it must please—and amuse you. He'll be a credit to us—our grandson, my beloved.'

11

Max spread the papers out on the yellow cloth and said, 'You sign there, and there and there, please.'

'I sign ther and ther and ther,' Julie repeated. 'I see. Where's the pen?'

He watched her sign, writing like a child, carefully and slowly—Julie Goodman—three times. Once a blot gathered on her pen and fell upon the thick white paper. She said, 'Oh, blarst it,' under her breath.

Max said, 'That doesn't matter. Leave it.'

She laid down the corroded pen, obviously with relief, turned to Max and said, inconsequently, 'Ted's away. He's gorne to Basingstoke to see 'is uncle and arnt.'

'Really.' Max simulated interest in Ted. 'When do you sail for Canada?'

'Nex' month, I bel'eve.' She paused. 'I don't know that I want to go. I don't bel'eve I would go at all—if things were different.'

'How—different?'

She looked at him, her dark eyes sullen and gloomy. 'If you were different, if you'd be nice to me, Max.'

Something told Max that this was the time to gather up the papers quickly, the time to say something cool and noncommittal, and go. He wanted to go, and yet something held him fast, staring into Julie's eyes, stupid, inarticulate, and almost frightened.

'I have tried to be nice,' he said, weakly. 'Really Julie, I never meant to hurt you.'

'Hurt me!' She laughed. 'No, you didn't mean, your sort never do. You only treated me as if I was something not like you at all. As if I belonged to a different place—was different, commoner, beastlier.'

'Not that,' Max said. 'Julie, you make me feel that we —my father and I—have been impossible.'

'Don't drag in your father,' she said, 'for God's sake

leave 'im out of it. An' don't say "Impossible". That's one of your toff words, that is.'

Max said, 'I'm sorry,' and turned to gather up the papers. His heart was beating heavily; in his temples a pulse throbbed, his hands were cold. Julie laid her hand on his arm, holding it with a firm, warm clasp. He shook it off and said, 'Don't, Julie, don't.'

'Why not?' She came closer, he dropped the papers and watched her.

'Why not? Max, be nice to me.'

'I've told you—I tried to be nice,' he snapped. Max who had never spoken unkindly to a woman in his life!

'I'm crazy about you, Max. Oh, I know about Ted, and Ted's all right, but you—you've just got me, and—God, I can't get you out of my 'ead.'

'Julie, you mustn't talk like this. It's not—it's not fair. Not fair to Ted, or my brother. I must go.'

Her hand tightened on his arm, her face was very close to his; he could feel the warmth of her, sense the passion which rose in her and rushed towards him. He knew that he was being swept along a wave which might fling him upon the rocks, knew that he was allowing himself to be drawn into danger, sucked into a whirlpool where muddy water eddied and circled. He knew that even now he could make an effort and go—and knew with complete certainty that he would stay because she wanted him.

'Ted,' she whispered, and he felt the breath from her mouth hot on his face, 'leave Ted out of it. Ted's all right. Bert—Bert don't count. There's only you an' me, Max. Put your arms round me, Max, just once. You do like me, don't you?'

He said, talking as if he were drugged, 'I don't know, Julie. I don't know.'

She caught his hands and laid them round her neck, bent forward and pressed her lips to his. They were hot, hungry, almost rapacious. She kissed him again and again, drew him closer and held him to her. He could feel the generous curves of her body, feel the rise and fall of her bosom against his chest. She whispered, 'Max, kiss me,' and again, more insistently, 'Kiss me—Max.'

Max caught her to him more closely, kissed her passionately, insatiably, again and again. Then drew her to the big, dusty arm-chair and sat down, pulling her on to his knees.

'Love me a little bit?' she said softly. 'Do you?'

'I suppose so,' he said hoarsely. 'I want to take you out and give you everything you want in the world—clothes and jewels and—oh, everything.'

Julie lay in his arms, her eyes like those of some great cat, sleepy, but with something tigerish in their depths. 'Go on,' she said, 'tell me.'

'Kiss me, Julie. Again, again. Is this what you meant when you said—life was there to be lived?'

'Something like that,' she laughed softly. 'You great kid. Never loved anyone before? Go on!'

'Never—never.'

'How old are you?'

'Twenty-three.'

Again that soft laugh which half frightened him. 'It's a shame to tike the money. Like taking jam from a baby. Never mind, let's be happy.'

'I want—terribly—to make you happy, Julie. Anything —anything in the world.'

She laid her face against his, drew down his head and whispered softly.

The waves caught him, carried him unresisting into the whirlpool, threw him this way and that, numb, suffocated, dazed, and blind. Time did not exist, the whole world was empty except for himself and Julie.

The pale September sun was throwing golden shafts of light down the grimy little street, the children had ceased playing and had been called home by raucous-voiced mothers to tea.

One by one men passed the window, going home, their day's work over. Max leant against the table and stared blankly before him. His face was very white, his eyes heavy. Julie lying back in the arm-chair watched him and laughed softly.

'What's the time?'

Mechanically his fingers sought and found his watch. 'Nearly six o'clock.'

'Good job Mum's gorne to Wandsworth and Dad's working overtime!'

He shivered, pressed the back of his hand to his eyes, then came towards her and held out his hand.

'Julie, please forgive me. Can you forgive me? I didn't realise that I was such a swine.'

'Go on,' she said, 'you silly kid, don't be a date! D'you love me?'

Max gathered his courage together with a violent effort.

'Julie—that's the awful part of it—I don't love you. I want to see you again—I'd give you anything in the world—but I don't love you. Now you know what a brute I feel.' She held out her hand, took his, and spoke almost as a mother might speak to a child. 'Garn,' she said, 'you're frightened, that's all. You're just a great kid, Max. It's all right. Smile, dearie, smile! You got to go, eh? When shall I see you again?'

'See me?' he said. 'Oh, yes. Tomorrow, Julie. I'll meet you anywhere you like. Not here,' he glanced round the crowded room, 'not here.'

'No, not here. Lemme think, Max. Sit down, dearie. Let's think—I know. A friend of mine, old chorus girl, has a nice house off the Tottenham Court Road. She lets rooms. It's Nineteen Mitton Street. I'll be there at three. That suit you?'

He nodded, moistened his dry lips, and said, 'Yes—three—Nineteen Mitton Street. All right, Julie. I must go.'

'Take your precious papers, Max. Here—give me a kiss. Gor! call that a kiss! I don't call that kissing or letting it alone. Till tomorrow.'

That night Max could not sleep. All through dinner, it had seemed that his father was determined to be more than usually fastidious, more than ordinarily selective. He had dismissed some man to whom Max referred as 'second rate', adding, 'I dislike anyt'ing which is second-rate.' Once Max had mentioned Frankie. Emmanuel had smiled and said:

'Frank is all right. Don't call him that horrible name—Frankie. It reminds me of the two ghouls and that terrible young woman.' He shivered with exaggerated disgust. 'Oh, that man-eating tigress!'

'I should think that she is the best of the lot of them,' Max said and felt that he had added disloyalty to his other crimes.

'An expression I detest,' Emmanuel said. 'The best of a bundle of dirty rubbish isn't worth anyt'ing, Max.'

Nineteen Mitton Street was no better and no worse than twenty other houses in its vicinity. It stood sandwiched between a small restaurant and a turner's shop where table legs, door knobs, rolling pins and newel posts were displayed. Max rang the bell and was admitted by a woman with metallic golden hair, and heavily made-up eyes, who wore a wrapper much trimmed with lace which was crying out for a visit to the laundry.

'I have an appointment,' Max said, 'with a lady.'

The woman smiled. 'I guessed that,' she said, pleasantly, too pleasantly; and opening a door on the left of the passage called, 'Jule—here's your gentleman friend come.'

The room at Camberwell had been unpleasant, but this room was terrible, it filled him with a horror which was indescribable. It was dim, and in the corners seemed to lurk the dreadful secrets of other people who had occupied it. The furniture was heavy, funereal, and oppressive. The walls were covered with trails of hot red roses, caught up at intervals with festoons and bows of bright blue. In the darkest of the dark corners stood a bed, a bed which sank in the middle, which—to Max—seemed blatant, bestial, and terrible. Julie stood by the black marble mantelpiece watching him.

'Hello, Max.'

He felt that he ought to go forward and take her in his arms, that he ought to feel glad to see her, grateful to her for coming. He felt nothing except horror, fear, and an intense longing to get away.

She said, 'You're looking as if you'd lost a shilling and found a tanner. Call and ask Lily to give you a drink, that 'ul buck you up a bit. Tell her to bring a bottle. You can finish it another time.'

Another time—another visit to this dreadful house! Max clenched his hands, and with a violent effort went to the door and called, not realising what he called.

'Bring a bottle of whisky, will you, and some soda.'

'Certainly, dearie. Pay for it now, will you?'

'Yes—yes, I'll pay for it now.'

Julie said, 'Yes, Lil, he'd better pay for it now, dear.'

'Half a quid, dear, an' sixpence the soda.'

Max forced himself to smile, and said, 'Well, the soda's cheap enough.'

The highly decorated bottle contained a brand which was unknown to him. It burnt his throat, but it took some of the horror away, made the room seem brighter, made Julie's smile something which was warm, alive, and seductive. He put down the glass, and went towards her, his hands outstretched.

'Julie, dear,' he said, 'it's so good to see you again. You're very beautiful, very wonderful.'

She smiled. 'That's better. Bit stand-offish, weren't you?'

'Just a fool,' he said, 'that's all—a confounded fool.'

He felt her arms round his neck, felt her kisses on his face, heard her whisper, 'I'd like to 'ear anyone else call you that, Max. I'd knock their 'eads off for them.'

Emmanuel was indulging in what his workmen stigmatised as 'a ramp'. At Campden Hill nothing pleased him. He found fault with the polishers, he eyed the restored and beautifully carved frames with disgust, and was so carefully polite to everyone that Barker, who had been with him for years, whispered to Mason, the head carpenter, 'Stand by for the crash. He won't be right until he's had a damned row with someone.'

The crash came over a small swinging mirror. Emmanuel had bought it and sent it to the workshops to have tiny wooden knobs fitted at the top of each column. He had chosen the pieces of rosewood from which they were to be cut, had given minute instructions, and even a detailed drawing. He found the work finished, stared at it, and asked blandly, 'What are the wooden turnips at the ends of the columns?'

'Those were turned to scale,' Mason said, 'from your drawings, sir.'

Emmanuel smiled and fingered his short clipped side-whiskers.

'I must have made a mistake, Mason. These were evidently made for a bedstead or a newel post. They dwarf the mirror.'

'Can't get them any smaller, sir.'

'Really? A pity. The piece can't go out as it is—obviously. Well, well, it's my own fault for having an army of incompetents about the place. What was the name of that excellent man who used to work here—Iron—Brass—I forget.'

'Steele, sir. Started for himself off the Tottenham Court Road.'

'Steele! What a workman. I wish I could get Steele beck. I must make him an offer. Not that you are not good, Mason, but you're limited—terr-ribly limited. Give me the drawings, and what wood is left. I will take them myself to that wonderful Iron.'

'Steele, sir.'

'I beg your pardon—Steele.'

Mason swallowed something which apparently stuck in his throat. He, like the rest of the staff, adored Emmanuel, but admitted that he could, on occasion, 'be'ave like a perfec' pig, nothink else'.

He said, 'What Steele can do, I can do, Mr. Gollantz.'

'Can you?' Emmanuel stared at him in surprise. 'Then give me an opportunity to see what Steele can do, and you shall copy him, Mason.'

So Emmanuel drove to Mitton Street, descended from his carriage, and interviewed Steele, the turner. He found the man intelligent, found also that his stock of old and well-seasoned wood was remarkable. Time flew, and it was not until nearly six o'clock that Emmanuel was bowed from the shop, and found himself out again in Mitton Street. He stood, swinging his ivory-headed stick, whistling a mournful little tune, reflecting upon the price which he had offered Steele for his stock of old oak, when the door of the house next to the turner's opened. The sound made Emmanuel turn, and then stand erect and immovable, his face stern, his hand clutching the cane which he had swung so lightly a few moments before. Max. Max, who stood for a moment to say 'Good-bye' to a woman, a woman whose voice reached Emmanuel. 'Good-bye, darling. That whisky's gorne to your head a bit, hasn't it?' Then Max's voice, thick and strained, 'Not the whisky—you, Julie. You've gone to my head. Until tomorrow.'

'Three o'clock, dearie.'

The door closed, and Max came down the steps, one hand sliding along the dirty railings. Emmanuel stepped forward.

'I have the carriage here, Max. Let me give you a lift home.'

Max stopped, stared at his father, swinging a little on his heels. His face was ghastly, his eyes heavy and glazed. He opened his mouth as if to speak, then closed it and said nothing.

'Be qvick, please,' Emmanuel said, 'I have no particular desire to be seen in this—unpleasant street.' He took his son's arm and led him to the carriage. Max moved like an automaton—mechanically and without volition. During the drive home neither spoke a word. Max sat, his eyes closed, his hands limp; Emmanuel leant back in his corner, frowning, very stern, and immovable.

'Come into my room, Max, please.'

Max followed obediently. His father produced a small glass, poured into it some dark fluid, and handed it to his son.

'Yorkshire relish,' he said, 'Please drink it, then listen to me.'

'I don't want Yorkshire relish . . .'

'Drink it.' Max swallowed the stuff and miraculously his head cleared.

'What was that place where I saw you? Wait, I'll tell you. A brot'el. Who was the woman? Again I'll tell you. Your brother Elchernon's wife. How pretty! How long has this gone on? How long hev you played this most unpleasant game?'

'Not long—only yesterday.'

'Yesterday, today, and tomorrow! Are you in love with her?'

'Yes—I mean I don't know.'

Emmanuel nodded. 'Then you are *not* in love with her!' He came and laid his hand upon Max's shoulder. 'You must pr-romise not to see her again. Max. Pr-romise me.'

Max moved uneasily. 'I can't do that, Father. It's not fair.'

'Not fair! Not fair!' The words burst from Emmanuel in a tone of concentrated disgust. 'Fair to whom, please? To this woman, to me, or to yourself?'

'To myself and to—Julie.'

Emmanuel sighed. 'I hev made you very English, Max. Presently you will say that you must do what is cricket, or play the game, or some other admirable and idiotic cliché. What nonsense!'

'She has been very . . .' Max paused and sought for a word, 'very generous.'

'Chenerous! God in Heaven! Am I chenerous when I sent out invitation cards to my exhibitions? No, I send them to all the people I know! So does she. Max, I know that type so well—any man, any fresh man is fair game to them. Had I allowed myself to watch her, as you did, I, old as I am, would have served. They take men as drunkards take whisky. Some kinds are better than others, but all kinds are—whisky.' He spoke more softly, his voice was almost tender; however harsh the words might be, the voice robbed them of their sting. Max could not hear it, Max felt sore and angry. He was a man, his father was trying to keep him in leading strings.

'Max,' Emmanuel said, 'look round. Go and walk through this house and tell me what you find. Beauty and dignity. All your life has been spent among dignified t'ings. Beautiful t'ings. You couldn't possible hev liked that brot'el, it wasn't your ideal of a setting for yourself, was it?'

'One takes what serves,' Max said.

'One does not'ing of the kind. I take only the best, always. Take what serves!' He laughed. 'Where would my business be today if I had followed that axiom! I am a Jew, always a Jew, and Jews are very wise. They want to get somet'ing out of everyt'ing. You are getting not'ing out of this nesty, vulgar intrigue with your brother's wife. Listen, Max, I know that you're a man, I know too, that men hev appetites, thet they get hungry. They want warmth and love, even if they pay for it.' He paused and went on, his tone less grave, 'So—take a mistress. You shall hev enough money to keep her suitably, I don't promise in tremendous luxury. Make a bargain with some pleasant woman, who likes you and for whom you hev an admiration. But let it be a good bargain. Get somet'ing more from it than just cheap physical setisfaction. To be forced to make love—that's a figure of speech, Max—because there is nothing to talk about, is such a dreadful bore! It's good to drink, and drink deeply, but not to be forced to drink early and late, day in and day out, because there is not'ing else to do.'

Max stood up and walked feverishly up and down the long room. Emmanuel watched him, half-smiling, half-regretful.

'I can't think of any woman who attracts me, Father,' Max said. 'You're very kind, but . . .'

'No, no,' Emmanuel said, 'I hev still anot'er alternative. You don't like the idea of an establishment. Very well. Then there are other women. Free lances, but still exquisite, charming, delightful. T'ink, Max, could you call—this woman exquisite, charming, delightful? Again, each time you see her, she makes a new link of the chain which holds you. Holds you—not by love, or admiration, but by base t'ings. Then one day will come threats, and a declaration of war. T'ink it over, decide which it shall be—a woman you will keep, or a lady who will admit you to her house on certain occasions. I shall say not'ing. I shall agree. But, I cannot and will not face your being dregged down, lower and lower, until you not only hate her—that will come quickly—but you will hate yourself. That is what I could not watch.'

'I should like to think over what you have said, Father. I can't think here—I'm not quite myself, I'm afraid.'

'One t'ing more, and I hev done, Max. I said before that

you were a Jew. In this country there is a prejudice against us. Down in their hearts Englishmen despise us. What Frank says in the vernacular, they all say at some time or another. The dirty Jew, the scheming low Yid! I am so proud of my race, that for nearly sixty years I hev tried to make my English friends t'ink not only well of me, but of Jews because of me. Suppose this story gets about— as such stories eventually do—listen to what will be said, "Max Gollantz is keeping his brother's wife as his mistress," or, "His brother married beneath him, he left her—but she was good enough for Max." And again as the verdict, "Well, after all, that's what one expects from a Jew, they're a dirty lot." And you, Max, will be a traitor to me, to yourself, and to your race. Not a nice picture?'

'I'll think over what you've said, Father. I don't think I will come down to dinner, if you'll excuse me.'

Late that evening, Max came down to his father. Emmanuel looked up from the letter he was writing and smiled. To Max it seemed that he must have forgotten everything to be able to smile so easily. He sat down, near the desk and laid a letter before his father.

'You're right,' he said, 'quite right. If you care to read that letter please do. I'm ashamed of myself. I'm not going to be quixotic and say that the blame rests entirely with me—it's fifty per cent to us both.'

Emmanuel looked at the thick envelope before him. "I don't like letters, Max. They're silly t'ings. One is ept to get sentimental and weak.'

'I'm sorry, Father, to use an expression you dislike, but it's only fair to write.'

'As you wish. I won't read it, Max. It's a private letter after all. Give it to Judson to post, please.' He picked up a letter which lay at his elbow and said, very briskly, 'While you are here, Max, you might attend to this. Schechter writes to me from Berlin, that the furniture, pictures, and books of old Baron von Zeissel are to be sold next week. There is a Hobbema, a small and rather inferior bronze of Caracalla, and an unsigned group which he believes to be a Chardin. The rest you can ignore, unless there is somet'ing which attracts you particularly, then risk it. You could leave tomorrow, I think?'

Max nodded. 'Certainly, if you wish.'

'Hev a nice time, Max. Don't keep your nose to the grindstone all the time. I will see you in the morning.'

Book Three

Max and Angela

12

Max moved his deck chair, so that it stood in the long shaft of shade thrown by the tall cypress, sat down, crossed his long legs, and turned his eyes again to the blue waters of Como which lay before him. He sighed, a sigh of deep content, and wondered why he lived in London when all this beauty was his for the asking.

On the right of his chair, under a striped awning, Emmanuel sat asleep. Max watched his father. Sixty-eight. He didn't look his age; he looked no age, any age. His hair was beautifully white, his skin fine, pale and unwrinkled as ever, his wonderful hands, the right one with its huge carved emerald ring, lay folded upon his knees. His clothes—a little smile hovered about Max's lips—were exquisite as ever; just a little theatrical, just a shade too perfect, but characteristic of Emmanuel Gollantz.

'Don't wake him, Max.'

He turned and met Rachel Leon's bright dark eyes. Her eyes were still bright, still danced with humour though she was past her seventy-first birthday. A pile of papers connected with the Women's Suffrage lay on her ample knees. Rachel had come with them to Italy to recover from her exertions for the Cause. She had wielded a seven-

pound hammer in Whitehall, she had—by sheer weight—
overthrown two policemen and reached the floor of the
House of Commons; and three times she had walked with
dignity to Bow Street from Trafalgar Square, an amused
and delighted policeman on either hand. Magistrates had
found something humorous in this massive old Jewess who
was brought before them, and who, in spite of fatherly
remonstrance from men young enough to be her sons,
remained entirely unrepentant. Then the temper of the
Administrators of the Law had changed, they had become
impatient and irritated, and had warned her that she was
impudently ignoring the Law and taking advantage of it by
reason of her age. Max, standing in the Court, had watched
her furious face, had listened to her denunciation of him
when he walked forward to pay her fine, and had wondered what fresh tactics she would resort to.

One morning, Hermann Leon had driven to Emmanuel's house, his kindly old eyes full of tears, his voice
shaken with distress. Rachel, 'and she is over seventy,
Emmanuel,' he had quavered, had been sent to Holloway
by a magistrate who declared that he would bring her to
reason by the most drastic measures which the law permitted.

Max had been sent off to Holloway, instructed to spare
no expense, to pull whatever strings offered themselves,
but to bring Rachel back with him.

'A most unrepentant old lady,' one in authority had told
him. 'I had an idea that Jews were a meek race!'

Rachel had been indignant at the idea of freedom being
granted to her. Even when the doctor suggested that the
hospital would be a suitable place for her, she had received his offer with scorn. She worked out her sentence,
attended the breakfast given in honour of her release, and
only consented to accompany Emmanuel and Max to Italy
because they told her that Hermann had suffered intolerably during her incarceration.

'I won't wake him, Rachel.'

'He only woke once,' she said, 'really woke, in all his
life, and that was when your mother was alive. The rest
of his life he has dreamed that he was a mixture of Moses
and Beau Brummel, with a dash of Lord Chesterfield. It's
been a most engaging mixture, too.'

'He has always had high standards, Rachel,' Max said.

She nodded. 'Yes, yes. But all his standards were set by
his antiques, my dear. He said, "Nothing but the best

shall come into my warehouse," and gradually he applied that to his life. He made himself mentally, morally, and physically, selective. His make-up is all priceless qualities —a perfectly clean heart—and a perfectly clean, fine linen shirt over it; a sound, honest dealing brain to match that beautiful hair which covers it—and so on.'

Max turned and looked again at his father. There was a very great and real affection between them, a great understanding, a great friendship.

'He's very clever, Rachel,' he said, 'I never forget how clever he has been in directing me, and Frank.'

'Wise,' Rachel corrected, 'not clever. He was born wise, he never made himself clever.' She heaved a large gusty sigh. 'I always thought that he might marry me,' she said, 'indeed, I think he would have done if your mother hadn't come from Paris and dined with old Davis and his wife that evening. If he had done, if he had married me over forty years ago, Max, I shouldn't be planning how to break up Churchill's meetings now.'

She moved so that all the papers fell to the ground from her knee.

'Leave them,' she said, 'it's a lot of nonsense. If I'd had children I'm damned if I should have wanted a vote. There it is—you must ache for something. What do you ache for, Max?'

'I don't know that I ache for anything,' he said. 'I can't think of anything.'

'You don't know—you can't think,' Rachel said. 'Do you ever try to find out, ever try to think?'

'Why should I? It might make me uncomfortable.'

'You ought to marry, my dear.'

Emmanuel stirred, opened his eyes and watched them. He got an intense satisfaction from watching Max. Max was all he had hoped for and more, Max had atoned for Algernon, had atoned for everything. Max knew how to enjoy life, he was neither sensualist nor prig, he never censured and yet it was impossible to believe that he condoned. He was sufficiently handsome without being conspicuous, hard-working, and yet found time to play. Max was a sane person, and Emmanuel loved sanity.

He listened and heard Rachel's voice, still full and rich for all her years, saying. 'You ought to marry, Max. You're —what is it?—thirty?'

'Thirty-one.'

Emmanuel spoke. 'I was married long before I was

t'irty, but then, I found your mother. Yes, Max, you ought to marry. Years ago, we had a party for Frank, I remember. He was t'irteen. I was talking to a little girl, she said that she liked me, and one day hoped to marry me.' He chuckled. 'I said that Frank would be more suitable. She thought for a minute, then said that Frank was too young, but suggested that if she married Max she might still live in the same house with me and see me every day. I was intensely flettered. Know who she was, Rachel?'

'No, Emmanuel.'

'Enchela Drew. Poor Walter Heriot's grenddaughter.'

Max rose. 'You've wakened up terribly bright, Father,' he said, 'but remember that Angela at thirteen and Angela at twenty are two different people. However—I'm going down to meet them all now, they've been over to Bellagio. Shall I remind her of her suggestion at once?'

'I should be very heppy, Max.'

'I'll give it my careful consideration. Take care of Rachel, Father.'

Rachel turned in her chair, which creaked protestingly, and watched him as he walked away. She turned back to Emmanuel and smiled.

'Not given you much anxiety, has he?'

'More now then he's ever done. He's going to find one day thet he's lonely, Rachel, and thet will be terrible.'

'He's lonely now,' she said. 'And with Frank more or less engaged to Ann Wilmot, William Drew dancing attendance upon that girl of Tom Wentworth's, with even fat Sir Walter dashing off to Paris with that red-headed hussy, it's making him realise just how lonely he is.'

Max walked slowly down the hill. He stopped to look in a shop window where embroidered shawls were hung like gorgeous flags, he wondered if he could find an excuse to buy one for somebody, then made an impatient movement and walked away. There was only one person he wanted to buy lovely things for. He was going to see her in a few moments, and she would be kind and friendly and—just as kind, just as friendly to everyone else. His father had found the weak spot in his armour. He, too, remembered Frank's thirteenth birthday. Remembered how old and rather superior he felt at twenty-four, how he longed to escape, and how the kid's games had bored him. Mrs. Drew, Walter Heriot's elder daughter, had talked to him, had said how the children enjoyed a party, how nice it was to watch young things, and that they were only young once. She had pointed out a slim child with long black silk stockings and a very abbreviated skirt who stood beside Emmanuel, and said that that was her little daughter, Angela. Max had looked and wondered what he could say, and found that he had said nothing, only stood and stared.

'Thirteen,' Gwendoline Drew said, 'it's dreadful how they shoot up.'

Max said, 'They do, don't they?' And had seen Emmanuel laugh and wondered what the child had said to him. He wanted, suddenly and idiotically, to go and take her away, make her talk to him and make him laugh as his father had just done. Gwendoline was babbling again. 'Walter says that she is going to be attractive.' She giggled. 'Walter should know.'

She had moved away from Emmanuel, and Max had followed her with his eyes, and wished that he dared ask her to dance with him. He had felt that he was a fool, that she would think him as old as her father, then remembered that her father was dead.

He had seen her again quite often. Once at a theatre party, where he had never been able to speak to her; again when she was sixteen and had been down to Ascot with Emmanuel, her brother William, and Walter. They had come back and dined at Regent's Park. She sat next to Max. He was the only person who had changed into evening clothes.

She said, 'Do you feel singular, or should we?'

He said, 'We—can't feel singular, it's a contradiction, isn't it?'

She laughed, and threw back her head, so that the shafts of light from the candles caught her smooth, fair hair and made it shine like dull gold. He had asked stupid questions about her school, and she said that she had left and was going to Germany to be finished. She said that William said that she would be 'finished' if she got as fat as the German girls. Max wanted to ask where she was going, and if he might write to her, and found that he dare not for fear she remembered how old he was and thought him a senile fool, and an unpleasant one at that. He was twenty-seven and felt dreadfully old. He only heard of her destination because she told Emmanuel and said, 'You will write to me, won't you?' Emmanuel bowed and said, 'I can't help myself, Enchela.'

Max wrote and sent a huge box of French sweets from

Paris. He signed himself, 'Your affectionate uncle, Max,' and hoped she would tell him when she wrote that he was too young to be her uncle. She didn't, she only thanked him for the sweets and said that they were the nicest she had ever tasted.

Then he heard of her only at long intervals, heard that she was studying the violin seriously, and that her master said she was brilliant.

Not until 1912 did he meet her again. They came to Como, Emmanuel, Rachel, Frank, and Max, and Frank said,

'You know that the whole clan is going to be here—the Drews, and the Wilmots, and the Wentworths. Rather fun, eh?'

Frank had asked Emmanuel if he could be engaged to Ann Wilmot, and Emmanuel had said that he was too young, but everyone treated them as an engaged couple and seemed to accept the situation.

Max had gone to his tailor's and bought new suits, to his bootmaker's and bought new boots, and had visited his hosier and bought a dozen expensive ties. Emmanuel had a villa, but the Wilmots and the Drews with Ann Wentworth stayed at the Grand, where they had a suite and were treated as if they were royalty.

Max had seen Angela, talked to her, and envied Frank and Charles Wilmot who were twenty-two and nineteen. Angela had not changed very much, he thought. She smiled more, laughed more easily, seemed very gay and as if she found life amusing. He asked her about her music. She said that she was 'very, very bad—really', and Max had said that he didn't believe it.

Now he was going to meet the boat from Bellagio, he was going to remind her that she was coming to dinner—with the others—up at the villa, he was going to give her some pretty message and say that it originated with Emmanuel.

He leant against the railing at the quay-side and watched the steamer come across the lake. Nearer and nearer it came, he could see the little group at the fore of the ship—Charles in a blue blazer with a splash of colour on the pocket, Ann Wentworth, very tall, with a green scarf round her hat, William, shorter than the others, in a bright brown tweed coat, Ann Wilmot, who was called 'Morrie' to distinguish her from the other Ann, Frank tall, straight, and very attractive, talking a great deal, as he always did—and Angela.

Max turned and saw Gwendoline waving a handkerchief from the balcony of the hotel, then let his eyes drift back to the boat. He saw Angela throw back her head, heard her laugh come over the water to him. Then she looked towards the shore, saw him waiting and waved, all the rest of them waved, and Max took out his yellow and white silk handkerchief and waved back. He wasn't waving to them all—only to Angela.

They were landing, all calling out remarks to him which he couldn't hear. They crowded round him and said that he must come to tea at the hotel.

'Do come, Max . . .' 'We're the only people who have tea . . .' 'It's not good tea but it's hot and wet.' 'Oh, come on, Max, Rachel and Emmanuel can get on very well without you,' and Angela saying 'I'm sure you're terribly *de trop* with those two, Max, only you can't see it.' Frank laughed and said, 'Have a heart, Maximus.'

He was walking along the hotel garden with her, under the palms. She stopped and leant her bare arms on the low stone wall. Max watched her and saw that she smiled. He longed to know what made her smile. Presently she turned and said, 'It's lovely, isn't it? I wonder if there is a lovelier place in the whole world, Max?'

He said, 'I don't know—it's wonderfully beautiful.'

She said, 'Yes—yes.' Then added in a queer excited whisper, 'It's wonderful to wake up one morning and find that the world is marvellous, isn't it?'

Max knew that his heart beat more quickly. He wanted to tell her that he had loved her for seven years, and couldn't find words. He only said,

'Is that how you feel?'

'Yes. I do think the world is wonderful—marvellous.'

'I'm always hoping that I shall think that one day.'

She laughed softly. 'Fall in love, Max dear.'

'Is that the touchstone?'

She came a little closer and touched his arm with the tips of her fingers.

'Max,' she said, 'I remember when I was a little girl, at a party of Frank's, I saw you standing in the doorway, talking to Mother. I said to Emmanuel that I liked you, and that I could talk to you if you'd let me. Then when I met you again, you were terribly grown up and sent me a box of heavenly sweets and signed your letter "Uncle Max".

That did make me laugh, because you're not really much older than I am.'

Max said, 'Yes—I know. Go on—Angela.'

She turned back to the lake, with the tips of her fingers still resting on his arm, and said, 'When I was little I used to have secrets—such silly things all about nothing. But they were precious because they were secrets, and I never told them to anyone.' She paused and laughed again. 'I always felt that I could tell you secrets, and now I'm trying to it's so dreadfully difficult.'

Max caught her fingers in his and held them tight. He wanted to say, 'Stop—let me tell you my secret,' but the words wouldn't come. Instead he said, 'Tell me your secret and I'll tell you mine, Angela.'

'Have you got a secret too?' He nodded. 'How queer— nicely queer. We're alike then. I couldn't tell anyone except you. Max—not "Uncle Max".'

He said, 'No—please, my dear, not "Uncle Max".'

'I'm in love with someone who loves me too.'

Max felt that the palm trees waved their arms, that the bells of the churches rang, and that a salute of guns was fired. Not church bells—all the bells of Heaven, and the stars shouted, and the sun stopped still to listen. He felt that he was falling very gently, that the world didn't exist, only the blue sky remained above him because it was the colour of her eyes.

'There! Tell me yours, Max.'

'Just exactly the same, my dearest. I've had the same secret for nine years, Angela.'

'Max—haven't you told her?'

'I've never been brave enough, Angela. I always thought that I was too old.'

She looked at him, her head on one side, gravely. 'Oh no!' she was emphatic, 'you're not too old.' She smiled. 'My man—poor angel—is much much older. He's twenty years older than I am.'

Someone, not Max Gollantz, said, 'Is he—twenty years? That's a long time—twenty years.'

The bells had ceased, the stars had forgotten to shout together, the sun and the moon moved slowly on as they had done since the beginning of time. The lake was less blue, the sky was hot and cruel. Max Gollantz stood all alone in the world which was emptied of everything.

'That's a secret, Max.'

'It's a secret, Angela. You haven't told your mother or anyone?'

'Not yet. I can't tell them yet.'

He felt sick and giddy, as though someone had struck him over the eyes. He tried to conquer it, to force himself to be wise and normal.

'Promise me one thing—don't marry him, whoever he is, until one of us has seen him, talked to him. Charles or William or my father or'—it was terrible to say it—'or—me.'

'No, I shouldn't marry him without bringing him to see you all. You'd love him, Max, he's wonderful. So clever, so kind—such an artist.'

They had turned and were walking towards the hotel door; to Max it seemed miles, a stretch of desert over which one travelled for years. He said, 'Talk to me about this again, Angela, will you? I do understand, I'll do anything I can, always, you know that.'

'I will—bless you. I'd like you to come over and meet him. Now, Max, tell me your secret.'

'Come over?' Max said. 'Over where?'

'To Vienna—that's where he lives. That's how I met him, when I went to learn the violin. Now, Max, tell me your secret!'

He stopped, took out his cigarette case, and lit a cigarette with great care and attention, then blew out the match and dropped it into a flower bed.

He smiled. 'My dear,' he said, 'don't think me an awful sneak, but I can't. I've just gone all shy, and idiotic. I should only make you and myself uncomfortable if I tried to tell you.'

'Oh, Max, how mean! Do I know her?'

'I don't know,' Max said slowly, 'I don't know if you do or not.' Then he caught her hand. 'Come along, they'll have drunk all the celebrated English tea and eaten all the cakes. You know what a hog Frank is for cakes.'

13

To Max, it seemed that everyone assumed that he had proposed to Angela in the hotel garden. When they reached
the sitting-room, the whole party appeared to watch them
with expectant eyes and a slightly overdone brightness.
Frank said, 'Hello, you two, you have been a time!' William
said, 'Almost missed the last of the tea, Max, and there
aren't many cakes left.' Mrs. Drew, placid and inclining to
stoutness, smiled, 'Max won't mind, I expect . . .' implying
that Max had other and better things to atone for the loss
of a few sugar cakes.

Max said, in the same bright spirit, 'On the contrary,
Max minds very much. Pass what's left of them, Frank.'

During the days which followed, he puzzled them, and
knew that he did so. His attitude was non-committal. It
might mean that Angela had refused him, or that she had
accepted him and that they had agreed to wait; or, again,
it might mean that he was biding his time, fairly assured
that his offer—when made—would be accepted. Angela,
too, was difficult to understand. It was evident that she
wished to be with Max. Wherever they went—and they
made their excursions in an excited crowd—she was to be
found with Max. She smiled, she looked contented and
happy, even, sometimes, a little more than usually ani-
mated.

Emmanuel noticed her gaiety, listened to her laughter
and smiled. 'Enchela,' he said to Mrs. Drew, 'is in high
spirits. I wonder why? I wonder if it is not somet'ing which
will please us all very much?'

'I've wondered too,' she said, placidly. 'I can't think why
they don't confide in us. But that's the modern girl, Emmanuel. They're charming creatures. Much nicer, I am
sure, than we were at that age, but you must let them tell
you things in their own time. Otherwise you hear nothing
at all.'

It was Frank who finally stepped in and voiced the questions which had hung on all their lips for days. He was walking from Cadenabbia one evening with Max. Together they swung along the dusty white road, stopping, as Max always did, to look along the avenue of cypress trees towards the little fountain at the far end. It sprayed diamond jets towards the moon which hung like a silver apple in the dark sky.

'This is good,' Frank said, sniffing appreciatively. 'The world's a good place, old Max, eh?'

'An excellent place if we don't ask impossibilities.'

Frank whistled the refrain of a popular song. 'That's the answer to all one wants—which are not impossibilities,' he said.

'I'm afraid I'm not up in the latest songs, Frank. I don't know the words.'

Frank sang in his pleasant young baritone voice. ' "Health, Wealth, and the girl you love. What can a man want more?" '

'I agree. What indeed?'

'Oh, *come* on, out with it, you old oyster! We're all hoping to hear it. Grandfather will get heart disease if you don't let it out. Rachel sweats at the thought that a romance is in the offing, and me—well, I'm bursting to order new clothes—all regulation and so forth—and shine as your best man. Come on—be matey.'

Max came a little nearer and laid his hand on his nephew's arm. He whistled softly, a whistle which conveyed that the evil moment had come and he must face it. 'Frank,' he said, 'as a favour, because, in spite of the fact that I'm your uncle, we've been—are—pretty good friends, don't help them to imagine things which don't exist. They all hope that Angela is going to marry me. I hoped it too —more than any of you could have done. She isn't. That's all.'

'She turned you down! Go *on*.'

Max laughed. 'That tone of surprise is most agreeably flattering, Frank, thank you. No, she didn't turn me down. I didn't ask her.'

'Then,' energetically, 'do. Go and do it now! Good God, Max, you old ass! Get on with it!'

'I think not. Now, this is between ourselves, don't let it get round, will you? She doesn't want me. She—she is in love with another chap.'

Frank stood still, pulling his arm from Max's hold. 'Another chap!' he repeated. 'Max, my dear old bean, you're

crazy. Who is it? Not Charles? Not—damme, it's not—
me?'

'It's not you, Frank. Sorry to shatter your hopes. You
don't know him. None of us know him. I can't tell you
any more; I, literally, don't know any more.'

'Who told you?'

'Angela told me herself.'

Frank walked on in silence. He hated to think that Angela, the nicest girl in the world except Morrie Wilmot,
should have hurt, or been the means of causing hurt to,
Max, who was, unquestionably, the nicest man in the world.
He kicked up a little more of the soft dust than was quite
necessary, took his huge and very hideous pipe—they were
fashionable that year—from his pocket, and proceeded to
fill it with a certain vicious intensity. Finally he spoke.

'Hope you're not too hard hit, Max.'

'Oh, not *too* hard, I expect.'

'I'm damned sorry. Whoever the feller is, I bet he isn't a
patch on you.'

'Thanks, old boy. Unfortunately Angela thinks him several patches better than I am. It's painful to my vanity, but
she's probably right.'

'Better than you! I'd like to see him!'

'I don't know that I should care to—not particularly.
Well, let's turn to something more pleasant. Your career,
for example.'

Frank's career had been discussed at length. Emmanuel
wanted him to come into the business; he had visions of
new developments, new openings, and Frank should find
his niche and make money. Max listened, said very little
and kept an open mind. He, himself, had made a success
of his work. He could work with Emmanuel and yet never
allow himself to be swamped by his father's somewhat
overpowering personality. He liked beautiful things, he enjoyed working out decorative schemes, he found the work-
men decent and, in the main, industrious. But, in his
heart, he doubted if Frank would find that the business of
making money for Gollantz and Son was sufficiently amusing. Frank loved to be amused. Not that he couldn't and
didn't work; he never failed to give Emmanuel satisfaction
in the matter of school reports and results at the univer-
sity. Even now he would come into the offices in Grafton
Street, or to the warehouse on Campden Hill, be interested, ask questions, and sometimes make suggestions and
tender small pieces of advice. Emmanuel took this as a

sign that his heart was in the work. Max felt that it only interested him because he himself was not a furniture designer, an antique dealer, a picture expert or a decorative artist.

Now, Frank pulled hard at the ugly pipe and said, 'Honestly, Max, I don't believe that chairs and tables are my job.'

'We deal in quite a number of other things, you know.'

'Do you? Yes, of course you do. I don't think they thrill me.'

'It's tremendous fun, sometimes.'

'Poorish fun, Max.'

'Not a bit of it. You're just a Jim Hawkins looking for gold.'

'Who the devil is Jim Hawkins?'

'Stevenson—*Treasure Island*.'

Frank nodded. 'Oh, yes, I know. Can't say Stevenson says a lot to me.' He walked on puffing in silence, then knocked out his pipe on the palm of his hand, stuffed it into his pocket, and with something of an effort, said, 'What I really want is—the Army, Max.'

'The Army,' Max repeated. 'Surprising feller! I didn't know that was where your inclinations lay. I don't know how your grandfather will take that. The British Army. He was born an Austrian, y'know.'

'Naturalised years ago, he told me so.'

'To please my mother, remember. Why didn't you give us this wish of yours to deal with sooner?'

'I don't know—fear, p'raps. You know, in this family everything means a council, and pros and cons all weighed and discussed. Rachel and Hermann drawn in, Julius Davis allowed to say what *he* thinks, Walter Heriot all pomposity and heavy breathing, and then the old man being charming, as hard as nails, having already made up his mind before the discussion starts. I just can't face those tribal gatherings, Max. I'd rather leave it and lose what I want. I would really.'

Max nodded. 'We do rather indulge in discussion, I suppose. It's the Jewish instinct, I fancy. To return to the Army—not much money in it.'

'Surely we have enough? The old man's terribly rich, isn't he?'

'Certainly, very rich. But I fancy he would like you to be rich too.'

'Jewish instinct again?' He was sorry the moment the

words had been spoken, he put out his hand and touched
Max's arm. 'Sorry—really, I didn't mean to say that. Only
money really doesn't mean much to me. The family has
enough. Morrie's people are rolling, too. What's the good
of grubbing about for a lot more?'

'I don't believe,' Max said slowly, 'that it's money as
money that really touches my father. He regards it as the
current symbol of success, and he adores success. I like
success too, I must admit.'

'Success is all right, but happiness, enjoying life means
more, Max.' He said suddenly, 'What was my father like?'

Max started. Frank had never asked questions, never
been told about his father. Emmanuel had always said
that he didn't remember him, and that it was well to let
sleeping memories die in their sleep. Max answered the
question by another.

'Do you remember him?'

'A little. He had thick light hair and played the violin.
He was amusing, but I never knew when he was angry
and when he was just teasing. He used to call me "the
Young Hope of Israel". Taught me to hate Jews like
hell.'

'Still hate them?'

Frank laughed. 'You ass—you're one, the old man's
one—I'm one myself. Do you remember my father, Max?'

'Of course I remember him. I adored him, thought Algy
the finest, most dashing feller in the world. Candidly, I'm
afraid he was a bad hat, Frank. Not the most succsssful
effort of the head of the house.'

'Algy—Algy . . .' Frank said. 'That wasn't his name?'

'Short for Algernon.'

Frank shook his head. 'He wasn't called that at home.
My mother called him . . .' he paused, then said, 'I've got
it—Bert. Herbert—Albert . . .'

'Albert. He changed his name.' Some impulse made him
ask, 'Do you remember your mother?'

'In patches. Dark hair, and very white teeth and laughing a lot. Terribly nice to me. Did you know her? Of
course you did. Like her, Max?'

'Yes,' the words came slowly, 'yes, I always liked her—
very much.'

'Where is she?'

'I couldn't say. Somewhere in Canada. She married,'
Max said it without hesitation, 'a rancher called "Ted".'

'Ted—what?'

'I don't think I ever knew; if I did, I've forgotten.'

'Then she divorced my father?'

Max said quickly, 'Divorced—yes, that's right—divorced him. Best thing she could have done. Algy wasn't much use as a husband.'

'Queer,' Frank said, 'to think that they're both alive somewhere and I shouldn't know either of 'em if I met them. Does he still play?'

'I can't say, I've never seen him since the first day I saw you. Never heard from him, never want to—now. He went over to Germany, I think. He was going to take Europe by storm. I've never heard that he did.'

'P'raps he's changed his name again,' Frank suggested. 'That kind of thing might get to be a habit, eh? Oh, well—Max,' suddenly, 'put in a word for me about the Army when you get the old man alone, will you?'

Max nodded. 'All right. Mind, I don't promise that he'll see eye to eye with you over it.'

'Let's chance it, shall we?'

The next night, when Frank had gone down to dance at the Grand, Max spoke to Emmanuel. Emmanuel had a trick of taking his atmosphere with him, and even in an Italian villa he contrived to make the room where he sat look not unlike his room in Regent's Park. The desk was smaller, the massive silver inkstand—which had been brought with them—dwarfed it; the carved chair in which he sat was old and dark, with a velvet cushion and great tassels which hung down at the corners. Round the room were evidences of his occupation, a cigar cabinet, a silver cigarette box which had once been the jewel case of a king's favourite, two old Waterford decanters which caught the light and winked with irrepressible Irish gaiety; and here and there were books in mellow leather covers, tooled in gilt, impressive and beautiful. Emmanuel raised his head as Max entered, the light caught his white hair, touched the polished linen shirt, and twinkled as it found the small diamonds in his cuff links.

'Not dancing, Max?'

'Going down presently, sir. I wanted a word or two with you, if you're not too busy.'

'Sit down, I'm not busy. Only writing to persuade that impoverished Italian count that his painted furniture is only deteriorating in this climate, and that its value will follow suit. He'll sell in anudder week or so. What is it, Max? Have a cigarette?'

Max sat down, crossed his legs, pulled the knees of his trousers up and helped himself to a cigarette. 'It's Frank —his career—future.'

'Ah ! Young Frenk. His career is surely settled. You, me, Frenk, and Julius—with a small allotment of shares —can make a company.'

'He doesn't want to sell chairs and tables,' Max smiled, 'he doesn't think it is his job.'

'Not his job—and, please, what is his job?'

'He fancies the Army, sir.'

'The Army!' Emmanuel ejaculated. 'The British Army?'

'What other?'

Emmanuel took up his penholder and balanced it on his forefinger, then shook his head. 'No, no, Max, I don't t'ink it's possible. He is too near to me, and I was an Austrian. He might, one day, hev to fight. Might hev to kill his own blood relations—horrible!'

'I fancy that the little show in South Africa was the last time the white man will fight the white man,' Max said. 'It's unlikely that he would see fighting nearer than India—at worst against the Russians.'

Emmanuel grinned, looking suddenly very young for all his sixty-eight years. 'The dirty Russ!' he said. 'If that were true, I am almost persuaded to let him be a soldier. No, Max, that is fentastic. Soldiering in these days is not a career, it's an expensive amusement.'

'Perhaps. Still, it's a good life for a man. We can afford to indulge this particular expensive taste.'

'We?' Emmanuel's tone changed. 'How, please—we?'

'I am quite prepared to allow him eight hundred a year.'

'You! What is your income, Max?'

'More,' Max said, 'than John Burns would be prepared to agree I had a right to. You're very generous, Father. As a partner I do very well; Simon Davis does even better for me in—speculations. I'm not so rich as my father, but I can afford to get Frank what he wants most.'

'I don't like that word—speculations, Max. Investments, not speculations. You'll lose it all one fine morning, I know. Still, eight hundred—it's not a great deal for a soldier. I shouldn't like Frank to have to pinch and scrape. It's undignified.'

The idea of Frank attempting to pinch or scrape amused Max. Frank who never gave a second thought to the money he spent! He nodded.

'I agree, a small purse doesn't go very well with the

Guards uniform. What a gorgeous affair it is! I never see them going down Whitehall without a little thrill of envy. You'd have made a fine Guardsman, sir.'

'Ah!' Emmanuel tasted the thought and found it pleasant; instinctively he threw out his chest, and squared his shoulders.

'Ah! Perhaps years ago—I was a fine swordsman. One day when you are older, I shall tell you how I came to London wit' my arm in a sling, and for what reason. The Guards—my grendson in the Guards. Ha!'

'Or any other fine regiment,' Max said. 'Remember the pictures of the Lancers at Omdurman?'

'Grend, grend. Und the Scottishmen—remember never to say Scotch, Max, unless you speak of whisky. The kilts. The man who played the begpipes efter his legs were broken! In Vienna, you hev seen the officers there? Vonderful men, but to my mind never qvite what the English soldier is. Grend men—t'ink of Gordon, that small Roberts, that fine Herbert Kitchener—Max, I almost wish that I had been a soldier.'

'Quite a good deal of young Frank is—you, sir.'

'True, Max, true. I shall t'ink over this idea of mine, to make him a soldier—as he likes it. I shall talk it over with Rachel and, when I get home, with Hermann and Julius.'

Max rose. 'Not a council, Father! Don't let them argue you out of it.'

'Argue me out of it! My dear Max, what queer expressions. I like to hear the opinions of others, it solidifies, stabilises those which I already hold. You're going? Give my love to Enchela, please.'

Max walked down the hill towards the little town. The sound of a band reached him, coming sweet and subdued through the still night. Below him lay the lake, quiet and untroubled, and in the distance the lights of Bellagio were reflected in its still waters. Max sighed, wondered if he really wanted to dance, and knew that he wanted it very much. He wanted to dance with Angela Drew, wanted to hear her voice, to feel her hand in his, to feel the touch of her hair as it brushed his face.

'Very stupid,' he mused, 'only making things hurt more. Far better if I had the pluck to clear out, get back to England and work like the devil. Not that work would drive her out of my mind—she's in far too deep for work to exorcise her. It's lasted too long, it's grown part of me.

It's a life sentence; it's—oh, damn it, it's just love, I suppose.'

He wondered about the other man, tried to imagine what he was like. Drew a mental picture, which satisfied him at least, though it reflected small credit to Angela's taste. Max saw a stout, long-haired, badly dressed fellow, sentimental, and not too well shaven. The kind of man women thought romantic. He painted the portrait slowly and carefully, taking a slightly sadistic pleasure in allowing one or two small and unimportant good features—mental or physical—to creep in. He felt that he was being more than just to the unknown man; that, in admitting that he might 'know his job' or even be 'decently educated', he was making concessions of a very high order.

Then the game ceased to amuse him. He had reached the hotel, and stood in the doorway of the ballroom, watching the dancers. In the distance he caught sight of Angela smiling at Charlie Wilmot as she danced. Max sighed. Pictures, even convincing caricatures, were no help. There she was, and somewhere in the world was the man she loved and who loved her, and he, Max Gollantz, stood outside and watched it all passing by.

He half turned, deciding that he would go back to the garden, that he would make his plans to leave for England; then almost regretfully, he turned again and walked down the long room to where Gwendoline Drew sat, placid, comfortable and undisturbed, watching the dancers.

'Damn it,' Max thought, 'I can't run away. Frank is going to be a soldier, my father is sitting up there at the villa wishing he had been one, but I have been through it, and I can still prevent myself from running away.'

Later he asked Angela to dance with him. She said no one danced so well.

'Nice person to dance with, Max,' she said, 'terribly safe. You never let one get bumped about, do you? You're like that about most things—driving a car, dancing, diving— you do things awfully slickly and cleanly.'

He said, 'My dear, you'll make me intolerably conceited.'

'You're not conceited enough. You ought to get some of Emmanuel's or even Frank's. Are all the family except you conceited?'

'All the family—there aren't any more of us. Just us three.'

'Frank's father, your brother?'

'I don't fancy we include him. Anyway, he'd prefer to be left out. He hated Jews.'

'Did he?' She seemed interested. 'Isn't it queer how some people do? A funny illogical dislike, like mine for parsnips. I've never eaten one in my life, and never shall. I know people who hate Jews.'

Max wanted to correct her, to say that she meant that she knew one person who hated Jews, and that person's opinion mattered a great deal. Her voice had given her away, it had become coloured, softer, more personal. He knew his own was cold, and thought what a fool he was, as he answered:

'Really? Probably the Jewish race will survive.'

'I know, I know,' she said, eager to take away any hurt which she had inflicted. 'I only quoted it as an example. It's an unreasoning thing'—she laughed—'like my parsnips. I don't hate Jews. I never could.'

'As one myself—thank you,' Max said.

'Max, are you cross about something?'

'Cross, no. Perhaps realising that I'm getting old. I'm past thirty and I feel twice that age tonight.'

'Darling, thirty is nothing at all! Forty is nothing . . .'

Max thought, 'Then he is forty or more, confound him!' and wished that the unknown man wouldn't keep intruding. Why couldn't he take the goods the gods provided—Angela, a good floor, a tolerable band—and not twist the knife in his heart and allow this man of forty or over to spoil everything? She was talking and he had missed half the sentence; again he thanked the 'other fellow' for nothing.

'. . . nicer, far nicer. I would never dance with Frank, or Charlie, or even Bill—and I adore Bill—if you asked me to dance with you.'

They had stopped, and stood near one of the long open windows. Max threw back his head and felt the soft night air from the lake.

'Let's go out,' he said, 'it's so hot in here.'

She sat down on a seat near the wall which bordered the lake; Max stood and looked down at her. She said,

'What are you staring at, Max?'

Without coming nearer he said, 'I'm looking at you, Angela. I've been looking at you ever since you were a little girl in short frocks and very long black stockings. I don't know if I ought to tell you this—I'm past being able to argue things out, they've got too big for me. That night, when you told me the world was a wonderful place. I believed you. I could have told you why—simply because you were in it.'

She made a movement as if she would have stopped him.

'My dear, don't stop me. I'm not going to worry you. You can only love—well—the person you do love. It won't come to order. It's not even hard luck on me—I'm not asking for pity. Only—I can't stop loving you because you don't love me. Loving you has become a habit, you see, it's been going on for so many years. This man—I don't know anything about him except that he's a foreigner, a musician, and that he's over forty . . .'

'Who told you how old he was?'

He laughed. 'You did, my dearest, just now. Your voice told me when you took up the cudgels for the elderly fellow. But don't decide anything in a hurry. Nothing that is irrevocable. I'm an antique dealer and it's my job to be suspicious that everything may be a fake, until it's definitely proved to be genuine.

'I am not trying to catch you for myself; I'm not trying to belittle the other man. You said I drove a car—slickly and cleanly. I can generally get past most things on the road without making a hog of myself or upsetting other people. Just remember that, Angela, will you?'

He came and sat down beside her, took her hand in his and smiled at her. The worst was over, he could speak naturally again.

'That's all,' he said, 'I shan't talk about it again. It's only that now you know that I love you—though you'll never know how much, because I don't really know myself —you can demand anything, and know that I shall think it a privilege to serve you in any way.' He laughed. 'I am, always, your devoted and obedient servant, Max Gollantz. Now come back and dance.'

She stood up, her hands clasped. 'Oh, Max, I do so wish it hadn't been you—who were to be hurt.'

'Honourable scars,' he said, 'I'm very proud of them. I don't think, in the cool light of reason plus that very theatrical moon, that I ought to have told you. I'm always wise after the event. Most of us are.'

14

Max passed a sale catalogue over to Emmanuel as they sat at breakfast in the garden of the villa. Emmanuel laid down the peach which he was peeling, glanced at the little book, stared at Max, and said,

'Well? What about it?'

'Looks interesting, I thought.'

Emmanuel, with a slight air of regret, abandoned the peach and took up the catalogue. He scanned it, his face blank, then handed it back to Max.

'It belies its appearance,' he said. 'Mostly rubbish.'

Max turned to the section devoted to pictures.

'There is a Ribera here,' he said, 'No. 765.'

'A fake. I've seen it. Crowther asked my opinion of it five years ago. I gave it. He has never liked me since.'

'Pair of Chelsea figures, eight and a half inches high,' Max read, 'decorated fruit and flowers. Sounds as if they might be the goods.'

'Limoges, and poor at that.' Emmanuel divided the peach with concentrated attention, then said, 'Why don't you say that you want to go home, Max? I'm too old, I know you too well, to fancy for one moment that you don't know that stuff is rubbish. When do you want to go?'

'Tomorrow, perhaps.' Max paused, then said impulsively, 'Today would suit me best of all.'

'Then go today,' Emmanuel said evenly, 'vhy vait? There is a letter here from Julius, suppose that it says that he wants you immediately. There is a—Raeburn on the market. No, not a Raeburn, they always publish the buyers' names in the *Daily Mail*—a Vernier, that is better. Pack and go this morning, Max.'

Max met his father's eyes across the table. 'Thank you, sir. That will suit me. You don't want to ask me the reason?'

'I know it, Max, but if you should like to tell me, I am listening.'

'You know? I thought you probably did. I'm not whining, only—I might find it all a bit easier in London, working.'

'You won't, not really, Max.' His voice sank, and the words came very softly and gently. 'I know, my dear. I've found a face—always the same face—staring at me from Chippendale tables, from Gainsborough portraits, from Hepplewhite chairs, even tangled in the folds of old brocade. It's—it's—terr-rible.'

He stretched out his hand towards Max, who took it and held it.

'It's terr-rible,' Emmanuel said again, 'but don't let it break you. That wouldn't be quite fair to me—I'm a selfish old man, and I hate pain. What hurts you—automatically hurts me. What was it that poor Valter Heriot used to say?—I hev it! "Kepp your top lip very close." Thet's what you've got to do. Unfortunately, that won't stop the pain. Poor Max!'

'Oh, I don't know,' Max said, 'I'm not the only fellow it's happened to. I'll go and pack. You'll read Rachel the extract from that letter, won't you?'

'Most certainly. I shall read it very fully.'

A few hours later Max called in at the Grand and was told that the whole party had gone over to Como, and hoped that he would follow by the next boat. They had left minute instructions as to where he might find them. Max felt suddenly that he did not want, after all, to go back to London. He wanted to see Angela again, wanted to show her the cathedral and to point out the especial bits which he knew would either interest or amuse her. After all, he could put off his going until tomorrow . . . Then he decided that he couldn't face it, that today or tomorrow or any other day would be just as bad, and he must go. If he stayed—things hurt; if he went—they would probably hurt just as badly, but he could fling himself into his work and get so dog-tired that he could scarcely think.

He wrote a note to Gwendoline Drew, ending with 'give all the kids my love, and tell Angela to let me have her address in Vienna. I may go there in a month or two.'

A week later, when he was back in London, and doing the work of two men in his anxiety never to leave himself time to think, she wrote to him. He read the letter slowly and carefully as though each word was precious, and smiled. It was what his friend Terrence O'Reilly would have called a 'darling letter'. It was filled with amusing bits of news about everyone. It brought the news that Frank was to go to an Army crammer's, that Rachel was champing at the bit, longing to get home to plot fresh onslaughts upon the House of Commons, and that Emmanuel was well, and had actually come down to the Grand, ordered the orchestra to play the 'Blue Danube' and had danced it with her to the admiration of everyone.

'. . .And I feel selfish to write of the lake, or the sky, or the mountains to you in London. I often feel selfish about you, Max, though it is illogical and foolish and probably only a kind of weak conceit. Do try to be happy, and better still content. Does it sound still more conceited if I say that I know it's hard for you? And does it sound like competitive sentiment to say that things are not quite easy for me sometimes?'

He folded the letter and put it away carefully in his pocket-book, only as he folded it did he remember that she had not sent the address for which he had asked.

The whole party returned as Max was leaving for Holland, *en route* for Germany and—later—Spain. When he returned Angela was back in Vienna, and life settled down into its accustomed groove.

He did not see her again until the September of 1913. Emmanuel had decided that he wanted to see England, and gathered a kind of family caravan round him. He drove, with Mrs. Drew, Rachel Leon, and Hermann in a massive Rolls-Royce, Max followed, or, as a matter of fact, usually proceeded—in his Fiat—while Frank, with Morrie Wilmot and Charles, came very much last in a French car of doubtful ancestry, which Frank had bought from a friend with whom he was now not on speaking terms.

They had reached Newquay, and Frank was hailing with delight the fact that they would be able to dance that evening. Emmanuel had taken his letters, and was seated reading them oblivious of everything and everybody. Max had taken his, and was glancing over them, bored and wondering why on earth he had come, and why Frank and Morrie—who were supposed to be deeply attached to each other—must always argue about everything. Rachel Leon was snorting over the injustice of sentences passed upon her sister suffragists in the 'Vote', Hermann

was staring out at the sea, his eyes dreamy and rather
sleepy. Gwendoline Drew opened her letters carefully
with a paper-knife which she took from her handbag, and
proceeded to read them slowly. Max, his letters read,
watched her idly. Suddenly she looked up and met his
eyes; her own were troubled, her brows wrinkled.

'Anything wrong, Gwen?' Max asked.

Emmanuel, from force of habit, lowered the letter he
was reading, and said, 'Not'ing wrong, I hope?' and continued reading.

'Nothing wrong, Max—she's apparently not ill.' Mrs.
Drew glanced again at the letter. 'No, she doesn't say
that she is ill, so that's all right.'

She paused and read slowly from the letter. Max saw
that the writing was Angela's, and instinctively pulled his
chair a little closer to Mrs. Drew's, he wanted to be the
only person to know what Angela had written, the second
person at any rate.

'She says,' her mother read, 'that she is arriving in London tonight. That means that she is there now, because
this was forwarded from town. She says, "I felt that Vienna was too stuffy, suddenly. I heard of this royal
procession which is visiting the beauty spots of England—
and felt jealous, full of envy, hatred, and malice. So I
braved your righteous wrath and decided to come home. I
know it's ridiculous of me, but please don't be cross with
me." As though I had ever been cross with either her or
William in all their lives. This is so like Angela—Charles
says that the place where her soul longs to be is always
the place which she is away from at the moment.'

Max said, 'Someone else said it before Charles.'

'About Angela?'

'No, no, Gwen dear, probably before Angela was
thought of. Well, here is Angela in town and here are you
and Charles in Newquay. Shall I wire her to come down?
Or better still, shall I go and bring her down?'

'In the car, Max.'

'Unless you'd prefer her to walk for the sake of exer-
cise, Gwen.'

'My dear, how ridiculous you are! I meant—isn't it a
great deal of trouble for you to take? Won't you miss
this nice rest by the sea?'

Max kept his voice unmoved, he hid the excitement
which made him want to rush out of the lounge and order
his car that very moment.

'Rest,' he said, 'Have you heard the plan which Charles has evolved for our pleasure tomorrow? Or rather it begins tonight. We are to dance, early—quite early tomorrow we are to bathe, then take a motor boat and scour the coast. After lunch, he has planned that we take a good long walk over the moors to some farmhouse he knows of, where we are to be regaled on cream and splits, whatever they are. We come back in time to bathe again, dine, and dance. At ten the next morning, we leave for Tintagel. Rest!'

'I thought that was the kind of holiday you liked, Max.'

'I may, when I am as old as my father or Rachel and can disregard Charles' time-tables. At the moment, I am —between ages. Why not let me leave tonight, bring Angela down tomorrow, and meet you at Tintagel?'

'Could you do it in one day?'

'Gwen dear, would your soul be shocked to its core if we did perhaps stay one night at some highly respectable place—Exeter or even here?'

'Max,' she was shocked and a little hurt that he should suggest it, she believed herself to be essentially modern, 'of course not. Stay where ever you like—so long as the beds aren't damp. Why should I mind?'

Max rose. He felt ridiculously young, and so happy that it was almost terrible; he wanted to laugh out loud and make idiotic jokes.

'Well, I'll get a move on,' he said.

'Not yet, Max, you can't go before dinner,' Gwen cried, distressed. To miss dinner was to Gwendoline Drew nothing short of a calamity.

'Where are you going, anyway, Max?' Charles asked, laying down *The Tatler* which he was reading.

'Your mother has mislaid her younger offspring. I am going to fetch it.'

'Angela!' Charles said. 'She's in Vienna.'

'Misinformed—she's in London.'

'Gosh!' Frank ejaculated. 'Isn't that like Angela!'

'Why is it like Angela?' Morrie demanded. 'What makes you say that?'

Emmanuel laid down his last letter. 'Morrie and Frenk,' he said, 'if you must argue again—go out on the sends or the beach or whatever it is and let the Atlantic Ocean judge between you. What is this, Max? Enchela is beck and you are going to fetch her? That is very nice, I shall be gled to hev her here. Vhy should he wait for dinner,

Gwen dear? There are hotels on the road. A young man can feed anywhere, it is only old people who must dine at special restaurants.'

Max smiled at his father; he always understood everything. 'I'll telephone to London, shall I? Say that I'm coming?'

'Please, Max. Let me know when you're through, and I'll come and speak to her. No, Charles, I will speak to her, surely as her mother I have the first right.'

Max walked out of the lounge, he felt that he held himself very erect, knew that he felt elated and rather proud. He wasn't going to try to make love to her. To have her with him during the long drive, to hear her talking and perhaps make her laugh—that would be enough. He felt a light touch on his arm and turned to find old Hermann Leon at his elbow.

'Hello, Hermann—want anything?'

The old man blinked his eyes before he spoke. His voice was thin and sounded as if he always spoke in a whisper. Everyone liked Hermann, he was kind, forgetful, intensely absent-minded, and yet—as Emmanuel and Max had reason to know—far-sighted and keen-witted.

'What for has she come back?' Hermann said softly.

'A sudden desire for England—didn't you hear what Gwen said?'

'Did you think that was true, Max?'

'Why shouldn't it be true . . . ?'

'I don't know,' Hermann said vaguely. 'Women don't always tell—all the truth. Perhaps she had a sudden desire for England, or what England stood for—but why?'

Max laughed. 'My dear old thing,' he said, 'you're trying to make a mystery. What for? It's all your imagination.'

'I know it's my imagination. I can imagine so many things that might make Angela—desire England. That doesn't matter, but don't wait to telephone. Let someone else telephone. Angela might say, "Has Max started? Not yet? Then stop him. I will come by train." Go now and let me telephone.'

'What is the matter with you?' Max asked with good-natured impatience. 'Do you think she hates the sight of me so intensely?'

Hermann shrugged his narrow stooping shoulders. 'Sometimes the people we like best are the people we

wish least of all to see. I don't know—I just wondered—
perhaps I am being foolish.'

'Wondered—what?' Max said. 'What did you wonder?'

Hermann blinked, stared at him, half opened his mouth,
then said, 'I don't know. Go and get the car. I will
telephone to London for you. Good-bye.' He turned and
walked away down the long passage which led back to the
lounge. Max watched him, saw his bent figure, saw his
white head turn from side to side, his eyes peering short-
sightedly at the palms in their 'decorative' pots. He thought
how queer it was. Hermann was queer and could give no
reasons for his imaginative fancies, and yet he had given
Hermann his own way. Hermann would speak to Angela
and would say, 'Max is coming, he is on his way now.'

Why should Angela want to come back to England?
Even if she was happy enough in Vienna—and Max felt
that old sting of hurt disappointment that someone else,
and not he, should be able to make her happy in Vienna
—she might want a holiday, might want the sight of the
English moors, the sound of birds, of seas washing against
grey rocks . . . It was easily explained. He thrust Hermann's imaginings from him, and began to give orders for
the car to be made ready. He would drive to Exeter and
stay there for the night, start early and get to London in
the morning. Two hundred and fifty-odd miles. Eighty
miles to Exeter. He looked at his watch, the time was only
four o'clock. He could get farther than Exeter. He decided to make no plans, to push on at a good pace and
see where half-past ten or eleven o'clock found him. He
didn't want dinner, he could pick up a sandwich anywhere.

He went back to see if there were any further messages
for him. Emmanuel said, 'Give her my love and tell her
that I am longing to dance with her again.'

Rachel lowered her paper, and said, 'If you have time
bring down the last issue of *The Vote*, will·you, Max?
Angela will get it, if you have scruples.'

Frank lifted his head from the map over which he was
poring. 'Max, which way are you going?'

'Bodmin, Okehampton, and Exeter, old man.'

'I shouldn't, Max. Listen . . .'

Morrie broke in. 'Don't listen, Max. He wants you to go
to Plymouth and take a by-lane, which you're certain to
miss. You stick to Bodmin!'

Frank scowled at her. 'If you'd let me explain, Morrie.
It's a topping way, Max, this of mine . . .'

Charles interposed, 'Take no notice, Max. You're right. Taunton, Salisbury, and Basingstoke.'

'Basingstoke-rot!' Morrie interrupted. 'Not Basingstoke, Charles, you idiot . . .'

Max held up his hand. 'It's all settled, my children. My mind is made up. Now, Gwen, any more messages?'

'You've had none at all yet,' Frank said.

Mrs. Drew said, 'Hush, Frank, let me speak to Max, please, my dear. No, thank you, Max. Hermann is telephoning to say that you're coming? Tell her to bring a thick coat for motoring and a pair of stout boots for walking, and she might bring down the other Thermos, it's in my bedroom on the top of the big wardrobe. Not the mahogany one, Max, the larger one—the one that came from her grandfather's place in Hereford. I think that's all, unless she likes to bring her violin, in case Emmanuel would like some music. She might bring some of Charles' songs with her . . .'

'He's only got a four-seater, darling,' Charles reminded her, 'and I want them to bring down my camera—the bigger one, Max. This little thing is no earthly.'

'I'll try to get them all in,' Max said, 'if Angela leaves room. Good-bye, all of you. Be good, kids.'

As he walked away, Morrie screamed, 'Max—dar-ling, some sweets! Real ones—exciting ones, please.'

He started on his journey, happy, contented and very grateful to Fate for having taken a hand in his affairs. The road was good, the car was ticking over very sweetly, Max glanced at the speedometer and mentally patted the car for behaving so well. He reached Exeter at nine-fifteen, the night was beautiful, and Max decided to push on. He didn't want dinner, and sandwich and a glass of beer was enough.

'Nice night,' he said to the waiter, as he drank his beer and munched the sandwich. 'Not going to rain?'

'Rain, sir, no, not tonight. Staying the night at Taunton, sir?'

'I was going to,' Max said, 'but I've a fancy to drive straight on to London. Quite pleasant, I should think.'

'Lovely trip, sir. Like to be doing it myself.'

Through the night he drove, steadily keeping up his average, never making great bursts of speed, driving for his own pleasure. It was no use arriving at Cambridge Gardens at four in the morning. If he got home first, bathed and changed, he might still be there by ten o'clock.

He felt the quiet of the night envelop him, wrap him round, and felt suddenly that it was too still, that the quiet was ominous, the silence unbearable. Resolutely he pushed the sensation from him. This was the result of a light supper and Hermann's croakings. He was as imaginative as old Hermann.

He tried to remember quotations which he knew about the night, even repeated some of them softly to himself. 'To steal a few hours from the night, my dear'—who wrote that? He had forgotten. Again, 'I heard the trailing garments of the night . . .' He thought how quietly they moved, those trailing garments. That was Longfellow. He didn't care for Longfellow much, but he found a good phrase now and then. 'Night's candles are burnt out . . .' that was better, so was, 'Hangs upon the cheek of night, like a rich jewel.' And best of all, he spoke it softly and lovingly:

'And he will make the face of heaven so fine,
    That all the world will be in love with night,
    And pay not tribute to the garish sun.'

How Shakespeare loved writing of the night, especially in that particular play. There were others—'I have night's cloak to hide me, and the mask of night is on my face.' Perhaps even more, he couldn't remember. Romeo and Juliet—the world's great lovers—a play of lovers for lovers, and night was the time for those who loved. That was why he was going to find Angela through the night.

His face was very gentle as he drove on. He felt then that he wanted nothing but that she should be glad to see him again, nothing but that their friendship should remain always a very real and precious thing. Love was not only giving and being given, it might bless him that gave, as well as the one who took what was given. Love could—if fate decided—live on itself and still grow and grow in beauty.

Max thought, 'It's not ideal, because—well, because one is only human, and one wants human companionship, human love, and all which goes with it. But I'd rather love Angela—even if she doesn't love me—than love no one. It's here—with me—I'm full of it, and I mustn't waste it, or let it waste me. "I wasted love and now doth love waste me." Shakespeare might not thank me for the adaptation, but it's apt enough in my case.'

The long road stretched black before him, as his head-lights caught it it shone like polished jet. The trees stood on either hand like guardians of the road.

'English trees,' Max thought. 'I wonder if there are such trees in any other country? Such kind, comfortable fields, such snug little villages tucked away in the hollows? My father said the other day that he loved it—loved every acre of it. That it is his "very kind foster-mother", who never made him feel a stranger or a foreigner. I suppose it's his love for it that has come down to me. It never seemed to touch Algy. Algy hated it—he hated a heap of things.'

He wondered where Algy was. He was forty-two this year. Queer that they'd never heard from him, heard of him. He thought that he was going to take the whole Continent by storm. Poor old Algy. And Julie . . . Max trod on the accelerator and sent the car rushing forward. Even now, the thought of Julie distressed him. He wondered where she was, how she was. Played with the idea that he might find out and send her a big cheque. Dismissed the idea, it wouldn't work. She might think—well, what wasn't true.

Better leave things alone—and yet he could never think of her other than kindly and even tenderly. Not love, not even the ashes of love, but—gratitude that she had trusted him.

The night was passing, the sky was shot with primrose and gold, with rose and faint banners of palest blue. The air was cooler, a little wind fluttered and died. The dawn was there—the night was over.

Past Basingstoke, on to Maidenhead, past the quiet Thames, the road beginning to be more crowded with market carts, on past Slough, into Hounslow, and so to the London streets, where early trams rattled past, work-men filled the pavements, and the early newspapers were on sale.

Park Lane, Baker Street, Regent's Park, and home. Max had not realised how tired he was until he got out of the car, and opened the door with his key. A quarter to six. It was no longer tomorrow but today when he would see Angela. He scribbled a note and left it on the hall table, saying that he was to be called at half-past eight, then, mounting the stairs to his own room, undressed and fell asleep.

15

Max put down his empty cup, turned on his elbow and prepared to telephone Angela. He felt vaguely excited and happy, and yet felt that his happiness was so tender, so fragile, that he must handle it very gently for fear it should break into pieces before his eyes. It might, if held in too strong a light, if examined too closely, vanish and leave him with nothing except disappointment.

Twice he lifted the receiver, and twice he put it back on its hook, then lifted it again and gave the number of Mrs. Drew's house in Cambridge Gardens.

He waited, was told that he should be put through to Angela—that she was awake and had expected him to telephone.

He waited. 'Is that you, Max?'

'Good morning, Angela. How are you? This is a delightfully sudden impulse!'

'Is it? When do you want to start, Max?'

'When can you be ready—ten, half-past?'

'Ten, please. I'm ready now.'

'Aren't you going to praise me for coming so quickly? I drove all night.'

'Did you? Kind Max—I'm glad you came, I wanted you very badly.'

'You're not ill? Not—unhappy?'

'I'm not ill—I don't think I'm unhappy—not really.'

There was a pause, then her voice came again. 'Don't worry. I haven't done anything—irrevocable. At ten, Max, and thank you so much.'

He waited, tried to speak to her, but she had rung off. Max stared at the telephone as if it was capable of answering questions, then flung back the clothes, and snatching up his towels went into the bathroom. He felt that his fears had become realities. His happiness had vanished. Her voice had been dull, miserable. Hermann had been right, her impulse to come home was something more than a desire to see the English country again.

He dressed hurriedly, gave orders for his car to be brought round, tried to eat breakfast and pushed it away after a few mouthfuls. It tasted of nothing. He watched the hands of the clock—creeping slowly—he compared the clock with his own watch—and wished that it might be half-past nine, with this awful waiting almost over.

Judson was attentive, Max wished that he had been less so. He wanted to be alone, to try and imagine what was wrong, to convince himself that nothing was wrong at all, he was fanciful, imaginative, idiotic. The clock hands crept forward. Then Judson told him that the car was at the door. Max felt like a prisoner who is reprieved.

He found her waiting for him in the breakfast-room. He came forward and held out his hands.

'Angela—my dear!' There was consternation, hurt astonishment in his tone. 'My dear—you're ill.'

'No, Max, not a bit ill. I know I look horrible— that's due to a bad night. Shall we go?'

He laid his hand on her shoulder. 'Tell me what it is— please tell me.'

She pressed her lips tightly together, he felt that she was afraid that they might tremble, and did not speak for a moment, then said, 'Do you mind if I don't talk here. In the car—when we're in the country. It's—it's not so difficult as in rooms, is it?'

'Very well. I'll see to your luggage.'

He drove in silence out of London again towards the country. He felt that again the silence closed in round him, suffocated him, terrified him. Once he turned to her and said with a kind of desperate moderation:

'Just tell me, on your honour, that you aren't ill?'

'On my honour, I'm not ill, Max.' Later, she said, 'Talk to me, please. I want you to talk. Tell me how everyone is.'

He tried to force himself to talk of them all, of Rachel's hatred of Churchill, of Emmanuel's hope that they might dance together, tried to give an imitation of Frank and Morrie arguing, and of her mother playing peacemaker. It wasn't very successful, for all the time he could remember her eyes as he had seen them when he entered the room at Cambridge Gardens, heavy, listless, and unhappy. He thought, 'I must go on talking because loving gives things, and she asked me to talk. It's all I can give her at the moment.'

They passed Maidenhead, and Max realised that his stock of small talk had run out. He tried to think of some fresh subject, when her voice broke into his thoughts.

'Thank you, Max. Now, let me talk to you, will you? Go on driving. I was glad you came, because you're the only person who knew, and presently, you'll be the only person who ever will know. It's—it's finished, Max. I suppose I'm not a very clever person, perhaps I haven't learnt enough. I don't think really, though, that I made a mistake. I think we both didn't understand. He thought that I was wiser than I am. He thought that things I did —meant other things, when I hadn't meant them to.

'It's—been a shock—perhaps to my vanity. You see, he thought that I'd done it all to make a fool of him. What is it Morrie says? Lead him up the garden. I didn't—I promise you, I didn't.'

He said, 'Angela, my dear, don't talk like that—it's unbearable!'

'Max—I've got to talk to someone, don't be cross.'

'Good God,' he said, 'cross! I'm only hurt—for you.'

'It was four days ago,' she stopped. 'Max, if you lived alone in rooms would you think—things, if I came to see you sometimes?'

'Me? I should only think it was terribly nice of you to come at all.'

She touched his arm with her finger-tips. 'Perhaps it isn't fair to take your opinion. You're such a nice person."

She sat silent for a long time, while the car sped forward, leaving London miles away, heading for the country, and—Max felt—the peace which at the moment seemed so far away from both of them. He wanted to cry to her to go on, to tell him her story quickly and get it over; he wanted to stop the car, take her in his arms, and say that whatever the story was, he loved her and wanted her. He felt the words pushing to the forefront of his brain, clamouring to be spoken. But the cool judgment of the Jew was too much for him. It wouldn't do, that might be taken by Angela as an advantage which he was trying to take. Better to sit still and wait—and never before had Max felt how intensely hard it was to sit still and wait.

'I've heard Emmanuel call people "raw",' Angela said suddenly, 'that's what I am, Max—raw. I was ignorant,

and ignorance probably made me silly. It was all wonderful—all new—beautiful. A kind of new world which was
made for two people, and I was one of them. I know that
women are supposed to make a kind of game out of
being in love—they pretend not to care, they have all
kinds of rules and regulations. Like golf. It seems so easy
at first, you hit balls so easily. Then the pro. tells you that
it's all wrong, and with every lesson it gets harder and
harder.

'I did see him a great deal. I couldn't see why I
shouldn't see him. I didn't see why I should pretend to be
bored with him when I wasn't. Then someone—said something. Not to me, but someone else repeated it. It worried
me. I told him—we were having tea. He laughed, it didn't
seem to worry him much. He said, "I expect quite a lot of
people think that." I felt angry, and I showed that I was
angry. I have a beastly temper, Max. Then—oh, I don't
want to remember the rest—I want to forget it all . . .'

Max, without taking his eyes from the road before him,
said, 'Better tell me, Angela. I mean now you've got so
far, you'd better tell me the rest.' She sat stiffly upright,
he could feel her rigid body beside him.

'Very well—if I can. I let my temper get out of hand,
I suppose I was hurt because he took it all so coolly. I said
that if we were engaged, openly and everything, people
couldn't say things—like that. Then, he said that being
engaged wouldn't make any difference, that he had been
married. He didn't love his wife, he hadn't seen her for
years. She wasn't the right type to marry an artist. He
said that artists must be free, that they couldn't be tied by
conventional things—that I might as well live with him
and be happy as he didn't want to marry me.'

Max pressed his foot down on the accelerator and the
car dashed forward over the level road. He said nothing
but felt his hands close on the wheel, felt his muscles
tighten as if something which was flesh and blood, not
vulcanite, had been under his fingers.

'I—I don't know what I said, Max—I can't remember,
and then he lost his head, and . . . I can't tell you any
more. That's all. Except that I know—in part that I was
to blame, because I was so ignorant, so stupid about
things.'

Max licked his lips and swallowed something which
stuck in his throat.

'Stupid, eh?' he said. 'How—stupid?'

'I suppose men are different from women,' she said, 'it's—it's more difficult for them to . . .'

'To behave decently? I wonder if that isn't one of the clever things men have thought out and given to the world as a truth, Angela?' He slowed down the car, ran it to the side of the road under a great oak tree and stopped it. 'Look here,' he said, 'this is awfully difficult for me— for both of us. I don't want you to be forced to say anything that you'd hate saying.' He put out his hand and took hers. 'My dear, don't for God's sake look so wretched —don't shiver, Angela. It's over, darling, you're home, you're going to people who love you. Listen . . .'

'I am listening, Max.'

He tried to keep the words—'I'm years too old for her, and anyway she doesn't love me'—running as an undercurrent in his brain while he spoke. He wanted to beg her to marry him, to let him wipe away every past thought which hurt her, waited—perhaps most of all—to go back, find the man and kill him, tear his throat open with his bare hands and shout into his ears why it was necessary that he should die. Again the coolness of the Jew asserted itself, and he spoke evenly and with apparent calmness.

'Listen, then,' he said again. 'I don't want to know— details. Only—it was all pretty beastly, eh?'

He felt her fingers tighten round his. 'Pretty beastly, Max.'

'But,' his face was very white and she saw the sweat on his forehead, 'but—oh, damn, why are words so difficult to find!—but you weren't hurt?'

'Hurt?' she repeated.

Max saw a scarlet fog before his eyes, leant forward and laid his hand on her shoulders, clutching at her, holding her in the grip of his fingers.

'Hurt . . .' he repeated, 'hurt, yes. God, Angela, answer me, can't you?'

'Max—don't hold me! Only bruises—my shoulders, my arms—you're hurting me now.'

He loosed his hold, she watched his face twist into a foolish grimace, saw him catch his lower lip in his teeth to stop its quivering, then he buried his face in his hands and began to cry. She watched him, horror-struck. Max—crying. Max who had always been so level-headed, so wise, so immeasurably kind, crying like a child. She could hear the great, hoarse sobs tearing their way up through his throat, shaking him as they came. The positions were

reversed; before Max had been grown up, and she had felt
a child, a foolish, terribly frightened child. Now Max was
hurt, frightened—she had heard the fear in his voice, seen
it in his eyes when they stared into hers—and she was the
elder—miraculously. She was there to comfort him, to
smooth away the fear which possessed him. She felt
maternal, protective, and anxious.

'Max dear—Max, don't. I can't bear to see you so unhappy. It's terrible. My dear, I'm all right. Bruises—they're
nothing. I was stupid, let my nerves get the better of me.
I'm safe—with you again. It's all right.'

He lifted his head from his hands, shaking his head
almost as if it hurt him, staring at her with bloodshot eyes,
looking like a man who is drugged and stupefied.

'I know . . .' he said. 'I know you're safe with me—with
us. Only, I can't bear it. I can't bear to feel that he—is in
the world. Someday he might meet you again. I want to
kill him, so that he never can meet you again.'

'My dear, don't talk of killing people. Please, Max . . .'

'But you—hate him?'

'Not quite,' she spoke very slowly and carefully, she
might have been speaking to a child. 'It wasn't entirely
his fault, perhaps. He was—is still—dreadfully sorry, unbearably ashamed. No, I don't quite hate him.'

'God!' He narrowed his eyes suddenly. 'Is still—what
do you mean by that? How do you know—is still?'

'He wrote to me this morning.'

'You won't answer it?'

'I don't know—not yet at any rate. I couldn't.'

'You won't see him again—ever?'

'I don't know, Max. I can't promise.'

Again that movement of his head, as if the pain was
unbearable.

'You—you won't ever give in to him—be his mistress?'

'No, Max. I can promise that. But I can't nurse hatreds.
This is my own particular hurt. It's my own unhappiness. I
wanted to tell you, because I felt so lonely, so cut off from
everything. You see—I was very, very much in love, Max,
for the first time in my life. I don't want you to plan vengeance—I don't want you to plan anything. I want you to
stand by me when I tell the family that I've been working
very hard, and that the heat tried me, and that I wanted
to come home for a little. That's all.'

Max nodded, his control had returned, his voice had lost
its almost hysterical note. 'I see. Just the father confessor

—as I've always been. I'll do it, I'd do anything for you. I've no right to demand anything from you. You reserve the right to go back again, if you wish, to see this fellow—to—take up things again?'

'If I think it's right, Max. I won't go on hating people —people who have said they are sorry, who regret foolish things. However I was hurt—and I'm not hurt—however much I'm frightened—I can't go on hating, and looking for revenge. It's not in me, Max.'

'You can't marry him, and you won't be his mistress?'

'I wouldn't marry him—now, if I could, and I shall never be his mistress.'

Max nodded. 'Very well. Let's push on and get luncheon. Then, perhaps, you'll look better again. Angela, dear—don't be frightened, and don't blame yourself. No man need behave like a brute unless he allows himself to. No man—unless he wants to misunderstand a woman's motives—is forced to do so. Unfortunately, my dear. I not only love you, but I am in love with you. That complicates things.' He leant forward and touched her hand with the tip of his fingers. 'Remember, Angela, that I'm a Jew. I never, never realised what that gave me, until now. Never understood that a Jew—is different. You can talk about not hating, you can look forward to a day when you can forget things. I can't. So long as I live the world will be less lovely because that man is alive and breathing the air, so long as I live I shall hate him, and so long as I live I shall wait and wait—and wait. Then, one day, I shall find a way to pay him what I owe him! That's not theatrical nonsense, Angela. It's just—me.' His hand laid more heavily on hers. 'It's—it's been a bit too much for me, my dear.' He laughed. 'You'd have done better, perhaps, to tell my father instead of me.'

'I shan't need to tell Emmanuel,' she said. 'Emmanuel will see. He's like that. Max, I can't bear this talk of hating, it hurts me, it frightens me.'

'Then why did you tell me?'

'Because I was frightened, I had to tell someone. It was weak—foolish. I'm sorry that I did.'

Again his eyes narrowed, she saw his mouth harden, tighten into a thin line. 'It's too late, Angela. You forgot that I loved you. I've loved you for years, my dear. I suppose, at the back of my mind, there is a feeling of jealousy. This fellow—you've loved him, and you've never loved me. You've been in his arms and never in mine. He wanted you—oh, don't stop me!—and tried to take you, I never dared to do that. He knows actually more of you than I do, than I ever shall know.' He turned back to the driving wheel, and started the car. 'God, it's unbearable —just unbearable—that he should still be alive.'

'I wish I'd never told you, only I've always told you things. I ought to have said nothing.' She burst out with sudden passion, 'Oh, do you think that you're helping me, sitting there with a face like stone, talking of hate, and killing and jealousy! You say that you love me—isn't it ten times more difficult for me than for you? I've lost something that was very precious. I've seen my illusions—and my illusions about myself—smashed to bits. You've lost nothing, Max. I'm not different, I'm the same. You sit there, with a face like stone, and talk of revenge. For what? Why must you be revenged? Because I gave him something which I was never able to offer to you, because he—rightly or wrongly—tried to take more than I offered, but still something which never touched you in the least.'

Max, driving steadily again, his eyes on the black shining road, said, without turning, 'All right, Angela. Let's say that it's filthy, insane jealousy, and leave it at that.'

'We can't leave it at that. I thought that from you I should get help and comfort and understanding for myself. Now, you want to drag in a third person—a man you don't even know.'

'That's right, I don't even know his name,' Max said. 'That's a safeguard for him at all events, isn't it?'

They drove on, and during luncheon at Exeter Max talked of ordinary things, kept his voice level, and never once allowed his misery to become apparent. It was difficult for both of them. For years they had been friends, more than friends. Now, there was a barrier between them which neither of them could break down, there was a ghost which stalked between them and made itself felt whenever they tried to get back to their old comradeship.

What had been, when she told it, a confidence and a tribute to Max as proving her faith and trust in him, became a guilty secret between them. Max watched her tired eyes, her white face, and as he watched—remembered. She looked at him across the table, noticed how tightly his lips were set, how impersonal was the expression in his eyes, and knew that he was trying to drive out an image which hurt and wounded him. She had travelled from Austria, longing for the kindness and under-

standing which Max had never failed to give her, no matter
how small the happening which worried her. When she
had heard his voice over the telephone, she had felt that
now Max was coming everything would be made sane again.
For days, she felt that she had lived in a world which was
filled with madness and the idiot imaginings of her own
mind.

Ever since she had first met the Austrian violinist, had
heard him play, and listened to his colourful and enthusias-
tic conversation about the music which she loved, Angela
had felt his attraction. The attraction had grown into
admiration and friendship. They loved the same things, they
could talk together about his hopes and hers which were
all bound up in the music which seemed the greatest
thing in their lives. She had never had a friend who felt
as he did. At home they had always regarded her music
as an accomplishment to be cultivated, now she had found
someone who believed it to be the one aim in life which
was worthy of pursuit.

The friendship had grown and developed and one day
he had told her that he loved her. She listened, and
answered quite frankly that she loved him too. She had
never learnt to hide her feelings, to smother her impulses,
she saw no reason why she should not say to the man who
loved her that to be with him was happiness.

'I'm too old, my dear—I'm old enough to be your
father!'

'Age—age is a stupid thing,' she said, 'it means nothing.
You and I are the same age. We always shall be.'

For two years they had met and talked, they had
heard music and made music together. She had told Max
about it, because she was so happy. Only occasionally had
she—wondered, only at rare intervals had she compared
the man she loved to her brother, her cousin, and to
Max, and then had felt mean and disloyal. He was different, she had known it—admitted it—and felt that he had
a right to be. He was a genius, a great artist, not to be
bound by small conventions of dress or conduct.

She had felt that it was right and natural that she
should go to him, as it was impossible that he could
come to her. She had gone to his rooms as she would
have gone to her brother's, to Max's had he lived away
from his home, with no thought of possible censure.

Then someone had come to her and spoken, had said
what people were saying, had repeated the gossip of the

small English colony, and Angela had laughed. She went to his rooms, and during tea told him what she had heard.

'It's stupid, isn't it?' she said, 'but perhaps it might be better if I just let everyone know that we are engaged. One woman had actually said that she believed that I was your mistress.'

'I fancy lots of them think that, my dear. Being openly engaged wouldn't make any difference.'

'But you said . . .' she began, and then that temper of which she told Max had got the upper hand, and she talked as her grandfather, old Walter Heriot, might have spoken to anyone who angered him. The man listened, then threw back his head and laughed.

'Why did I never make you angry before? You're adorable. Go on—go on—I'm enjoying it more than I can tell you. I never said that I should marry you. Marriage isn't everything,' again he laughed, 'there is always "our art to hold us together"—tighter than any vows made before a parson.'

That snapped the last of her self-control, and she began to cry. He came to her, caught her in his arms and began to talk softly, to whisper and beg for forgiveness. She had lain in his arms wondering if she was waking from a dream. Then he changed—she couldn't remember why, but she had looked into a face which she saw clearly for the first time. A face which was florid, and coarse, with a little network of scarlet veins round the nostrils, and a skin which had lost its fineness and had become thick and hard. His hands, which she had thought so beautiful, became cruel and inquisitive, clutching her, holding her fast so that she could not escape. It had been like a nightmare, when you try to cry out and find that you cannot make a sound. She had tried to cry out, tried to twist herself out of his grasp, the hands which she had thought the hands of a genius were too strong.

'Don't be a fool—keep still, can't you?'

Then she had twisted herself away, and he stood looking at her, his head bent, his mouth half open, panting a little.

'You fool—you've only yourself to blame. There is a remarkably ugly name for girls who—behave as you've done for the last two years.'

She said, 'It's all over. I'm going home.'

He stuck his hands in his pockets. 'Very well, go, damn you—get out.'

She had come home, wanted Max, and Max had come. She had talked to him, and—everything was changed. Max had cried, talked of murder and revenge. And now—she looked across the table towards him—he was different. Hard, and cool and impersonal.

'Do you want coffee, Max?'

'Not unless you want some, Angela.'

'I don't . . .'

'Shall we get on, then?'

16

Emmanuel was puzzled; more than that, he was slightly annoyed. His touring party was not behaving as he had planned that it should. Frank and Morrie continued to quarrel. Certainly the quarrels were nothing and they never appeared to like each other any the less for them, but Emmanuel disliked the perpetual bickering which went on. Rachel, from whom he had hoped to gain a good deal of amusement, was absorbed in her wretched papers and textbooks on Parliamentary Law. Hermann mooned round, did and said nothing in particular. Apparently he was content, even happy, but no one would have thought it unless they had known Hermann very well.

And now—Emmanuel sighed and moved restlessly in his chair—Angela had come back. Max had every opportunity to make the running, to dance attendance, to make himself indispensable—and Max was behaving like a fool. He was never with the girl; he went off with Charles and William Drew, who had joined them, stravaiging all over the countryside, leaving Angela at home. Now Max announced that his friend O'Reilly was coming to continue the tour with them. That was the last straw—a man with a name which, Emmanuel felt, he could never possibly pronounce. Emmanuel flung his cigar with some violence into a bush, and stared at the Atlantic Ocean as if he held a

personal grudge against it. Max had gone with Charles and
William to Boscastle; Rachel was in her room planning
some nonsense which would land her in prison again, he
shouldn't wonder; Frank and Morrie had departed to
some mysterious cove to bathe, and Gwen was writing
letters—which meant she had gone to sleep until tea-
time.

He was alone, and he hated being alone. It was his
tour, he had insisted that he, and he alone, would pay the
bills, and this was how they all showed their gratitude!
By leaving him to stare at miles and miles of deadly
uninteresting sea and a few gloomy-looking rocks.

'Bude!' he ejaculated, only he pronounced it 'Pute,' 'I
vish that I had stayed in London!' Then he saw Angela
walking along the hotel garden and his annoyance disappeared. His hand went to his tie, he glanced down at
his beautiful shoes, and gave a hitch to the knees of his
immaculate trousers. 'Enchela!' he called, 'hev they left
you, too, all alone?'

'I don't think I wanted to go, Emmanuel,' she said, 'I
didn't feel like it.'

'Tired? You look tired.'

'Perhaps—yes, probably tired.'

Emmanuel patted the chair at his side, then tilted his
chair so that he could reach the electric bell. He would
order tea, he would show them when they came down
clamouring for that meal that he had stolen a march on
them all.

'We'll hev tea,' he said. 'Tea always does all women a
gr-reat deal of good. I want to talk to you, please. You
know, Enchela, that I never like to beat round bushes,
don't you? Is dere anyt'ing wrong between you and Max?'

'No, darling, nothing.'

'When you look at me like that, with your eyes very
wide open, and say, "No, darling, not'ing," Enchela, I
know that you are speaking half the truth. Your grendfather used to say that helf a truth was the whole of a lie.
Max isn't himself, neither are you, and together you are
making my holiday—spoilt. That isn't very kind of either
of you, is it?'

'Have you spoken to Max?'

'No, not a word, because I knew that you—being a
woman—could speak for yourself and him, too. Don't you
want me to speak to him?'

'I'd rather you didn't, please.'

Emmanuel leant back and smiled. 'Then there is somet'ing wrong! Never mind, let us hev tea and forget it. I'm an old man and I mustn't expect that you children will confide in me any more. That's the lonely part of old age.' Then turning to the waiter he said briskly, 'Tea for two, and please see that it is very, very nice, and very quick.'

Angela watched him, and smiled, and said, 'Emmanuel, what an old fraud you are, with all that rubbish about lonely old ages. You're not only old but inquisitive. That's one of the most horrible traits of old age.' Then, more seriously, she added, 'Darling, don't bother about Max and me. It's all really all right. Only—I was impulsive and didn't stop to think. That's all. Now, we're both paying for my selfishness.'

Emmanuel nodded to the waiter his approval of the tea, and began to pour out. He did it with the same neatness and beautiful courtesy as he did most things. He liked pouring tea, it showed off his hands, and demonstrated the excellence of his memory. Emmanuel always remembered who took sugar, and how much they liked to each cup.

He sipped his tea in silence, watching the girl who sat beside him with her hands clasped round her knees, his face very soft and kindly.

'Enchela,' he said at last, 'please forgive me, but there is someone—not—Max?'

'There was.' She added, 'Emmanuel, perhaps they'll have a little piece of me—always.'

He nodded. 'Yes, yes—just that little tenderness for the beginning of t'ings. I understand so well. It's the soft light in the sky after the sun has gone. I know. Would it hurt you to talk to me about—t'ings?'

'I don't think so. I'd almost like to, if you will let me leave unanswered the questions that are too difficult.'

'My dear, I'm not a member of the Inquisition! I'm not merely curious, I am devoted to you—and to Max. I don't love many people, though I like a great number. I never want to make the mistake of thinking that my age, which is not'ing, gives me the right to offer opinions. Only when I love people, I do want to be sufficiently brave to say, "I made this and this mistake, if my experience is of any help to you, allow me to relate it to you."'

Angela laid down her cup and turned towards him.

'You're going to tell me that I am making a mistake in not marrying Max?'

'No, no! I don't even know that Max hes esked you to marry him. Max is often a great fool. I know—because you hev told me—that there is someone else. He's a foreigner, eh?'

'That's surely not a crime in your eyes, Emmanuel? You're one yourself!'

'A crime! Enchela, don't be childish. Of course I am a foreigner—but I didn't marry or want to marry an English-woman. I married a Frenchwoman.'

'A foreigner in relation to you, then,' she said quickly.

'Not qvite. You see, to the Austrian—the Frenchman is less a foreigner than a man of another country. To the English—all people not English are foreigners. It is qvite true that the English—and I like them—are the most insular of all nations. They are so sensitive . . .'

'Sensitive!' she said. 'I should have thought that was the last thing attributed to them. I thought it was regarded as an axiom that they were insensitive about everything.'

Emmanuel waved his hands, dismissing the idea. 'Axioms are mostly r-rubbish,' he said. 'Let me tell you, if I can, what I mean. First let me state again my premise: the English are at once sensitive and intolerant. Suppose I bring home an old friend of mine—Reismann—and he brings with him his son. They are both clever—learned—erudite. Both kindly, well behaved and at heart, gentlemen. All right. They come to dine. I ask Charles and William and Max to dine with me. Or perhaps luncheon is better. It is luncheon. They arrive—we are waiting for them. Reismann comes in first. He wears a long frock-coat, with a waistcoat which shows a gr-reat deal of shirt front, his trousers are baggy, his boots hev perhaps seen trees, but never felt them. Behind him comes his son Frederick. He is a tall fellow, his hair sticks out at the back like an old hairbrush. The front is too long. His collar is the kind that men wear in the evening, with little wings at the side. His tie—it's a dr-readful tie. It is in checks, a kind of bastard tartan. He wears a gold watch-chain, very thick and shining. His coat is rather light tveed, too tight over the beck, too tight in the sleeves, too many pockets. His trousers are tight where they should be loose, loose where they should be tight. His boots are br-right brown. He is very gled about his boots. No—don't interrupt; let me go on, please.

'Charles looks at him and his eyes frown—not his face, only his eyes. William says, "Good God" silently, but I can hear it. They are both very nice indeed to Frederick. Charles makes a joke, one of those light, rather charming jokes that Englishmen do make. William laughs, I laugh—no one else. Frederick looks puzzled and begins to argue that Charles' story couldn't be true. He quotes Nietzsche to prove it. While he speaks he lays his knife and fork at r-right engles to his plate. William notices it. I am unheppy. These men are my friends. I like them, I understand them, that makes me a little confused and my ears get hot. The luncheon is over—Reismann and his son take their leave, Charles and William and Max say "Good-bye". They don't esk Frederick to dine with them at their clubs, they don't say, "Play golf? Let's fix up a game—foursome? What is your telephone number?"

'We go beck to my room. Max says that he should think they are clever men, Charles says, "Rather—so should I," and William says, "You can see they are!" I say, "Will you all hev another drink before you go?" and we don't mention Reismann and his son again.'

Angela took a cigarette from Emmanuel's case which he had laid open on the table. He leant forward and lit it for her, carefully, ánd watched her inhale the smoke.

'I think that is a caddish story, Emmanuel,' she said. 'It's a true one.'

'Can't you see that if you really loved anyone, their ties, their collars, their—yes, even their table manners wouldn't matter? Not if you loved them enough.'

'Only,' Emmanuel said gravely, 'if you lived on a desert island. In England—with English people—the more you love them, the more their clothes, their boots, and their social behaviour would metter, my dear. I can bear most t'ings, I can bear the enger of an Englishman, but even I should fear his polite disapproval of my clothes or the way I ate my food.'

'Oh, well, I'm not going to marry a—foreigner, so this doesn't affect me, Emmanuel.'

He took her hand in his, his voice was very gentle, he might have been talking to a child who was hurt, trying to soothe away the pain.

'My dear, somet'ing hes heppened to you. I shan't esk you what. If you wanted me to know, you would tell me. Only remember these t'ings. Don't let unheppiness eat into you and leave a great throbbing scar. Try to look further

than tomorrow morning, and never believe that you can
make people happy by anyt'ing you can do. People make
themselves heppy—you hev to live the day efter tomorrow, and life is sufficiently full of pain for all of us, that
there is no need to edd to it.'

With that queer lapse into childishness which was so
characteristic of her, she said, 'Emmanuel, I'm so sick of
everything! I do hate it all.'

He nodded. 'I know, I know very well,' he said. 'I hated
everyt'ing—even Max—once.'

'That's how I feel now. I hate everything—even Max.'

The tour through England continued, and gradually she
seemed to be happier with Max. She sat beside him when
they drove from place to place, she went off for long
tramps with him. To Max it appeared that she forgave
him for knowing what he had never asked to know, and
that she was allowing him to slip back into his old place.
He ceased to be actively unhappy, because he learnt how
to fight the demons which attacked him in his bad hours.
He learnt that, when he was alone, he had to be constantly on his guard against his thoughts which were sign-posts
along a dangerous road. Music—Austria—mixed marriages—those were the names printed on the sign-posts,
and when he saw them he leant to turn his thoughts very
swiftly down a by-path which led nowhere in particular,
but away from the danger zones.

They had seen Aberdeen, come south by Edinburgh,
and dropped down to Whitby. Emmanuel was growing a
little bored by it all. He began to wish that they had
planned a less extensive tour. O'Reilly failed to amuse and
interest him. He began to complain of the hotels, to decry
the climate and compare the countryside unfavorably
with that of France and Italy.

'Make the most of it, sir,' O'Reilly said one evening as
they sat in the hotel at Scarborough, 'it might be all
changed one day.'

'The climate, the hotels? Then—Thank God!' Emmanuel said fervently.

'No, the English countryside. One day . . .' O'Reilly's
eyes grew dreamy and speculative, 'one day, we shall go to
war, and after that . . .'

Frank sat upright, his whole face shining. 'You don't
mean that?' he said. 'A real war! Bit of luck that I chose
the Army, eh? Bit of luck for me, and for the Army.'

Max said, 'I think you're wrong, Terrence. Wars are

finished. We all recognise that they're an illogical way of
settling a quarrel. I've always said that, ever since the
South African show.'

'Illogical?' O'Reilly repeated. 'But after all, so's hanging,
but it still goes on. Nations, in the mass, are illogical.'

'That's true,' Rachel said, 'illogical to the core. Otherwise would women be suffering in prison today? The whole
attitude of the Government towards the suffrage is illogical. They haven't a leg to stand on.'

Charles looked up from his evening paper. 'That's right,
Rachel, let 'em have it. By Jove, I am sick of that wretched
"Get Out and Get Under" that the band's playing.'

The band played on, Charles returned to his paper,
Frank and Morrie quarrelled quietly in their corner, Max
and O'Reilly discussed the possibilities of going fishing,
William came back with a handful of letters and began to
distribute them.

'Mother—bills, obviously,' he said. 'Max—looks like a
summons to me.' William's wit was always heavy. 'Emmanuel "billydoos"; that's all—except one for Angela—
nasty squirmy fist, old thing.'

Emmanuel took his letters. 'Thank you, William. I don't
t'ink, perhaps, that comments upon letters are qvite per-
missible, my boy.'

'Sorry, Emmanuel.'

They all read their letters, it was an unwritten law
among them that everyone read letters without asking
permission or making excuses.

Max finished his—they were very dull—and watched
Angela. He knew that he watched Angela too often, that
he was constantly apprehensive about her, that he had
grown to fear unhappiness for her, to wonder from what
point that unhappiness might come, and to dread it far
more than if it had threatened himself. He saw her take
out the closely written sheets and lean back in her chair to
read them. He saw her fingers tighten on the flimsy paper,
saw her eyes close as if she hated what she read. He
wanted to get up, snatch the paper from her and beg her
not to read it. Then, suddenly, before she reached the end,
she folded the sheets, slipped them back into the envelope
and put the letter into her bag.

Max felt that a weight had lifted, at any rate the letter
was out of sight, she had not even read all that the
fellow had written. Emmanuel had finished reading his

mail, too. He was asking questions of O'Reilly who was in the Foreign Office.

'War,' he said, 'it's a curious t'ing. A kind of netional hypnotism. A war, a good war must take a lot of organisation, O'Reilly.'

'A devil of a lot, sir. Kind of jig-saw puzzle. You get bits here and there, stick 'em together and they look like nothing. Then one day along come the extra bits, and hey presto, the puzzle isn't a puzzle any longer.'

'Is there going—really—to be another war, Terrence?' Morrie asked.

'One day. This year, next year, sometime . . .'

'Never!' suggested Gwen Drew comfortably.

'Oh, don't say never,' Frank begged. 'All my hopes are founded on a war.'

Emmanuel had gone back to his own thoughts. 'The pieces?' he said. 'How do you get the bits of this international jig-saw, please?'

O'Reilly smiled. 'Agents, sir. Continental agents. Clever fellows who take risks for money. Not often for anything else. They send in this and that—a gun here added, an officer talking there, someone opening a letter intended for someone else—so it goes on. They're clever fellows. Someday, Max, I'll show you some of their dodges. They don't send the best stuff in letters, y'know. They're up to all sorts of tricks.'

'You mean spies?' Max said.

'If you like to call 'em that. Agents is a nicer word, though I've never seen why a spy shouldn't be a most respected person, if he's on the level with his own people.'

'Who will the next war be with, Terrence?' Morrie asked.

They all began to answer her at once. Charles said—the Irish, and Terrence laughed. William said he fancied Russia, while Frank said that a fellow had told him that China was going to sweep the Western Hemisphere, and flood the world with yellow faces. 'The yellow peril,' he added, 'that's what it means.'

Morrie said, 'What rot, Frank. China—they're too far off. I should think Turkey, wouldn't you?'

Gwen Drew shivered. 'Oh, it's a horrible thought. Perhaps—France?'

Emmanuel said, 'Not France—she won't fight us. Neither will Germany—America might. O'Reilly, what do you think?'

Terrence said, 'I'm not asked to think, sir. I only take what's sent me, docket it, and try not to think. You see it's all speculation. Today what is impossible might be an accomplished fact tomorrow. It won't really bear speculating about.'

Max watched Angela, and thought, 'Supposing we did go to war—with Austria? What would she do? What should I do? Suppose—a war came, and I could meet him and kill him?'

But the thought remained with him all the evening. Even when he danced with Angela, he felt that the idea was still in his mind. She did not talk very much, but she did not seem to be actively unhappy. Max had learnt to ask no questions when she was silent, only to accept what she gave and leave it at that.

The party was scattered over the huge hotel. Emmanuel demanded a room which overlooked the sea, so did Rachel and Gwen. Hermann must have absolute quiet. Charles and William only asked that their rooms should be near the bathroom. Morrie wanted plenty of lights, and invariably declared that the bulbs were worn out. Max only asked for a window which opened easily, and Angela—without expressing any conditions whatever, usually occupied the best room of all. O'Reilly, having only joined them after their tour had started, took what he could get and was apparently easily satisfied.

That night, when they departed to their several rooms, Max found himself wandering down a long corridor with Angela.

'Are you over here?' he asked.

'I'm one five seven,' she said, 'and Morrie is one five four.'

'And I,' Max said, 'am one five eight. You'll be able to call me if you hear burglars.'

'I will—that's a promise. Good night, Max.'

'Good night, my dear.'

He sat reading, his thoughts only half on the book, while the other half was filled with wonderings and speculations about the girl in the next room. He heard Morrie come in to say 'Good night,' heard the door close, and from his window saw the broad beam of light shining out into the darkness. She was awake. He turned back to his book, and read steadily but without much comprehension for an hour. He went to the window, and found that the light still shone from the window next door. He leant out, breathing the cool air, thinking unhappily that things could never be the same again. Before—it hadn't been ideal, she had never loved him as he hoped that she might, but she had trusted him, confided in him, liked to be with him. Now, when they drove together, they drove in silence. She wasn't unkind, she wasn't cold, she was only impersonal. He felt that she drove with him because he kept silence, and she liked silence in these days better than the sound of voices. Silence—he listened intently. There wasn't silence in her room now, she was talking to someone. He listened again. Not voices, not even the sound of one voice—but a noise—a dull, stifled sound, intermittent and persistent. She was crying—alone—in the night—crying as a child might cry who was frightened, and who has been forbidden to call for anyone to still its fears.

Max waited, listened, and heard the noise persisting. He left the window, walked to the door and opened it, looked up and down the long corridor. It was dark and silent. He stood for a moment undecided, then switching off the light in his room, closed his door softly and walked to the door of Angela's room. Very softly he tapped upon it, and after a second heard her voice.

'Who is that? What is it?'

He opened the door and went in. She was sitting in a big chair, wearing a dressing-gown over her nightdress. Her face was stained with tears, and her eyes met his—miserable and frightened. He came forward and knelt by her chair.

'Max—what have you come for?'

'I heard you crying, I couldn't bear it. Angela, it's—it's breaking my heart. I can't—I can't stand it. Tell me what it is. What's happened?'

'Nothing, Max.' Then, 'Go back to your own room. I'll be all right.'

'My dearest, I can't. Try to tell me. Surely things can be put right?'

She did not speak, only covered her face with her hands and began to cry softly. Max stood up, pulled a chair near hers, and sat down.

'Something in that letter today?' He waited and she did not reply. 'He wants you to go back? Is that it?'

'Conditionally, Max. On his terms or not at all.'

'To go back to him—are those his terms? I see. You don't want to go back?'

She made a little puzzled movement. 'I don't know. I

suppose half of me does want to go back desperately. The
other half knows—knows that it just wouldn't work. I
know myself, I should demand things. I should resent not
having them, I should hate to be—really nothing. It's all
wrong, if I loved him, all of me, I shouldn't care. Then,
there is my work—I do love that wholly, Max. I can't just
work anywhere. Some people might, I can't. I might have
to go back because of the work. Then—he will make it
impossible. I do love him, really and truly, I love the side
of him that I thought I knew. The other—I don't know. I
told you that I blamed myself a great deal. It's like being
torn in two. My pride, my intense hatred of being
second best, my work, then my love—that I can't fight
against—for him. It's a miserable business.'

'Poor Angela,' he said, 'it's a wretched muddle.'

'I'm muddled,' she said, 'it's me. I'm not really single-
minded, Max. I don't want to give in. I do want to work. I
want his friendship—his brain—his intelligence—his
knowledge. I want to fight against anything else that he
has to offer.' She stopped and gave a miserable attempt at
a laugh. 'What I really want is protection against myself.'

He pushed back his chair a little. 'Angela,' he said, 'you
want protection—well, you can have it without asking. I
can give it to you. Say that you are engaged to me. It's
sometimes useful to have a man to fall back on as a kind
of buffer. Be engaged to me—until you are certain. Then
you can go and work with me as a kind of unseen moral
protective. I won't stand in your way, not in anything. If
you come back and tell me that you know yourself, that
you don't mind second best for him, I'll not try to stop
you. If you come back and tell me that you are sure that
you don't want second best—or anything, that you're
safe and assured in your own mind, you can break it off,
or I will break it off for you.'

She shook her head. 'That wouldn't be fair, Max—not
fair to you.'

'That's my business, Angela.'

'It might not work out right.'

'Try it—if you must go back.'

'I think—sooner or later—I shall go back. Half because
I want to see him, half because I want to work. Oh, it's not
him, it's not his voice or his hands or his eyes; it's what he
stands for, what he meant—once. I can't break things off
and throw them on one side. Being engaged to you might
safeguard me—in one way, it couldn't touch me in anoth-

er.' She broke off and looked at the little clock on the mantelpiece. 'You must go. It's half-past two. There would be an awful row if anyone found you here. Good night, Max, and thank you . . .'

17

They were back in London, the summer was over and the autumn had very definitely arrived. Max had never known the time when the house of Gollantz had been so busy, when people had clamoured so insistently for antiques, for pictures and for new ideas in interior decoration. He was sent here and there, to huge houses in the provinces, to out-of-the-way sales of furniture, to the Continent—anywhere and everywhere where he might be likely to find goods suitable for the firm to sell to the ever-increasing list of customers.

He saw very little of Angela, or of anybody for that matter. Sometimes O'Reilly would come in the evening to talk to him, and they would sit in Max's comfortable room and discuss everything under the sun until the small hours. But usually, after a hard day's work, Max was too tired to want to visit other people, especially as at the moment very few of them interested him in the least.

Angela still absorbed most of those thoughts which were not actually concerned with his business, and the rare occasions upon which he saw her were mentally marked in his memory with a star. She was always kind, always anxious to hear what he had done and what he had planned to do, but she never referred to the interview in her room, never confided in him concerning her own affairs, and Max resolutely refrained from hinting even vaguely that he was hurt by her silence. She had a right to keep silence, she was not forced to discuss her affairs with anyone. Her silence and his consequent ignorance only hurt him because it marked the change in their relationship. Now, Max reflected, they were companions, once they had been close friends.

He heard of her more than he saw her, indeed it seemed to Max that the whole of his world discussed and referred to no one else but Angela.

Gwen Drew, returning from a drive with Emmanuel, stayed to tea and talked of her, of her music, and what this and that person had said about it.

Frank and Morrie chattered of dances, of themselves, and of Angela.

Frank chuckled. 'I think she likes old Charles, y'know.'

Morrie said, 'What rot—Charles likes her, but she doesn't give a damn for him.' Being Charles' sister, she could not see him as attractive to another woman.

'She danced with him nearly all last night, my good child.'

'Frank, don't be so Victorian. He's her dancing partner!'

Frank shrugged his shoulders. 'Anyway, I shall go on thinking my own thinks about it. Bet you they're engaged by this Christmas.'

'Bet you a fiver they're not—or any other Christmas!'

'Max, make a note of that bet, will you, old thing?'

Morrie giggled and threw her cigarette into the fireplace. 'If anyone wants my opinion, I think she likes Emmanuel the best of the lot of you. Where is she tonight—I ask you?'

'I'll tell you—she's gone to see *Oh! Oh! Delphine* with him.'

Morrie spread her hands with a gesture of triumph. 'There! How would you like Angela for a stepmama, Max?'

Max felt the blood rush to his face. For a moment he hated Morrie.

'Charming,' he said. 'Now if you two have finished scrapping and talking tripe, perhaps you'll leave me in peace?'

Charles came and talked of her. Max wasn't sure that Charles wasn't in love with her. He looked at the straight, clean-run young fellow and had it in his heart to hate him —as he had hated his sister. Charles walked round the room picking up things and putting them down with a clatter, talking, talking, talking until Max felt that his head would burst.

'Thats' nice, Max—that bit of old iron or whatnot, isn't it? I say, that's a nice snap of Angela. Where did you get it? I'd like one—think you've got the negative? Eh? Where is that old inkpot you used to have? She's terribly attractive, isn't she? Funny kid—I feel years older sometimes. I'm really a year younger. I don't think age comes into things much, d'you?'

'Comes into things—what things?'

Charles wagged his head. 'I don't know—just things. I must push along. Coming with us tomorrow? Not? We're going dancing. Angela's coming, too.'

'No, I'm not coming. Too much to do. Go on, Charles—clear out.'

Then William, who regarded himself at twenty-two as the head of the family, and was serious and very heavy. He sat down firmly, and Max knew that when William sat down he meant staying. His staying powers were astonishing.

'How's things, Max? Very rushed at our place, y'know what the City's like! The devil an' all. Hard life, very hard life.' He tugged his waistcoat down and looked like a child playing at being grown up, his round pink face serious. 'Worries crowd in a bit. The mater leaves almost everything to me. Wish we could get rid of that place in Dorset. Awful expense. Wish Angela would get married. Ever asked her, Max?'

Max stared at him, then said, 'Mind your own damn business, Bill.'

William looked back at him unmoved. 'That's what I am doing, my lad. She's doing no particular good at the moment. Dancing every night with Charles, and if she isn't with Charles she's out with Emmanuel, and if it's not Emmanuel it's your bright pal, O'Reilly. If it's not him, it's a little undersized Italian who plays the fiddle day in day out. I wish she'd settle down . . .'

Max said, 'Why not settle down yourself? She's only twenty-one.'

'I've got responsibilities, she hasn't. I was only saying to a fellow this morning . . .'

Max cut him short, 'I'm sure you were, Bill. At the moment, I wish you'd clear out. Talk about the devil—it's the devil to have an office off Bond Street, and have you all regard it as a dumping ground for gossip about Angela. For God's sake leave your sister alone.'

William stared at him with round blue eyes, very wide and hurt. 'Steady the Buffs!' he said mildly. 'What's the matter with you? Surely we can drop in for a chat without your going in off the deep end like this?'

Max ran his fingers through his hair. 'Oh, my God!' he said, 'can't you see that I'm not here to chat? I'm here to work. All I get is a series of detachments of people arriving full of speculations and complaints about Angela!'

'Very well.' William assumed an air of grave and offended dignity. 'Very well. My mistake. Apparently you're not interested in Angela.'

'No, I'm not,' Max snapped. 'Let Angela marry whom she pleases, and leave me alone.'

He turned back to his desk and tried to concentrate upon some estimates which lay before him. The figures danced before his eyes, they were a meaningless jumble. Why had he lost his temper—and with poor Bill, of all people? He mustn't let his nerves get out of hand, he was letting all this chatter about Angela get too much for him. It seemed that the whole world knew her movements, her likes and dislikes, except himself.

William stood at the door, his hat in his hand. 'Bye-bye, Max. I think I once heard an old saw—that's the word, isn't it?—about someone who protested too much.'

Max glanced over his shoulder. 'Think what you damn well please, Bill. Forgive me, I'm a bit rattled. Good-bye —some other time . . .'

That evening, Max sat at home while Emmanuel went off to a theatre. Emmanuel loved plays, loved to dine with a pretty woman, or order a dinner with great care, to eat it—conscious that everyone looked towards him and his companion with interest not unmixed with admiration. He was still one of the most handsome men in London despite his sixty-nine years. His figure was upright, still slim and flexible. His hair was perfectly white, and no one except his hairdresser knew the trouble which was taken and the time which was spent to prevent a tinge of yellow appearing in it. Now, facing Angela Drew across the table at the Berkeley, he smiled contentedly. She caught the smile. 'Happy, Emmanuel?'

'I am with you, Enchela.'

'Thank you. I doubt if being with me is sufficient reason. Doesn't the very pleasant dinner contribute?'

'Perhaps—but very little. I could tell you some poem about a glass of water, only I don't remember it very well.'

'You are a happy person, aren't you, Emmanuel? Have you always known just what you wanted, and gone straight for it?'

He thought for a moment. 'I t'ink so. You see if you don't know what you want, then you can't grumble at what you get, can you?' He pushed back his glass and leant his arms on the table. 'Enchela, shall I tell you what is wrong with you? You are esking for too much—you are esking for the best of both worlds, and you'll never get it. You can only live—live, I said—in one world at a time. Choose which one, and next time, when perheps you have another chance, you can choose the other one.'

She moved impatiently. 'But that's where you are wrong, Emmanuel,' she said. 'I can live in two worlds—I do—I have done for a long time. It's not a bit satisfactory, it's like trying to be two people at once. It's like *Alice in Wonderland*. I hate it. What I want is someone who would make me stay in one world for good.'

'Poof!' he said. 'You'd hate anyone who made you do anything, and you know it. You'd never forgive a man who tried to make you do t'ings.'

Angela looked at him for a moment, her eyebrows drawn into a frown, her whole face puzzled. 'How funny,' she said, 'just for a minute, you reminded me of someone I once knew. I wonder why? Never mind—anyway, you're wrong, Emmanuel, when you say that I should never forgive. I forgive too easily, that's my trouble. Or perhaps I forget—I don't know which. It's much easier to go through life hating quite violently and contentedly, you know.' She paused, then said slowly, 'I believe things would be easier for me—oh, I'm being quite frankly selfish—if I got married.'

'Married,' Emmanuel said, 'perhaps. But, my dear, he'd have to be a very wise man, or a very adoring one, to be able to get much happiness with you—yet. You would forever be making declarations of independence, you know.'

She sighed. 'I suppose I should. I wonder if all this independence is really worth much? Sometimes I don't think it is. I believe that you can love two people at the same time, don't you?'

'No,' he said, 'and neither will you when you're older. It's an idea that men and women hev always played with. Two loves—no, my dear. One is first, the other second. One is fundamental, the other is extraneous. One is—part of you, the other is dregged in, super-imposed.' He glanced at his watch. 'We must go, unless we are to miss the beginning of *Mr. Wu*. I believe that it is t'rilling.'

As they drove along the Strand, she said, 'We still

haven't decided about my marrying someone; you're not much help, Emmanuel.'

He smiled in the semi-darkness of the car, and took her hand in his. 'Well, I can only offer myself as a sacrifice—would you care to merry me?'

'No,' she said, very firmly, 'I wouldn't. Why? You don't want to marry me, do you?'

'Not in the least—what a conceited little thing you are! And you don't even listen. I said "sacrifice myself". Well, who else is there?'

'I think,' she said, slowly and softly, 'I think I want to marry Max.'

'And I t'ink,' Emmanuel said, 'that it is more than likely that Max wants to merry you. Here we are. Now let us go and see Mr. Lang as a suave and sinister Chinaman.'

At the end of the second act, she said, as the curtain fell, 'Emmanuel, I don't think I like this much. Would you mind, awfully, if we went home?'

Emmanuel, who would have much preferred to lose his dinner than miss the last act of a play, said that he didn't mind in the least, that she should come home and he would open a bottle of champagne by way of celebration.

When they reached Regent's Park, Emmanuel turned to her as they stood in the hall and said, 'Which room? The drawing-room, my room, or Max's room?' He bent down and looked at her more closely. 'You're very white, darling, aren't you well? Tell me, please?'

'I'm all right. That play tired me.' She touched his arm with her finger-tips. 'Your room—and may I go and speak to Max first. I'm going to do a dreadful thing—I'm going to ask him to marry me, Emmanuel.'

'He esked you first,' Emmanuel said, 'didn't he?'

'Yes. I said "No"—but I've changed my mind.' She laughed unhappily. 'I wonder if he has changed his?'

'If he hes, then he's enough pluck to tell you. Go along, my dear.'

She ran upstairs, and tapped on the door of Max's room. She was frightened, her heart was beating uncomfortably fast, she felt that neither her voice nor hands were quite steady. She tapped again, more loudly, and Max's voice said, 'Come *in*—I said, "Come in!"'

He was seated at his desk, the light from a reading-lamp shining on his hair, his head was bent over a drawing which he was making; from where she stood she could see the light, firm lines—a door, with decoration over it.

She closed the door and leant against it, her hands pressed behind her touching the smooth polished wood. It felt cool, reassuring, firm.

'Max . . .' she said.

He lifted his head and looked towards her, then shut his eyes and opened them again. He laughed. 'Angela, it really is you! I thought I was dreaming. Didn't you go to see *Mr. Wu* with my father?'

'Yes,' she said, 'we went. I didn't like it much. We came home. I wanted to talk to you.'

His face changed, the smile, the light in his eyes, the air of delight disappeared. He stood facing her, quite still, his face expressionless. She saw that his fingers gripped very tightly the pencil which they held.

He said, 'Yes—please do.'

Instantly she felt his fear, understood it, and felt intense sympathy for him. Poor Max—he had suffered badly; he still suffered.

She said, 'It's all right, Max. It's not anything that will hurt you. It's—me.'

He licked his lips, nodded and said, 'Yes—it's you. What is it?'

'Do you still love me enough to want to marry me?'

The pencil dropped from his fingers. He bent forward as if to see her more clearly, screwing up his eyes as if a sudden light hurt them.

'What do you mean?' he asked. 'Angela, what is all this? I don't understand. Please tell me quickly.'

'I'm asking you to marry me.'

'You mean that?' He turned back to the desk, moved his papers, pushing them together into an untidy heap, speaking while his hands were busy with them. 'No one told you to come and say this, did they? You came because you wanted to come?'

'Yes, Max.'

'Because you . . .' he stumbled over the words, 'love me —more than you did at Scarborough?'

'Yes, Max.'

At last he came over to where she stood, took her hands in his and drew her to his chair beside the big desk. 'Sit down,' he said, 'sit down, darling, and tell me. I'm so stupid, I don't understand. I want to take you in my arms and never stop kissing you,' he laughed, 'that's what I want to do. But—I want to know what made you come. I want to know what has happened about—other things. I won't let you do things today and be sorry tomorrow. Tell me.'

She picked up his pencil and rolled it up and down the desk while he stood watching her. When she spoke her voice was steady, though she never turned and faced him. 'I'll try,' she said, 'only if I begin to cry, don't think it means anything. I'm just tired, that's all. You see, I've been rushing about, dancing and riding and motoring and going to theatres—doing anything to fill in the time. I thought that you'd perhaps come too, Max, and you never did. Everyone else came—except you.

'I thought that what I wanted was to crowd things out, other things—the things that made me unhappy. Only they only crowded closer. I did try dreadfully hard. Then, I began to see that I'd got to do more than just drug myself. You remember all the more vividly when the drug's worn off. You see, one side of me still—wants him, Max. Only one side, and that's not the happiest side of me; though it's only the best—or what I think is the best side of him that I want. Oh, I'm making such a muddle of this.'

'That's all right, Angela, I understand. Go on.'

'Then I knew that I was afraid of myself. Afraid that one day, I should just give in and go back. That after one of his letters, I shouldn't be able to fight, that something would snap. I want anchoring, Max. And I didn't like any of the anchors that offered. Charles, or O'Reilly—they wouldn't have done. You see, you've always been very dear to me. I've always loved you, and always wanted you to share things. I didn't know how much I wanted you, until after we'd finished that holiday, and I didn't see you every day. I used to go and play with little Carera, and thought that would help, and it didn't help a bit.

'Letters come and come, and they batter things down, they reproach me, they terrify me. I can't tell anyone except you. I keep saying that it's not the real me that wants to go back to him—and it's true. The real me wants to play, to make music, to be happy and content. I can't think of anyone in the world who could make me content except you, Max. It seems so mean—the way I put it—as if I wanted to use you. It's not that really, this will pass —it must.

'Are you willing, to help me over it all, to make me feel safe, and happy, and to look foward to a day when it will all pass, and we'll be in smooth water again? The real me —the Angela you've known for years—is still here, asking you to marry her, telling you that she loves you. It's only the other me—the new me—who gets miserable sometimes and wants things back that are much better dead and buried decently.'

She was crying now, he saw the tears on her cheeks and heard the loneliness and the fear in her voice. He came nearer and knelt beside her as he had done once before.

'Angela, darling,' he said, 'don't cry or you can't hear what I want to say to you, and it's very important. There —listen . . . Will you marry me?'

'I want to.' Suddenly she twisted round and put her hands on his shoulders. 'Max, you'd trust me, always, wouldn't you? If ever I said that I wanted to go back to see him—listen, listen, just to see him, to make things sure in my own mind before we were married—would you trust me?'

'To go back and see him,' he said, 'to make sure that everything was over. My dear—that's asking a lot, isn't it? I'd trust you—you know that; could I trust him?'

'If you trusted me, really, I should answer for everything else. If I knew that you trusted me, I should see that no one betrayed your trust.'

'I see. Yes, I think—I am almost sure that I could. Not yet, Angela, not too soon. Let me get used to knowing that you love me, first.'

'I promise. Oh, Max, you will take care of me, won't you?'

He put his arms round her and held her tightly. He felt her tears on his cheek, heard her sobs as she clung to him and whispered, 'Max—don't let me go. I've been so frightened . . .'

'I won't ever let you go. Angela, you'll really marry me? Soon?'

'Soon, Max. Next year—we'll have our holidays together, shall we?'

'You really love me?'

'I do—really—and,' very softly, 'I do like you so awfully, too.'

Emmanuel was standing waiting with glasses and a golden-topped bottle when they went down to him. Max stood, his arm round Angela in the doorway, his pleasant face shining with happiness. Emmanuel looked at him. and thought how proud Juliana would have been of him.

Max said, 'Father—I've got some great news.'

'News! I knew it first. Max, be careful, the girl has a

mania for esking people to merry her. She suggested that I should this evening.'

Angela said, 'Max, he's a horrible liar. Anyway, if you hadn't been such a fool I shouldn't have been driven to desperation. I told Emmanuel that I wanted to marry you. Now he'll hold it over me for the rest of my life.'

The bottle was opened, and Emmanuel poured the champagne into the glasses neatly and deftly as he did everything. 'There,' he said, 'please drink, and let your toast be—The heppiest old man in the world. That is me, Max. I've wanted this for such a long time. Angela, I love you very much, and I could never t'ink of anyone nice enough for you but Max. Max—I love you very much, and I could never t'ink of any girl nice enough for you except Enchela. May the God of my Fathers bless and keep you both.'

18

Everyone appeared to believe that they had arranged the engagement. Gwen Drew smiled and nodded and said, 'Well, Max, I hope you realise how much you have to thank me for? You don't—for men are ungrateful creatures. Never mind, I'm sure it's all very nice.' Rachel said, 'I'm glad, Max. She's a fine girl, has her head screwed on the right way. I take something to myself for that. She has a good working idea of women's real position in the world, and that is a most satisfactory basis for marriage—so far as marriage ever is satisfactory.'

William grinned. 'Thank me, young-fellow-me-lad, thank me. I put the idea into your head. You acted under the instructions of a wiser man than yourself—only you didn't know it.'

Charles sighed—Max was rather sorry for Charles—and said, 'Congratulations, Max, and all that. I blame myself, in a way. I let you see how keen I was—it roused the emulative spirit in you. Hard luck on me, but one man's meat was ever the cause of acute stomachache to another.'

Even Frank and Morrie Wilmot descended upon him at the office, sat on the desk, smoked innumerable cigarettes, and argued over his head at each other.

'Morrie and I agree . . .' Frank said.

'Agree? Surely not!' Max interrupted.

'Shut up, Max,' Morrie said, 'Frank agrees with me, that we engineered this. Remember the day we came in here?'

'I can scarcely remember a day when you did not come in here . . .'

'About a week ago, Max. When we told you that Angela was keen on Charles.'

Morrie screamed, 'You mean Charles was keen on Angela! Mutton head!'

'Anyway, we believe that what we said gave you the idea that you rather fancied Angela yourself.'

'And,' Morrie added, 'you went and jumped in with both feet before poor old Charles began to get a move on at all! Personally, I fancy that Charles is as sick as mud over it.'

'In addition,' Frank said, 'seeing as how all this family joy is really owing to us, we think that you owe us something. Something not gaudy or ostentatious, but—solid recognition.'

Max lifted his well-marked eyebrows. 'Such as . . .? Don't be too bashful to ask, Frank, will you?'

'Leave it to me.' Morrie jumped off the corner of the desk upon which she sat and came round to Max's side. 'Do you know that car of Frank's? That bloodsome bag of hammers in which I have to be driven round town?'

'You don't have to.' Frank was indignant. 'You're always nagging me to take you! Have to—I like that!'

Morrie disregarded him. 'There is a car—a real car— which can be bought and would do me credit, almost as much credit as I should do it. Now, what about it? Frank's broke—so am I.'

'It's second-hand—only done eight hundred miles, Max. A peach of a car. Standard—lovely little bus. Lend me the money, will you? Honestly, it's the chance of a lifetime, it is really.'

Max sighed. 'You're a couple of blackmailers! I never had a car at your ages—I walked, or took a bus.'

'We want to buy a bus!'

'I've got to pay for Angela's ring, damn you!' He laughed. 'I'll make a bargain with you. Keep out of here for a fortnight, and I'll give you a hundred quid—now?'

'Oh, done with you, Max. Done every time. Thanks awfully—we'll go and touch the old man for the other hundred. Bye-bye, Max, and our united blessings!'

Emmanuel behaved like an open-handed patriarch. He was delighted, and showed his approval by showering gifts upon them both. Already he had begun to consider the rival merits of houses, to discuss soils, drainage, and outlook. His attitude towards Angela was a mixture of a doting father and an elderly lover. He made no attempt to conceal his love and admiration for her, and never lost an opportunity of taking her out with him and introducing her to his friends.

Max, himself, was happy, his whole life was flooded in sunshine, and if sometimes there appeared on the horizon a little cloud no bigger than his hand—he resolutely looked in the opposite direction. He told himself that if he could make her happy, then he could make her forget. If he could make her love for him a solid, established thing, then she would never have to go back to make certain that the other man belonged to the past. He decided that if he failed to do this—then his failure would be due to some fault in himself, and he would deserve to suffer in consequence.

Angela was content, she told herself that she was quite consciously happy. Max was charming, devoted, amusing. He had not made the mistake of never leaving her side. His work occupied him for many hours each day, even his evenings were sometimes filled with business engagements. He was attentive, but never obtrusive; he was affectionate without being sentimental; he was solicitous without being tedious.

Each day, when she opened the letter which never failed to come to her on her breakfast tray, Angela felt that her affection grew, felt each day that life without Max would be a miserable business. She looked forward with increasing pleasure to his coming, to their evenings together. He loved gaiety, he danced well, appreciated music, and was always ready to find fun in small unexpected excitements of the more simple kind. There were bad days—days when she carried about with her a long, thin envelope, when she stared at the sloping writing and put off reading its contents as long as possible. Then, when she read them, there would come the old insistent longing, some phrase would remind her of days which had been full of sunshine and laughter, or some harsh, angry protest would make her shiver suddenly with apprehension.

Those were the days when Max found her silent and absorbed. When she would sit and listen, but he would know—because he loved her so dearly—that her mind was full of other things.

'I'm boring you, sweetheart. You're tired?'

'No, Max. I'm all right. Don't take any notice of me. It's just—been rather a bad day.'

'Have you told him about us?'

'I've written today. Oh, I know I've been a coward and put off doing it. I am a coward, you see, Max. I told you that I was.'

'You're afraid of what the answer may mean to you?'

She drew a deep breath. 'Just a little.'

Max stood up and walked up and down the room in silence. At last he came and stood before her, his face white and unhappy.

'If I did what perhaps I ought to do—I should tell you not to read the answer when it came, and to read no more letters that came from that source. I wonder if you'd respect me more if I did?'

'I might respect you—I don't suppose that I should obey you, and I should love you rather less, I'm afraid, Max.'

'But he frightens you, he makes you unhappy!'

'No—I frighten myself, I make myself unhappy, my dear. Oh, Max—try to be patient. It's only a little bit of me—wants him. The big bit of me wants you, and our life together and the future. I can't think of a future that didn't hold you.'

He laughed softly. 'You are the future—for me,' he said. 'Oh, Angela, if only I could talk to you—as I want to talk. If I was a poet, and could use phrases and voice wonderful thoughts! I feel that when I can't—I let you down every time. It's colour, light, starshine and moonshine I want to turn into words for you—and I can't, because I never learnt to talk that way. All I can tell you is this—that when I see you smile, and laugh and being happy, I'm content. But when you sit and stare straight in front of you, when I know that all I say only reaches you through a fog of other thoughts—well, darling, the world isn't a very pleasant place for me.'

She stretched out her hand and took his. 'Sorry, Max. I'm not a very satisfactory person. Believe me, I don't like myself much.'

'Don't you? I like you so much that I make up for it. Don't worry, we'll come through together.'

He walked home that evening with his mind full of her. His footsteps rang out clear and sharp against the frosty ground and seemed to beat out questions to which he could find no answers. He wondered how far he might help her, wondered if there was any way in which he could prove the other man unworthy of the half-regretful affection which she gave him. That wouldn't really help, because in the proving—if it were possible—he would find an element of self-indulgence, and Angela would realise it. In exposing his rival he would, of necessity, injure himself in her eyes.

'It will pass,' Max said softly, 'it must. Every time I can manage to speak of him, think of him sanely, as something which doesn't belong to the present, I've made a step forward. Gradually, he'll become unreal, dim, and then sink down into the water and be forgotten and not leave even a bubble on the surface. After all, I'm a fortunate fellow, I mustn't expect too much from the gods . . .'

At Christmas, Emmanuel spoke of their wedding. He was impatient, and suggested that they might be married early in January.

'Jenuary,' he said, one evening when Angela and Max were sitting with him in the big dining-room, 'Jenuary is a nice time. The South of Frence is an ideal place for a honeymoon. Even further—Efrica—follow the sun.'

Max watched Angela's face, saw that she pressed her hand against her mouth, suddenly, and held it there. She didn't want to marry him so soon. Very coolly he said, 'January, eh? I don't know. Perhaps Angela couldn't be ready so soon.'

Emmanuel said, 'Ready! Of course she can be ready! Get most t'ings in Peris as you go through.'

'I don't think January is a particularly nice month for a wedding,' Angela said, 'it's so cold. I don't want to be a bride with a red nose, Emmanuel. The papers make brides look sufficiently hideous without taking a hand in the process oneself.'

'The papers?' Emmanuel repeated. 'You're not going to wait for the papers to do you justice, are you? They never will—they aren't able.'

She smiled. 'Very pretty, darling. But all the same—I don't want a chilly wedding. You'd wear a coat with a fur collar and look like a blue-faced impresario. Let's wait for

warm weather, when you will look your very beautiful
best. Then if I change my mind at the last minute, I can
leave Max at the altar steps and marry you instead.'

'Poof!' he smiled back, 'I don't know that Max is right to
get married in a church at all. Why shouldn't you be
married in a synagogue?'

'Because I'm not a Jewess, and because Max doesn't care.
It's my wedding, and I'm not going to be at a disadvantage
on that day. I shouldn't know where I was, or what was
expected of me. All your Jewishness is tradition, I don't
believe that any of you have been inside a synagogue for
years.'

As Max drove her home, he said, without turning his eyes
towards her, but with them fixed on the road before him,
'You don't want to be married in January? It's too soon,
eh?'

He heard her quick indrawn breath before she answered, 'It is—awfully soon, Max, isn't it?'

'Too soon?'

'Yes, I'm afraid so.'

'I don't see what we have to wait for, after all.' He felt
that tonight he wanted things settled, felt that his hopes
had become insistent, his love too strong for waiting.

'We have to wait—for me, Max,' she said. 'Oh, my dear,
don't let's go into it all again! I don't want to spoil things,
I don't want to come to you with reservations and in-
completeness. I do want everything to be perfect.'

'I may be all wrong,' Max said, 'but it seems a pity that
all this can't be explained. I must wait—indefinitely—while
my father, your mother, and everyone else, look upon me
as some kind of curiously cold, undemonstrative fish.'

He knew that she moved away from him, that her arm
ceased to press against him. When she answered even her
voice seemed distant, removed.

'Very well, Max. Tell them—I don't mind. If it will
make you happier or more content. It might be easier to
end things now—then you can tell everyone anything you
wish, and have no scruples.'

He laughed miserably. 'And what would you do?'

'Do I come into it? I should do whatever I wished—as
you did.'

'I'm talking nonsense,' Max said. 'It's not likely that I'm
going to risk driving you back to that blackguard, is it?'

'Doesn't it strike you that—you are driving me back,
when you talk like this? That's just what you are doing,

Max,' her voice became soft and appealing, 'Max, don't, my dear, don't. I'm trying so hard, and it's so damned difficult. I've got a duty to you, and a duty to myself. I only want to be certain of myself. It would be quite easy to allow you all to make me rush into things. If there are difficulties, bad patches, let's get them over before—not have to face them afterwards. Can't you see that?'

'Duty! It's a poor substitute for love, Angela.'

'It would be, if I offered it as a substitute. I don't.'

'As a kind of makeweight, then. God! how I loathe sharing you!'

'You don't, Max. What is yours is all and entirely yours. The other—it all happened before you and I loved each other, really loved each other. The love I give you is growing—it's alive; the other—oh, can't you see that I'm only waiting for it to die?'

'The prolonged illness and the evident strength of the patient make it a little difficult,' he said. 'In addition, I have to face the possibility of a recovery, haven't I?'

'I think that love, when it begins to die, is the one thing that never recovers. And when it's dead—Max, it's the deadest thing in the world.'

He stopped the car at the door of her house. 'Well, let's hope that one morning you can ring up and tell me that the blinds are down,' he said. 'It would be even nicer if I could hear that he—and does it ever strike you that I don't even know his name?—was lying inside a house where the blinds were drawn. Nicer still, if I could have had a hand in killing him.'

'Good night, Max.'

'Good night, Angela'. He made no attempt to get out, only sat there waiting for her to go. He felt that everything was hiding behind a hot scarlet fog, that neither he nor Angela were quite real. The whole thing was an elaborate dream. Presently he would wake and shiver at the remembrance of the hate which had shaken him. He leant over and opened the door. She sat still for a moment, then pulled her coat more closely round her and got out.

Max thought, 'She's going—I can't let her go—I must speak to her.' He made a violent effort, felt that he forced himself to wake, and speak.

'Angela—Angela!'

'Yes, Max.'

He got out and stood beside her. 'My dear, forgive me!

It's only that I get so desperately hurt. It's as if this—this fear waited for me, sprang at me and got me by the throat. Sometimes I can fight it, but tonight I hadn't any strength left. I do try so hard, Angela. I do want you so badly.'

She lifted her hands and held the fur collar of his coat, looking up at him, her face white under the glare of the street light.

'Poor Max, I do understand. I do love you so much. I want peace and safety so much too. I'm certain that my way is the only way to find them. Don't let fear come into it—fear and hate make so many things possible. And, Max, don't talk of killing—I can't bear it. I feel that you're killing me.'

'Angela—marry me soon—next week—don't wait for anything. Let me take care of you—I'll keep you safe always.'

For a moment he fancied that she was going to agree, he knew that she came nearer to him, held him more tightly, then her hands lost their grip, and she moved away.

'Max, please,' her voice shook a little as she spoke, 'please don't. It's tempting me too far. I'm not strong enough to fight against it. Not yet—trust me that the moment,' she laughed, 'the blinds are really down, I'll marry you. Are you coming in?'

'May I—just for a minute or two?'

She turned to the table in the hall, while he took off his coat, and began to sort the letters which had come by the late post, talking as she did so.

'Mother is dining with Rachel and Hermann, I wish the wretched Government would give Rachel the vote. She's wearing herself out fighting for it. William has gone to watch a fight—I think I should like to see a fight, Max. Carpentier and Bombardier Wells—someone like that. Would you take me? Charles says that . . .' she broke off suddenly and Max saw that she held a letter in her hand, saw, too, that it was bearing a foreign stamp. Then her voice went on, evenly again, 'Charles says that if they allow a black man . . .'

Max said, 'It's all right, Angela, read it. Let's go and sit down. It's cold here.'

In the drawing-room, she stood by the fire balancing the letter in her hand, as if she weighed the contents. Max lit a cigarette, watching her as he did so.

'Give me one, Max. Thanks—that's lit.'

He said again, 'It's all right. Read it.'

'Don't you mind?'

'Not more than I mind it coming to you at all.'

She went over to the window, he heard the sound of the envelope being torn open, the rustle of paper, then sat in silence, staring into the fire. Once he heard her turn a page, and then came the crackle of paper crushed suddenly.

She came back and stood before him. Max looked up and tried to keep the fear from his eyes.

'I can say, "It's all right," ' she said. 'Don't worry, Max. The blinds are coming down, they're almost down now.' She made an impatient movement, and began to speak as if she expostulated with someone. 'Oh, I hate cowards, perhaps because I'm one myself. But whining—I loathe whining. Be sorry, regret things—but either put them right, or don't whine. No, not you, Max, I was thinking aloud. You know women still worship heroes—or the men they believe to be heroes. There's a good deal to be said for the "strong silent man" after all.'

He managed to smile as he spoke. 'Regretting things, Angela?'

'Don't we all regret pleasant things, happy things that are over? Even if there are lots of other even more pleasant and happier things waiting. I hate to see the curtain come down on a play that I've loved, even though I may be going to an even better one the next night. Besides, Max—and oh, don't be hurt!—the first things always seem so wonderful. Perhaps because one had no knowledge—no power to make comparisons. Ignorance made one believe that it was bliss.'

'You're a cruel little beggar, aren't you?' he said.

'Am I? I don't mean to be. Perhaps I'm only talking to myself most of the time. I wish I had been made so that I could hate—nice, easy, whole-hearted hate. The kind that only wants a little puff of wind to make it blaze into a flaming fire. I add up mental accounts and say, "Yes, that debt to me is so much. It ought to be paid. It shall be paid!" Then I remember that I *did* borrow a sum here and a sum there, and was given presents this day and that day. I add it all up again, and see that there's nothing owing on either side, and that it's ridiculous to try to extract payment, when there isn't any debt.'

'You're a long way from me tonight, Angela,' Max

said. 'I think those letters always pull you away from me,
don't they?'

She nodded. 'Perhaps. That's why I must wait until
they don't pull any longer. Yet, do believe this—I'd do
anything in the world to make you happy. Anything.'

'Would you?'

Again she nodded. 'Yes.'

'You can—if you mean that. Write and say that these
letters must end, write and say that it's all over and
done with. Or let me write and say it for you. Promise me
that you'll never see him again, never read another line he
writes to you. You can do that.'

'That wouldn't be any use. That would be leaving things
still alive. That wouldn't kill anything. I should remember,
and you'd know that I remembered. I want things dead
and done with. I don't only want to turn my eyes away,
and run the risk of one day looking back and finding that
they were still beautiful. Writing, as you ask, might please
you, or you might try to believe that it did, but it wouldn't
change me.'

Max came closer and took her hands in his, he bent
down and looked into her eyes.

'Perhaps you're right,' he said. 'I'm trusting you. I'm
trusting my whole life to you. I've put it in your hands.
Do what you can with it, and don't hurt me more than you
can help. Help me to believe that whatever you do, you
love me, and want to marry me—one day. Try to keep
close to me, don't let things pull you away too far, my
dearest.'

She took her hands from his and laid them on his shoulders, pulling down his head until his mouth met hers. Max
felt her lips on his, felt their soft pressure not once but
many times, as if she could not bear to let him go.

'My dearest . . .' she whispered, 'I'm so afraid that you
may get tired of waiting, that I may lose you. Don't let
me lose you, Max. I'd die. I've thought so often about it all,
I get muddled, half crazy with fear—for you, for myself.
I don't trust myself sometimes, you know. It's all the un-
certainty. I've even thought of asking you to take me
away, asking you to—live with me, to see if that would
help. I wondered if I were your mistress, if that might kill
everything. But I daren't. I was so afraid that I should
remember too much, that it wouldn't be only me and you
but you and me and—someone else.' She caught her
breath in a little gasping sob. 'But I've always been certain

of one thing. It would never be any use going back to him and trying to forget you. I couldn't do that, Max—ever. I couldn't watch the blinds come down—for you. They never would—never.'

'Poor baby,' Max said, 'it's pretty awful—for both of us. Just tell me that you are certain that it's going to be all right one day. Give me that to take home with me.'

'It's going to be all right, Max. Soon—now, quite soon.'

Book Four
❦

The House of Gallantz

19

At the end of April Max went to America to decorate and furnish one of those impossibly luxurious houses which are the dwelling-places, if not actually the homes, of millionaires.

In many ways he was glad to go. He had begun to feel the strain of an engagement which was prolonged for a reason which was known only to Angela and himself. When he was with her he found it difficult to forget what held them apart, the consciousness made a barrier between them. Max found that he grew to attribute every change of mood in Angela to the arrival or non-arrival of those letters from abroad. He was not able to accept the fact that she was gay, without adding the mental note that no letter had arrived that morning. If she was silent, if she seemed absorbed or tired, he immediately concluded that he knew the cause of her depression. The thought filled him with anger and hatred, which made itself evident in his words, which influenced all he said and did.

When he told her that he was going to America, she seemed quite content and made no protest.

'You're not sorry that I'm going?'

'In one way, terribly sorry. In another—oh, Max, can't

you see how dreadfully difficult things are growing. Perhaps I shall manage better alone. Perhaps you'll come back and find me clamouring for a wedding.'

He frowned. 'Things haven't been easy, have they? I haven't found them easy.'

She sat very still, and to Max it seemed that she was waiting for something, seemed that she listened intently, as if trying to catch some faint sound. When she spoke her voice was very quiet.

'I'm happier than you are,' she said, 'because I keep saying—"It's coming; any minute now I shall know it's all over." Every day it's easier to look forward and not look back. Doesn't that help, Max?'

'Yes, it helps.'

The night before he sailed, he dined with her. Emmanuel had wanted a huge farewell dinner, and not all Max's protestings would move him. He outlined his plan to Angela; she listened and smiled.

'Lovely,' she said. 'I do hope it goes off well, and you'll all enjoy yourselves.'

'I hope that you and Max will enchoy it, too.'

'We shan't be able to accept the invitation, darling. We're going off on our own somewhere to dine.'

'But I'm giving this dinner for you both!'

'It's sweet of you, but—it's his last night. Emmanuel, if you were Max, wouldn't you want your young woman to yourself, your last night in England?'

Emmanuel pursed his lips. 'Perheps—but perheps I should be glad to show her off to a lot of people! Like to see her making a big splesh!'

'Ah,' she said, 'that's because you're still terribly Oriental. Max is—what is it?—Occidental, isn't it? Put off your dinner, darling, or make it the night before you planned and we'll both come to it and be shown off properly and behave prettily.'

So they dined together at a quiet restaurant, and Max felt for the first time for months that things were well between them. She was gay and happy, she laughed and talked, asked questions and was obviously interested in his replies.

'I don't believe you mind my going a bit,' he said, 'I haven't seen you so happy for months!'

The smile died from her lips, he fancied that she looked round nervously as if she expected to see someone standing at her elbow.

'S-sh!' she whispered, 'don't, Max.' She leant nearer and

whispered, 'I'm almost afraid to remember that—it's almost over, darling, almost finished, and when you come back—oh, my dear, I'm so sick of waiting. It's going to be wonderful—a new, clean, bright world just for us.'

'You mean that?'

'I mean it. Max, suppose I told you that I wanted to go back, just once. No, don't interrupt me, listen. Wanted to go back to prove to myself, and to—other people. You wouldn't mind too much, would you?'

'Go back,' he said, stupidly, 'Angela, not go back, my dear!'

'I shouldn't go unless I was certain. Quite, quite certain. I might want to—make a kind of formal burial, a state funeral.'

'Suppose you weren't certain when you got there?'

'I should never want to go unless I were. I couldn't risk it. I love you too much. I'm not deciding irrevocably, Max. Only just—providing for a contingency, that's all. Could you bear it?'

'I don't know—it's difficult. It's not that I shouldn't trust you, but I couldn't trust him. I've watched you so often, known that pity—your pity—springs up so easily.' He rubbed the end of his cigarette on the plate before him. 'Angela, I'll put off going for twenty-four hours. Marry me before I go.'

'Then—you could trust me to go to Vienna?'

He stammered a little, 'Trust you—I've told you that I do that already—told you it's not you—it's other things . . .'

'The other things would still exist even if I were married to you.'

'Yes, but—I don't know—it would be different.'

She laid her hand on his. 'Max, dearest,' she said, 'what you're trying to say and getting so uncomfortable about is this. If I were married to you, I should belong to you. That's what you're trying to say. I should have been yours —physically. My dear, I'm yours now—mentally and spiritually. The other surely isn't nearly so important, is it?'

He frowned and made an impatient gesture. 'I know,' he said, 'I know that is the answer, and you're right, absolutely right, but—I don't know—I can't explain, it's no good trying to.'

'You know that mentally and spiritually I'm yours, Max, absolutely, that no one else comes into it—except a stupid little bit of regret or remembrance or sentiment that I am

trying to kill as quickly as I can. You know it's that weak
place in my armour that prevented us being married
months ago. So long as that is there, I won't and can't
marry you. I love you too much. I shan't go to Vienna
until that has gone, disappeared, healed. For my sake and
for yours. If I do go, I shall go armed so well that nothing
can touch me. Perhaps going at all is only a gesture—I
don't know. It seems to me that it might be a final con-
firmation for me, it would make me so certain, so sure.'
She spoke more softly, so that her words came to him in a
whisper. 'Max—before I didn't know, I was foolish, I made
things possible—and I didn't love you as I do now. I can
safeguard myself. If I can fight the mental side, surely the
—other isn't difficult. I'm not a sensualist. I couldn't bear
to give myself to any man except you in the whole world.'

'Couldn't you . . .' he stared at her, his eyes worried and
troubled. 'You mean that?'

'You know that I mean it. But now—yet—I can't marry
you. I want just a little longer. It's better to wait just a
short time, and be certain. I won't let either you or myself
be tied and then remember and regret and ruin everything. Listen, Max, I've given you everything that I have to
give—because I loved you and believed in you and trusted
you. Everything but—that one thing. We're terribly close,
even when we quarrel; we're still loving each other all the
time. You've made sacrifices for me—oh, I've noticed them
all, and loved you for each one. You've let me fight this in
my own way, and I'm grateful. I only want you to let me
finish the fight in my own way, I want to crown myself
the victor. If it will make you happier, make you believe
in me more firmly—I'll give you the only thing I haven't
given you, tonight.'

Max lifted his eyes and stared at her again, unbelieving,
almost afraid.

'You mean . . .?'

'Darling,' she said, 'you know perfectly well what I
mean. Don't be difficult. Only—if you tell me that it will
make you happier, that's my only reason. You know me
well enough for that.'

'And you'd marry me when I came back from the
States?'

'The moment I was quite, quite certain.'

'But—Good God!—you'd hate me if I said, "Yes".'

'Hate you? My dear, should I offer such a thing if I

thought your saying "Yes" would make me hate you? I want to make you happier, that's all.'

Max wiped his forehead and then began to twist his handkerchief into a rope with nervous fingers. She saw him lick his lips, drink his wine as if he was parched with thirst. When he spoke his voice was husky.

'I'm afraid . . .' he said. 'I've got so much. Your love ought to be enough. I might lose you if I said yes. I daren't lose you, Angela.'

'You shan't lose me, darling. I promise you that.'

'You—you wouldn't love me less?'

'Why should I?'

He was nervously clasping and unclasping his hands, his eyes turned from her, his face white. 'It ought not to make any difference, but—I don't know—somehow, it does when you love anyone as I love you. It's illogical, it's not very commendable, but there it is! You do love me enough because it's a big sacrifice, I know that.'

'Is it? I'm glad to be able to make a sacrifice for you.'

'You're not afraid?'

'Terrified, Max—but dreadfully anxious to make you happy.'

He stopped twisting his hands together, sat upright and looked at her, the strained look gone from his face. She smiled at him, serene, confident, very young, very lovely, and full of courage. Suddenly the gravity left his face, and he smiled back at her.

'Oh, darling,' he said, 'that was a close call. I wonder if the devil is ever tempted by angels—how he must hate himself! I don't think I even began to love you until this minute—darling, beloved, wonderful Angela. What have you got that the fairies gave you as an extra birthday present? I'll tell you—it's a touchstone for turning rather inferior love into something that's like Blake's tiger—burning bright. Burning with a very clear, sharp flame, darling. Listen—you must go anywhere, at any time you wish—I don't say that I shall like it. I can't promise that I shan't go through hell; but I believe you know better than I do. You're wise, my dearest, terribly, abominably, uncannily wise.'

'Max . . .' She smiled still, but her eyes were puzzled.

'Sweetheart, I'm only very inferior stuff after all,' he said, 'but I do try to live up to you. Say you forgive me . . .'

'There isn't anything to forgive.'

'Isn't there? I wonder . . . You've made me feel even less satisfied with myself than I was before. Very good for me.'

'I seem to have made rather a mess of things,' she said. 'Sorry, Max.'

'Blessed—I adore you.'

She looked round the restaurant, throwing back her head as if she felt the air oppressive. 'Max, couldn't we get out of here? It's hot, there are too many people. It's cold outside, but the car is closed. Let's drive out where there are trees and open places—this is so near, all the time. The walls are so dreadfully close.'

She lay back in the corner of the car, while it carried them out of London, towards the open fields of Kent, where the keen air cut like a knife, and came clean and sweet from the hills. A few miles outside Sevenoaks Max stopped, and they sat in silence watching the stars over the bare tree-tops.

'Max . . .' she said at last, 'I'm afraid I was just childish and rather silly. But I did mean what I said, and I don't want you to make any more sacrifices for me. You've made enough. You're sure you're not making one now, not being—just noble?'

He slipped his arm round her. 'Of course, I'm making a sacrifice,' he said, 'but only sacrificing the rather more unpleasant side of me. Not the Max that I care for you to know, darling.'

Her head lay on his shoulder, and in the half light of the stars he found her lips and kissed her. She moved nearer to him, and lay in his arms, quiet and content.

'Happy, Angela?'

'I'm with you, Max.'

'Damn the United States of America!'

'Yes,' her voice was sleepy, 'oh, yes—damn them!'

Max sat very still, listening to the sound of her breathing. When, at last, he switched on the light and looked at the clock, he found that it was almost two o'clock. Gently he took his arms from her and laid her back, covering her with the rug, tucking her up as he might have tucked up a child. Once she opened her eyes and smiled at him, murmuring, 'Oh, don't wake me—Max—what did you say?— damn the United States.'

He turned the car and drove back to London. She did not move until they were crossing Westminster Bridge, when she sat up suddenly wide awake and asked what the time was.

'A quarter to three, sleepy head.'

'Oh, Lord! We shall have to tell lies and say we've been dancing. You can't say that I've been asleep, it sounds so uncomplimentary to you.'

'Asleep for nearly three hours—more, quite a lot more.'

'And it's today, and you sail this morning. Poor Max! Poor Angela.'

'Ah, tonight made a great many things easier, darling.'

She snuggled against his arm as they drove up Park Lane. 'It was nice and happy, wasn't it?' Suddenly she laughed softly. Max glanced at her and asked why.

'I don't think I ought to tell you. If I wasn't quite abandoned I couldn't . . . It's my unfortunate sense of humour, Max.'

'Go on, tell me.'

'I did keep part of my promise,' she said, 'I did stay with you all night, didn't I?'

The next morning at breakfast, her mother asked her where she and Max had been the night before. 'I heard you come in. My dear, it was dreadfully late. After three.'

'Dancing, Mother.'

William looked up from bacon and eggs. 'Dancing—where?'

'A place you don't know,' Angela said, 'a perfectly good new place. I'm not giving it away or by the time Max comes home it will be overrun by you and your mob, Bill dear.'

On July 20th, Angela announced that she was going to Vienna. Her mother, wide-eyed and a little anxious, said, 'To work, darling? But I thought you and Max were going to be married! Max won't like you beginning to work again, will he?'

'Not going to work, angel, just going to clear up some bits and pieces. I'm only staying for a week. Max is going to meet me in Paris on the way home.'

'Max is going to meet you in Paris? Angela, is that quite—quite nice?'

'I think it's lovely, Mother.'

'Quite—convenable?'

'Oh, that! Yes, for me and Max, it is. I shall stay at one hotel, and Max will stay at the Edouard Sept, where he always stays. All quite nice and conventional, bless you.'

When she told Emmanuel, he started and said, very slowly, 'Peris—thet's where you are going to meet Max, eh? Enchela, I don't like Peris very much. One gets disappointed in Peris—I don't know why. Why don't you meet him, or let him meet you in Vienna?'

'I don't want him to come to Vienna, Emmanuel.'

'Lausanne?'

'Right off his track, darling. Besides, I want to see Paris with Max.'

He sighed, 'All right, hev it your own way. Then when you get back, you'll get married?'

Her face was all alight as she answered. Emmanuel saw the change and decided that Max was a lucky fellow.

'Almost at once—so find us a beautiful house, Emmanuel. Not too big, but terribly nice. That will keep you nicely employed until I come back.'

Max, in the huge New York Hotel, read her letter. He sat with his shoulders hunched, his eyes anxious and apprehensive. He was very thin, the heat had tried him, and the work had been very heavy and worrying. Now, he had booked his passage home and her letter had come. He read it for the third time.

'. . . . Don't worry, my dear, I am only going to finish the burial arrangements. It's all over, Max, and the coast is clear for us. This visit is only to "put the lid" on everything, to tie off the ends, and make the announcement to all my friends that I am going to marry you. Then, with that lid firmly soldered down, I shall come to meet you in Paris. You get there on the 28th, and I shall arrive the same day. Don't come to meet me. Let me go to my hotel first —the Meurice, which Emmanuel believes to be the only hotel in Paris fit for me—and then I will come to you. I want to shed everything I have worn in Vienna—every single thing—and then we can begin, really and truly begin. Don't be unhappy, don't worry, I have learnt so much wisdom, and I do know myself so well now. Just believe that July 28th is the first day of a new world for both of us.'

Max sailed on the 21st. He remembered that that was the day upon which she was to leave for Vienna. Vienna—he wiped his forehead, and pushed the thoughts which rose in his brain away from him. On the boat he feverishly filled every moment. He played deck games, he bet on the ship's daily run, he played cards and always won.

'Lucky fellow you are, Gollantz!'

'I suppose I am lucky, yes.'

An American shifted his cigar to the other corner of his mouth and said, 'What's the old saying? Lucky in cards—unlucky in love, eh?'

Max picked up his cards and sorted them with intense concentration. The wretched old saw ran in his head like a tune. Unlucky in love. He tried to lose that night, took risks, overcalled, bluffed—and still won. He went to his cabin miserable, anxious, and feeling that sleep was miles away. The voyage was a nightmare. His brain never ceased to wonder, and speculate. When he slept it was only to be terrified by nightmares, to wake sweating with fear. Angela in Vienna—with him—alone—saying that she was going to be married. He imagined scenes, imagined that her resolution grew weaker under protestations, pleadings, and arguments. He saw her remembering the things that had once been wonderful, looking back on them with regret, trying to put the clock back.

The morning of the 28th—Max sat in the carriage *en route* for Paris. Paris meant Angela—meant the end of his torture. Perhaps a letter would be waiting for him. She might be in Paris now, that moment. Or—his brain seemed to contract—suppose she wasn't there? Suppose circumstances had been too strong for her, and she had stayed in Vienna? Suppose—she daren't come back? Suppose that a letter was waiting, telling him that same story that she had tried to tell him once before on the Western Road?

'Pretty beastly, Max.'

Then his own words, months later. 'It's not that I don't trust you, I don't trust him.' What a fool he had been to let her go. He might have cabled and begged her to wait. Now—it would be too late. He put his hand to his mouth to stop himself talking aloud, he wanted to shout, to curse, blaspheme. His face felt cold when he touched it. He got up and stared at himself in the mirror on the carriage wall. His reflection stared back at him, white faced, the mouth half-open as if he had been running and still panted for breath, his eyes fixed and glazed. Not a real face—the sort of face you saw in the papers when they published photographs of murderers. A face which was brutal, and half-mad—a mad murderer. Max sat down again, and again wiped his face.

'A mad murderer. If she's not there, no one shall stop me. I'll spend my life finding him—to kill him.'

He knew that he whispered the words over and over,

clenching his hands as if they gripped the throat of a man, as if they were squeezing the life out of a human being, the thumbs pressing inwards, the fingers curved and constraining.

With a great effort he leant back and rang the bell for the waiter.

When the door opened the waiter appeared through a haze. Max rubbed his eyes and wondered where the man had come from.

'Bring me some brandy,' he said, 'very quickly.'

The brandy made things less terrible, the edges were blunted. After another he felt almost normal. Paris. He gave his luggage to a porter and went to the buffet. Paris was going to be difficult, she might not be there. That would be horrible; the waiting would twist him a bit. Two more brandies might dull the edges of things again.

The hotel. He asked if there was a letter waiting for him. Some letters had been taken to his room. Any telephone message? None—they would enquire. Max said:

'No, don't enquire. You've reserved me a sitting-room as well as a bedroom? Then send up a bottle of brandy, and if anyone calls . . .' he stopped.

'I don't think anyone will call,' then turned and went up to his room. He looked at the letters, the writing moved up and down as he watched it. Angela—from Vienna. He sat down and held it in his hand. He was shaking. He poured out some brandy and drank it, then looked at the letter again. From Vienna. How did he know what was in the letter? It might be the end of everything. It would be. That was why she had written from there. To tell him. He laid the letter down—he daren't read it—not yet—it must wait . . .

An hour later, he heard someone knocking at the door. He lifted his head and called out that he didn't want to see anyone, he wanted to be left alone. The door opened. Max sprang to his feet, leaning against the table. Angela saw him—tall, white-faced, with eyes that stared, swaying as he stood; saw his mouth half-open, stupid and uncontrolled.

'Max . . .' she said, 'Max, darling, what is it?'

He said, 'Don't tell me—I know about it—I—I—I'll go and kill him.'

She came over to where he stood, put her hands on his shoulders and pushed him back into his chair.

'My poor sweetheart,' she said, 'oh, Max, I'm so sorry, I

didn't know it would be so difficult for you. There—it's all right. I'm back with you. It's all over. I'm quite, quite safe. Look at me, Max, look at me.'

He fumbled to find her hands and held them. 'I'm half mad,' he said.

She bent down and laid her head against his. 'Not even half mad, Max, only—you poor darling—very, very drunk. It's all right. I know what to get for you. What a blessing that I have a brother who goes to dinners in the City!'

She rang, gave her orders, and turned back to Max. He sat, his head pillowed on his arms; she bent down and listened, then smiled. He was asleep.

20

Max gathered the papers together and handed them to his secretary.

'As soon as you can let me have them, please.'

'Yes, Mr. Max.'

'I should like everything cleared up before Bank Holiday.'

'Yes, Mr. Max.

As the girl went out, Frank came in. He nodded to her, said, 'Hello, Miss Gibbons. Max slave-driving you as usual. Why don't you strike?'

He didn't wait for her answer. Frank never did wait for answers to anything. He came forward and sat down by the desk.

Max shook his head. 'No time, my son, this morning. Working like a black!'

Frank said, 'That's all right. Listen to me, when are you and Angela going to be married?'

'August the 20th. And we don't want a silver salver, Frank. We've got three already.'

'I wasn't altogether wondering about your wedding presents. Max, I should hurry things along a bit if I was you. Morrie and I are being tied up tomorrow at ten.

Registrar's office at Marylebone. P'raps it's a bit different for us. I shall be shoved out pretty quick, y'know.'

'Shoved out!' Max said. 'You're not taking this scare seriously?'

Frank lit a cigarette and grinned. 'N-n-no! Dear Uncle Max—not likely. A storm in a haystack or whatever it is. My lad, it's here! I know. I hear things, and that's why Morrie and I are taking no chances.'

Max looked at his nephew. He was a handsome fellow, a decent lad for all his love of amusement and his apparent dislike of anything approaching work. He said, 'Your grandfather will be very angry, you know. He'll say that both you and Morrie are too young. He's right, you're only twenty-two, and she's—what? twenty-one. It's non-sense, Frank. Crazy nonsense. Like one of those rags that you and Morrie indulge in!'

'All right. I tell you, I don't intend to go away—and it's a cert that I shall go—and leave Morrie kicking her heels round town without some kind of a contract to keep her. It's here—right here—now. In another three days—whew!—we shall be in it up to the neck. Better rush that wedding of yours, Max.'

'You're going to tell your grandfather?'

Frank grinned. 'I'm so damned busy, that I thought you might do that job for me. Break it gently, start by saying how I've improved, and how I yearn for responsibility. That's your ticket, Max.'

Emmanuel was very angry. He said that every man who assumed that war would come was a traitor. He stated that both Frank and Morrie were irresponsible chil-dren, and that he should attend the ceremony at the regis-trar's office and declare it illegal.

'Is Frank at home? He is? Then send for him at once. I will not hev him hiding behind you, Max. Listen to that once and for always, please.' Frank came, he lounged against the door-post and grinned, utterly unrepentant.

'Well, Grandfather—why the turmoil, shemozzle, or row?'

Emmanuel faced him scowling. 'Frank,' he said, 'I hev to forbid this nonsense going further. Never in all my life did I hear of such—such stuff! War—and with whom, will you please tell me?'

'Pretty well everyone, I fancy, sir. Germany's just aching to have a cut at us, and Austria will join her.'

'Now, that I know,' Emmanuel said, heavily sarcastic,

'now that Sir Edward Grey hes told me, I will go on. To assume a war is coming is to be a traitor—do you know that? You don't, well, that's why I tell you. And how will marriage with a little girl help t'ings suppose that there should be a war? What will you and Morrie live upon? Perhaps you t'ink upon me, I shouldn't wonder?'

'I think that you'll help materially, sir. Morrie is twenty-one, she's got pots of money.'

'You'd live on your wife! Thet's very pretty, Frank.'

'Not live on, sir—only fifty-fifty.'

'She is a child. So are you.'

'She's just a year younger than Angela. You're all bursting your collars for Angela to marry Max!'

'What is this—bursting collars?' Emmanuel said. 'I don't ever burst mine. Frank, I forbid it. Once and for always—I will not hev it.'

Frank stood upright, and came over to his grandfather's chair. He sat on the edge of the desk and looked down at him.

'Listen,' he said, 'and this is going to be awfully private and awfully important. I'm a soldier, and whether you like it or don't like it, there is going to be a war. Now wars are nasty, sticky things—all sorts of things and all sorts of people get into sticky messes. Men go away, and they do all kinds of queer things, and women get left at home and do a damn sight queerer. That's what Morrie and I are after—playing for safety. You see, we're very fond of each other. I don't think she's an archangel, as Max thinks Angela. She doesn't think I'm Galahad as Angela does Max.

'When I saw what was blowing up—people talk, y'know, and we hear things—she said that if it came to anything like a show, we'd get married first. Candidly, I wasn't terribly keen. We're having a jolly good time as we are, and we are both pretty young. But when Morrie talked—and believe me when Morrie gets going she has Christabel Pankhurst licked to a frazzle—I saw that she had got a real idea. I stopped in my mad career and listened, and gave in. She's right, oh, she's so dead right. Believe me—that's twice I've said that—and Grandpoppa, when you're a bit older and know more of women, you'll realise that when a woman wants to do anything—it's better to down tools and let her have her own way. If you don't nothing but trouble comes of it.'

He stopped and laughed. 'That's all badly done. Honest

Injun, I'm awfully fond of Morrie, and she likes me quite a lot.'

Emmanuel, his head in his hand, said, 'Awfully fond—likes you quite a lot. Ah! Might that perheps mean that you're in love with each other?'

'You might take it, sir, that it does.'

'What a generation! I cannot imagine saying anything like that to your adored grendmother! Well, Frank—hev it your own way. I shan't come, because I don't like hole-and-side marriages at r-register offices. But come here afterwards and we'll breakfast together.'

'Bless you, my child,' Frank said, 'I'll go and break the glad tidings to my bride. No doubt she is sitting at home shivering with apprehension.'

'More likely,' Emmanuel said, 'she is dining at a restaurant, preparatory to going on to a night club.'

When the door closed, he turned to Max.

'You're not going to hurry on your marriage, Max?'

'I don't think it's necessary, Father. I'm not a soldier, and even if this scare is more than a scare I don't anticipate that I should be wanted. Do you?'

Emmanuel shook his head. 'I don't know,' he said, slowly, 'I can't see. If it comes—it will be very, very difficult for us. You see, I'm not English, you're not quite English. But we shall hev to stand by the people who hev been our friends for all these years.'

Frank went to France on the 18th of August. Emmanuel went down to the station with Max and Morrie. Morrie, very excited, very talkative, and very white round the lips. Emmanuel, it seemed to Max, leant more heavily on his stick than he had done a week before. He struck Max for the first time as an old man, and a very tired old man at that.

Frank laughed a good deal, talked of rags and great times; Morrie laughed even louder, talked even faster.

'It's a great stunt,' Frank said, 'make the jolly old Hun waltz back to the tune of the "Blue Danube".'

Morrie said, 'That's not German, it's Austrian, you fool.'

'Near enough—they're all alien enemies.'

'Play it as a two step, then, not the old pom-pom waltz.'

Frank turned to Max. 'Keep your eye on my missus while I'm away.'

'He'll want both eyes, my son,' Morrie said, 'and he

won't want to take them off Angela. No, I shall shake a loose leg—two loose legs.'

Max caught Frank's eyes watching her, something in them made his heart contract a little, they were hungry and a little afraid.

'Damn pretty legs they are too, Morrie,' Frank said. 'I must go—we're off. Good-bye, Grandfather. Bye-bye, Max. Good-bye, Morrie—and have a good time. Write and tell me what you're doing and send me some new records every week.'

'I'll have a good time—take care of yourself, Frank. Manage some leave soon, won't you?'

'You bet I will!'

Driving home in the car, Morrie smoked hard. Once she looked out at a long line of soldiers marching, at the crowd watching them.

'Damn silly this war business,' she said, 'we're overdoing it, I think. People will get bored with it.'

Emmanuel said, 'I t'ink that is very likely, my dear. Terribly bored.'

The night before his wedding Max dined with the Drews. Gwen, when she left them, said gravely:

'Max, you must go early. Before twelve, you know. You mustn't see her on the wedding day until you meet in church. It's *so* unlucky.'

He closed the door behind her, and stood watching Angela in silence. Tomorrow . . . He sighed and came back to her, sat down, and took her hand in his.

'Well, sweetheart?' he said. 'I've got a confession to make.'

She smiled. 'Have you? It's the correct thing to do the night before you are married, isn't it? Go on, I'll try to be charitable.'

'I shall have to cut down our honeymoon, Angela.'

He felt her hand close more tightly on his. 'Go on, tell me.'

'This morning,' he said, 'O'Reilly has fixed a commission for me. Not actually fixed it himself—but through a man he knows.' He stopped, then said, 'I don't want to go in the least, Angela. I hate it.'

'I hate it too, Max. Only—you can't let Frank and Charles and Bill go, and stay at home, can you?'

'I feel it's a little inconsiderate of fate to engineer a war at this particular moment. I feel, too, that after all, other men don't have to leave *you*. That's what makes me kick.'

'I feel that it's easier for other women—who aren't married to you.' She laughed, softly. 'Oh, Max—if it wasn't so tragic, it would be funny. We've waited and waited, and you've been so patient and good, and now when everything was right—dead right—this comes. It's—it's not quite playing the game on Fate's part, is it? How long shall we have?'

'Ten days—ten whole days.'

'Ten days,' she said, 'it's not very long.' She threw back her head, as if flinging away thoughts which disturbed her. 'Well, let's make the best of it. One might as well make a virtue of necessity. Does Emmanuel know?'

'I told him today.'

'Emmanuel's getting old, Max,' she said. 'I always used to think that he had no age at all, that he was just—Emmanuel, that he would go on and on for ever, treading very lightly in his beautiful patent boots, with his gold-headed cane and his wonderful coats. Lately he's leant rather heavily on his cane, hasn't he?'

'Frank's going upset him more than he liked to show.'

'Frank's going upset Morrie more than she cared to show either.'

'Yes, poor kids. It's hard for my father, after all he isn't an Englishman. Somewhere—he may have a son fighting against us. I think he remembers that often.'

Angela nodded. 'Frank's father? How old is he?'

'Algy? He's—let me think—forty-two or three.'

'Ten years older than you are.'

Max said, 'Of course he may not be fighting, but it's rather a nightmare to think that I might have to kill my own brother or Frank—his father.'

'Would you know him again?'

Max considered for a moment. 'I think so. Not very tall, with fair hair that was a little too long, rather curly. Blue eyes—bright blue. Good hands, he used them a lot when he talked. Got it from my mother I think. A voice that sounded terribly energetic, vital—rather an impelling sort of voice. I saw him last when Frank was about eight. He was only about thirty then, but I believe I should know him. Algy was—probably still is—rather a bad hat, but he got me every time. Funny, fascinating fellow. He thought that he was going to set the Continent on fire—but we've never heard of him. I often wonder what he's doing now. Probably teaching young women to play the fiddle.'

He laughed. 'I don't know why we're wasting time talking about my brother, who isn't a very reputable person after all. Darling—what's the matter?'

'I think I'm tired. Excitement and rushing about. I've had to get so many clothes that I didn't want.' She came to him and put her arms round him. 'Max—don't leave me alone, I don't want you to go away—ever. Let the war rip, it's not our war. It's different for you—not like Bill and Charles, they're English, you're only half English. Stay in England with me. There are such lots of things you can do. They don't want every man to go. You speak dozens of languages—get O'Reilly to get you a job as Interpreter. No one can say anything when you're just married. Max, don't go, I can't bear it.'

'My dear, don't. Just think how you'd hate me.'

'I shouldn't. Think of Emmanuel, he's so old—he relies on you.'

'That's not fair, Angela. You're tired, all this damned dressmaking, and shopping. You'll feel quite differently tomorrow.'

She let her arms fall to her sides. 'All right. Let it go at that. I shouldn't have said it. It was mean.'

All the eagerness had gone from her voice, to Max it sounded dull and hopeless. She turned away and walked over to the piano, sat down and began to strum a ragtime tune. She didn't look at him, only hammered at the keys as if she was playing away her unhappiness. Max followed her and, leaning over the piano, watched her intently.

'You're glad that we are going to be married?'

Still playing, she answered, 'Terribly glad, Max.'

'Love me?'

'My dear, you're everything that really matters in the whole world. I'm twenty-two and you're thirty-three; but you're my child, my son as well as my lover. It's a funny complex feeling—makes me feel dreadfully old and dreadfully young.' The tune had changed, from the ragtime she had slipped into a little melody which came very softly and tenderly as an accompaniment to her words. 'That day in Paris, Max, I was so glad that I could take care of you, if only for a few hours. Poor miserable little Max—I felt like a mother who has found a lost child. Do you remember the night when I went to sleep in the car? When you held me close and kept me warm? That's what I want always. Hold me close—only just sometimes let me slip out and take care of you. Not for very long because I'm a selfish young woman and I like being taken care of myself.' She brought her hands down and crashed out chord after chord, triumphant and victorious. Then left the piano and came back to him. 'That's all right—I've played the devils to sleep. It's after eleven and you must go . . . My dear, tomorrow, and all the tomorrows that God sends! We're going to take life in our hands and make it give us happiness—aren't we? It doesn't matter what you've done before, or what I've done before—what we've felt or thought or feared. Tomorrow is the beginning, Max—the beginning of everything.'

The next day, Max stood waiting for her in a church which was strange to him, ready to listen to a service which he did not understand and which was no part of the religion of his fathers. He looked down the long, rather dark church, caught faces that he knew here and there. They had all come—Jews and Gentiles. The Jews anxious to make no mistakes, anxious to conform outwardly to the forms which the English church demanded; they were grave and courteous, attentive and very quiet, but Max felt that under everything, they were a little contemptuous.

Emmanuel, the light catching his white hair, his back less straight than Max remembered it a few months before, his eyes darting this way and that, his mouth soft and kindly. Max smiled at him, Emmanuel caught it and sent one flying back in return. Exquisite Emmanuel, Max thought, with a heart as white as his linen, and as soft as the beautiful *crêpe de Chine* handkerchief which showed in the breast pocket of his immaculate coat. He saw Rachel, splendid in purple satin, old and fat but retaining a great dignity. Wearing on her breast the badge which proved that she had suffered in prison for the Cause in which she believed. By her stood old Hermann, thin and stooping. Hermann had walked into church wearing his hat, and had been spoken to by one of the ushers. He had been terribly confused, even ashamed. Rachel had smiled and whispered to him. Max was sure that she had bidden him to bow the knee in the House of Rimmon.

He saw Charles Wilmot, strange in a new uniform with a broad leather belt and another strap which crossed his shoulder. Max felt that the new leather creaked when he moved, and that Charles got immense satisfaction from the sound. Morrie came down the aisle and sat next to Emmanuel, who smiled and took her hand in his for a moment. Her face was very white, her lips scarlet. Max could see the cosmetic on her eyelashes, and the mascara on the lids. Artificial and attractive, her smile a little forced, her eyes hard.

Gwen, with a crowd of Drews and Wilmots, followed by the cousins from Dorset and Gloucestershire. Tall women strode into church, entering the pews allotted to them and falling upon their knees devoutly, burying their faces in white kid-gloved hands. The men red-faced, the young ones in uniform, obviously envied by their elders. More Jews—Davises and Bernsteins, Lowensteins and Francks—resplendent, handsome and excited.

Terrence O'Reilly touched his arm. 'They're here—look.'

Down at the doorway, Max could see a sudden flutter, caught a glimpse of light dresses, of William Drew, solid and dependable, giving orders in a whisper which came sibilant up the church. People turning round; the little crowd at the door arranging itself, a mass of colours at the back—the bridesmaids, and in front someone in white, standing very still beside William.

He whispered to O'Reilly, 'Do I go and meet her?'

'No, you heathen, stand where you are and look pleasant.'

A priest—two priests—he remembered that one was George Wilmot, a cousin. Choir boys opening books, turning over pages. A new tune from the organ. Something about the Garden of Eden. The little procession moving up the church, everyone singing, the choir boys' mouths opening and shutting, emitting a piping noise. He turned and found that she was close to him. He took a step forward, and found her eyes watching him through her veil. He fancied that her mouth was grave, though her eyes smiled. O'Reilly dug him gently but firmly in the back with his finger and whispered something. Words—he tried to follow, but they all seemed mysterious. Too many of them—the priest talked for hours. He watched Angela. She stood quite still. Even her hands were steady. Max knew that his own shook a little.

'Max Emmanuel Julius . . .'

He had forgotten the 'Emmanuel' and 'Julius', the sound of them was unfamiliar, he felt that he was pretending to be someone else.

'Angela Gwendoline Mary . . .'

He couldn't hear what she said, it sounded like 'A-mum-mum-ey'. Probably they wouldn't be properly married now. That would be a nice business. He looked at her again. She had given her flowers to someone to hold, the veil was turned back from her face. Her hand was cool, he held it tightly. Then with unexpected suddenness they were walking away from the choir boys. He began to walk down the church, felt her hand on his arm, heard her whisper, 'This way, Max—to sign the register.'

He said, 'Oh, Lord, yes. I remember you told me.'

A voice like treacle saying, 'Here-ah, and here-ah, please. For the last time, Mrs. Gollantz—the last time!' Emmanuel writing his name, Gwen Drew writing hers, hundreds of people all signing their names. He stood wondering what happened next. Saw Emmanuel turn to Angela, hold out his hands.

She said, 'Darling—Max first, unless he hates the idea.'

He said, 'What idea, Angela?'

Her face held up to his, the loveliest face he had ever seen—radiant.

'Sweetness, don't be a perfect fool—kiss me!'

The organ again—louder than ever. Walking down the church, his hand in hers. People smiling, he felt that he grinned like an idiot. A crowd at the door, and Angela whispering, 'Run, Max—run. Never mind me, I'll make a bolt for it.'

In the car he sat back and looked at her. She laughed.

'I never hope again to see such a perfect ass of a bridegroom. Poor Terrence was almost crying!'

'It's the most awful ordeal I ever went through. Terrible —devastating.'

'It's considered necessary, Max.' Then she leant forward, 'Good morning, darling, and a happy new world to you!'

21

Angela sat in the drawing-room of the house which Emmanuel had found for them in St. John's Wood and yawned. She found life boring at the moment. Max was training in Lancashire, and even a long daily letter to him still left her with a good deal of time to occupy. Gwen had begged her to 'take up some work' and Angela had asked 'What work, Mummy?'

'Work in a hospital, or making bandages.'

Angela screwed up her eyes for a moment, then said, 'I don't think I want awfully to make bandages—or work in a hospital, dearest.'

Her mother had obviously been disappointed. 'Very well, my dear, only I should have thought that you would have liked to do something for the war.'

'Did you? No—I don't think that I do. I'd rather be free to see Max whenever he can come home.'

She remembered the conversation now, and clenched her hands suddenly. She wouldn't work in a hospital; she couldn't bear to watch wounded men, and think that one day, Max might be lying in one of those beds. She wouldn't make bandages or roll lint, and know that one of the bandages might be used to hold Max's life in his body. She didn't even want to feed and help to clothe Belgian refugees, who stammered tales of war and horror and made it all so terribly close.

She would stay at home, write long letters to Max, be at hand when he managed to put through a long-distance call, or free when he managed to get a few hours' leave and came tearing back to London.

Sitting there on an afternoon in October, her hands clenched, she tried to drive away by force all the terrors which came crowding in upon her. Repeating that Max was still in England, that he might never be wanted, that the war might end before he was called overseas.

Max—she smiled as she said his name very softly, then said again—'Max Emmanuel Julius' and thought how ridiculous it was that those names should belong to him —pretentious, high-sounding names, not a bit suitable for him. She remembered their wedding day, and the mess Max had made of the part which he had to play, remembered how he had muffed his positions, his words, his duty in the vestry. Some of the Dorset and Gloucester cousins had been a little shocked, had felt that she was marrying a man who was a heathen. She had loved him, and she didn't care what he was, what he believed, what he did; he loved her and that was enough.

Then the long drive down to Devon and the sea. Max had wanted to stay somewhere for the night, and she begged him to push on. She wanted the sight and sound and smell of the sea. Wanted to feel that the sea washed

away every trace of remembrance, and left only the consciousness that she and Max were together. Max had
nodded and said, 'All right, I'll get down to it then.' He
had driven like a fury.

'Max, you're driving like the devil!'

'That's what you wanted, wasn't it?'

She had laughed and slipped her arm round his neck.
'I want to leave them all behind—people and devils.'

As they drove, the big car eating up the miles, she had
sat silent and wondered if—there was anything left? If—
when they were alone—some faint ghost might walk,
might stand before her and force her to remember? She
had dug her nails into the palms of her hands and forced
the thought away from her, driving it back and calling
silently, 'There only is one person—Max—Max—Max.'

During dinner, she had talked and laughed, had drunk
Max's health, and made him ridiculous speeches. She had
teased him, and turned everything into a sort of ragtime
tune. They had gone out on to the big balcony and looked
at the sea, with a long silver track upon it leading to the
moon.

'Max—let's bathe!'

He had said, 'Now, sweetheart? It's nearly ten o'clock.'

'Ten—rubbish—it's no time at all. We make our own
time. Clocks don't tick for us. Let's bathe!'

They had run down to the sea, and she had stood at the
end of the silver pathway and looked right along it. She
had thought as she stood there, that now—the present
minute—was perfect, tomorrow—one couldn't be certain
of tomorrow or the day after.

'Tomorrow—next week—next month—next year—
Max might not be everything. I might not be everything
for Max. Now, I'm enough, and he's enough for me.
Things might come back—days full of sunshine, nights
when someone else played for me, long afternoons when we
lay on the hill-side and talked—they're dead now, or I
think they're dead—they may only be lying doggo. I could
swim out along that silver track and take perfection with
me, and leave perfection with Max. If I'm brave enough to
realise how afraid I am of ever losing it.'

Aloud she called, 'I'm going to swim to the moon, Max.'

She heard him laugh, ran into the water and began to
swim. On and on, along the silver track, and presently behind her came the steady rhythm of Max's strong strokes,
gaining, gaining, gaining. She knew that he would keep be-

side her, that he would make her turn back before she began to flag. She saw his dark head gleaming at her side.

'Not too far, Angela, you've got to get back, you know.'

'Don't let's go back. Let's go on and on and never go back.'

She thought, 'Now I must act—he won't let me go,' and stopped swimming, so that Max shot ahead. She felt herself sinking, Max hadn't noticed.

'Oh, damn it,' she whispered, 'I wish I wasn't such a good swimmer. It's going to be awfully difficult.'

Down and down, noise and roaring in her ears, pictures coming very quickly like a cinematograph. Then a cry from Max, a cry so full of agony that it reached her above the roaring of the water.

'Angela—I'm coming—here, darling.'

His hands catching her, holding her, his voice speaking, telling her to hold on, not to leave go, assuring her that he'd have her on land in a moment. She felt that his will was beating her own down, forcing her to obey, making her obedient to him. He was swimming hard, faster than she had ever known a man swim.

'It's all right, Max, cramp—I can manage.'

'No, keep hold of me—don't leave go.'

He was standing on the firm sand, catching her in his arms, carrying her away from the sea.

'Put me down—please put me down.'

He knelt beside her, holding her hands in his. Suddenly she began to cry, couldn't stop crying, felt that something had snapped and she was left without control.

'Max—don't let me go—don't ever let me go. Keep it— just you and me.'

Ever since, her love for him had absorbed her. She wanted no one but Max. The days were long dreary deserts only broken by his letters, his voice on the telephone, or the wires which he sent her. She was never actively unhappy, but consciously trying to make the time pass until she should see him again.

She wrote him long letters, half-romantic, half a jumble of the slang which she had always used. She sent him ridiculous parcels, foolish bits of rhymes about his old dog and herself. She bought him new ties, new socks, new handkerchiefs and laid them away ready for that time when the war should be over.

Once she tried to tell Emmanuel what Max meant to her.

'You see, Emmanuel, other people don't really count. I don't read the Casualty Lists, for fear I should believe that Max's name could ever be in one of them. I don't think about the war at all if I can help it, because I want to try and stave it off from Max. It's really a war between Germany and the rest of them and—me. They want Max, and I want to keep him. It's Max they're trying to get, because he is so terribly important.'

Emmanuel added. 'If vishes were horses, Max would ride into Berlin on a cavalry charger tomorrow, eh?'

'I don't care a hoot about Berlin, all I want is for Max to ride home to me.'

The maid brought in tea, and Angela wondered if Max got good tea up in Lancashire, and if she could get cook to make him some of the small cakes which were so delicious, hot and buttery. She wondered if he could heat them if she sent a box full, otherwise they weren't terribly good. The telephone bell shrilled and broke in on her thoughts. She put down her cup, hoped it might be Max and felt certain that it wasn't.

'Mrs. Gollantz?'

'Speaking. Yes.'

'Mrs. Frank Gollantz wishes to know if you could come round, madam. She's had bad news.'

'Her husband—wounded?'

'Killed, madam.'

She drew a deep breath. 'I'll come at once.'

As she drove to Morrie, she thought that the war was closing in on her, coming nearer. Max's nephew killed. Frank—it seemed only a few weeks ago that she had danced with him; only a month—or so it seemed—that they had bought records together in Bond Street.

Morrie was standing before the fire in the ultra-modern drawing-room that Max and Emmanuel hated—all black and green, vivid, screaming green. Furniture that was painted gold and picked out with red. Frank roared with laughter at it, said it was indecent, had compared it to the reception room in a house of Easy Virtue. Morrie turned as Angela came in and stared at her.

'Heard, Angela?'

'Yes, darling.'

'Pretty bloody, isn't it?' She stood frowning, as if the

news puzzled her, then said, 'Angela—what *am* I to do? I don't see what I am going to do.'

'You're sure it's true?'

'War office telegram—they regret to inform me—like the coal merchant when he can't send me what I order! Could I go out there, Angela?'

'I don't think so, Morrie.'

'Anyway, what's the use if I did. They've probably blown him to bits.' She sat down, her hands between her knees. 'Give me a brandy and soda, will you? God! how I hate them! This is the beginning—we've only been at it since August. I felt awful when I heard Pastern, and Geoff, and "Mud" Baxter had gone—but I never thought that it could touch me. I don't know what I'm going to *do* without Frank . . .' She snatched the glass from Angela's hand. 'I'll tell you what it will do to me, it's going to make me hate every woman who keeps her man after this. I shall hate you soon, Angela—hate you like hell. I don't know why I sent for you—you can't do any good—don't wait, Angela, old thing. Sorry to have dragged you out. I'm better by myself—better get used to it quickly.'

Emmanuel shut himself up in the big house in Regent's Park and refused to see anyone. Max came home for twenty-four hours and after much persuasion, got his father to see him. He was wretched, he had loved Frank very dearly, and felt his loss keenly. He found Emmanuel calm, dispassionate, and very quiet. He said very little, talked of the future arrangements for Morrie. He did not break down, only sat dry-eyed and apparently unmoved.

'Good God,' Max said, 'I shall be glad to get out there to get at the brutes.'

Emmanuel held up his hand. 'No, Max, no. I won't hev you talk that way. In Germany, in Austria today t'ere are t'ousands of men and women talking that way about us in England, and for the same reason. It's no good hating anyone—the machine is working by itself now, we can't stop it. We're all caught in it and we've all got to move with it. Hating will only oil the wheels. Tell Morrie that I am here if she would like to see me—perhaps next week, but I don't want to see people, Max. Not even Enchela. Give her my love, she'll understand.'

He went back to Angela, and told her that his father was hard hit, that he was old and rapidly growing older. She listened and nodded.

'I'll go and see him one day, when he wants me.'

In the first week of November, Max went out to Flanders. He and Angela spent his leave together, driving out into the country and sitting side by side in the car, not talking a great deal but conscious that they were very close. Together they went to dine with Emmanuel. The big table seemed too vast for the three of them, Emmanuel's gay courtesy a little overdone. He looked from Max to Angela and smiled. 'Not only I am growing old,' he said, 'Enchela is too.' He leant over and patted her hand. 'Don't take t'ings too hard, my dear, it never helps anyone. It's not a t'ing which heppens only to you or to me, it's heppening all over the world. Not'ing really big ever heppens only to one—or one. Death, birth, love—belong everywhere—to everyone.'

'And hate,' Angela said, 'that, too.'

'Supposing that we are silly enough. Es bringt nicht gute Frucht, wenn Hass dem Hass begegnet.' He smiled. 'There, should anyone hear me quoting that I shall be put away in the Alexandra Palace as a spy! But it's true.'

'Oh, yes,' she said, 'I'm sure it's true. It's as true as the saying that it's darkest before dawn, and that long lanes have turnings and clouds silver linings and all the rest of it. What concerns me is that the winter is going to be so damned long, so are the lanes, and the clouds seem to be so inkily black. However, we shall all come through—on one side or the other. I don't quite mean Germans or English top dogs, Emmanuel darling—for once I'm thinking a little further than that.'

Max left early. He hoped that she might not wake, that he might leave her sleeping, but as he tip-toed across the bedroom, she said:

'It's all right, Max. I'm not asleep. Don't get cramp in your toes.'

He came and sat on the bed and watched her. 'I wish you didn't make me such an infernal coward, darling. I do hate and loathe leaving you so.'

She nodded. 'It's hell, isn't it. But—remember that there isn't anyone but you, never can be, never could be. Everythings else is gone, finished. It's you—you—you—all the time. I just—quite literally—adore you, Max.'

'It's fifty-fifty, Angela.'

She sat up in bed, and picked up the mirror from the table beside her. Looked at herself, frowned, powdered her face, and combed her hair. Looked again intently then said, 'I look a hag, don't I? I believe I'm going to have a baby, Max. How do you feel when you're going to have a baby?'

'Angela . . .' he put his arms round her, 'Angela, really? Oh, my poor little love. How do you know? I mean are you certain?'

'I don't know, I'm not certain, and you won't tell me how one does feel. I suppose after all you can't be expected to know. I only know that I feel rather cheap—and that I don't really mind much feeling cheap. I suppose that's what they call the "exaltation of motherhood". It might be rather nice, Max—only you'd always have to love me best, or I should put it out to nurse and have it abducted and you'd never see it again.'

'I should probably hate it because you'd love it too much.'

She came and cuddled into his arms, watching him while he drank his coffee and ate his hot roll. Not even the Army had trained Max to eat an English breakfast. He ate in silence, only at intervals she felt his arm tighten round her, and knew that the parting hurt him as it hurt her. Then he began to speak, quickly and methodically. She was to see Sir Nathan Bernstein—he was the best man in London, she was to do everything that he told her, to deny herself nothing.

'Except you, Max, and I can't help myself there, can I?'

'Darling—shut up and listen. You're to spend all the money you want. If you want anything and can't get it go to my father. Do just as you like, don't give a damn for what outsiders want you to do—except your doctor. My father knows all my affairs, business, everything. Above all, don't be afraid. I'll come back, and all the wonderfulness will be as it was before.'

When he had gone, she lay back on her pillows and repeated softly, 'All the wonderfulness will be as it was before.'

During the winter she lived in a perpetual state of fear, every letter which came she felt would be the last. So many men killed, it seemed impossible that Max could be missed! The sight of a telegraph boy with his face turned towards St. John's Wood sent her flying home, shaking, and not able to look towards the hall table where the letters and messages were laid.

Her mother shook her head over her evident anxiety.

'It's not right, Angela, you mustn't think only of Max, there is yourself to think of, the child.'

'The child is Max's. If Max is all right, the child will be all right. I've got the rest of my life to worry over the child —I may only have today to worry over Max.'

Morrie came to see her, demanded cocktails at three in the afternoon, laughed, and was gay with miserable eyes.

'Going to have a baby, Angela? Wish I was. Rather fun, I should think. If anything will ever be fun again, except what one can knock out of life to the noise of a band, and the clink of ice in a glass. I tried "snow" the other day—man I know had some. It only made me feel ghastly sick. I've got a new car—like to come out with me? It's a corker. I did sixty-five yesterday—easy as pie. Come and try it.'

'And do sixty-five? No thanks. I've got to think of Max Junior. It might upset him.'

Morrie said, 'Oh, mustn't do that—they'll want Max junior for the trenches in another eighteen years. He'll be the last man left to fight in the bloody old war! Kitchener says five years—I say fifty-five.'

'You don't know any more than Kitchener does,' Angela said, 'no one knows. Good-bye, Morrie—don't do sixty-five in—or out of the car. You look as if you were going right over the speed limit, darling.'

'I am—I'm going while the going's good. Let it all rip!'

In the early part of 1915, her old fears began to creep back. Max fighting—in the trenches, going over the top, hand-to-hand fighting with the enemy, and—Max and—someone else face to face. Max recognised—she remembered that his picture had stood in her room in Vienna— her name spoken, and Max ceasing to be a number in the Army, ceasing to be just a bit of the machine, becoming a private individual with a personal hate. Not killing because it was war, but killing because it was his own quarrel. She lay awake at night and with closed eyes saw them wrestling together, heard her own name shouted, heard Max cursing under his breath, throwing away his revolver —or whatever they fought with out there—using his hands, pressing his thumbs into a windpipe, stilling the struggles which became less and less determined and then ceased. Max rising, wiping his hands, and looking down on the twisted, suffocated body that had been the man she had once loved.

Max coming home on leave, telling her, knowing that

he had murdered a man, and dreading that his spirit
might not lie quiet, but come and stand between them. The
nightmare came again and again, and during the day it
followed her, stood at her side and killed what little joy
she had in life.

All her love was for Max, no one else mattered to her;
and the thought that, through her, Max should suffer again
was unbearable. One evening she dined with O'Reilly who
had been refused by the Army ten times but was always
trying again. He had his work in Whitehall, worked hard,
kept immense hours, but that wasn't enough. Women
handed him white feathers in the street, and he took them,
raising his hat and thanking them.

'It's lousy, Angela—God, how I loathe it. I can't explain
that my heart goes on strike, can I? I wish I'd had a
wooden leg, or had lost an arm!'

She said, 'After all, Terrence, you're lucky, you've got
a legitimate grouse against things. I haven't. People tell
me how lucky I am, that I'm fortunate to have a husband
who is still alive. Only if he wasn't alive, I shouldn't be
here to be lucky or unlucky. I'd get out!'

He looked at her over the table, shifting the flowers so
that he might see her better. Her eyes were heavy, her
mouth—Terrence had always told Max that her mouth
was the most lovely thing about her—drooped, there were
little hollows in her cheeks. Somewhere between August
and this new year she had lost her girlhood.

'All the same,' he said, 'you are lucky and don't forget
it, my dear.'

'Do you back horses, race, and all the rest of it?' she
asked suddenly.

'I do. Why?'

'How many men are there fighting now? Thousands—a
million, perhaps?'

'More—taking them all round.'

'What would you say the chance was of a particular
man of one nationality meeting a particular man of another—actually meeting and killing him?'

'Not the outest outside chance,' he said. 'I wouldn't bet
on such a chance. Why—what's the idea?'

'It's not probable?'

'It's the sort of thing that a man knows happened to a
fellow who was the cousin of another fellow who once
knew his tailor. That's what it is.'

'I see—thanks, Terrence.' She smiled. 'What's your job exactly? You never talk about it, do you?'

'Mine isn't the kind of job that is talked about much,' he said. 'It's sniffing round, collecting bits and pieces here and there, laying a hand on this fellow and keeping an eye on another. Getting bits of paper which tell me that Frau Wassermann has had another baby and that her cat was fighting another lady's cat last week. That means that somewhere, someone has found out how many guns were shipped off to the front last week and where they were bound for. That's my job.'

'Spies,' she said, wrinkling her nose.

'Don't be supercilious, my dear. A damned fine lot taking them all round, so long as they play fair with the fellow who employs them. If they get what we want, we say, "Thanks very much. Don't talk about it, will you?"; if on the other hand they get nabbed, we say, "Nothing to do with us. It's your trouble and not ours. More fool you to get caught." It's heads we win, tails they lose every time. No—personally, I respect 'em.'

'Suppose they don't play fair?'

He grinned. 'They lose then all right. Someone's sent to catch 'em, and when found—they are distinctly—made a note of. If they're wise guys they don't wait to pack. They get out.'

'How—get out?'

'Any old way—a jump in the dark into nowhere. My dear, let's talk of something more pleasant. I hate that part of it all.'

'I hate all the parts of it,' Angela said. 'Drive me home, Terrence, it's late, and I must get to bed early. I've been sleeping badly.'

The telegram lay on the hall table as they came in. Angela saw it, walked forward and picked it up. She turned to Terrence and said, 'Well, here it is. What's the betting?'

He said, 'A hundred to one against. For God's sake open it, Angela.'

She tore it open, read it, leaning one hand on the table to steady herself. 'Wounded—it doesn't say seriously. How can I find out, Terrence? Now—I don't want to wait until the morning.'

'I'll go down to the W.O. No, I don't think you'd better come. It's—a bit twisting to be there. You're better here. I'll be fearfully quick. I'll telephone to you.'

She sat down, her face very white, and said, 'Tell someone to get me a drink will you? I feel so deathly sick.'
When he came back with some brandy, she had laid her
head on the table beside her, and lifted it when he
touched her arm. 'I'm better now, thanks. Oh, Terrence,
if it's really only something slight, how wonderful to think
Max is out of it. Go on—telephone me at once. Bless
you. Out of it—back—I don't care what it is—I'll get
him well. Out of it, Terry—hurry, please hurry.'

22

Max came home and was sent to a wonderful hospital in
Park Lane, where all the V.A.D.'s were highly decorative
and a pleasure to look at. There were two awful days
when the surgeons hinted that his leg might have to come
off at the hip, when Angela went from St. John's Wood
to Park Lane every few hours seeking fresh news, when
she sat in a beautiful waiting-room and twisted her gloves
into a damp rope, or sat at home and tried to concentrate
on making his leg better. Sat making bargains with God,
saying over and over, 'Let his leg be all right and you
can have ten years of my life,' or, 'Don't let them take it
off. Let me break my leg tomorrow and they can take it
off to make up for Max.' Regarding God as a Shylock who
must have money or a pound of flesh as an equivalent.

On the third day, she sat by his bed and held his hand
very tightly, knowing that she was desperately tired and
past feeling anything at all.

Max said, 'It's all right, sweetheart, it's going to stay
where it is. I shall only be a bit dot and carry one; not
badly, only enough to do me in for tennis. I've got off
cheaply.'

She looked at him, her eyes heavy and tired. 'That's
wonderful. And it will keep you out of this damned war,
won't it, Max?'

'Oh, I don't know that. They might find me a job of

sorts. It's going on for years. I shan't be here all the time, let's hope.'

'All right,' she sighed, 'only you'll kill me if you go back. You might as well know that now. I just can't stand it—my nerve's gone to bits.'

He held her hand more tightly, spoke soothingly and gently to her, tried to comfort her, to assure her that he would be tied by the leg for a long time, and that even when he was well, even if the mysterious people he referred to as 'they' found him a job, it wasn't likely to be the trenches again.

'You can't hop over the top with a gammy leg, darling.'

'That's something to thank God for!'

When she left him, one of the V.A.D.'s spoke to her. They had known each other in the days before the war. The girl said that Max was divine, that they all thought him the 'sweetest thing' and had been frantic when they thought his leg might have to go.

Angela listened and smiled. 'Divine—sweetest thing—frantic,' she repeated. 'Honestly, Helen, I wonder if you, any of you, know what it's like to be frantic?'

'My darling child, wait until you're in a hospital and watch all these lovely boys come back smashed to bits. It's heart-rending. Poor Pip Masters died yesterday, y'know. I almost wept! Still,' she patted her fair hair, 'one can only do one's bit, after all. We're working for the living, we've got to remember that. Let's hope when it's over, they'll make the devils of Germans pay . . .'

Angela pulled on her gloves. 'Yes,' she said, 'it will be a great comfort to us all to know that Germany pays up—so much a head for every man that's been killed, won't it? Good-bye, Helen. Be nice to my Max.'

She got home and found Morrie waiting. Morrie hurt her these days. She was so beautifully dressed, always so busy doing nothing, her mouth—that scarlet gash in her face—twisted down at the corners as if she laughed at everything and mocked everything at the same moment. Her eyes, plastered with mascara and eyeblack, were hard and very bright. A disturbing, miserable person, Morrie Gollantz. She put down the glass she was holding as Angela came in, kissed her and said, 'Sorry—half my lipstick's come off on you. It's beastly stuff. The only decent one comes from Paris, and it's the devil getting it over in these days. You're looking rotten, Angela. How's the great Max?'

'He's going on all right. The leg hurts a good deal, but he's awfully good. They're not going to lop it off, thank God.'

'That's good. D'you mind if I have another drink? No, thanks, I loathe tea. Darling, you do look rotten.'

'If I look half as rotten as I feel, I must look unbelievably foul. I literally feel like death, and don't much care.'

Morrie put down her glass and came and sat down beside her cousin. Angela looked at her and wondered what anyone could do for Morrie, wondered if anything in the world could wipe that look from her face and make her what she had been a year ago. She thought, 'I get sick of everything, I get frightened because I think too much. Morrie has gone further than that, she's too frightened to let herself think at all.'

'I've got a spot of news, for you,' Morrie said. 'It's going to make the Gollantz family sit up and hate me, I'm afraid. Aunt Gwen will be shocked to death, Charles and Bill will turn their faces to the wall, but after all, it's my business. I'm going to be married in a month.'

'Married? Morrie, who is he?'

Morrie going to be married. It was going to hurt Emmanuel, even hurt Max a little. They had both loved Frank, both felt his death terribly. Now, after five months —Morrie was going to marry again.

'George Stansfield—you've met him, haven't you?'

'Lord Stansfield—yes, I've met him.'

Morrie laughed. 'Go on,' she said, 'tell me that you've heard of him, too! We all have. George is like me, a bit notorious. Still, he suits me, and I'm going to marry him. He can't go to the war, he's rotten with T.B. He's trying to get through things, so am I. He hates everything—so do I. We ought to make a pretty good pair.'

'Are you in love with him, Morrie?'

'In love—my dear, I leave that to you and Max. No, George amuses me, and I amuse him. It's a very sound basis, believe me.'

Angela leant back in her chair, she wondered what it felt like to marry a man because he amused you? Probably it hurt a good deal less than marrying a man who absorbed you, who filled your mind and left no room for other things. She remembered what it had felt like to be with Max again, to hold his hand, to watch his face—even the pain which had shown on it had been something personal. Each time his face had twitched with pain, she had fet it too, and been glad that she did. Through the dullness, through the weariness, she had known that Max was home, alive, that she was with him again. The war had receded, the whole world had seemed to be something removed from her; the real, tangible thing was that Max was home.

'You know best, my dear. Only—and I'm not preaching —he is a bit of an outsider, isn't he?'

Morrie shrugged her shoulders. 'I expect so—judged by the Gollantz standards. Though, from what Frank told me, they had one rather inky sheep in the fold. They might remember that when they discuss my marriage. You could remind them, Angela, tactfully and quite nicely. Well, I'm off. Come to the wedding—bring Emmanuel, he's so decorative. Bye-bye, my dear.'

She sat there after Morrie had gone, thinking, wondering. She thought, 'Max is going to be all right. God listened to the bargain I made. I wonder if He's going to take ten years of my life? Or if I shall break my leg tomorrow? I'd rather break my leg, if it's all the same to Him. I don't want to lose ten years with Max. I don't mind—not a lot—losing a leg. Tomorrow Max will be a little bit better, and the day after better still. Presently, he'll be almost well and we'll go into the country. Emmanuel can lend us his house on the Downs behind Brighton. Then when he's better—really better—when he wants to do more work for the war I can keep him at home because of Max Junior. He'll arrive in July and I won't let Max go until it's all over. I've a right to insist on that. Afterwards—p'raps when he's got used to being at home, when he sees how nice Max Junior will be he won't want to go. He can do war work in England, something at the War Office, or interpreting or something.' She laughed. 'God's all on my side! He shan't go out again. That's another nightmare ended. Ever since I first loved Max, I've been praying for things to end . . .'

She realised that her face was damp, that she was shaking, feeling deathly ill. With a great effort she got up and rang the bell.

'Oh, ma'am, you're ill!'

She nodded. 'I believe I am. Ring up Dr. Bernstein, will you, and ask him to come round quickly. Tell Gibbons to take the car round and bring Mr. Gollantz back.

I want to speak to him. Tell Gibbons to hurry—but not to alarm Mr. Gollantz.'

'The Master, ma'am?'

'Mr. Max! He's in hospital—no, his father. Gibbons knows the address.' By the time Emmanuel came, she was in bed, and wondering how she could have imagined that she felt ill an hour before. An hour ago—that was nothing. This was—she set her teeth—just hell.

She said, 'Hello, Emmanuel darling. I'm afraid I've made rather a mess of things. Mother's coming and I'm going to have Bernstein round. I thought so much about Max—that I'm afraid Max Junior got jealous at being left out.'

Emmanuel sat down stiffly, she thought that his hands folded on his gold-headed cane looked like parchment. She sniffed. 'How nice you smell.'

'My dear, don't vorry,' he said. 'Not'ing metters except you—not even Max Junior, perheps you're wrong, perheps it's'—he sought for a word—'influenza!'

She smiled. 'Splendid. That's what I want you to tell Max, Emmanuel. You see—I might be kept here for a few days, and I don't want Max worried. Tell him that I've got 'flu, and that I can't come to a hospital until there isn't a scrap of infection left. That attitude will appeal to Max. He wouldn't care, but he'll think of all the other men, and not want me to give it to them. Promise, Emmanuel—faithful?'

'Will you not vorry, will you be very good and do all that you are told, if I pr-romise to tell lies for you?'

'Promise—honest Injun . . .' She sought under her pillow for her handkerchief and wiped her forehead. 'Sorry, Emmanuel dear—I'm afraid I shall have to tell you to go. It's—rather beastly.'

He bent down and kissed her, his lips felt cold and dry —old lips.

'Enchela,' he said, 'you'll be all right. I'll look after Max.'

'Don't tell Max,' she whispered, 'he's rather braced about Max Junior.'

'Officially you hev influenza, my dear. The God of my Fathers bless and keep you.'

Three days later, Nathan Bernstein stood by her bed and thought that he had never seen any woman look more beautiful. Thin—even a little haggard—pale, with shadowed eyes and a mouth which had lost its colour, but still beautiful. She looked up at the tall, sallow-faced Jew, with his intelligent eyes and full red mouth and tried to smile.

'Hello,' she said, 'how is Max? I don't believe I even asked yesterday?'

'Max is going on well,' he said, in his soft lisping voice, 'he thends hith love to you.'

'You told him I had 'flu?' she whispered.

'Yeth—thath all right.'

'I'm better, but—well, I've rather messed things up, haven't I?'

He spread his large white hands with the short pink nails and square tipped fingers. She thought he looked like an Eastern carpet seller.

'Iths a pity,' he said, 'I'm thorry—better luck nexth time.'

'There can be a next time?'

He nodded gravely like a toy mandarin in a china shop. 'Yeth—yeth—thirtainly. You're a young woman, throng, healthy. Max is young; once he gets over this leg buithness he'll be fit as ever. Why not . . . No reason at all. This—you can put down to worry—the war . . .'

'I see. Thank you.'

She lay still, and remembered that she had tried to make bargains with God. Ten years—her own leg—but she hadn't mentioned Max Junior. 'That's what comes of trying to make bargains,' she thought, 'you can't tell how they're going to turn out. It does seem a bit mean all the same.'

She was not consciously unhappy; somewhere deep in her heart she felt that she and the baby together had offered a sacrifice for Max, that between them they had saved him. Been scapegoats thrown to the war god instead of Max. Lives were wanted, pain must be suffered, she and the child had joined forces against Fate to save Max. She held fast to the idea, thinking that even if it were not true, her belief might reach some power, whose sense of justice might be touched. He—whoever He was and wherever He lived—might say, 'There's something in it. She's right; let Max Gollantz off lightly. The score against him is wiped out.'

When her head ached so badly that she felt sick and nauseated, and the nurse watching her white face offered drugs to ease the pain, she refused them. The headaches were part of the bargain; she mustn't shirk things. If it was worth doing, it was worth doing well. When she lay awake at night and sleep eluded her, she closed her eyes and simulated sleep, so that they should not offer her sleeping draughts. Part of the bargain—this lying awake. The first bargain hadn't worked out as she had hoped, she would manage better this time.

Every day she asked Bernstein if she could get up. She wanted to see Max.

Every day he shook his head and said, 'Not today, Mithes Gollanth—not today.'

Three weeks—a month—and one sunny afternoon in March, Emmanuel came to see her. He stared at her, his mouth working, his eyes filled with tears. She hadn't been allowed to see him before, and he had not imagined that she would look so ill.

'Darling, don't get wet eyes. I'm terribly well now. Sit down and tell me things. How's Max?'

Emmanuel blinked and sat down slowly. 'Max,' he said, 'is so well that in a few days they are sending him pecking back home. All t'ose nesty goyem girls will be furious; they think he looks romantic, hope that he will live up to his looks. I saw him this morning, and he sent you a special letter by me.' He took a letter from his pocket and held it in his hand.

'Give it to me, Emmanuel.'

'Vait,' he said, 'one minute, please. This morning, I br-roke my word to you. I told Max.'

'What did he say? Did he mind awfully?'

'He said—t'ese are his words, "My poor darling, how r-rotten for her." I t'ink that he minded very much for you. That was all. I t'ink that you are—all.'

The next week, he was home. Hopping on crutches, able to get up and down stairs if he took time and no one objected to the noise. For hours he sat by her bed, read to her, cut up her food and waited on her hand and foot. To Angela every moment was precious. He was home, he was well or almost well, the war for the present was out of sight, and they were together. She was happy, and being happy began to recover, and Nathan Bernstein rubbed his hands over her and purred like a huge cat.

She tried to get Max to talk of Morrie and her wedding. Max shrugged his shoulders and said that it was Morrie's business and not theirs. Emmanuel had, it appeared, also shrugged *his* shoulders. He had insisted that the income which he had paid to Morrie, as Frank's widow, should be continued.

'He feels,' Max said, 'that he owes that to Frank. I think he's right. Whatever Morrie does won't alter my father's responsibility as regards Frank's wife.'

'She's doing it because she's so miserable,' Angela said. 'I've never known anyone take anything so hard. It's terrible.'

'If I know George Stansfield,' Max said, 'she'll be still more miserable married to him. He is the most bounding fellow I ever met.'

In the October they were back in St. John's Wood. All the summer they had lived within sight of the sea, they had bathed, and played like two children. Each day, as Angela saw that Max was stronger, that his leg was ceasing to give trouble, she felt that their present life was too good to last, that he would become restive and want to go back. When those thoughts came, she remembered her idea of paying a debt, and would repeat again and again to herself, that Max was paid for. The Gods couldn't ask anything more from Max or herself.

At dinner one evening the bomb fell. He had been out most of the day, had lunched with O'Reilly, and only got back before dinner.

'Angel,' he said suddenly, 'do you realise that except for a slight and most becoming limp, your husband is well?'

She thought, 'It's come—well, I'll fight for him.' Aloud she said, 'Well? I suppose you are fairly well. You've been taking life easy, Max.'

'That's not why I'm fit. I really am well again, and you know it.'

'That means that you want to work? All right, Emmanuel will be very glad. I know he has lots of schemes for you.'

He laughed. 'Pictures—furniture—carpets—old silver —houses! Darling, no one wants those things now. Everyone wants to sell them, not buy them.'

Angela lifted her glass and finished her wine. The fight was beginning, the buttons were off the foils. She was ready. She would attack first.

'You mean,' she said, 'that you want to do war work. Go back to the front?'

'That's what I should like to do.'

Very calmly, her voice quite even, she said, 'I once told you that if you went back I should kill myself, Max. I should. I won't go through it again.'

'There is no question of going back,' he said, and she thought that she caught a hint of coldness in his voice. 'They won't have me—this damned leg would let me down. It's not good enough, I should be more bother than I was worth. I must get something else to do. I have a job offered to me. I was talking to O'Reilly this morning. Intelligence Department.'

She leant back, feeling that a load had been lifted from her shoulders.

'Intelligence,' she repeated. Then a conversation with O'Reilly came back to her, she said, 'Spy work, Max? That's what it is, isn't it?'

He made a little grimace at her. 'Oh, darling, don't call spades blasted shovels!' He laughed. 'It's catching 'em. Rather a good job, I thought.'

'Suppose you're caught?'

'I shan't be spying. I shall only be . . .'

'Spying on spies,' she said. 'I wonder if that will make them look at you in a more kindly light? I doubt it. I can't quite see—why—having done what was up to you— you want to go and mix yourself up in it again.'

Max lit a cigarette carefully; he wanted to gain time. He knew that he was going to be forced to face difficulties. Angela wouldn't want him to go, Emmanuel wouldn't want him to go—because Angela didn't want it. It was going to be difficult all round. He had made up his mind, he was going to 'be in it' so long as it lasted. He couldn't face walking about town, fit—except for an almost imperceptible limp—knowing that every woman whispered and every man thought, 'Why the devil isn't he fighting?'

He said, 'I don't want to—mix myself up in it, darling. It's one of the things that won't stand explanations. If I try to explain I shall sound melodramatic and stage-ily patriotic. It's just that firstly, I want to be in it, and secondly that I'm too big a coward to stay out. Briefly, that's the position. The very fact that my father is an Austrian makes it—to me—all the more necessary that I should pull my weight. You do see that, don't you?'

'Then I don't count?'

'You count more than anything, and you know it. It's just something that's bigger than I am.'

Angela got up, pushed back her chair so that the legs rasped on the polished floor. Max felt that she had meant them to rasp. She walked over to the big silver cigarette box on the mantelpiece and took a cigarette. Max remembered that usually she held out her hand and said. 'Chuck me one over, Max darling.' She puffed the smoke towards him in a huge cloud, looked at the end of the cigarette as if the fate of empires depended upon its being properly lit, then said:

'I see. Bigger than me—bigger than anything. Then, God forbid, that I should keep you away. It's like the Bible—about leaving fathers and mothers and everything else.' She half closed her eyes and looked at him. 'I can't see any especial reason why you should be fitted to play at being a policeman, can you?'

Max said, 'Languages; I can speak five pretty decently.'

'Oh, you're going to catch spies all over Europe? A big job. All right, Max, if you want to go, you must. I say that because evidently I can't stop you. Only, if you come back and find me developing into another Morrie just remember who's to blame, won't you?'

He came over to where she stood, took the cigarette from her fingers and threw it into the fire, then put his arms round her and held her close. She struggled, said, 'Max, let me go! Do you hear, Max—don't—I hate it.'

'No, you don't,' he said, 'and even if you do, I can't help it. I adore you, we adore each other and you know it. What are we hurting each other for? Getting further and further apart every minute . . .'

'Oh—hurting!' she said. 'I'm not hurting you, Max!'

'Yes you are—hurting like hell. Angela, listen, I must do something. I can't help myself. Frank's killed, and somewhere or other my own brother is fighting against us. Both take a bit of wiping out. You do see that, don't you?'

'Your father says that all this hate stuff is so foolish.'

'I know he does. He's looking at everything down miles and miles of years. For me and for you—it's here, with us. We can't look at it and get wonderful perspective. In another ten years, we shall have forgotten the hating, but just now it's too near us. I can't sit at home and air what from me would be a lot of cheap philosophy. It's not in me, Angela.'

She had ceased to struggle and lay in his arms quite still and passive.

'All right, Max. You've won. Not that you've convinced me, but if it's going to mean your happiness, I suppose

you've got to do it. I suppose you will come home sometimes?'

'I shall be at home for quite a long time. Even when
they think I'm to be trusted with a job, I shall be backwards and forwards all the time.'

'Until the other side catch you, and stick you up against
a wall. That's a pretty picture, isn't it?'

'No prettier, believe me, than some of the pictures I've
seen out there. Better than lying with your guts trailing on
the ground in a shell-hole, waiting for stretcher bearers
who may find you, and again, may not.'

She lifted her hand and laid it over his mouth. 'Shut up,
Max. I can't stand horrors, they're too much for me. I
hate it all—I should hate you if I didn't love you so
damnably.' She lifted her face and kissed him. 'Off you
go, then. Get your policeman's lantern and boots. Only
—let me catch you standing at an area door making love
to someone's cook, and oh, my hat, what a row I'll make,
war or no war.'

23

O'Reilly pushed some papers over to Max. 'That's all I
can let you have,' he said. 'I don't even know what the
fellow's like. Never seen him. He's worked in conjunction
with another fellow, a Swiss schoolmaster. Since the war
began he's been damned useful; kept his eyes open, and
sent us the results. Now—he's turned crook, he's double
crossing us. One message got mixed, it was evidently intended for someone else. Where ours went to, God only
knows, but I can make a good guess. It's got to stop—he'll
have to be nipped in the bud. Unfortunately he knows too
much. The very fact that he knows *what* information we
want, gives him a clue as to where our anxieties lie. Switzerland is full of wounded, sick and so forth, he's there,
and that's a happy hunting ground for him.

'I've heard tales from the French. I believe that a
French officer appeared in the English lines, listened most

intelligently. Only after he'd gone, it was discovered that this had been queer, and the other had been suspicious. Now, three weeks ago, his Swiss pal comes to London. Brings some—apparently—excellent information. He stayed at the Majestic. A girl in the laundry caught him. Handkerchief with a yellow stain on it. All these girls carry a little bottle of chemical for removing stains. Not supposed to, but they all do. She dabbed the mark with her dope. The whole thing leapt out! Invisible ink of sorts. The whole handkerchief a remarkably good map of the river with the big guns marked all along, and in the areas nearby. Lovely bit of work. Sent to the wash by mistake. Probably half a dozen others were already on their way to Switzerland.

'The boss of the laundry came to us. We managed to catch the fellow as he was leaving. He squealed on his partner. Swore he didn't know everything, didn't know where the information was going, only knew that it went.'

Max said, 'And what's happened to him?'

'We've got him where we want him. It's the other fellow who is causing the trouble. Take on the job of laying him by the heels?'

'What—bringing him back to England?'

O'Reilly laughed. 'I don't know that we're pining for him. Only we don't particularly want him lying about. No, you deal with him as you think best, Max. You're a free agent.'

'You mean that I can—do him in?'

The other pursed his lips and rolled a pencil up and down his blotting pad. 'I'm not advising you, not even giving you instructions. We don't want him running wild, he may not be alone.' He looked up and smiled. 'Go and make a report. If in the making of the report anything happens—we shan't blame you. On the other hand, if anything happens to you don't blame us. That's fair enough, isn't it?'

'I suppose so. Now—tell me, where is the fellow and what's his name?'

'He was in Lausanne, Heaven only knows where he is now. His name was—let's see—Houseman, with one or two n's, also Goodman, and last of all Riches. He's English—or was; I don't know his description. His partner is a man called Henby. Little, pale-faced fellow with glasses. They used to stay at a pension near the Lake called'—he turned back to his papers—' "La Rosabella". Fairly cheap place, I gather. Didn't run to stamped notepaper. At one time he had a woman with him. A Frenchwoman. She's left him, was working on her own until last week.'

'And now?'

'She isn't working anywhere—nowhere at least within means of communication. Freddy Marsters caught her. She's the Lady of the Sable Coat, with the buttons set in paste, you remember?'

Max shivered. 'God,' he said, 'I'd hate to try to catch women. Men are bad enough. I don't know that I'm keen on this job, Terrence.'

O'Reilly shrugged his shoulders. 'All right. Hand in your papers, Max. Angela dislikes it too much, I suppose?'

'What Angela likes or dislikes,' Max said, his voice suddenly hard, 'is her business and mine. Oh, damn it— I'll do it. What a brute you are!'

O'Reilly looked up and smiled. 'Poor old Max,' he said, 'it's so dead easy to annoy you. My dear chap, I wish to Heaven I could go myself. It's not all it seems. Think of it—these fellows can do more damage than a long-distance gun, a bombardment. I know it sounds pretty foul, but it's a damned good way to serve your country. Good luck.'

He travelled as Colonel Julian Weston. He was going to see into some of the conditions in the invalid camps, he was representing the Red Cross, and several American societies. Arriving at Lausanne, he went to an hotel, and again went through—with meticulous care—such papers as were in his possession. He had a letter of introduction to A. Riches from the interned Henby, couched in language which was guarded in the extreme and which yet implied that Colonel Weston was returning to England shortly and was a person of the highest rectitude. It hinted that Colonel Weston might be willing to carry news of Riches' health and financial condition to his old mother who lived at Andover.

Max shaved and bathed, wished that he could write to Angela, scowled at the writing desk as if it were to blame, and then went out into the clean, cold streets of the town to begin his search. He found the Rosabella, it was over in Montreux, a decent enough place overlooking the Lake. He called in at the tobacco shop nearby and stood talking for some moments to the proprietor. Max confessed that he knew but little of Switzerland and that the war made travelling a little difficult. He wanted to stay in

Lausanne and then move on; he fancied that Zurich would be a pleasant place.

'Zurich is a splendid place. Not difficult to travel to Zurich.'

Max laughed. 'Like a good many people,' he said, 'I like to see my way clear. I wanted a railway guide, but my hotel, which is very small, doesn't seem to have one.'

The proprietor wagged his head, railway guides were of no use, so many of the trains were altered. The war had altered everything. Max thought that it had, at all events, left his tobacco shop singularly untouched, probably his pocket as well. He wagged his own head in chorus, admitted that he was foolish about such things, but he liked to see how long journeys took, what towns were passed—in fact, he was a thorough old maid about his travels. Had the proprietor a railway guide?'

'No, I have no need for one. When I need such a thing I borrow it from the proprietor at the Rosabella. If you cared to mention my name, and perhaps drink coffee there, I am sure you might read the railway guide to your heart's content.'

Max, to hide his delight, bought more boxes of tobacco, more cigarettes, and several boxes of matches. He had hoped that he might have drawn the proprietor on to talk, to talk about the inhabitants of the Rosabella, but this was Fortune smiling with a vengeance.

He said that indeed he would drink coffee, he might even lunch there, and assuredly he would mention the name of the tobacconist.

The Rosabella was very clean, rather bare, but moderately comfortable. Max glanced at the stout lady in the reception desk, bowed and asked for coffee. It would be brought immediately. He wondered if he might stay to lunch. The stout lady corrected him and stated that they had midday dinner on account of the many English who stayed there. Max said that he preferred a midday dinner. He asked if the English still came there—didn't the war keep them away? The stout lady replied that indeed it did, but she thanked Heaven that there remained some who never went away, except for a small time, for holidays, and then returned quickly and with great contentment to the Rosabella. Max said that he didn't wonder that they returned, wondered if he should ask more questions, and decided that he could wait. He spoke of the tobacconist, spoke of him highly and with praise. It appeared that he was the stout lady's cousin. The railway guide was forth-coming, and Max retired to the lounge where he drank some inferior coffee and turned the pages of the continental guide, most of which he already knew by heart. He set his finger in the book, his eyes on the Lake which lay below calm and untroubled. The clear sky above and the Lake below gave him a sense of content. These things were not touched by wars, they remained permanent, lasting. The mountains—the Lake—the great rivers—stayed, only men came and went, suffered, were wounded and died. Perhaps men didn't matter so much as the mountains. They were so small—only affecting at most half a dozen other men or women.

He thought, 'If I finished there would only be Angela and my father. Other people would say, "Poor old Max," and go on with their jobs. If Angela lost me, or I lost her —that's the end of our world. I'm hers, and she is mine. That's what can make a world—two people.' He sighed. It was a pity there had not been a third person; Max Junior might have made the world fuller for Angela. One from one left nothing, one from two still left one. He sipped his bad coffee, lit a cigarette and turned back to the railway guide. He was conscious that someone else had entered the lounge. Two people. One an old lady on his right, who read an equally old novel, dipping her nose with its pink tip into the pages like an elderly bird pecking seeds from a garden path. The other, a man—Max heard him cough, heard him striking matches, smelt the smell of his pipe tobacco.

Max closed the guide, rose and began to walk back to the reception desk. The man was reading, half hidden behind a tattered *Weekly Graphic,* nothing visible except his legs encased in baggy tweed trousers and heavy brown boots. From above the *Graphic* streamed clouds of tobacco smoke. Max sniffed. This was no foreign brand, it was some strong and world-wide mixture, manufactured, he felt certain, within four miles of Bristol.

Carefully he tripped over the brown boots, and was rewarded with a smothered shout, the instant lowering of the *Graphic* and the stare of a pair of angry blue eyes, surmounted by bushy grey eyebrows.

'What the devil . . .'

Max smiled a smile in which apology and comradeship were carefully blended.

'A thousand apologies—I was staring at the view from the windows, I didn't see your feet. Pray forgive me.'

The blue eyes lost some of their anger, and the rather hoarse, booming voice softened. 'All right—corn on that left foot. Only corn I've ever had in my life! Damnable! As bad as gout . . .' the speaker grunted a laugh.

'You're too young to be troubled by gout, eh?'

Max said, 'One never knows what the future may hold, sir.'

'Staying here?' The question came like a rifle shot.

'In Lausanne,' Max said, 'in the world's most uncomfortable hotel. I came in here to borrow a railway guide and look at the view. What a view.'

'View! Oh, damn the view. I don't stay here for that. I stay here, because it's the only place where people appear to forget that there is a war. I want to forget it, too. Want to forget it most damnably—most damnably.'

Max nodded. 'Some of us do want to forget it.'

The old fellow—Max placed him at sixty, a well-preserved sixty, a sixty which could still do a round of golf, a ten-mile walk, and a *Times* leader every day—stared at him. His red face took on a deeper shade, his eyebrows drew together again. He coughed as if something stuck in his throat.

'You want to forget it, eh? I wonder why? I shall ask you in a moment, I warn you. If you don't want to answer me, you can get along now. If you do—well, I'm glad to have someone to talk to instead of a mob of cackling old women.' He leant forward and tapped Max on the knee with a gnarled forefinger. 'Can you imagine why I want to forget it? Take a look at me—how would you describe me, eh?'

Max looked at him, thought for a second, then said, 'Tough, sir, tough.'

The old fellow leant back, smiling for the first time. He nodded.

'And rightly,' he said, 'rightly. Tough as the devil, and you can't find anything tougher than his Satanic Majesty. I'm sixty-four—mark that—sixty-four. Boer War—Yeomanry—went through Ladysmith. Came home—made every youngster about the place a soldier. Took up Roberts' ideas like a duck takes to water. Trained 'em, taught 'em what the Empire and England means. Every penny I could spare, every moment the lads could spare was given to drill, marches, sham fights, and all the rest of it. Crack lot. Three years ago, I got French down to see 'em. He said to me afterwards, "Cranston"—that's my name— James Cranston—"Cranston," he said, "God knows how you've done it, but they're a smart lot. They're a crack lot. Damme, they are soldiers. Farm hands, village jobs, and you've made 'em a credit to their uniforms." That was French, sir, French. The war came—I told the W.O. what I'd got to offer. A hundred and seven fighting lads—a hundred and eight, with me at the head of 'em.' His face became suddenly purple, and Max saw his lips tighten and his throat work convulsively. 'What did I get in reply? A letter—signed by some Jack-in-Office—thanking me, and saying that the ranks were open to my fellers. They took 'em, split 'em up into a dozen regiments—half of 'em are dead now, poor boys. The rest of 'em are training for commissions. Me—James Cranston—they said that there was no room for me. Offered me an office job, or said that I might sit on committees. The front—no! That's why I'm here, sir. Stuck like an old maid in a boarding house, reading the weekly papers and smoking more to-bacco than's good for me. Heart sick and home sick. It's a silly story, and I'm a silly old fool to care so damnably. You'll forgive me for whining . . . ?'

Max looked at him, felt his heart soften towards the old man, wanted to make up to him in some way for the sting, the wound which had been inflicted upon him. He knew that he must begin by telling him lies, and for the first time Max hated his job, which made those lies necessary.

'I'm Julian Weston, sir,' he said. 'Boer War too. I got into this show, but a bit of shell got me soon afterwards. Hip—that's why I'm a bit lame. Now I . . .' he hesitated for a second, 'I investigate camp conditions, and enquire into the balance sheets of charitable concerns out here.'

'Dud job!'

Max said, 'Quite—a very dud job.'

'Care for a drink? You would? Come up to my room— it's got a wonderful view, I believe. I know nothing of the beauties of nature. Come and have a look at it.'

'You wouldn't,' Max smiled again, that very pleasant smile of his, 'come and take lunch with me? I'm fairly lonely, and I'm stuck here for a day or two waiting for a report to come along. Charity, I assure you, if you'll join me.'

The old man was obviously pleased, he scurried off to

change his old coat, and returned to Max in the hall, his
face wreathed in smiles. He talked of the South African
War, told anecdotes, recounted hardships which Max
knew as well as he did, but his pleasure in Cranston's enjoyment forbade his saying so. Only towards the end of
lunch did Max speak of the Rosabella. 'It's a pleasant
place, I should imagine,' he said, 'what are the people
like?'

Cranston frowned. 'The people,' he said, 'mostly wash-
outs. Duds. Horrible. Old women—young old women—
that's a nasty mixture, my boy! Painted faces, and badly
dyed hair. The men—puff—nothing much. I do manage a
hand of bridge sometimes. At the moment one of my
table is away, that stops the bridge. I won't play with the
women. Always been taught to be civil to women, and
their bridge would be too much for my civility! Old
Rogers, an old Scot, was chief engineer on a P. and O.
Got a dicky heart, he's one of us. Manning, he's T.B.,
poor devil, so they won't have him, and an Englishman
called Riches. Riches is away at the moment. Coming
back tonight. Come up and have a game?'

Max drew a deep breath and said that he would like to.
He licked his lips and asked about Riches.

'Riches . . .' he said, 'I used to know a man called
Riches. In the Gunners. Tall dark chap, with a little stammer. It's not the same man, is it?'

'No, no. Can't be. This feller is fairly tall—medium
height. Fair, wavy hair. I tell him that he has it curled!
No stammer. I sometimes think he has a faint accent.
Told him so. He's lived in Austria for years, that may
account for it. Took me a long time to stand it. Sounds
like a Hun. But he's a very nice chap. Plays a first-rate
game. He had a pal over not so long ago. A man called
Harding—was it Harding? I think so. But otherwise he's
a lonely feller. Can't get into the Army because he had—
still has—varicose veins.'

That evening, after a very poor dinner, Max walked to
Rosabella, and was shown into the lounge. Old Cranston
fussed about, evidently elated at having a visitor. He introduced Max to his friends, to Rogers, a sandy grey Scot
with an accent which you could cut with a knife, to
Manning, a thin, pale young Midlander with a pitifully
narrow chest, and to a small table with a pack of new
cards laid on its green baize surface.

Manning picked up the cards, stripped off the cover and said:

'Noo cards, eh? Not befower time an' all.'

Old Rogers sipped his whisky and water and said, 'Cut for par-rtners?'

They played well, Max realised that the three of them played as a means of keeping their wits sharp, realised too, that this nightly game was the one real pleasure left to them. They played slowly, and finished the game with very little comment from either losers or winners.

'Yew lost uz two tricks then,' Manning would say. 'If you'd led back clubs we'd have been all right.'

Or Rogers, busy shuffling, 'Ye played a grand hand there, par-rtner. Ah niver hope tae watch a prettier hand played.'

At half-past nine, Cranston remembered a letter which he must post. He said that he could give it to the porter in the hall, and went out of the lounge. A moment later he came back, smiling and rubbing his hands.

'Here's good news,' he said, 'Riches is back. He's just gone up to have a wash and he'll join us here.' He chuckled. 'We shan't know ourselves with an extra player.'

Rogers nodded. 'Aye—it's a great pleasure. Hoo is Riches? Ah thou him looking a wee thing pasty when he went away.'

It appeared that Riches was looking well, that he was laughing and joking with the proprietress when Cranston saw him.

'He's always laughing,' Manning said, 'I never saw sooch a chap. If he isn't laughing then he's sing-ging, an' if he isn't sing-ging then he's whistling.'

Max lit a cigarette, held the match overlong to make sure that his hand was quite steady, picked up a few cards and began to build a card house to assure himself. Cranston laughed and blew them all down again. Max didn't care, he had managed two decks all right. Riches—washing upstairs—coming down in a moment. Max's thoughts halted for a second, and the question came into his mind, 'And what then . . . ?' He shivered, and knew that he hated his job. Knew, too, that he must go through with it, he couldn't back out now.

He was sitting with his back to the door, and wished that he had chosen a seat which faced it. Too late now. He could hear steps coming along the parquet-covered corridor, could hear the sound of someone whistling a little, merry tune. Manning nodded.

'What did I saay?' he asked.

The door opened, a voice said, 'Well, my merry old gamblers, how is Monte Carlo tonight? Making lots of siller, Rogers? How's the cough, Manning?'

Cranston turned and looked towards the door. 'Come on, Riches,' he said, 'we have a guest tonight. Come and meet Major Weston.'

Max turned and faced the new-comer. He looked and felt that his heart had turned over in his body, that for a second it stopped, then started work again, beating like a sledge hammer. He saw the man in the doorway stand perfectly still for a moment, then saw that he exaggerated his surprise and shifted his eyes from Max to the table. Then he came forward and held out his hand.

'Forgive my sudden display of emotion, Major Weston,' he said, 'the sight of a stranger in this place plus a brand new bottle of whisky—well, it took my breath away. I feel that the festive air is for Major Weston, not to celebrate my return, Cranston.'

Cranston grinned. 'Confound your return,' he said; 'if we got a new bottle every time you returned, you'd be going off every other day—and you know it. Help yourself.'

For the next game, Max refused to play, he said that it was only fair that Riches should take a hand. He would wait. He sat back from the table and watched the new arrival. He knew that now his hands shook, that his whole body felt paralysed, numb, and cold. He hadn't changed much, Max thought. He still laughed a good deal, his hair was still thick and curly, though beginning to thin on the top and at the temples. How old was he now? Forty-four or forty-five. Once or twice he shot a glance at Max, and once Max saw his eyelid droop in a wink, as if he found the situation amusing. Max shivered again, and this time knew what made his blood run cold suddenly. This man, this laughing, good-humoured fellow, was the man who had betrayed not only his native country, but the country of his adoption as well. This was the man who had double-crossed the men who were his masters, whose money he accepted. This was the man that he—Max—had been sent out to deal with, to catch and put an end to his treachery. O'Reilly had said that he had a free hand, that he might do as he felt best and that he would be blamed for nothing but lack of success. This man was the son of old Emmanuel Gollantz, the father of poor Frank, and his own brother, and he, Max, had been sent out to make him pay for his sins, for his greed and his treachery.

Algy—Max remembered how he had loved him, how as a small boy Algy's pipes, Algy's prowess in beer drinking, Algy's clothes had seemed wonders invested in no ordinary being, but reserved for Algernon Gollantz. He clenched his hands stuck deep in his pockets to hide their trembling. Algernon did not seem particularly concerned or apprehensive. He was playing well, that was obvious from Manning's nods and smiles of delight. His hands were steady enough, he sipped his whisky and soda with evident enjoyment.

Max thought hard, tried to find a solution, to discover some way out. He, too, was bound to the men who trusted him. O'Reilly had said that these fellows, these men who served the two masters might cause as much damage as a bombardment, more than a big gun. Frank—Max wondered if perhaps Frank hadn't been killed owing to some information supplied by that 'French officer' who had visited the English lines and displayed such intelligence? That plan of the river, sent back by Algernon's partner— that might account for some bombs dropped on the Strand one evening, one evening when Angela might have been leaving a theatre with Emmanuel. He wiped his hands on his handkerchief—Angela smashed to bits, Emmanuel killed and lying bleeding on the pavement. He swallowed hard. If he could only remain single-minded, if he could blot out everything except Angela, Emmanuel, and poor Frank, things might be easier.

The game was over, Algy was laughing, saying that he could take them all on, separately or collectively, and beat them to smithereens.

'Now, Weston,' Cranston said, 'come and take a hand.'

'I think perhaps I ought to be getting along,' Max said, 'I have a good deal of work to get through.'

Riches yawned, 'O-o-oh. That damned train has made me feel stuffy. I want some air. It's only ten, d'you mind if I walk down with you, Weston?'

'I should like it immensely.'

24

The streets were empty, Algy pointed out a narrow lane which led to a path by the lake-side, and together they turned down it. Max thought, 'I'll say nothing yet. I'll leave the first move to him.'

Algy said nothing until he reached the lake-side, then he stood by the low wall and pointed to the left, beyond Chillon. Told Max where you could see the Jungfrau on a clear night, then turned his back to the water, leant against the wall, and said, 'And now, Max, what are you doing here?'

'I might ask you the same question, Algy.'

'Playing with my three old pals under an assumed name!'

'You play with them, apparently, every evening under an assumed name.'

Algy laughed. 'That's easily explained. Gollantz isn't a particularly good name in these days. It smacks too much of alien enemies.'

'Everyone stands it in England.'

'Ah, in England they'll stand anything! Stands the House of Gollantz where it did? Is it still the aristocrat of junk shops?'

Max said sharply, 'Let's leave the house of Gollantz out of it, shall we? It's smaller by one of its members.'

'Really? They took one of us for the Army? Ah! That may do me a bit of good. Which one?'

'Frank—your son. Last year—no, I'm wrong, nearly two years ago.'

Algy threw his cigarette into the water.

'My son,' he said, 'think of that. Hard lines on a man to lose his son.' He began to quote bits of poetry, bits of Rupert Brooke, bits of Kipling, even a bit of Henry V. Max listened and wondered how much of it was sincere; he felt certain that it would have made Frank terribly embarrassed.

He said, 'Let's walk on, shall we?'

Algy, without speaking, fell in beside him and they walked on in silence. Max wondered what he should say next. They seemed to have come up against a blank wall. Algy broke the silence.

'Well,' he said, 'let's have some explanation of your appearance here and the assumption of the name of Weston. It's making me curious.'

'I'm equally curious,' Max said. 'Let's toss up who tells first, shall we?'

'All right.'

Max spun a coin, and together they examined it by the light of a match. Max won, he pocketed the coin and said, 'Go ahead.'

'We'll sit down, shall we? It's not cold. Well, my story is simple enough. I tried to enlist—they wouldn't have me. Varicose veins. I was fed up. So I came here to give music lessons. I still play quite well. I haven't managed to gain the reputation I once hoped because luck has always been against me. I realised, when I decided to come here, that Gollantz wasn't going to gain me much popularity in the way of a name. I chose another. I go about giving lessons, sometimes go up to the sanitoria and play to the poor devils there. I just make a living and that's all —that's all I'm ever likely to do, worse luck. There's my story. Now—what about yours?'

Max leant back so that his shoulders touched the hard wood of the seat. He liked to feel it firm and resistant against his shoulder blades. He had no story ready, and he had never believed that his imagination was his strong point. Algy's story was so obviously false that it wasn't worth while telling him so.

'Me,' he said, 'oh, it's a dull business. I joined up, got hit in the hip. I couldn't go out again. They sent me here to look round and see how much use this place will be to us, if Switzerland comes in. They apparently think she may, very soon. I'm —prospecting, that's what.'

He felt his brother's eyes staring at him through the half light, knew that he scowled, and that he drew his breath sharply.

'You don't expect me to believe that, do you?' he said.

'Not really,' Max said, 'but then I didn't believe yours, either.'

'You didn't, eh? Go back and ask old Cranston, or Rogers, or Manning if it's not true. I was playing at a

camp—sick camp—only yesterday. Tomorrow I'm playing up there, above Montreux.'

'Is that your sole source of income?'

'You don't fancy that my revered father makes me a
princely allowance, do you? Not likely. If I'd settled
down and run errands and played at being an office boy,
if I'd married well and danced attendance upon him, then
I might have feathered my nest. As it was—not a penny.'

'Not a penny from my father. I know that.'

'Not a penny from anyone,' Algy said. 'I've no one to
look to except myself. God, I often wonder what my poor
mother would have thought!'

'I don't think,' Max said, slowly, 'that our mother's
ideas about you will bear speculating upon. Let's leave her
out of it. You say that you're all alone here?'

'Here!' Algy ejaculated. 'Here! Anywhere—everywhere.
No one cares a damn for me, no one cares whether I live
or die.'

'Come back to my hotel,' Max said suddenly. 'Let's get
the gloves off. I want to talk to you.'

He fancied that Algy shot a glance at him that was
half-relieved, half-suspicious; he said nothing; only nodded
and together they walked back to the hotel. He sat down
in the sitting-room, and stared round him, his mouth
twisted into something which might have been either a
sneer or a smile. Max, busy with the whisky and soda,
watched him in a mirror on the wall, saw how the thin
nose had thickened, how the cheeks were netted with little
congested veins, how the hands were less steady than they
had been at the Rosabella, half an hour before. He
brought the drink to his brother, took his own and sat
down opposite to him.

'Now,' he said, 'I'll tell you something. I have a letter
for you from a fellow called Henby. He's in hospital in
London. Millbank. I didn't know who Riches was, I didn't
know that I should meet you at the Rosabella. Mind, he
only knows me as Julian Weston—that's because of a
whole lot of things which are not in the least material.
Except this—that there is a Julian Weston who is a big
expert in chemistry and as he's at present otherwise engaged, they handed me his name to use.'

He put his hand in his pocket, took out his wallet and
extracted Henby's letter. He passed it over to Algy. Algy,
his face suddenly white, read it slowly.

'Have you read this?' he asked when he had finished it.

'No. I suppose the hospital authorites dealt with it. The man wanted a letter sent to Lausanne. The hospital people—in doubt I suppose—sent it on to my people. They handed it to me. That's all.'

'What's Henby in a military hospital for?'

'Can't say. How did he come to be in England at all?'

'Got a permit to go and see his old mother.'

'I suppose that he was taken ill, and as he was over on a special permit the military authorities thought they'd see that he was looked after.'

Algy glanced again at the letter, his lips pursed.

'He—he hasn't got into—a mess, has he?' he asked.

'Mess?' Max echoed, 'what do you mean by a mess?'

'I don't know, he's a silly fool of a chap. Goes poking his nose into all sorts of corners. Regular nosy fellow. I thought he might have got up against the powers that be. No harm in him, just mad on photography and all that sort of stuff.'

'It's a bad hobby—in war time,' Max said. 'Dangerous.'

He watched the figure in the chair before him. There was something rather pitiful in Algy to his brother. He probably was a lonely fellow. Then he remembered the French-woman, who had been working with him until a short time before. Perhaps he wasn't so lonely after all. But he was an exile, even if his exile was self-inflicted. Forty-four—and no one who cared a damn about him. Max thought suddenly that that was the best state for a spy, then no one was hurt except themselves. They took the risk. If they went under, no one else was hurt.

What was going to happen? If he informed the police, if he acted as he assuredly must act when he had a little more certainty behind him, Algy would be taken to Paris —or London—and that would be the end. Trial—Max knew how much chance there would be there. Not a ghost of a chance! Then, he would have to tell Emmanuel. No, perhaps Emmanuel might never ask and he could keep silence. He could pretend that he had never heard of Algy again. But he would know—he, Max Gollantz, would know that he had sent his brother to face a firing-party, to stand blindfold before the round black muzzles of the rifles, to be buried like a dog in a ditch. That would be what he had done and what he would carry about with him for the rest of his life.

He felt the sweat on his forehead and hoped that Algy didn't see it. He must decide one way or the other. Either

himself, Emmanuel and his brother, or his country, the
people who trusted him and believed in his honesty. He
must make his choice. He felt the room terribly close,
wished that he had stayed out in the open air, things
seemed less on the top of you in the open air. He glanced
at his watch, it was only half-past ten. If he worked quickly, Algy might be out of the town before morning. He had
decided. He would go home and say that he hadn't been
able to find the fellow, that he had gone before Max
arrived, and that he had left no traces. Then the thought
of Cranston, Manning, and Rogers came back to him. If
someone else came out and investigated they might turn
their investigations to that quarter. He could hear them
all talking. Rogers frowning and biting his short, stubby
nails.

'Ah only knaw that the last time Ah saw Mister Riches
was on the neight he left her-re wi' Major Weston. Ah
niver saw hum again.'

'Whatever there is tue know, Weston moost know it.'
That would be Manning. Well, he must risk that. If there
was a risk, he would take it on his own shoulders and
carry it. He'd tell Angela the truth and after that things
must take their chance. Angela—and Emmanuel. Those
were the two people who cared. Emmanuel would hear
things. Hear that Max had been sent out because O'Reilly
trusted him. Max had bungled things—that was the kind-
est word. Max had seen the man last—the man had gone.
It might not be Max's fault, but it looked queer. Max
could see his father piecing things together, trying to make
a complete whole. Puzzled and distressed he would ask
Max; would ask him, certain that he would speak the
truth.

Then, either he must lie and destroy Emmanuel's faith
in himself, or he must admit all that he knew of Algy and
Algy's trade.

He stood up. 'Come on,' he said, 'I'll walk back with
you.'

On the way, he began to talk very quickly, trying to control his words, trying to speak softly and to keep any
trace of emotion from his voice. He said, 'Algy, listen
carefully, I know all about it. I know about the French-
woman, about Henby and that letter, about the plans on
the handkerchief—everything. I know that you've double-
crossed us. You've tried to run with the hare and hunt
with the hounds. They sent me out to find a man called

Riches. I found him, and until I found him I didn't
know that he was my brother. If I had known, then I
shouldn't have come.'

He felt Algy's hand on his arm, pressing it convulsively, heard his voice whispering and fear-stricken asking,
'What are you going to do?'

'I'm going to give you money to get away. I'm going to
go back to England and say that I can't find you. That's
what I'm going to do.'

'But,' the voice quavered, 'they'll send someone else.
They know that I'm here. They'll find me.'

'Then—get away. I'll give you money. Plenty of
money.'

'I can't get away. Ten miles is the limit. My passport
isn't good enough. They're suspicious now, I think. It's
forged, Max. I only changed my name to Riches six
months ago.'

'Where did you come from first?'

'Vienna, then Zurich. In Zurich they have my photo
filed, I was Houseman there. I wasn't Houseman in
Vienna. I had to get away from there—for other reasons.
Nothing to do with the war.'

Max lifted the shaking hand from his arm. 'What do
you suggest that I should do?' he said. 'Don't stand still
under a lamp, you fool—walk on.'

'Leave me here,' Algy said, 'give me money—as much
as you can spare now. Send me some more. I'll give up
this—agency business. It's a rotten job, anyway. All I
want is to stay here and play and live decently. I should
never have been forced into this game except for my
father's damned meanness to me. Remember that, when
you get self-righteous.'

Max walked on thinking hard, then he said, 'That won't
do. They're after you. If it's not me, it will be someone
else. I can't let my own people down too much. I'm doing
too much as it is. Besides, Henby split days ago. No, you
must get away, Algy. Somehow or other, that's your side
of it. I can't do any more than provide the money.'

'Then take me back to England. You're rich, my father's
rich—let me stand a trial.'

Max laughed. 'Stand a trial—my good fellow, how
much trial do you think they'd give you?' He paused.
'Spies don't get long and elaborate trials.'

They were walking along the lake-side, Chillon was a
few hundred yards ahead. The night was very still, the

stars shone down into the dark water. Ahead Max could
see the mountains towering away, up and up into what
seemed to be infinity. The mountains—untouched, aloof.
Max felt suddenly very old, like the mountains—aloof and
detached. He felt that he played no part in the drama of
Algernon Gollantz, that he was only watching it from the
stall of a theatre. He thought, as he might have thought
in a play, 'What can he do? How are they going to disen-
tangle this mess? It's apparently impossible, but there must
be a solution somewhere.'

He watched his brother, pacing by his side, swaggering
a little. He felt that he was confident that a solution
could be found, that he would have a way of escape
pointed out to him. He was pale, but, Max felt, not de-
spairing.

'Good God,' he burst out suddenly, 'can't you think of
something to do? Can't you see what a damned infernal
mess you've made of everything? Why the devil couldn't
you have been content to stick to our own people, and
not get into the hands of the others? They don't pay badly, I know that.'

Algy snarled back, 'Keep all that moralising to yourself. I did what I wanted to do. Our people! Who are your
people, please? A lot of damned, hook-nosed Sheenies!
Our people! I did what I did for money, because my rich
father was too mean to hand me some of his. You've always had everything that he could give you. I suppose
you've always played the dutiful son. Did you marry to
please him?'

Max said, 'Marry? Who told you that I was married?'

'I heard: I forget who told me.'

Max snapped, 'Then forget anything about it, please.
Now—what are you going to do?'

Algy took out a cigarette and lit it, then threw the
match into the water and smiled at his brother.

'Do?' he said. 'Sit here, or hereabouts, and have a very
good time. You can send me all the money I want—and
you will send it. You can make up what tale you like for
your people in London. "Think I am dead, and even now
thou takest, as from my death-bed, thy last living
leave." That's your card. It's up to you to keep the lovely
name of Gollantz clean and bright. You can do it if you
want to. Do it to save your poor old father, and your
wonderful wife, eh?'

'I don't anticipate that my wife would care two damns one way or the other what happened to you.'

'No?' Algy drawled. 'I don't agree with you at all. If you have any better suggestion to make, I shall be glad to consider it.'

'I have,' Max said. 'I can only suggest what I should do if I were in your position. I'd take a jump in the dark.'

'Where to?'

'Into the Lake. Finish it. Don't talk about coming to England, don't buoy yourself up with ideas of trials, don't think that they'll leave you alone here once they're on your track. I told you that Marsters got the French-woman, they've got Henby, and they'll get you. I can't save you. I thought that I could. I can't. You've made too big a mess of things.'

'You are really seriously expecting me to consider that? My good Max, don't be a fool. If anyone goes into the Lake, it—most decidedly won't be me. If you're feeling so badly about things—go in yourself to save the family honour.'

'It wouldn't,' Max said. 'They'd catch you, even if I was dead. They'd be over here hot-foot, you'd be suspect at once. The only difference would be that you'd be taken to London, shot, and my father would have to face a fear-ful scandal. God, can't you see that I'm trying to find a way out? Can't you see that it's fearful for me? I'm going back on people who trust me, going back on my own country by trying to get you away. Damn it, you've got yourself into this mess—and I've got to get you out again. I can't do it, Algy. I don't know how to do it. I have tried . . .'

Algy shrugged his shoulders. 'Very well. I can't help either. It's up to you to go home and make these people satisfied. Tell them that I'm dead, say any damned thing you like, only keep 'em away.' He leant forward and thrust his face into Max's. 'If they do come, if they do find me, they shall have my papers, I shall destroy nothing. Mind that!'

'I don't care. Even if they know that you're my brother. I shall tell them that. They'll keep their mouths shut. I know them.'

Algy tittered. 'Quite, but will they keep their mouths shut quite so tightly over the letters—all dated and docketed—all numbered, and all signed—Angela? They're in the packet marked "Mrs. Max Gollantz", by the way. That won't be quite so nice, will it?'

'Mrs. Max Gollantz,' Max said stupidly, 'what do you know about my wife? You don't know my wife—what the devil are you talking about?'

'I know a good deal about your wife,' Algy said. 'I knew your wife—in the fullest and most Biblical sense of the word. I was rather in love with her, and she was terribly in love with me. When you see her, say that Albert sends his love and good wishes and say that he whistles "Auld Lang Syne" sometimes and thinks of her. Oh, my God, what a little prude your wife was in those days, Max. I hope you've taught her to be more amenable.'

Max nodded. 'That's no damned use,' he said, 'my wife told me all about it—told me everything—years and years ago. Even that she loved you. She didn't know you as my brother; one of your numerous aliases, eh?'

'Albert Goodman—the name I took before I left England. So now, perhaps, you don't want the authorities to go through my papers, do you?'

'I don't care a damn,' Max said, 'think that over, not a damn. Years ago—when my wife told me, she wasn't my wife then—I wanted to kill the man, whoever he was. Now, blast you, you've spiked my guns. I have a right to get rid of you—as a spy. That's law—international law. We're at war. I've got a free hand. I can't kill you for what's over and done with. I hate you, but I mustn't kill you. I daren't even kill you—as a spy, because I should be afraid how much—personal element came into it. It's got so twisted in my mind that I can't see straight. But what I can see straight about is this. Either—I give you five minutes with my back turned, to take the one getaway—that water there, or I take you now to the police. You'll be brought to London and—it's the Tower for you. I thought that brotherhood went for something—it goes for nothing at all. You love a man because he's decent, and straight, not because he's your brother. You've treasured letters for years to use against me—against my wife. That's what brotherly love goes for! Now—make up your mind—do what you like. London won't be pleasant for either of us. It would probably leak out and kill my father. I don't care—you can have which you want. This —or an early morning firing party.'

'You don't mean that?'

'I do mean it. Let's get it clear. This isn't revenge. You couldn't help falling in love with my wife. God, no one knows that better than I do. You lied about her just now, but I'll let that pass. But you're dirty even over something that might have been clean and decent. I'm thinking of what she might have done for you. You're crooked about your love affairs, you're crooked about your spying, you can't run straight in anything. Damn you, it's time the world was clear of you—it's overdue.'

Algy looked at the white face of the man who stood staring down at him. He shuddered; this was a stranger. He didn't know this creature with a ghastly face, with the staring eyeballs, the tight-lipped mouth, whose whole figure looked like that of some mechanical doll which was wound up to go, and which would go on until the wheels and springs ran down. Inhuman, cold, impersonal. He tried to touch his brother's hand, it was cold and felt as if it were made of steel.

'Max—it's impossible. I can't do it. It's too much. Shoot me!'

'No. I hate you too much. I daren't.'

'I can't face London and the Tower . . .'

'There is the alternative.'

'Max—influence—money—my father . . .'

'No use. We couldn't save Frank. He didn't ask to be saved by influence. Why should you . . .?'

Algy's voice became shrill. 'Then kill yourself—why make me?'

'My death wouldn't save you. They'd find you.'

'Why should I have to go—leave the world—while you go back to your trollop of a wife and . . .'

Max's hand shot out, he held his watch so that the light fell on it.

'Three minutes to go,' he said, 'make up your mind.'

Algy stood silent; Max saw that he shook from head to foot, his face was streaming with sweat, his eyes dull and heavy, lifeless. Suddenly he stood upright and began to speak very quickly, pouring out a stream of abuse and curses so that Max shrank back for a second. His mother, Emmanuel, Max, even old Hermann Leon and lastly—Angela. Max felt the nails of his fingers pierce the flesh as he forced himself to remain silent and still.

'Half a minute,' he said. 'I'm going to walk over to that seat. I'm going to turn my back. In five minutes, I shall turn and come back here. I shall make some marks

on the stones with my boot—you will have slipped. Don't
try to get away. The road is closed ten yards further on.
I can see that. This way—I shall be waiting for you.'

'I can't—damn you—blast you and all the rest of your
loathsome tribe.'

'Time's up,' Max said, and walked away to the seat.

He sat still feeling that his heart would burst, feeling
that if he might only die now, he could be grateful. He
tried to force his mind away from the struggle which
was going on by the Lake, tried not to picture his
brother in an agony of fear, trembling and sweating by
the low wall. He strained his ears to hear any sound
which might tell him that it was over. Forced himself
not to glance at the watch on his wrist, made himself wait
and wait and wait. A splash, a cry—Max stood up and
looked round him. There—ten yards from the shore—
he saw something moving. By the wall lay boots, a coat,
and waistcoat. He remembered that Algy was a good
swimmer—he hoped to get away by water.

Max thought, 'If he can—then he must. I can't do anything more.'

The figure was twenty yards from the bank, Max heard
a cry—'Max!' And again, 'Max!'

For a second he stood rigid, his hands clenched. Algy
was sinking—he wasn't going to get away. Max hesitated,
and again heard the cry, 'Max.' He threw off his coat,
slipped off his boots and leapt into the water, calling as
he did so, 'Coming, Algy—coming!'

He swam towards the shadow in the water, saw it sink
and rise again, saw it disappear, and redoubled his efforts.
His hip hurt him, he knew that he was out of training,
but he set his teeth and went on. The shadow had gone,
the water was undisturbed except for his own movements.
He swam round and round, scarcely conscious of his
heavy clothes, or of the fact that his own strength was
flagging. He heard himself saying, 'Algy—Algy' over and
over again without waiting for a reply. There was noth-
in. Algy had got away by water.

25

Max, almost unconscious of his own exhaustion, climbed back on to the pavement, picked up Algy's coat, waistcoat, and boots, and began to walk back to the town. He was shaken, weary, and past feeling either grief or relief very acutely. His brother was dead, he had forced him to kill himself. Algy had tried to double-cross him for the last time, had failed, and Max had tried to save him. Tried to save not Riches, the agent of two governments, but Algy Gollantz, his brother, whom he had once admired and loved. Now, Algy was dead, Riches the agent was dead, and Max must make a statement to the authorities.

Along the promenade he went, his boots heavy, his trousers dripping as he walked, his dry coat only accentuating the wet waistcoat and shirt which clung to him. He asked the way to the house of the British consul, hoping that his soaked garments might escape notice. They did, and he stood before the consul's house and rang the bell.

He was shown into a large room, half study, half office, and faced a good-looking elderly man with a beautifully trimmed beard. The man stared at him, then said:

'Sit down, won't you?'

Max said, 'Thanks, but I'm soaked through. I shall make a mess of your carpet. I've been swimming.'

The other showed not the slightest surprise. 'Really. Perhaps you'd like to change. I'll get my man to take you up to my room. My things won't fit, but they'll be dry.'

'That's very good of you. Thanks.'

'Not at all. Great pleasure.'

As he changed, Max thought that they had talked like two men offering each other a lift home on a wet night. He returned to the consul's room, found a hot drink waiting for him, and thought again how queer it was to drink

255

whisky and water, quite calmly, after you'd killed your brother.

Very slowly and with great care, Max told his story. Admitted who he was, and why he had come to Lausanne. Admitted, too, that Riches had been his brother, although he didn't know it when he was sent out. Confessed what he had ordered Algy to do, gave the two courses which were open to him, and explained how his courage had failed him when he heard the shout for help.

'You tried to save him, Mr. Gollantz?'

'Yes—I was too late. I'm not a very good swimmer since I went lame.'

'Why did you try to save him, I wonder? Perhaps that question is an impertinence?'

'I think just—well, I used to be very fond of him when I was a youngster.'

'Quite. It's a distressing situation for you. I should be quite resolute if I were in your place. Dismiss the matter from your mind. Every time it comes to you—drive it away. Now what can I do for you?'

Max drew a deep breath. 'His papers,' he said. 'Naturally, I don't want it to get about. My father is an old man, he's very proud—I should be glad if the papers might be left to me. You can rely on me to hand over anything which is important.'

The consul lifted a white, rather plump hand. 'Don't give it another thought,' he said. 'In the morning one of my men shall go down with the police, they can seal everything, and the rest shall be left to you. Now,' his manner became brisk and kindly impersonal, 'now, I think that bed is the best place for you. I think you might stay here—I can send for your things in the morning from your hotel. A couple of aspirin, perhaps?'

That night Max slept the sleep of exhaustion, and when he awoke in the morning found that he was still cold, that his bones ached, and that his head throbbed painfully. Hensley, the consul, came and visited him, pulled his beautiful beard and said that it seemed desirable that Mr. Gollantz should stay where he was. Max noticed that he never said, 'Do this,' or 'Do that,' but always suggested or advised, felt that such and such a course was wise, or that one or another action might be advantageous.

'The papers?' Max said. 'I want to get on to them at once.'

'Quite. I think perhaps that you might have them delivered here. They are all sealed with the official seals.'

The papers came, there were not many of them. Max reflected that secret service agents didn't usually carry about much in the way of papers. He found very little: last week's bill from the Rosabella, a few letters in cypher, a few scraps of manuscript music, and—carefully tied with tape, and directed 'Mrs. Max Gollantz', the packet of letters for which he sought. Max lay back against his pillows and held them in his hand. Angela's letters. 'She was terribly in love with me,' that was what Algy had said. Letters written before that evening at Menaggio, letters written before that morning when they had driven down the Great West Road together, letters which belonged to a time in her life in which he had no part. Queer—what a muddle everything had been. He looked back, saw himself and Julie, saw himself for what he was then, half-sensual, half-romantic youth. Remembered his disillusionment, his horror, his shame when he had found Emmanuel waiting outside the sinister house off Tottenham Court Road. The incident didn't reflect much credit on himself or on Julie, though, he remembered, Julie had made no pretence, Julie had held no illusions about herself. He should have remembered that she was Algy's wife. Out of all the world, Julie had come into his life, out of all the world, Algy had come into Angela's.

He thought, 'The whole thing is like a lot of circles which cut into each other. Some only cut in a little, take in a small segment, others cut deeper. Julie only took a small piece; Angela has cut in so deeply that she'll never, never get out again. There have been some bad times, bad times for me, times when I felt the waiting was unbearable; but I know her well enough to know that they were a thousand times worse for her. Now it's all over, Julie was over years ago—I shall never hear of her again —and Algy's over too. Only Angela and I are left, just us two—and my father.'

Then his thoughts began to wander; he found it more and more difficult to concentrate, more and more difficult to order his ideas. Hensley came in, suggested that it might be advisable for a doctor to see Max. Max didn't care; so the doctor came, and laid a top hat on the dressing table, and looked wise and made little exclamations in French with a strong German accent. The next day, someone—the doctor probably, Max thought—sent in a nurse, an English nurse. He didn't bother to ask why she was in Lausanne, but she soon told him. Sitting on the edge of his bed, she told him of all she was going to do for him—and then went on to tell him why she was there and what she had done.

'Soon have you right, Mr. Gollantz, better in no time. That's what I used to say to the poor boys in hospital. Used to cheer them up no end. Did Doctor Mangin tell you what was wrong? Didn't he? Then perhaps I'd better not. Nothing serious, not reely. That is—all illness is serious, but it needn't be dangerous. I'll make your bed presently and get you a nice cool drink. Then a little bit of dinner—you must eat, a nice wash—I always say nothing freshens a patient like a nice wash. Then I'll take this old temperature—don't you worry if it's up a little, always is at night. Then I'll tuck you up and leave you all comfy for the night.'

Max said, 'That will be nice. Thank you.'

'Don't thank me! I'm not used to being thanked. I've been nursing an old man here in Lausanne who never thanked anyone for anything. Y'see I was nursing the boys —bless them!—and overdid it a bit, nerves and so forth. Oh, I was ill for a long time. Then I took on this private job. He died last week. When Mangin sent for me, shall I tell you what I said?'

'Yes, do.'

'I said, "What! an Englishman in this God-forsaken hole?" I said. "Well, thank Heaven for that," I said. I've nursed all over the world, all kinds of people, rich and poor, high and low, and I still say—Give me an Englishman. They're more considerate, more grateful, and—well, in lots of ways they're nicer. You see, I'm a sensitive person. I can't stand rudeness or lack of refinement. A harsh word is like a blow to me, it is reely. Always was. When I was a child, my mother used to say, "Lily, I tremble for you with that temperament of yours. How you'll ever face the world, darling girl, I cannot think." Now what about making this bed? Can't let you lie here with all the sheet in wrinkles, can we? Let's get on with the job! I used to say that to some of the Aussies I nursed. I used to say, "The better I get on with my job, the sooner you dear things will be able to get back to yours, and that's getting the old Hun on the canter." '

For five days, Max stuck his teeth together and stood it all. On the fifth day he said to Hensley:

'Look here—how ill am I? Anyway, how long have I to stay here? I don't want to sound ungrateful, but this pottering doctor and this gramophone nurse are too much for me. Would it be terribly inconvenient for you if I got my wife to come over?'

Hensley pulled his beard. 'I gather,' he said, 'that the doctor is waiting to see if some patch—I'm not very clear about it myself—which is on a lung, or a breathing tube, or something, is going to ascend or descend. He and the nurse are engaged in watching it. That appears briefly to be the trouble. Apparently, your temperature behaves in a far from radical manner. But, by all means, send for your wife—I shall be charmed, Gollantz.'

Three days later, Angela came. She smiled at Hensley, thanked him for his care of Max, and then went to Max's room.

He had already regretted sending for her, already he had wondered how soon he must give an explanation of Algy's death, and his mind constantly went back to the packet of letters which were locked in his dispatch case. Whenever he turned his eyes to the case, it seemed that he could see the packet, that he could read the superscription —Mrs. Max Gollantz—with terrible clearness. Then, when she came, when she stood by his bed, nothing mattered except that she was with him again. The rest could wait; the rest retreated so far into the distance that it was lost in a dim haze. Only Angela remained, standing by his bed, holding his hand and smiling.

'This comes,' she said, 'of taking on work of which your wife disapproves. Now, when can I see this doctor?'

The doctor came, he clicked his heels together and bowed. He complimented Angela upon her freshness after a long and tiring journey; he complimented her upon having a husband who was such an excellent patient, and who would—it was impossible to doubt it—make an excellent recovery.

Angela smiled and said, 'Recovery from what, exactly?'

The doctor lifted his hands towards the ceiling. 'From what? That is difficult to explain. A very bad chill—a devastating chill. Fluid which has gathered here and there. We wait with terr-rible anxiety to know what this fluid will do, and what it may leave behind.'

'How long will it take it to make up its mind?'

'A day—two days—a week—a month, perhaps. Our

guide is the noises of the chest and the temperature, madam.'

Angela nodded. 'I see—it may be a slightly protracted business. Well, first of all, I can move him to a nursing home, I suppose, without any great danger? I can, that's good. It's quite impossible to inflict him upon poor Mr. Hensley any longer. In a nursing home they will provide a nurse, I take it. If they can't—well, I can manage. Unless you're very much attached to that starched young female, Max, in which case we'll keep her as part of the harem for you.'

Max said, 'Oh, Gosh! Send her back to nurse the poor devils of Australians. Apparently they adore her.'

So Max was moved, and another doctor was called in to consult with Mangin, another doctor who to all intents and purposes took over the case and pushed Mangin more and more into the background. For a fortnight, Angela nursed Max. She read to him the lightest of light novels which were all that he could listen to at the moment, and carefully concealed the fact that they set her own teeth on edge as she read. She amused him, made him smile, and chased away the shadow which lay in his eyes.

'Good news,' she said one morning. 'In another week we can go back to England. You're better. When old Mangin comes this morning, I shall tell him what a wonderful doctor he is. I can afford to be generous.'

Max thought, 'God, I'm better! I'm going back to England. I've got to tell her, tell her everything. She'll hate me . . .'

'Aren't you glad, Max?' she said, then more sharply, 'Max, you are glad, aren't you?'

He managed a poor attempt at a smile. 'Rather, darling. Terribly glad.'

Back in London, he sent for O'Reilly and handed him over a small packet of papers. Told his story briefly and without any embellishments. Told it as he had rehearsed it again and again.

'I found Riches. Talked to him to make certain. We were walking along the lake-side. He jumped into the water and tried to get away by swimming. He didn't swim quite well enough. I reported it all to Hensley. They found the body three days afterwards. Hensley has all the necessary proofs. There are the papers, O'Reilly, and now—I'm going to hand in my resignation. Please accept it. It's not really my line of country.'

O'Reilly took the papers and stuffed them into his pocket.

'All right, Max. I'll take it. I don't blame you, it's a hell of a job. I'm sorry, because you were so damned good at it. I always thought it was because you're a fairly simple fellow. Single minded and all that. Still, if you're through—that's that. Did Hensley see to the funeral and all the rest of it?'

Max cleared his throat before he spoke. 'I made myself responsible for that,' he said, 'Hensley handed the bills over to me. You see, in a way, I liked Riches—he was a very popular chap, all the old boys at the Rosabella thought no end of him. For their sakes, and his—and my own, I wanted things done decently.'

The days passed slowly. Emmanuel came to see his son, walking slowly and leaning more heavily than ever on his ivory-topped stick. Not that he was feeble; true, he stooped a little, his hair was silver white, and he could not read without glasses, but his mind was as clear and as active as ever. His clothes were still beautiful, his linen marvellously white, and the old air of romance still clung to him. He was the most handsome man of his age in London, and he knew it.

Max sat and stared at his father with something like terror in his eyes. As Emmanuel talked—it seemed to Max that he talked of everything except the war—Max could see Algy's face, white, terrified, and pleading, could hear Algy's voice calling desperately 'Max—Max!'

'Your work?' Emmanuel said. 'Shall you take that up again when you are well—qvite well?'

'I've handed in my resignation, Father.'

'Ah, for that I am more then glad.' He wrinkled his handsome nose. 'I never cared for it. Not a gentleman's work, Max.'

Max smiled. 'Extermination of vermin,' he said.

Emmanuel nodded. 'Nu, if you are able to judge what is vermin and what is not. I am told that sparrows are vermin. Personally, I like them. But even then—I don't invite a rat catcher to dinner, Max. No, I am glad that it's over.'

'That's most damnably offensive,' Max said, 'and you know it.'

His father nodded. 'I meant it to be. There must be something feminine in my composition. I have waited a long time to say thet. Now that I've said it I feel better.'

The years passed. 1918 dawned, and still the struggle
went on between the nations of the world. Charles Wilmot came home and went out again. A Charles who was
older, graver, who laughed less, and who was very kind
and tolerant to his sister, Morrie. He even appeared to
like Stansfield, and when the rest of the family cited
Morrie's looks and Stansfield's indifferent health as proofs
of the life which they both led, Charles always managed
to find some kindly thought, some decent action to atone
for the faults of both his sister and brother-in-law.

William Drew, grown heavily weighed down with his
position of authority, was less attractive. William seemed
to consider that the world should order its life in active
preparation for endless years of war, privation, and suffering. Rachel Leon, very old, very yellow, shapeless and
almost unable to move even with the help of a servant
and a bath chair, said that Charles had grown wider,
William only higher and more narrow.

She regretted the active days of the Suffrage, and had
thrown herself passionately into the Irish Question. In
those days, and during the days which were to come, odd
people came to Rachel Leon's house. Hermann died in
the spring of 1918, and with his death she threw restraint
to the winds. Her house was open to every man who was
'on the run', and with her house, her purse. She did not en-
courage visitors, Emmanuel came only very rarely; Max,
Charles, and William not at all, only Angela came and
went, saw everything and said nothing.

To Angela, the last month of 1917 and the first two
months of the New Year were heartbreaking. Max was
slipping away from her. She had no idea as to what had
come between them; she loved him as she had always
loved him. She had rejoiced that his work as an agent
was over, and had looked forward to a time of quiet happiness together. But Max had changed. Where he had
laughed, now he sat silent, where he had been interested
in everything she did and said, now nothing could arouse
anything but a temporary interest. Worst of all—most
hurtful of all—she realised that Max suffered, that he was
wretched and that he longed to come back on the old
footing of good fellowship, complete companionship, and
great affection.

Everything had been perfect; she had told herself that
no one in all the world knew what love meant as did
she and Max. Now it was gone, and Max was left changed,

cold, aloof, silent, only serving as a reminder of what once had been perfect. She had tried, still tried to break down the barrier which had come between them, without knowing what had built it, or why it had been built.

One evening in February she was dining with Morrie. Max had refused to come; he said that the fog did his chest harm, that he wanted to write letters and that Julius Davis was coming in to talk over a contract.

Angela, dressed too early, came and stood in his library. 'Not coming, Max?'

He looked at her, his eyes heavy and tired. 'No, my dear, I don't think so.'

'I wish you would.'

'That's kind of you, Angela. I'm not much addition to the gaiety of nations, am I?'

He turned back to his letters. Angela watched him, then came over, took the pen from his fingers, laid her hands on his shoulders, and forced him to turn towards her.

'Max,' she said, 'you don't love me any more. I wonder why?'

She saw his face twist as if some pain had hurt him, stabbed him; saw his lips tighten, the muscles of his jaw contract. 'That's not true,' he said.

'Not as you did once,' she persisted.

'More than ever.'

'I don't attract you any longer.' She laughed. 'Very well, Max. I won't pester you with unwelcome attentions, darling. Only—I'm not thrilled with this celibate existence. I'm not a plaster saint, only a very ordinary, healthy young woman. In common decency, I think I deserve an explanation.'

He stood up, put his arms round her, and for a moment held her so close that she could feel his heart beating against her. He stared down at her face, bent as if he was about to kiss her, then stiffened and stood upright again. He had gone again. For a second she had felt that she had won him back, now the barrier was up once more.

'You shall have an explanation,' he said, 'soon. I warn you, it will be difficult for us both. But—you're right, you shall have it. Soon.'

She picked up her bag and gloves, walked to the door and with her hand upon the handle, turned and said, 'Is it someone else, Max?'

'No,' his voice was dull and lifeless, 'there never could be anyone else. It's you all the time.'

The dinner finished early, she refused to go on to dance, pleaded a headache and drove round to Rachel's. She nodded to the old servant, and said that Rachel would see her, she knew that. Implied 'Miss Leon trusts me' and was admitted.

Rachel's drawing-room was filled with tobacco smoke, and through the haze Angela saw that she was not alone. Dimly, she made out two other figures, a young man and an old woman—a woman as old as Rachel.

Rachel stretched out a fat white hand. 'Angela—these are two friends of mine. This is Mrs. Max Gollantz.'

The old woman held out a hand, and Angela took it, feeling that she was being granted an audience with a reigning sovereign. The young man rose, bowed clumsily, and smiled. As he bowed a lock of his dark hair fell over his eyes, he brushed it back with his hand. Angela sat down and said:

'Can't I have some coffee, Rachel?'

Rachel said, 'If you want it. We're having tea. These people love tea.'

The young man laughed softly, Angela felt that he was afraid of his laugh being overheard. 'Tea,' he said, 'I wonder where we'd all be now, but for the Grace of God and that same tea?'

The old woman nodded. 'It's a great help. I'd rather know that men—with a just cause—fought on tea than on whisky. Poor fellows, half their sins come out of a bottle.'

The young man moved uneasily. 'Ah!' he said, 'their sins! The sins rest with the fellow at the other end of the corkscrew! We all know that!'

Angela leant back in her chair and watched them both. She wondered how they went on day after day, living down disappointment, treachery, lack of loyalty from their own people, lack of understanding from others. Without money, without arms, without discipline. And they went on. Old and young—the rich growing poor, the poor growing poorer still.

She thought, 'They're beaten; they must be beaten to-morrow, next month—the end will be the same. But still they go on. I can't face hardships, I can't watch Max growing away from me, I can't face losing what I've loved and treasured. How do they do it?'

She said, 'Tell me, how do you go on?'

Rachel glanced at her and said, 'S-sh, Angela. Don't ask those questions.'

The old woman lifted her hand, smiled and said, 'No, no, Rachel, let her ask. How do we go on?' she said softly. 'Because we want to, and because we must. Because you can't turn back if you love anything, anyone enough. We go because we have faith and trust and tremendous love which outweigh all the doubts and disappointments. There, my dear, is that any help to you?'

'Faith and trust and love—in what?' Angela said.

'For us—one thing, for you—another. Only be certain that you have those three things, or you'll lose your way.'

The young man said, 'I've seen a many lose their way, God help thim.'

'There is no tragedy,' the old woman went on, as if she had not heard him, 'except the tragedy of growing old before your work is done. I was born fifty years too soon. You and this boy here—you're young, you're lucky.'

The girl laughed softly. 'Lucky!' she said, 'I wonder? Sleep's a blessed thing, isn't it?'

She rose to go, the young man held out his hand, smiling.

'You're down on you're luck,' he said, 'but remember you an' me will see big things, big changes before we're thro'. Good night.'

'God bless you,' the old woman said, 'and a quiet sleep. Don't worry over things at night. When the morning comes you'll see clearly.'

Rachel kissed her. 'Good night, give my love to Max.'

26

Emmanuel sat at his desk. He had dictated letters, he had listened to Julius Davis complaining of the difficulties which beset them at every turn. Men were not to be had, and when you managed to find one you could never be sure how long you could keep him.

Emmanuel said, 'That's all right, Julius, never vorry. Get young women. T'ere are young women who will come into our business—decorators, painters, gilders—find 'em. No use to say you don't like the idea, none of us really likes new ideas, but we've got to hev them just the same.' He looked at the fat Julius and laughed. 'Poor Julius,' he said, 'you will not be edeptable, will you? Is thet vy you still vear that ship's cable over your stomach? Is that vy you still vear detechable cuffs to your shirts? It's 1918, Julius, go and get a thin, thin chain, pletinum and gold, and go to my shirt makers and buy some real shirts. You and I, we don't live in the Ghetto any more.'

Julius shuffled his flat feet. 'I'm a business man, not a dandy.'

'Dandy!' Emmanuel laughed. 'Good Julius, that word is dead! Now we say—knut—and that will be dead next year. Get Mrs. Max to tell you the new vords, please. Get along with you. Max is waiting, isn't he?'

'He's in my room. He looks ill, Emmanuel.'

Emmanuel sighed. 'Indeed he does. I t'ink that he hes come to talk to me about why he looks so ill. God grant that I may help him. I love that son of mine, Julius.'

Max came, he sat down near his father, leaning his head on his hand as if its weight was too much for him. Emmanuel watched him, then put out a hand and laid it on his shoulder.

'Come, Max,' he said, 'I am here. I am here to listen, to help, to do everyt'ing that a father can do for his son, and a man may do for his gr-reat friend. Is it money? No. Women? I don't need to esk. You hev taste, Enchela is perfection. Health? You're not well, but that is an effect not a cause. Let us get to the cause, if you please.'

Max sat upright, his face was white, and Emmanuel felt a little spasm of pain at the sight of his drawn face. Whatever Max had done, Max had suffered—still suffered.

'Father,' he said, 'I'm going to tell you the truth, and nothing but the truth. I may have to betray someone else's confidence. I shall do it, because it's necessary. Necessary to my story. You will never, never let it affect you. The part which—belongs to someone else, will you?'

'No, Max. I promise you thet.'

Max got up and began to pace up and down the long room, very slowly he began to speak, began to tell his story. Emmanuel listened, his hands clasped on his leather blotting pad, his eyes following his son. The story unwound itself, beginning with the interview in O'Reilly's office, the visit to the tobacco shop, the game of cards, and—the entrance of Algernon. For the first time Emmanuel moved, Max heard him catch his breath, heard him stir in his great carved chair, then the room was still again and Max's voice went on.

'. . . I heard him call—he called "Max, Max". I went in after him, but he'd gone.' Max came over and stood by his father's desk, stood very still, scarcely breathing, then he spoke, softly, 'I did my best—I honestly did my best, Father.'

'You don't hev to tell me that, Max,' Emmanuel said, 'I know you—I know that without you saying it. Is that all?'

Max put his hand up to his throat. 'Not all—the rest is the part that doesn't belong to me. The rest belongs to Angela.'

'Belongs to Enchela,' Emmanuel said. 'Then, perhaps you hed better wait to see if she is willing to share her belongings with me.'

Max made a movement of indecision. 'I don't know,' he said, 'all I know is that I am afraid to tell her. It's coming between Angela and me, it's making our lives terrible.'

'Ah!' his father gave a long-drawn-out exclamation. 'Ah, now I see a little. Let us go back. First to the part which does concern me. You had no hate for Elchernon as your brother, nor as an individual other than a man who had gone against your country, is that right? You did what you did—not to gratify a private quarrel, you can swear to that?'

Max nodded. 'Quite honestly. I wanted him to get away. I didn't realise how deep he was in everything. Too deep for me to get him out.'

His father sat silent, his head bent, his hands clasped before him. He looked like some carved figure. Max watched him, wondering where his thoughts were leading him. At last he turned, faced Max, and said:

'Yes—yes. I understand. It's terrible for you. That is where these insane quarrels between nations lead us. You begin by fighting other nations, you end by fighting your own brothers. Perheps it is the penalty which we—men like me—pay for leaving their own country, and adopting another. I don't know. Somewhere t'ere is somet'ing wrong, but I am not wise enough to put my finger upon the place. Well, that is the end of my son—and the war was the end of his son, also.' He smiled. 'I am fortunate that my house is not left unto me desolate, Max—I do thank God for you, very, very sincerely.'

'Even now, Father?'

Emmanuel rose and came over to his son, he laid a hand on his shoulder.

'Now, more than ever. Am I so poor a thing that I cannot understand? You—Max Gollantz—would try to save your brother, did try—and failed. But the other, the man who was made because of the war, who was created to meet the exigency of war—how can I blame him? I might as well blame a machine-gun for the damage which it does. I know that I leck somet'ing; I can never feel that burning patriotic sense which some men feel, but I could have found it in my heart to be less proud of you, if you had done less than what you believed was your duty. I hev known you so long, Max, so intimately, so well, that I can believe what you tell me. I never need to question what you say. Years ago, I was called the most honest Jew in England—perheps I was, perheps I wasn't, but I can certainly put out my hand and touch the man who is.

'The other point . . .' his voice stopped for a moment, then went on steadily, 'that my elder son is dead—that is difficult for me to explain. He was dead so long ago—years and years ago. He never liked me, and I, God forgive me, never understood him. To me he always wanted to be a one-eyed king in a country where all other men are blind. You see, Max, to say that a man is your son, or your brother, or your father may mean nothing at all. He must be, as well, your friend, your equal, your loved companion. You owe me nothing because I am your father—but you may owe me somet'ing if I hev been a good friend, if you like me, if we enjoy the same t'ings, and trust one another. The tie of blood is just not'ing at all, fatherhood, sonhood, motherhood mean not'ing unless they are becked with somet'ing which is added. If a son will say "Thet man is my father, and I am gled and proud that he is"—good! If a father shall say, "T'ere is my son, and I love him as a friend, and respect him as a man"—that also is good.' He sighed. 'Poor Elchernon, I don't know—perhaps if his wonderful mother hed lived, he might hev been a different fellow.'

Max said, 'And this story hasn't made you feel differently about me?'

'No, Max. Look at it this way, if you please. All over
Austria, perheps in Germany, are men fighting, who may
be my cousins, nephews, relations. How am I to know
that poor Frank did not kill—and with a good heart—
the son of my cousin—Ludwig Bruch? How am I to
know that you did not make the wife of my second cousin, Ferdinand Jaffe, a widow? You, here with me in my
business, are one person. Out there, in uniform, part of
this gr-reat organisation for beating another nation—you
are another. There will be moments of regret for you, I
am afraid, but for myself—there is no need to say it, yet
I say it for you, Max—Solachi.'

He bent down, took his son's face between his hands,
and kissed his cheeks.

'Now,' he said, 'tell me what hurts you, what is making
you so unheppy? If it is not your business to tell me,
then go and tell Enchela.'

Max twisted his hands together, his face was white,
and Emmanuel could see the beads of sweat on his
forehead. He threw up his head like a man who is
suffocating.

'I daren't tell her,' he said, 'I've waited too long. I'm
a coward when it comes to facing Angela.'

Emmanuel nodded. 'I know,' he said, 'love can make
us brave, or it can make us terr-ribly afraid. I know. If
I didn't know, I should tell you to make an effort, to
"take a pull over yourself", or somet'ing of the kind.
I may be wrong—but I am cowardly too, when it comes
to seeing you suffer. God of my fathers, you have suffered enough. Tell me, Max, tell me, and I will carry it
to Enchela for you.'

Max clenched his hands, and leaning forward in his
chair so that his face was hidden, he told the story very
carefully and slowly. His father listened, here and there
asking a question, making a sound of assent, or understanding.

'And, you see,' Max ended, 'she'll think—she's bound
to think—that I killed him because of her. It's inevitable
—and I can't face it. I can't face losing her, she's everything in the world to me, always has been, always will be.
I've thought, sometimes, that I might go and kill myself,
that I might leave her; anything so that I might keep something of her.'

'Have you the letters with you? Then give them to me. Is Enchela at home? Very well, then I shall telephone and esk her to come and see me. You—you will take the car, and drive anywhere you like, and be beck here in half an hour. When you come beck you will go and sit in the smoking-room, or where you like, until I send for you. Max, dear Max, never talk to me of killing yourself. There hes been too much killing—and how much good hes it done anyone? Now, go and wait and be patient and confident.'

Left alone, Emmanuel telephoned to his daughter-in-law, then sat and waited, his hands folded, his handsome face calm and unmoved. Only his bright keen eyes remained fixed on the picture of his wife as if he tried by steady watching to discover some message which she might send to him. His mind moved quickly, going back over the years which were past, reviewing his actions, noting his mistakes, trying to form some honest estimate of the motives which had governed him. At last he lifted the photograph and held it more closely, so that he could see it very clearly.

'My dear,' he said softly, 'the biggest t'ing in my life—after you—hes been pride. Sometimes it hes worked things right for me, sometimes all wrong. Even when it came to dealing with your affairs and mine, pride came into it and helped to force me to decide. Now—help me to tell this child the truth for my own sake, for her own sake, and for the sake of our son Max.'

He went up to his room, he washed his hands, brushed his beautiful hair, selected a clean handkerchief from his drawer, passed a clothes brush over the collar and shoulders of his coat, took a last look in the glass to assure himself that he looked—himself, then descended the wide stairs again and went back to his room.

A few minutes later Angela came in. She kissed him affectionately, sniffed critically, and asked what scent he used.

'The same as always,' Emmanuel said. 'Never hev I used any other, and you know it.'

'It's too strong, I think. Not the same brand. Anyway, what did you want me for, Emmanuel? You're a selfish old monster—how did you know that I wasn't terribly busy?'

'Because you never are terribly busy, except about not'ing. Listen, my dear, I sent for you because I wanted

to talk with you. Today, I have heard that my elder son
is dead. Elchernon—you never saw him. It is about him
that I want to speak to you. It is all very private, very
hurtful and very difficult.'

'Emmanuel—dear Emmanuel—and I made a joke
about your sending for me. Tell me—when? Does Max
know?'

Emmanuel nodded. 'Indeed yes,' he said, 'Max told
me. Max—killed him.' She made a sound half of pain,
half of relief. 'Now I know what has made Max so unhappy—poor Max. Oh, Emmanuel, tell me, explain. It
was in this secret service business? How I hated it all!
I always felt that no good could come out of it. I always . . .' she stopped and bit her lips.

Emmanuel laid his hand on hers. 'You always—what?'
he said. 'Tell me?'

'No-nothing . . . Nothing really, Emmanuel.'

'Tell me, if you please,' he said again, 'this may be very
important.'

'Nothing—only a silly idea of mine, that Max might one
day—kill someone I knew. I knew so many people in
Vienna who must be fighting on the other side now. I
always wondered if he might meet one of them. That's
all, Emmanuel.'

'And that,' he said, very slowly, 'that is just what did
heppen, my dear. Listen and be kind, for this is very
difficult to say. I am a very proud old man, and this hurts
me. My son, Elchernon, was a spy—and a spy who tried
to serve two masters. I am not concerned with the rights
or wrongs of spying, that is for internetional councils to
decide, but I do know that no man can serve two masters
—that was one of the truest t'ings the Christians ever
said. Max found him, not knowing that he would find his
brother. He tried to give him money to get away—Max
did, Max would hev gone against his own country to
save his brother. That was impossible, the passports were
forged. Then he told him—either London—a firing-party
—death—a grave with no name; or—he said—"Take the
chance that offers, jump," Max said, "in the dark. There
is the Lake." He—my son . . .' It seemed that he referred
to the dead man as 'my son' again and again, so that he
might make her realise how much it affected him,
'refused. He tried to intimidate Max. Talked of letters—
private letters which might affect Max's happiness.'

'Letters,' she said, 'what letters? Emmanuel, how does all this affect anyone—I knew?'

He held up his hand. 'Let me finish,' he said, 'I am telling this very badly. But I want no sympathy for anyone—not for me, for Max, or for my dead son. Max refused—refused to bring him to London for fear the whole thing should get around and I should be hurt. Again, Max pointed to the Lake. He knew that there or London the end would be the same. My son jumped into the Lake, and even then tried to get away. He was taken with—I suppose—cramp. He called for Max, and Max tried to save him. Perheps you know somet'ing of that? Yes, Max would tell you, of course. Now, Max is breaking his heart—for fear you may—not understand his motives.'

She moved impatiently. 'Of course, I understand them. It's terribly hard for Max. But—surely . . .' She stopped and stared at him, then said sharply, 'Emmanuel—what were these letters?'

'My son,' he said, 'had not used his own name, Enchela, not always. He died as—Riches. Once he had called himself—Albert Goodman. The letters,' he pushed them over to her, 'were in this packet, with your name on the outside—Mrs. Max Gollantz.'

She picked them up, looked at them, horrified, incredulous, then flung them down, and met Emmanuel's eyes squarely.

'Then Max killed him,' she said, 'he once said that he would. He waited until the war came. They say Jews don't mind waiting, don't they?'

Emmanuel did not move, only his eyes continued to meet hers, his mouth tightened a little, but his voice remained perfectly even and controlled.

'Ah,' he said, 'I was wrong, Max was right. He was afraid to tell you, he was afraid that you might imagine this—unspeakable t'ing, I—fool that I was—imechined that you were too big to t'ink such t'ings.'

Again she touched the letters with the tips of her fingers.

'It's obvious, isn't it?' she said. 'Max killed him—virtually—after he had told him about these. It was kind of you to tell me, Emmanuel, as Max knew me so well. Max would have done better to tell me, perhaps.'

'The obvious t'ing,' Emmanuel said, 'is what fools see. Surely, whatever Max is or is not, you and I are certainly not fools, Enchela. Sit down, and listen to me. This is important, and I am determined that we shall set it straight. For your sake, for mine, for Max's sake.'

Angela took a cigarette case from her bag, extracted a cigarette, leant over the desk to reach the match box, and lit her cigarette carefully.

'I don't think I want to hear anything,' she said. 'I was honest—in the beginning. I trusted Max—well, I shan't trust him again. After years and years—he's nursed this thing and he's won. I hope he gets some satisfaction out of it all.'

'You don't want to hear, eh?' Emmanuel said. 'Just the same—you will hear, you will listen. Do you t'ink that I am going to let my son lose what he loves best in all the world for the sake of what you want or do not want to hear? Sit down and listen to me!'

She looked at him coolly, 'Don't bully me, Emmanuel,' she said, 'I don't like it.'

'Sit down,' he repeated. 'Now, first, you said just now that you trusted Max. Hes Max done anything to forfeit your trust? Not'ing except what you like to call—obvious. Are you such a fool, please, as to believe that if Max had carried about with him a grudge all these years, he could have found no way of gratifying it? Are you such a fool as to believe that he could not hev found this man years ago, if he had wanted to? Hes Max felt that this man—my son—came between you since you were married? You don't believe that, you know that he has never entered Max's mind, except as something which perheps once hurt you. Did Max rate your love, your honesty, your decency, your refinement so low that he believed you married him—still loving another man?'

He turned more towards her, and she saw his white hand come closer towards hers along the desk top. His voice changed, softened, it was full of colour, he slipped back into sentences which were reminiscent of the East, he went back to his youth, became romantic, sentimental and gentle.

'Dear child,' he said, 'let me tell you. Suppose even that Max had been filled with hate when he knew of t'ose letters—are we to wonder very much? He adores you, he worships the ground where your feet tread, you are his sun, his moon, his Rose of Sharon. But—remember, too, this—when his brother called, when Max heard his own name, he had no thought of hate, of patriotic duty, of

anger—that disappeared as the mists disappear in the
morning sun. You believed sufficiently in Max to stand
with him in that strange church and let him make vows
which he only half—perheps—understood. You took him
for a husband, a man who is not of your race, who comes
from stock which is poles apart from yours. He said, "I
will love you, and cherish you, I will give you all the
money I hev"—not that Max cares much about money!
He said, "I will worship you with my body as long as we
shall go on living." And yet, Max risked losing that body,
losing you this side of eternity, to go into the Lake and
try to save a man who was his enemy—in every sense of
the word. To believe Max, when he makes vows in a
strange church, to believe that you can trust him with
your body, with your life, with your thoughts, to be
willing to have his children, to share his roof—and then
to doubt him over this,' he pushed the packet of letters
away with the tips of his fingers, 'is illogical, foolish—not
like you, Enchela.'

'Oh, Emmanuel,' she said, 'you talk too much. You talk
too softly, you make it all impossibly romantic. You'd
better let me alone to think it all out.'

He picked up the letters, threw them up and down,
catching them on the palm of his hand, the very gesture
was scornful.

'Tell me,' he said, 'for what reason do you t'ink that
my son—my elder son—kept these letters? Did he keep
them because he loved them, loved them because they
were all that he hed left of you? Was that it, do you
t'ink? Tell me, too, why did not Max, knowing what
they were, destroy them? Was it because he felt that they
might hev some value to you, and as such must be
guarded—even if the guarding them hurt him? Tell me—
when you told my elder son that you were going to be
merried—you did tell him thet?—why did he not say,
"To Max Gollantz? Thet is my brother!" No, he kept it
secret. I wonder why?'

'One can go on speculating for hours,' she said. 'What's
the use of it?'

'Then,' Emmanuel shrugged his shoulders, 'if it is use-
less—let us leave it. I will tell you quickly what I think,
if I may. If Max were harder, more scheming, less loving,
and—not qvite so stupid, these letters would never hev
come to England at all. If Elchernon had been kinder,
braver, more loving—they would never hev been kept at

all. He is dead; that is over. They say that we must speak no ill of the dead, and indeed, it is a thing which I dislike to do very much. So because we must speak no ill, and because—and I am speaking of my own son, my dear—it is difficult to speak good, let us say nothing. Let us say that he belongs to the past—that he is lost in obscurity.

'Once, a long time ago, I loved him, perheps not as much as I should hev done, but still—he was my son, and he was like his dear mother. Once, a long time ago, perheps, you loved him a little, much, a great deal—I don't know. It is over for us both. We hev someone who is dear to us, very dear to us. I don't t'ink that Max hes ever—let us down. If he hes I hev forgotten. Why would he begin now? Leopards don't change their spots. Let me ring for tea, and let me talk to you and tell you some very private t'ings, if I may. T'ings which no one hes ever heard me say.'

27

When the tea was brought, Emmanuel drew up a chair to the little table.

'Please pour out,' he said, 'I love to have a beautiful woman pour out tea for me.'

He turned to Judson who stood near the door. 'If Mr. Max comes,' he said, 'say that Mrs. Gollantz sends her love and she and I are discussing the summer holidays, and cannot be disturbed. He is to have tea in the drawing room.'

He sat down, took his cup from Angela, sipped it and put it down on the stool at his side.

'I will try,' he said, 'to be very qvick and not weary you. This is my story, you will make of it what you can —out of your understanding and perheps the little love you hev for me. Years ago, I came to London; I came because my father hed been rich, and hed died poor. I could not bear to accept pity. I was terr-ribly proud. In

London, I met your grendfather, Walter Heriot. We were
friends, but at the beginning, I almost lost his friendship, because my pride could not take what he said. He
was all kindness and simplicity; I was alert to find slights,
and keen to watch for sneers. He was a gentleman, I was
very anxious to show him thet I was one also. I need not
have worried. He understood t'ings like that soon enough.

'Then, I married. I married the most lovely, wonderful
woman in the world. I said that I would marry in three
weeks. It doesn't metter why I said it,' he shrugged his
shoulders, 'but it was because of an indiscretion. I said,
"Three weeks I shall be married," as a gesture. Pride
again. Well, I married. I adored my wife, and she loved
me. I went away to travel and find t'ings for my work—
she begged to come. I said it was impossible. That was
pride—I trusted myself more than I trusted her. I said
that I knew what was fitted for my wife.

'I said that I knew what was good for my wife, I said
that my wife must hev only the best; I never t'ought
—Juliana will find the best in everyt'ing, Juliana knows
what is best, she will make everyt'ing which she sees
beautiful—because she has let her eyes light upon it.
No—I, Emmanuel Gollantz, knew!'

He drank his tea, handed Angela his cup to refill,
took it, and thanked her. She waited, and still he did not
speak. She said:

'Emmanuel, go on.'

'Yes—I shall,' he said, 'only this part is very hard. If I
did not love you I could never tell you. When I came
home, I was very happy, my wife told me that she was
going to hev a child. Only—she would not promise that
the child was mine. She had not taken a lover, you will
understand. She had—oh, it is so hard to make you
understand—she had been bored, unheppy, and the man
was an—adventure. That was all! I t'ought—what should
I do? I loved her, I could not face life without her, and
—listen to this—my pride said that people would talk.
They would say, "Gollantz could not keep his wife's love,"
"Poor Juliana was so bored with Emmanuel that she took
a lover." That decided me—pride, Enchela, pride.

'The child came; he was like her, I still did not know.
It was my pride which made me accept him as my son,
which made me give him everyt'ing in the world. I
used always to say, "My son will do this," or, "My son
will do that." Max was born, and I lost my beautiful wife.

Then Elchernon began to hate me. He hated Jews, he hated me, my clothes, my work, he hated everyt'ing about me. I said, "And why not? This is proof that he is not my son." I let him go. I was just—but, Enchela, justice is a poor t'ing to offer a boy, it's a cold t'ing, a hard t'ing.

'Years efter, Max found him again. He was going avay—he was leaving his son, poor Frank. Max went to find Frank, he came home with a picture of the boy. He was exactly what I hed been when I was a little boy. Can you imechine what I felt? I sent for him, I wanted my grendson. I was filled with pride. Here was the beginning of a family, the House of Gollantz! I bought him from his mother's people—I boasted that he cost so and so many pounds an ounce, that he was the most expensive child in the world!

'So all my life that hes gone on—pride, pride, pride. And now, what hev I left? I am seventy-four—old, almost ended. Pride is part of me, never can I get away from it. My business is wonderful—it must be, my goods are the very best—they must be; my house, my motor-cars, my food, my clothes, my box at the opera—the best. And what hev I left? My son—who was really my son— is dead, my grendson is dead, I have lived for years without the sound of my wife's voice. Such a divine voice, Enchela!

'Max is left—all I hev. I always t'ink that I lost other t'ings because I t'ought the worst, never the best. Now, let me try to help you if I can, and my dear, I am doing it so humbly. If you could see into my heart, you would see that it is shivering for fear I shall offend you. Pride— for you too, hev it. You wanted everyt'ing to be so perfect for you and Max. I remember when he was ill, and you—my poor beloved—were ill too, you wanted that Max should be saved everyt'ing which should make his homecoming, his recovery less perfect. It was good, but there was that little pride, that "I can do it! I will do it!" We did not t'ink that perheps we hed no right to deny Max the truth about you. Now—this; and with this you may either lose Max, or keep him for ever. Your pride is hurt. It was hurt when Max began to do Intelligence work, so was mine. We didn't t'ink that it was a good enough job for Max Gollantz, did we? We judged; we couldn't trust that Max went into it clean, and would come out of it clean. Now, you cannot believe that Max acted as he did—in spite of those letters, not because of them. They were—yours. You are—and you know it— the important t'ing in his life, and therefore those letters you t'ink must be of greater importance to Max than his duty. Because they were yours. A little packet of letters, and he didn't even open them to make sure that they were really yours, he didn't try to verify the writing, just accepted them; yet to you they blind him to everyt'ing —duty, decency, honour, everyt'ing. Because of them you forget all that Max hes been, is and may be. Pride, my dear, just pride. Go on and you'll find that one day you are like Emmanuel Gollantz—very poor, very lonely, pretending to be a great svell, a figure, and really depending upon two people in the whole world to make him heppy. All over this pecket of letters written by a little girl to a man who—even t'ough he was my son— couldn't behave like a gentleman.'

He walked to the desk and came back with the packet in his hands. He held them out to her.

'Look,' he said, 'fency the happiness of t'ree people depending on this. It's silly, already?'

She looked at the little packet, then took them from him and held them in her hand. 'They were written,' she said, 'by a little girl who was quite unbelievably happy, because she thought that—your son loved her. Even the fact that he didn't, couldn't quite take away the—the— flavour of what had been.' She looked up at him and smiled. 'There is a lot to be said for the Spring, Emmanuel.'

He nodded. 'Indeed, yes. But it's a cruel time, efter all. It's so hot one day, so cold the next; the light is so clear that it shows up all the shabby petches on one's clothes, and the storms of rain find all the weak places in one's boots. Spring is so certain of itself, it's so headlong. But—while it's still Spring with you, you can never see it. But,' he paused, 'never mind the Spring, Enchela, I want to know about Max.'

'Max?' she said. 'Max? Oh, my dear, Max is safe. It's so true, all that you've said about that damnable pride of mine and yours. All my life that has been the background for everything, only I never faced it. I suppose that I couldn't really believe that letters—letters of mine —could be of anything but primary importance to Max.' She laughed, 'Now you have shown me that they weren't —I'm not certain that I'm not just a little hurt about it.'

'Then I may send for him, and you will tell him?'

She stood up, leant over the fireplace, and dropped the little packet into the flames. Emmanuel watched and forgot for a moment how much he disliked people to burn paper, forgot that it dulled the fire, forgot that it blew about the grate the moment the door was opened and made the place look like a street market on a windy day. The old man and the beautiful young woman stood side by side watching the little packet catch fire, blacken, curl at the edges, and finally turn to ashes in the heart of the fire.

Angela sighed and said, with her eyes still on the flames, 'There! That's over. Now, you won't bully me any more, will you?'

'I never meant to bully you!'

'Oh, yes, indeed you did. You said that you would be gentle, but that if I was difficult, if I showed fight, then you would break me. Admit that, Emmanuel, be truthful. If there are two people in the world who can be truthful with each other it's you and I. We both suffer from the same thing—pride; enormous, overwhelming pride. We both love success and swagger, and light, and the upper seats at feasts; we both love possessions, and place and pomp and power. If Max ruled me, I shouldn't love him half so much, as some women might. I rule him, and he knows it. That's one reason why Max will be such a success. Shall I tell you the other reason?'

'Please do.'

'He is the son of that rather attractive, altogether delightful old fraud, Emmanuel Gollantz.'

He looked at her, frowning, serious, and a little puzzled.

'You're a qveer woman,' he said, 'almost a hard woman, aren't you?'

'Hard?' she said. 'Why, yes—if to be hard means to live in the present and not in the past. If hard means to make the best of the world in which I live and not look back regretfully on a world where I once lived. Look at women who aren't hard—look at Morrie Stansfield. She's miserable. Wretched, trying to make believe —because she is always looking back. She can't only look at Stansfield, who adores her, she looks back past him— and sees ghosts. Yes, I suppose I am hard. So are you, Emmanuel—if I am. I'm much more like your daughter than Max is like your son.'

'We're alike in one t'ing,' he said, 'we both love Max.'

'Ah—yes. I love Max, and I shall love Max's children. I shall make them all very happy. I used to want to express myself through a violin, you know. That's over. To play well would have meant to strip down my emotions so that they quivered and hurt and made me suffer. I couldn't face it. I realised years ago that I'm not cut out for suffering. Certainly I'm never going to look for it.' She threw out her arms. 'I'm cut out for success. I shall express myself through Max and his children. His sons will laugh at your business, Emmanuel, and think it—potty and provincial. They'll make it international. Oh, my dear, what a brute I am—go and find my poor Max and send him to me. Not too quickly, please. Give me —five minutes.'

Emmanuel walked to the door, then turned and said, 'Enchela—one t'ing.'

'Yes, Emmanuel.'

'My business—is—already—interenational, remember.'

She nodded, still smiling, then as the door closed turned back to the fire, and stared down at the ashes as if she would have read what was written upon the charred sheets.

'That's the end,' she said. 'It wasn't very beautiful really, it wasn't even very real—but being the first meant something, I suppose. Bits were lovely—early mornings, long talks about nothing in particular, longer talks about dreadfully serious things about which neither of us really knew anything. It could never have been very glorious, or it could never have ended so ingloriously. It never ousted Max, it had no real place at all—for years in my life. There isn't any regret for the man—he wasn't worth regretting. Perhaps I regret the girl who believed that it was all true. I suppose I made Albert—I must have made him, to see him as I once did. I'm probably hurt that my handiwork didn't turn out better. Ah—it's over. I don't look back at ghosts—especially when my own mortals are so beloved and so infinitely worth loving.'

The door opened and Max came in. He stood for a moment, uncertain, then she turned and held out her hand.

'Max,' she said, very gently, 'my poor frightened Max. Come here. It's all right—I understand everything, only—why didn't you come to me?'

'I daren't,' he said. 'Years ago I told you that I trusted you, didn't I? I still trusted you. I told you years ago that I didn't trust him. Perhaps I was still—frightened of him.'

'A poor bogy of your own making. Max, put your arms round me, hold me tight, promise that never, never will you go away from me again. Let's begin again, my dearest—the whole world's in front of us. It's yours and mine for the taking. Let's take it.'

Three months later, Emmanuel sold the house in Regent's Park. He said that he found London too stuffy, that it held too many people. Max believed him, Julius believed him, only Angela knew—and not because he ever confessed it to her—that he left because the house had become too painfully full of memories. He bought a huge Georgian house fifteen miles out of London, it had park land, stables, a home farm, and vast gardens.

Emmanuel said, 'It's a grend house—lots of room in it. It has thirty bedrooms. It hes four lawns, and two hard tennis courts. It hes places for six cars. It's wonderful.'

Angela said, 'What on earth do you want a house of that size for? You can't sleep in more than one bedroom, you can't play tennis, and you have only two cars. Why all this waste room?'

He took his cigar from his mouth, and blew a cloud of smoke towards the ceiling. 'I t'ought that you and Max might come and live with me, perheps.'

'You thought!' she laughed. 'You determined that we should! You bought this immense place for that reason—and no other. Pride, Emmanuel, pride. You want a place to plant the—House of Gollantz.'

'But you will come?' For the first time his voice was anxious.

'Certainly we shall come—if it's a sufficiently nice place. I want to find a suitable setting for your descendants.'

In 1919, Angela's first son was born, and named Max Emmanuel; in 1922, her second son, William Hermann. Emmanuel was delighted. The children were beautiful boys, strong and healthy. He felt that the House of Gollantz was indeed founded.

Max, going backwards and forwards to London every day, found that his life was filled with contentment. He loved and admired his wife, he respected and loved his father. They were, he often told himself, the happiest people in the world. Angela had wiped out definitely and completely in a few seconds the only thing which had

ever come between them. She had never referred to the
matter again, never allowed Max to see by the smallest
sign that she remembered it. She was gay, amusing and
always, to Max, the most attractive woman in the world.
He felt sometimes that he understood her less than Emmanuel did, felt that there existed some subtle bond of
sympathy between his father and his wife which he did
not share, but that delighted him. He never considered
himself a particularly clever fellow, he regarded his father
as the wisest man he had ever known, and rated his
wife's intelligence above that of all other women. It was
right, natural and altogether delightful that they should
understand one another so well, it was even—to Max—
rather charming that they sometimes appeared to regard
him as younger, more immature than themselves.

He had his own work, work which interested him, and
in which he had made and still made a great success.
The firm of Gollantz had never been so prosperous, its
bounds were extended each year, and its balance sheet
never failed—even in the worst times of trade depression—to show a very considerable profit. So extensive
had it grown in 1920, that Max and his father decided
to float the decorating and furnishing branches as a Company; and with William Drew watching their interests
calmly and carefully it seemed likely to rank among those
ventures which are regarded as 'gilt edged'.

Emmanuel paid what were almost state visits to the
offices and warehouses. He only appeared in the most
exclusive sale-rooms when some picture, some piece of
silver, or some beautiful furniture was in danger of being
lost to America. Then, dressed in his rather eccentric
clothes, leaning on his gold and ivory-headed cane, he
would make a superb entrance, and smile as he heard
the whisper go round, 'That's Emmanuel Gollantz! He's
come to beat the American dealers.' His knowledge was
unsurpassed, his taste unquestionable, his business instinct
never at fault. He was respected, consulted, admired, and
even feared. No one, except Max, knew the requests
which were made to him, the confidences which were
given to him, the secrets which he shared and never
betrayed. His charity was wide, wise, and unostentatious,
but it was known—and Emmanuel desired that it should
be known.

In 1926, when he was eighty-two, he was told officially
that he was to be offered a knighthood. He told Max and

Angela as they sat at dinner in his favourite restaurant. Max was going on to an official reception to some foreign potentate who was reputed to be interested in Art; Emmanuel and Angela were going to the opera.

Emmanuel said, taking a letter from his pocket, 'Today, I hev heard that I can be a knight. Hev you ever heard of such a t'ing! If I did not know that these people were incapable of fun, I should t'ink it a joke. Sir Emmanuel Gollantz! My name, in itself, is fentastic, but to add a title—would be to make it ridiculous. What do you t'ink, both of you?'

Max laughed. 'I should be inclined to leave it.'

'Wait until they offer Max a baronetcy,' Angela said. 'I agree—a knighthood is too small for you, Emmanuel. It would be a ha'penny head and a farthing tail.'

'My name being the—head?' he said.

She lifted her glass, and smiled at him over the table. 'Has it ever been anything else?' she said.

Later, Max escaped from his long, very dull and very stuffy reception and went to wait for them at Covent Garden. As he stood in the entrance, his eyes mounted the stairway down which he knew they would come. He felt a thrill of satisfaction as he watched the crowd of men and women. These were the people among whom his sons would take their place, as a matter of course, in the years to come. More than fifty years ago his father had come to England, unknown, poor, and a nobody; now, because of his integrity, his wisdom, and his personality, he was known, sought, and honoured. He would leave to his grandsons a heritage which was more than a great estate, a splendid house and a huge banking account. He would leave them a position which he had won, a name which was respected because he—Emmanuel Gollantz—had never sullied it in the smallest degree.

Looking up, it seemed to Max that the crowd on the stairs parted a little to allow two people to walk with greater ease; or else—he smiled—it was that those two people did walk with greater ease, that they contrived to pass through the crush of people, that they automatically became separated from the smaller people round them.

His wife—beautiful, smiling, and, at thirty-four, still very slim, very straight, very young. She had her hand on Emmanuel's arm, had turned to him to ask some question. Then, looking down the stairs, she seemed to Max to be searching the faces below for someone. Their eyes met, and he realised that she had been looking for him, for she sent what he always called 'her special smile' towards him, and he felt a sudden warmth in his heart. She spoke to his father, he knew that she said, 'There's Max waiting for us,' knew, too, that Emmanuel was glad that he should be there. Max watched them coming slowly towards him, for Emmanuel refused to hurry for anyone. He saw people look, whisper to each other, and knew that they were saying, 'There goes old Emmanuel Gollantz with his daughter-in-law, old Walter Heriot's granddaughter.' He knew, too, that Emmanuel was conscious of the glances, of the whispers, and that both gave him great satisfaction. His white head was held high, he had squared his shoulders, and bowed with tremendous dignity and once or twice not a little condescension to people who greeted him. His white frilled shirt, his high white folded tie, and the collar with the long points—for he had decided some years before that he could afford to return to the style of dressing which pleased him most—gave him an air of belonging to a former period. The cloak which hung from his shoulders was, Max remembered, a copy of the identical one which he had worn when he first came to London. Max continued to watch them and smile; they were two people of whom any man might be proud.

As they made their way down, Emmanuel sighed. 'I shan't come here again,' he said, 'I'm too old. I don't feel old, but I know that I am. Eighty-two, think of it, Enchela.'

'Nonsense,' she said, 'that is your latest affectation—being an old man. You know that you love it all, you love to know that people watch you, that you make a little stir, that men admire you, and that women envy me for being with you. You're eighty-two, and your pride increases with your age. I tremble to think what you'll be like at a hundred.'

His fingers tightened on her arm. 'Yes,' he said, 'and for the first time in my life, I begin to feel that my pride is justified. It's less personal, it's not for myself—it's in you and Max and the boys. I am thankful to have that pride. I should be terr-ribly ungrateful if I lecked it.'

She looked up at him and saw that he looked tired—content and happy, but weary. After all eighty-two was a great age. She must make him go South for the winter. The sunshine would take that look from his face, would dispel that dreadful frailty. Max was coming towards them, and she felt that Emmanuel would be glad to drop her arm, hand her over to Max and lean more heavily on his cane.

Suddenly, from a little group on their left, she caught a whispered conversation. 'Oh, say—tell me who is the divine old man? That's surely one of the English aristocrats I've heard about!'

'S-sh, my dear,' the second voice was purely English, 'he'll hear. That's Emmanuel Gollantz. He used to be called the most handsome man in London.' The American girl whispered emphatically, 'Used to be! I'd say that he still was. He makes all the other men look like ten cents.'

Angela glanced at Emmanuel, the weariness had left his face, his head was held at its accustomed angle, his lips smiled a little. He smiled at Max, but did not relinquish her arm. His voice was very clear when he spoke; to Angela it sounded strong, vital, and full of life.

'A very wonderful evening, Max,' he said, 'made all the more wonderful by the fact that I had Enchela with me. I am very grateful to you for allowing me to have her with me. No, no—I will take her down to the car.'

GARDONE,
ITALY, 1929

All Futura Books are available at your bookshop or newsagent, or can be ordered from the following address: Futura Books, Cash Sales Department, P.O. Box 11, Falmouth, Cornwall.

Please send cheque or postal order (no currency), and allow 55p for postage and packing for the first book plus 22p for the second book and 14p for each additional book ordered up to a maximum charge of £1.75 in U.K.

Customers in Eire and B.F.P.O. please allow 55p for the first book, 22p for the second book plus 14p per copy for the next 7 books, thereafter 8p per book.

Overseas customers please allow £1 for postage and packing for the first book and 25p per copy for each additional book.